Cheryl Adam spent her childhood in rural Australia where her love of storytelling began. Her dramatic excursions into foreign countries where she was evicted, kidnapped, abandoned, made homeless and discriminated against, helped develop her deep empathy for immigrant women. She married in Africa, had five children and returned to Australia after a 17-year absence. Cheryl became a student again at 46, completing three degrees in visual art as well as being a carer for her husband. Her concern for marginalised women and the environment took her to the Philippines where she taught homeless women how to create useable art from plastic bags, assisting in the development of a cottage industry. This experience inspired her to begin writing and to enrol in a creative writing course at Holmesglen TAFE in Melbourne. *Lillian's Eden* is her first book. She is a proud grandmother and looks forward to writing more books.

T0308095

LILLIAN'S EDEN

Cheryl Adam

First published by Spinifex Press, Australia, 2018

Spinifex Press Pty Ltd
PO Box 5270, North Geelong, Victoria 3215
PO Box 105, Mission Beach, Queensland 4852
Australia

women@spinifexpress.com.au
www.spinifexpress.com.au

Editors: Pauline Hopkins and Susan Hawthorne
Front cover photograph: *Summer Breeze* by Alice Dalton Brown, 1995,
oil on canvas, 50" × 70". Used with the permission of the artist.
Cover design by Deb Snibson, MAPG
Author Photograph: Teresa Cannon
Typeset in Australia by Helen Christie
Designed and typeset in Berling
Printed by McPherson's Printing Group

A catalogue record for this
book is available from the
National Library of Australia

9781925581676 (paperback)
9781925581706 (ebook: epub)
9781925581683 (ebook: pdf)
9781925581690 (ebook: Kindle)

This project has been assisted by the Australian Government through
the Australia Council, its principal arts funding and advisory body.

To my children –
thank you for believing in me.

Meeting Aunty Maggie

The truck rattled over potholes and shook its way down the gravel road, leaving behind the whine of the sawmill, the school bullies and Eric's infidelities. The whole bloody mess. Lillian concentrated on the pudding hills that rolled along beside them in an attempt to stop the vomit that threatened to explode from her body and ooze down the side of the truck. Another corkscrew bend and they disappeared into dense bush. Ancient tree ferns swished as they passed.

She was used to taking a back seat to Eric's family. That bunch stuck together like burrs. They had always made her feel like an outsider. This time it wasn't her fault. His mother had caused it all. It had shocked Lillian the way his mother had treated her when she first arrived in Australia. A shy young bride, fresh off the boat from England, naïve and in love. If only the isolation hadn't overcome her perhaps things may have been different.

It was too late now. Lillian looked at Eric's face through the haze of dust coming up through the floorboards of the truck. Women loved him and he loved them.

"Make sure you only talk about how unhealthy the mill is for the children. Steer clear of family matters," Eric shouted over the roar of the engine. Lillian nodded. Of course she'd leave family matters alone, what did he think she was, a nincompoop? They all had so much to hide. But what was she going to talk to his old aunt Maggie about? How could she win her over? She didn't know her from a bar of soap and Eric hadn't been in contact with her since he was fifteen and yet here they were on their way to Eden to ask her for a loan.

"Potholes!"

Eric's warning snapped Lillian from her musings. She stretched her leg across the seat to hold Bubs in place and braced her arms against the dashboard. The truck juddered through the corrugations shaking every inch of Lillian's skinny frame. Ahead, a grader pulled to the side of the road to allow them to pass. Eric lifted his finger in thanks. The road surface smoothed, giving Lillian's stomach a moment to settle. Evidence of a bushfire clung to the blackened trunks of eucalyptus trees that edged the road. Sheep clumped in their shade. It was a hot day. After thirteen years in Australia the heat still bothered Lillian. She didn't sunbake. She burned. Eric loved the sun; he was always tanned. She looked at Bubs asleep on the seat beside her a thumb in her mouth and a piece of Lillian's old nightdress clutched in her hand. Bubs called it a 'coff-coff'. The 'coff-coff' had to go, Bubs was nearly five. Lillian would make sure she left it in the truck when they reached Aunt Maggie's.

They came down a hill and around a long sweeping bend into Cann River. The main street was wide enough to drove cattle through. They passed the Cann River hotel and drew into the only petrol station in town. A general store and a farm supply shop was the rest of the town. A loaded log truck was refuelling at the station. The petrol attendant gave them a nod and Eric raised his hand in greeting as he climbed from the truck. Bubs spied the hotel.

"Could I have a glass of lemonade, Dad?" Eric held out his arms and she jumped into them.

Lillian stayed in the truck with her thoughts. She wanted her children, Splinter and Johnny, back. They should be living with her, not relatives, but to get them back they had to move away from the sawmill. The responsibility of bonding with Aunt Maggie weighed heavily. Lillian didn't want to think about what would happen if their mission failed. They had nothing to sell; most of it had gone in the fire. The other option was robbing a bank! If Aunt Maggie was anything like Eric's mother or any other member of Eric's family she was a lost cause. Deep in thought, Lillian stared ahead oblivious of the petrol attendant who was busy cleaning the bugs off their windscreen with a rag and a watering can. A tap on the window brought him into focus. He grinned and winked at her. Lillian lowered her head.

The bush had changed to rainforest and the hills were steep and the road narrow after Cann River. By the time they reached the New South Wales border the brakes were hot and smelled of burning bread. Eric seemed unperturbed. He'd carted logs over this terrain many times. Another half hour and they crested a hill and through a clearing, on their right, saw a small town nestled on a low hill that separated an indigo ocean from a large bay glittering in the sunlight. Boats bobbed in the harbour. A lighthouse perched on the end of a cliff. The view was beautiful.

"Eden!" Eric yelled. Lillian's heart lifted. It was a few more twisting miles before they entered Eden, saw the lake and ocean and the shops on the top of the rise. Lillian went over what they had planned to say to Aunt Maggie. No one in Eric's family had even mentioned the old lady before. They are a strange lot, she

3

thought. Lillian never voiced her thoughts to Eric; he didn't like her to criticise his family. The aunt was about eighty and a bit senile, Eric had said. It didn't matter to Lillian. She would go along with anything if it meant getting her children back.

The truck screamed in protest as Eric ground through the gears for the haul up the hill that would take them into Eden's main street. The 1938 Bedford was only twelve years old, but had been used to cart logs and was not well-maintained. Eric had won her in a bet. The stink of fuel filled the cabin. Bubs wiped her eyes with her 'coff-coff'. Eric made a hard turn left before entering the main street then headed down a dirt road towards a tranquil sea stretching to a passenger ship on the distant horizon. Lillian wondered if it was on its way to England; her homesickness had never left her.

A surge of seagulls rose above a barricade of ti-tree at the bottom of the road and spilled over the edge of a high cliff. To quell her nerves, Lillian concentrated on the row of timber houses with shaded porches, all owned by Aunt Maggie, and tried to guess which one she lived in. Eric had said it was on the left. It had to be, as apart from the two houses on the right, which they'd already passed, there was only a vacant block and what looked like a disused tennis court. A stone's throw from the cliff edge, Eric swung the truck to the left, bumped up a bank and entered the driveway of a small cottage. A climbing rose scrambled along the fence that separated Aunt Maggie's house from her neighbour. Roses were Lillian's favourite flowers. She crossed her fingers hoping it was a good omen.

The truck rattled to a stop a few yards from an old lady kneeling on a sugar bag, cutting grass with a pair of sheep shears. Taking in the stout form shrouded in black, Lillian turned to Eric. "You said she needed looking after? She looks quite hardy to me."

4

"Just stick to what we planned," Eric said tersely. He opened the door and jumped from the truck and walked towards his aunt. Lillian struggled with the passenger door then gave it a kick. It grated open. She climbed out, reached up for Bubs and lifted her down. Lillian held onto Bubs's hand and stood behind Eric.

"Hello, Aunt Maggie, it's been a while." Eric lifted his hat and flashed his disarming smile.

The stout form sat back on her heels and peered up at him. Her brow wrinkled, recognising a family resemblance. It was one of her brother's children. Howard wore glasses and Grahame had shifty eyes. "Well goodness me, it must be Eric." Her eyes narrowed. "You look like your father. What are you doing here?" Her eyes suddenly widened. "Has your mother died?" Her voice was bright, eyes full of hope.

Eric cleared his throat, embarrassed. "No, I believe she's well, thank you." He removed his hat, wiped an arm across his brow and motioned towards Lillian. "You haven't met my wife, Lillian."

Lillian moved towards Aunt Maggie. Should she offer her hand to an old lady on her knees? Was she supposed to call her Aunt Maggie? She forced a smile. "Um, pleased to meet you, Aunt Maggie." She rushed the name and gave Eric a quick look.

The old lady grunted onto one knee, broke wind and tried to stand. Eric put his hand under her arm and helped her up. "Thank you, Eric." Lillian saw the eye of a hawk sweep over her and Bubs, and thin lips stretch past jowls in a smile. "Come in. I'll get the kettle on." She stopped suddenly and drew a sharp breath, wincing in pain. "Of course, I'll have to make a fire first It won't take long; I'll just get some wood." She took a few steps towards a pile of wood under the overhang of her shed and crab-scuttled sidewards losing her balance. Lillian's arm shot out to save her. It was waved away.

Aunt Maggie steadied her feet. "It's nothing, just the usual heart turns. I'm not used to surprises." She put her hand on her heart and turned dull eyes on Eric. "I'll be able to chop the wood and gather some kindling in a moment, just need to catch my breath," she coughed and smacked her chest. Lillian raised an eyebrow at Eric. Perhaps their visit was too much for the old lady.

Eric stood to attention. "I'll sort that out for you, Aunt Maggie. You and Lillian go and make yourselves comfortable." He looked at Lillian and nodded towards the door. Unsure what to do, Lillian went to take Aunt Maggie's arm, but the old lady had moved ahead with a sturdy pace. In her wake Lillian noticed the uneven heels of her worn shoes. No wonder she staggers, she thought.

A lone rose bush stood by the back door. Lillian noticed the freshly turned earth around its gnarled base. She bent and breathed in the fragrance of a bloom and closed her eyes on a memory. The act sparked Aunt Maggie's interest as she opened the door.

The smell of mould assailed Lillian's nostrils as she followed Aunt Maggie into the house. She saw Aunt Maggie's eyes narrow towards Bubs's feet as they aimed for a faded blue Persian carpet. Lillian pulled Bubs back and steered her towards the worn linoleum. An elegant rosewood sideboard dominated one wall. On its top, a crystal decanter full of amber liquid caught the sun's rays that had found spots in the grime on the window behind it. Three family photographs in dull silver frames and an ornate silver tray kept the decanter company. At the end of the room was a sturdy chaise longue, which Lillian guessed from its hollows was where the old lady spent most of her time. So did the tabby cat asleep at its end. There was a picture on the wall of a dark haired garlanded woman, not unlike Lillian, dancing among roses. Lillian walked over to the chaise longue.

"Don't sit there. I'll get chairs from the other room." She bustled off. Lillian followed. "Stay." Aunt Maggie flung the order over her shoulder.

Lillian pulled up like a sheep dog. Grunts of exertion and scraping chairs came from the adjoining room. After a moment's hesitation Lillian called out. "Perhaps I can give you a hand?"

"In a minute."

There must be a reason she doesn't want me in there, Lillian thought. She gazed up at the ornate ceiling, yellowed and covered in cobwebs and at what she had first thought were broken streamers, leftovers from a forgotten Christmas, to find they were flypapers stiff with dead insects. Revolting! If she was going to visit Aunt Maggie to clean her house as Eric had suggested, then she wouldn't be touching those – he could pull them down. Averting her eyes from the gruesome hangings Lillian looked at Bubs who had settled herself on the floor near the cat. She wouldn't be a trouble. The picture on the wall caught her eye. It was crooked. She straightened the picture and exposed a line of dirt and cobwebs where the picture had been. Pulling a handkerchief from her sleeve she began to wipe the wall.

"Don't do that!" Aunt Maggie stood in the doorway with a mahogany dining chair in each hand, disapproval on her face.

It wasn't a good start. "I was just admiring your picture." She felt her cheeks flush as she shoved the handkerchief up her sleeve.

"Here, you can put these near the chaise longue and I'll organise the tea tray while we wait for Eric to light the fire." Aunt Maggie disappeared through a door at the end of the sunroom. Lillian arranged the chairs a distance from the chaise.

Bubs stroked the cat. It stretched, shot out its leg and swiped her hand. "Ow," she pulled her hand back. "It scratched me." She held her hand up for her mother to inspect. Lillian looked around to make sure Aunt Maggie was out of sight and flicked the cat off the chaise. She'd never liked cats. In the orphanage the housemistress's cat had watched her beatings. The cat swished past Lillian, nearly colliding with Aunt Maggie carrying a packet of biscuits and a tin of powdered milk.

"Scared of the visitors are you, Puss?"

"He scratched me," Bubs said, squeezing out some blood and holding her arm up. Aunt Maggie brushed past her without a glance and put the packet and tin on the sideboard.

"Cats know people who like them. I only like people who like cats."

"Splinter likes cats," Bubs said.

"Who's Splinter?"

"She's my sister."

"Her name's really Louise," Lillian butted in. "We call her Splinter because she's skinny and of course this is Bubs. She's our youngest that's why we call her Bubs. And there's Johnny, our eldest …"

"I'm nearly five. My name's Maureen," Bubs interrupted. She was rewarded with a brief nod.

It was obvious to Lillian that Aunt Maggie had had more contact with cats than children and that Bubs, who hadn't stopped staring at Aunt Maggie, needed entertaining. Fishing in her handbag, Lillian pulled out a colouring-in book and some pencils and gave them to Bubs. Once she was settled, Lillian turned her attention to Aunt Maggie. The old lady was giving the silver tray on the sideboard a wipe with her sleeve. "Lovely tray," Lillian said. It was all she could think of as a conversation opener.

"Tennis trophy." Aunt Maggie reached into the sideboard and took out eggshell china cups and saucers delicately painted with birds. Lillian was about to ask the tray's history when to her horror Aunt Maggie blew into the cups. The husks of daddy-long-legs rose into the air. Lillian watched as the old fingers clawed at stubborn residue left in the cups from visitors long gone, and put them on the saucers. She shook broken biscuits, joined by webs, onto a plate and arranged them with garden-soiled fingers.

Then Aunt Maggie collected a billycan of tank water from behind the door, alive with mosquito lava and strained the water through a tea strainer into a jug. To this she added powdered milk, which she mixed with a teaspoon. Lillian swallowed. Eric hadn't warned her of his Aunt's lack of hygiene. A tug on Lillian's cardigan dragged her attention away from Aunt Maggie's grubby activities down to the concern on Bubs's face.

"Mummy?"

"What is it, Bubs?"

Bubs frowned and pointed at the plate of broken biscuits. "They look ..."

Lillian grabbed Bubs's chin, tilted her face up to hers and enlarged the whites of her eyes. Bubs plugged her mouth with her thumb.

"Your rose bush looks healthy," Lillian said, above the clatter of cups.

"I don't like them in vases," Aunt Maggie replied. Lillian nodded in agreement, eager to please. Her vases were always full of flowers.

"Tea things are ready, now we just have to wait for Eric." Aunt Maggie dropped onto the chaise longue, raising a cloud of dust. She leant back on an overstuffed cushion, squashing the picture of a pyramid and an Arab on a camel. Her eyelids lowered to half-mast and she purred like a ship's cat. "So, are you still living at the farm with, what's-her-name, Eric's mother and his brother Howard?"

Before Lillian could reply, the thumb came out of Bubs's mouth. "Not the farm, we live in the sawmill where daddy works. Johnny doesn't, he lives with Aunty Mavis in Sydney and Mummy sent Splinter away because she coughs. Grandmother's nasty, so is Uncle ..."

"Bubs!" Lillian was half out of her chair, her mind a dither of explanations.

Flecks of gold gleamed in Aunt Maggie's mud-coloured eyes. She leant forward. "Nasty?"

The breath Lillian took was audible. Aunt Maggie's eyes narrowed. Lillian gave a nervous laugh and helped herself to a biscuit off the plate, which she then handed to Bubs. "Go and play outside for a while, there's a good girl."

Bubs looked at the biscuit. "I don't like spider biscuits."

Lillian gave her a shove. "Give it to your father then, but I want you to play outside while I talk to Aunt Maggie." Lillian felt a pang of remorse at the hurt look on Bubs's face as she stomped out of the room. She closed the door behind Bubs, anxiety gnawing, aware of Aunt Maggie's expectant gaze. If only Eric would come inside. He was good at spinning yarns. Lillian sat down, back straight, waiting for the interrogation.

"You're English." It wasn't an accusation. "My father was born in Ireland," Aunt Maggie said. "In the north, but he didn't like the English. High and mighty lot, he used to say. They act like they're better than us, put on the dog, you know, sound plummy. You'll have to speak like us." She scratched at a piece of dry food stuck to the front of her black dress.

A plummy cockney, that's a laugh, Lillian thought. "I'll try," she said. "My father was French." The information was offered to earn her some brownie points.

"Perfumed frog eaters. Arrogant lot." Aunt Maggie pulled a face. Lillian quelled her irritation and hunted for a saviour.

"Eric's sisters speak well. Actually, I think they sound rather English, particularly Patricia." It was a mistake to mention Patricia. Lillian instantly regretted it when she saw the gleam in Aunt Maggie's eyes.

A dismissive hand flicked the air. "I've never had much time for Miss High and Mighty." Patricia had called her a miser for not having electricity. She wasn't in Aunt Maggie's will.

Lillian's ears pricked. No one in Eric's family ever criticised Patricia.

"What do you think of her?" Aunt Maggie said, lowering her eyelids.

Two red spots appeared on Lillian's cheeks, 'give away spots' Eric called them. Lillian's brain raced for an answer. What could she say? She hadn't been prepared for questions about Eric's family. Living in the mill hut and the children was what she wanted to talk about. She had to tread carefully.

Hard-eyed, Lillian paid tribute to her undeserving sister-in-law. "Yes, Aunt Maggie, Patricia was most welcoming. I've only met her a couple of times. We stayed with her and her husband, Theodore, for a week when I first arrived in Australia. That was about thirteen years ago. They have a lovely home as I recall, a beautiful view of Sydney Harbour." Lillian's dark eyes found a spot over Aunt Maggie's shoulder. God, her first meeting with a member of Eric's family had been a disaster.

2

Disclosures

Eric's arm had swept towards Patricia as though she were royalty. "Lillian, this is my sister, Patricia." The tall elegant woman had touched Lillian's hand and flicked cool blue eyes over her. Her smile had been condescending. Lillian had felt like a scullery maid at an interview. During the dinner, under Patricia's quizzing, Lillian said her mother owned a sweet shop and she was planning to come to Australia as a Second World War looked imminent. That Eric had said Patricia might be able to help her find work in Sydney. Patricia had raised her eyebrows at Eric and tittered. Then she had turned to her husband with an amused smile and said, "There are charity groups who meet new arrivals and find them lodgings. I doubt Theodore would have many contacts for shop assistants, would you dear?" She dabbed the twitch of her lips with a linen serviette. "But of course we'll do our bit for the war effort, if there is one, and my little brother's new relations." Under the table Patricia's husband had squeezed Lillian's knee, which resulted in Lillian knocking over her glass of water. Eric had glowered at her. Patricia had rushed to mop the mess. Lillian's first meal with Eric's family had left her mortified.

"Biscuit?" Aunt Maggie nudged the plate of broken biscuits towards Lillian. She was disgruntled; it showed in the scrunch of her face. "I don't like big houses and my view is better than Sydney Harbour." She pointed at the filthy window and endless expanse of sapphire ocean beyond. "Miss Uppity and that husband came begging once, wanted to start a business, stock-broking or something. I made short shrift of them." Her eyelids lowered and the line that was her lips, stretched. "The family only come to see me when they want something."

Lillian squirmed under Aunt Maggie's gaze and cursed Eric. He should be talking to Aunt Maggie, not her. The old lady was no fool. If she called him in she knew he would just look at her with contempt. Failed again, his eyes would say. Of course he never failed. Bloody Patricia, she thought.

"We don't live in a grand house; we live in a sawmill hut," Lillian said with a catch in her voice. "We lived with his mother when I first came to Australia and then we decided to start a farm of our own in Buchan, but we lost it in a fire. After the fire we had to move back to Eric's mother's farm." Being forced to go back to Eric's mother had been a humiliating experience for Lillian, something she could never forgive Eric for. "That's why our son, Johnny is staying with Mavis. He needed a school and we didn't know how long we would be at River Bend with Eric's mother or where we were going to settle. We had to start all over again after the fire." Lillian studied the grime on the window. "She's not the easiest person to live with you know." It was out before she could stop it. Her eyes swivelled to Aunt Maggie.

"Not all there," Aunt Maggie said, tapping her head with her finger.

The old lady's response surprised Lillian. At River Bend, Eric's family had always been guarded around her, making references such as 'you-know-who' or changing the conversation to farm talk or the weather if they were talking about a family member when Lillian entered a room. It had made her feel like an outsider. Now this Aunt was agreeing that Eric's mother was difficult. It was encouraging. Lillian's chin went up. "I was against Johnny going to Eric's sister Mavis. Mind you, I feel sorry that she can't have children of her own." It wouldn't do to let Aunt Maggie think she was without sympathy for a childless woman. Aunt Maggie gave a shrug. Lillian could have given them all to Mavis for all she cared.

"I suggested Johnny do a correspondence course, but Eric was adamant he should go to Mavis because she lived near a good school. He wasn't concerned about Splinter because she was a girl. I think children should be with their parents. I hate them being away."

Memories of the orphanage and the aching loneliness she had felt as a seven-year-old surfaced. She swallowed. "Johnny's been there eleven months already."

A heaviness filled Lillian. Would Johnny grow to love Mavis more than her? She looked at Aunt Maggie, her eyes filling with tears. "Two weeks ago I had to give up another child and send Splinter to live with my mother in Melbourne. I miss her dreadfully."

Her voice faltered and she took a moment to gain her composure. She couldn't fall apart now, not before Aunt Maggie knew how desperate they were. "Splinter's had a dreadful cough ever since we moved into the mill hut. The doctor said she has an allergy to sawdust. He said she could die if she stayed at the mill. I had no choice but to send her to my mother."

It was too much for Lillian; she pulled her handkerchief from her sleeve and blew her nose. Aunt Maggie made a tutting noise. Disconcerted, Lillian stumbled on. "I'm finding it hard to cope without Splinter and Johnny. Bubs is about to start school, but she's too scared to go on her own." The enormity of their situation pressed heavily on Lillian. It was all she could do not to throw herself on her knees and beg for help, but she sensed that she needed to win Aunt Maggie's respect and begging wouldn't do it. In an effort to control her emotions, Lillian reached for a piece of biscuit and put it in her mouth. The biscuit crumbled like a dead thing and stuck in her throat. A spasm of coughing followed. Aunt Maggie jumped to her feet, grabbed the billycan and poured the last of the water into a cup and handed it to Lillian. Eyes streaming Lillian gulped a mouthful and managed to take a breath. "Sorry, that went down the wrong way." She lifted her glasses and wiped her eyes with her handkerchief.

"Couldn't you have rebuilt your farm after the fire?" Aunt Maggie said, with no sign of compassion.

A fly droned in the silence. Hope did a nosedive. She'd just poured her heart out and it hadn't made any impression on Aunt Maggie. She might as well admit failure and tell Eric he should talk to his aunt. A squeal of laughter from Bubs outside penetrated Lillian's thoughts. She hadn't heard Bubs laugh like that since Splinter had left. She looked out of the window. Bubs was chasing seagulls across the yard. It was a beautiful day, the air was clean, no film of dust between land and sun. Lillian took a deep breath. "We didn't own the farm, we leased it. After the fire the owner decided to sell and we didn't have enough money to buy it." And Eric had an affair with my best friend. The thought had popped into Lillian's head from nowhere. Cora was the last person she needed to think about. Lillian blocked her out. "The children were all born on that farm." A sadness came over Lillian. "I made a lovely veggie garden. We had a big orchard. I used to sell my preserves and chutneys in the local store." Her eyes suddenly hardened. "It would have surprised Eric's mother. She told me I would always be a burden on Eric because I was from London and didn't know anything about farming." At the mention of Eric's mother, Aunt Maggie leant forward. Lillian gave a nervous laugh. "She said that when I had just arrived in Australia. I'd never been on a farm before. It's all in the past though. It must have been hard for her, being a widow and struggling with a farm." Lillian hoped she sounded sympathetic.

Aunt Maggie snorted. "She made herself a widow."

Lillian's eyes widened. "What? How?" Eric's father had drowned in a flooded river. No one could be responsible for that; Lillian had seen his grave on the farm.

Her own father had drowned when his ship hit a mine. She had told Eric when they had first met at Portsmouth. When all the ships from the British Colonies were gathered for the Naval Memorial service for sailors lost in World War One. Drowning was something she and Eric had in common. Didn't they?

Aunt Maggie stared at Lillian, her hands folding and unfolding in her lap. "Well …" she hesitated. "Eric would have been fifteen when my brother drowned. It was a few days before he ran away to join the navy."

Lillian did a quick calculation. Aunt Maggie had it wrong. "Eric said he was thirteen when he searched for his father's body?"

Aunt Maggie tossed her head. "Well, whatever." She brightened suddenly. "I was there the day he searched for the body. Brave boy. Tied a rope to his waist and the other end to a tree and flung himself into raging waters. Huge trees with roots like talons hurtled down the river." Aunt Maggie licked her lips. "Eric searched for hours, diving amongst those trees. When he crawled out of the water he was covered in cuts and rope burns. A terrible mess. I covered him in iodine. They didn't find his father's body, of course, only a jacket and a shoe on a rock." She gave a cackle. "Had them all fooled."

Lillian blinked. "Pardon?"

"All a long time ago and probably best not remind Eric," Aunt Maggie said. She gave Lillian a sly look. "You can pour me a small brandy." She indicated the sideboard with her hand, then tapped her heart. "I've got the flutters. Not used to visitors. You'll find a glass in the sideboard. Brandy's in the decanter."

Lillian poured the brandy, her mind a whirl of questions she couldn't ask. She looked at the photograph on the sideboard to see if it was a picture of Eric's father, but it was of a young woman, corseted, in a long sleeved, high-necked dress. Lillian picked up the photo. "Is this you, Aunt Maggie?"

"My sister, Elizabeth," Aunt Maggie said. "She died young. She's buried in the Eden cemetery. I haven't visited her grave for a while. Too far to walk. Suppose the weeds are high." She gave a sigh. Lillian replaced the photo and handed Aunt Maggie the glass of brandy. Her eyes lit up.

"That's a good pour." She had a sip. "Keeps the heart going. Now, tell me why you aren't living at River Bend? Eric's a farmer, I would have thought what's-her-name, Eric's mother, would have needed him on the farm?" There was a smug look on Aunt Maggie's face as her eyes bored into Lillian's.

A dull ache started behind Lillian's eyes. She was going to get the third degree, there was no putting the old bugger off. Of course Aunt Maggie wouldn't believe Eric preferred to work and live in a sawmill rather than on the family estate. Hadn't Lillian told Eric that? What would he do if he found out she'd told Aunt Maggie about his brother Grahame? Not that Grahame deserved to be protected. Lillian nibbled at her fingernail. A cool wind picked up and rattled the windows. "Weather's changing," Lillian said.

Aunt Maggie flashed stubby brown teeth. "A southerly is on its way." She peered at Lillian over the top of her brandy. "Don't you get on with Eric's mother?"

There was a tightness in Lillian's chest accompanied by a shortness of breath. It occurred when she was anxious, a leftover from her childhood when her house had been bombed. The wardens had taken two days to dig Lillian out of the wreckage. She steadied her breathing. "No, it wasn't Eric's mother I didn't get on with. Well, a little perhaps, but really it was Eric's brother, Grahame." She looked at Aunt Maggie anxiously. "Eric doesn't like me to speak about it."

"He'll never know." Aunt Maggie purred.

Old eyes watched Lillian wrestle with her thoughts. There was no way Aunt Maggie was going to let her off the hook. Not that Lillian could blame her, the family hadn't visited in years and if hanging out the dirty linen was the price Lillian had to pay to get the old lady's help, she would comply. This was a trade-off. The old lady wasn't the feeble minded old duck Eric had led her to believe. She remembered the first time she had met Grahame, the way he had looked at her, pressed himself against her and kissed her on the lips. It had made her skin crawl. He was such a contrast to Eric's other brother, Howard. Howard had hardly touched her hand. She'd liked Howard, at the beginning.

The chair creaked as Lillian stood up. "I need to make sure Eric's still busy." She went to the back door and looked outside. Eric's axe rose and fell, splitting wood that Bubs picked up and added to a small pile. Satisfied, Lillian returned to her chair. Aunt Maggie wriggled into the chaise longue.

"After Grahame sold his farm in Queensland he came to River Bend," Lillian began.

Aunt Maggie sat forward. "I never liked him as a child."

Another family member she doesn't like. Lillian took heart. She waited, hoping Aunt Maggie would say why she didn't like him.

"Go on, what about Grahame?" Aunt Maggie urged.

"He pulled my pants down." Bubs said from the doorway.

Lillian jumped to her feet. "I told you to play outside. You shouldn't be listening to adult conversation."

"Daddy told me to come inside because he's bringing the wood in." Bubs looked hurt.

"Ship shape and ready to go," Eric said, walking in behind Bubs with an armful of wood. "I'll have the stove going and kettle on in a jiffy." He grinned at Aunt Maggie, expecting a thank you, which didn't come. He raised his eyebrows at Lillian.

"We were just talking about names given to roses and how none of them have boys' names," Lillian babbled, smiling at Bubs. "Aunt Maggie was suggesting a few." She turned to Aunt Maggie and held her breath. Aunt Maggie's eyes darted from Lillian to Eric and after a moment's hesitation, she nodded. Lillian let out her breath. "You'll have to tell Aunt Maggie what it's like working in a sawmill, Eric." Maybe talking about the sawmill would steer Aunt Maggie away from Grahame and open the way for Eric to explain their financial difficulties. And if Aunt Maggie asked him about Grahame, Lillian could always say Bubs had mentioned him. It wouldn't be a lie. Anyway, it was time Eric was put through the wringer.

Leaping to her feet Aunt Maggie steered Eric towards the kitchen. "You can put the wood in the wood box and light the fire while I go and fill the kettle." She gave Lillian a conspiratorial look and darted down the back steps with the kettle and made for the tank stand.

Left alone in the sunroom with Bubs, Lillian pulled her close and whispered. "Don't go repeating anything you hear adults say. Do you hear? Not even to Dad." Bubs nodded.

Aunt Maggie came in the back door with the kettle and disappeared into the kitchen. The fire took hold and Eric shut the grate. "All finished," he said, taking the kettle from Aunt Maggie and putting it on the stove. He stood up and wiped his hands down his trousers. "I was wondering if you'd like ..." His voice trailed off as a pair of sheep shears was slapped in his hand.

"Here, off you go and finish clipping the lawn. I'll call you when the tea's ready." Eric cast startled eyes towards Lillian as Aunt Maggie propelled him towards the door.

A hysterical giggle rose in Lillian. There was no thwarting the old girl. Lillian smiled at Bubs. "Go with Dad, there's a good girl." She put her finger to her lips and Bubs nodded.

Settled on the chaise longue again, Aunt Maggie filled her mouth with a biscuit and looked expectantly at Lillian. "Now, what were you going to say about Grahame?"

Lillian sighed. "The girls went with Grahame to gather sheep from the top paddock. Grahame left Splinter to guard the flock and took Bubs into the bush to see if there were any strays. According to Bubs he stood her on a tree trunk and took her pants down, then touched her girl parts. She told him she didn't like it and started to cry so he lifted her down and she ran off. Splinter said Bubs looked scared when she came out of the bush. She told Splinter what had happened and they ran home to tell me. Eric was home that weekend. He worked at the mill during the week to help the farm. It was in debt." Lillian's mouth went into a line. "All our money went into that farm and we've never had so much as a brass razoo back." Eric's family had brought Lillian nothing but misery. "They're a mean grasping lot," she said. Aunt Maggie's head snapped back. Realising her mistake Lillian leant forward and lowered her voice, "Eric beat the daylights out of Grahame, you know." The gasp from Aunt Maggie nearly floored Lillian. Her teeth hadn't been cleaned for years. Lillian fished for her hanky and wiped her nose.

"Tell me about the fight," Aunt Maggie said, eyes widening, unable to contain her excitement. It was a long time since Lillian had had female company and such an attentive audience. She would deliver what was expected of her.

"It wasn't a contest. Eric had been the navy's champion boxer. Grahame was no match." Lillian shivered. "Eric's fist pounded into Grahame's face. I heard his nose crunch. It poured blood. Then Eric was punching Grahame in the ribs. I heard them crack. He doubled over, and then Eric hit him again. Grahame went down like a sack of bricks and just lay on the ground all curled up. I thought Eric had killed him. His mother and Howard arrived then." A stillness settled on Lillian as she remembered the look of fury on Eric's mother's face.

Aunt Maggie tapped Lillian's knee. "What did what's-her-name say?"

"She blamed me," Lillian said. Aunt Maggie sat back, mouth open. "She overheard the children telling me about Grahame. She accused us of lying." Lillian's lips pressed together.

Aunt Maggie bristled. "He was a peeper as a child. His sisters had to stuff the key holes and pull curtains when they were dressing." Aunt Maggie's support eased Lillian's anger.

"While Grahame was in hospital Eric and his mother had a set-to. Eric told her he wasn't putting any more money into the farm unless Grahame left." Lillian looked into Aunt Maggie's eyes, now two glistening beads. "She told us we had to leave the farm, said the money Eric put into the farm was her due because he'd run off to the navy and left her. She said Howard and Grahame were the only ones who had helped her and she wasn't sending Grahame away."

Aunt Maggie nodded sagely. "That was to do with their father," she said.

"What do you mean?" This thing with Eric's father was intriguing Lillian. Maybe she should get up the nerve and ask Eric again. From another part of the house a grandfather clock struck three. Aunt Maggie swung her legs off the chaise.

"Come on, the kettle must have boiled by now. Call Eric and the child," Aunt Maggie said, as she bustled off to the kitchen.

21

3

Reward

Lillian and Eric sipped tea and ate broken biscuits in the sunroom while Aunt Maggie lay back on the chaise longue like a contented dowager. It was obvious to Lillian that Aunt Maggie was not going to divulge her afternoon confidences to Eric. She was relieved, but they were still far from calling their visit a success. Eric plumped Aunt Maggie's cushion and refilled her cup of tea. Lillian wanted to laugh, he was so obvious.

"I've been thinking of working on the Snowy River scheme, make good money there," Eric said. "Could save a few bob and move the family away from the mill. I don't think the old Bedford will last the distance though. I bought it second-hand. You need a good truck for the Snowy. If I could get a deposit together I could buy a new one." Eric gave Aunt Maggie a rueful smile. She pursed her lips. Eric's smile disappeared.

"Why don't you ask Patricia and her husband for a loan?"

Aunt Maggie said. "They have a view of Sydney harbour." Her eyes slid towards Lillian. Cunning old minx, Lillian thought.

Eric grimaced. "I did pay them a visit actually. I borrowed a friend's car in case the Bedford didn't make it. Drove all night. Went to Theodore's office. He kept me standing in front of his desk, hat in hand like a beggar. I was only asking for a loan not a handout. I even offered him a share of the truck's contracts." Eric's brow beetled. "He said he wasn't interested and I should move back to River Bend. Arrogant mongrel." Aunt Maggie tutted. "Excuse the language, Aunt Maggie." He lit his pipe and took a long drag, then blew a stream of smoke into the air. "The mill is not a healthy place to bring up children. There's a lot of drunks around. Lillian's probably told you about spiders as big as dinner plates that come in the hut. We often have visits from goannas and snakes. You can hear Lillian's screams over the mill saws," he laughed. Lillian blushed. It wasn't funny. She remembered how sick Bubs was after being bitten by a redback spider. She'd spent two days in hospital.

"I'd have shot the snakes with my gun," Aunt Maggie said. Lillian's cup stopped on the way to her mouth.

"Good for you," Eric grinned.

"Why don't you move back to River Bend if you're in such a fix? Surely your mother needs you?" Her eyes widened, full of innocence.

The grin went off Eric's face. Grahame was still living there. He put the pipe in his mouth and chewed on the stem.

Indignation surged through Lillian. Aunt Maggie was baiting Eric and enjoying herself. Had the woman no compassion? This wasn't a game; it was about their children. Lillian stood up. "River Bend is in debt and can't afford us a livelihood, that's why we're not going back." She picked up her cup and saucer and Eric's, and put them on the tray. "We should be making tracks soon or there will be a lot of kangaroos on the road." Her voice carried a reprimand for Aunt Maggie. The chaise longue creaked. Lillian looked at Eric, saw his jaw clench and knew she had jumped the gun. Their failed visit would be blamed on her. The cups rattled on the tray as she carried it over to the sideboard and placed it next to the photo of Aunt Maggie's sister. The photo tweaked an idea. "Before we go, Eric, perhaps we could pay a visit to the cemetery? Aunt Maggie's sister is buried there and she hasn't been able to weed the grave. Maybe we could do that for her?" Aunt Maggie leapt to her feet.

"That would be lovely, Lillian." It was the first time Aunt Maggie had said her name. Lillian sent the dead sister a message of thanks. "I'll get you a garden fork from the shed."

The cemetery was next to the beach. The dead had beautiful views: a lake to one side and a long expanse of golden sand and foaming sea in front of them. There were rock pools, cliffs and ti-tree. The sky was full of sea birds. Lillian and Eric found the grave, a blue granite monument five feet high with names etched in gold on all four sides. It was quite grand. They set to work clearing weeds and pig face. Bubs wandered off and collected flowers from the other graves.

"You shouldn't have interfered," Eric said. "I was about to ask her for the loan. You ruined everything." He snatched at a weed, lips thin.

"I was letting you off the hook. Did you want to tell her why we left River Bend? It doesn't bother me if you do. I don't understand why you protect Grahame."

"It's not something you discuss with women. I forbid you to mention Grahame." Eric gave Lillian a hard stare.

She looked away. Next time she wouldn't let him off the hook. At least she'd made a connection with Aunt Maggie. He hadn't. That connection needed to be nurtured. They shouldn't be asking for a loan on their first visit, they should come back in a couple of weeks. Even if it meant Lillian would have to manage without Splinter and Johnny for a little longer. The suggestion had to come from Eric though. Lillian worked at the roots of a stubborn weed. "Aunt Maggie told me the family only visited her when they wanted something." The weed pulled free of the grave. Lillian looked up at Eric. "Did you know Patricia asked her for money and she refused?"

"Cripes," Eric said. He gazed at the sea in thought. "I think we should visit her again before asking for a loan."

"That's a good idea," Lillian said.

Eric gave her a long look. "What did you two talk about all afternoon?"

"Her rose garden, Splinter's illness, Johnny living with Mavis. Everything you said to talk about." And as an afterthought Lillian added. "You, hunting the river for your father when you were thirteen."

"Why did you bring that up?"

"I didn't, she did. Said how brave you were. Although she seemed to think he hadn't drowned?" Eric went still.

"There were rumours he'd done a bunk," Eric said. "Someone thought they saw him in New Zealand a year later. It was a lot of nonsense, but I think Aunt Maggie believed it."

Lillian's eyes widened. "Why didn't you tell me all this?"

"I don't like discussing my father."

Lillian saw his jaw harden. Best let sleeping dogs lie, she thought. The day would come when she would ask Aunt Maggie all about it. Her back ached from bending. She stood up and stretched. "Well, I think that will do me for today. What do you think? Leave it for the next visit?" Eric nodded and picked up the garden fork.

"I'll get Bubs, and we'll go and tell Aunt Maggie what the grave looks like," Lillian said.

Aunt Maggie ushered them in with a big smile and a smell of brandy. Lillian handed back the garden tools.

"Sit," Aunt Maggie said. She took three sherry glasses from the sideboard and a bottle covered in dust. "A little pick-me-up for the road." She looked at Bubs. "Would the child like me to squeeze a lemon and make some juice?" Bubs pulled a face and shook her head. Aunt Maggie uncorked the sherry and filled the glasses. She handed them around then lifted her glass. "To good health."

The sherry was sweet. Lillian rolled it around her tongue enjoying the taste. They only had sherry at Christmas.

"How does it look down there?" Aunt Maggie asked.

"It was covered in weeds and pig face," Eric said. Aunt Maggie's face screwed up. "I'll bring Lillian back next month and we'll give it another go."

"Next month?" She turned to Lillian. "I have something I want to ask you, Lillian. As you know my heart's not the best," she gave it a tap, "and I was thinking it would be nice to have you closer. My tenants next door are moving, building a house on a property somewhere. If you would like to move in, rent free of course, you could keep an eye on me?" Two scraggy eyebrows elevated.

Had she heard right? Lillian looked at Eric, stunned.

Eric put his sherry down. "That's very generous of you, Aunt Maggie, I'm sure …"

"This is up to Lillian, Eric. I don't want a man looking after me." Eric ducked in his chair.

"Of course I will, Aunt Maggie." A huge surge of happiness went through Lillian's body. She pulled the old lady into her arms. "Thank you. I would love to live next door. I'll take great care of you." She could hardly believe it. A home, at last, her children back. Taking care of Aunt Maggie would be a piece of cake.

Aunt Maggie went pink. She peeled Lillian off her. "Just a minute I need to get something from the kitchen." She bustled off. Lillian looked at Eric and her eyes filled with tears.

"I'll still need a new truck," he said.

"You can't ask her now," Lillian hissed.

"You heard her, she needs us," he said.

Aunt Maggie came back from the kitchen and went over to Lillian. She took Lillian's hand and folded her fingers over a pound note.

"This should cover your fare on the mail bus. You needn't wait for Eric to bring you. I want you to visit me next week." She looked at Bubs and pursed her lips. "The child can come if she has to." Aunt Maggie patted Lillian's hand. "I'm sure we still have lots to talk about." One eye closed and half her face screwed up.

Eric cleared his throat. "Moving to Eden means I'll certainly need a truck. Eden is a distance from the mill and if I get a job in the Snowy I'd only get home once a month." He fingered the cleft in his chin and looked thoughtful.

Aunt Maggie's eyes narrowed. "Plenty of jobs at the Eden cannery."

Eric grimaced. Cannery workers stank of fish. "I suppose fifty quid would get me some spare parts and I could try and fix the truck myself. Keep it going a bit longer?" He didn't look happy.

Aunt Maggie put her hands on her hips. "I'll walk you to the truck."

Panic filled Lillian. The selfish so and so. If Aunt Maggie reneges on her offer, Lillian would burn his bloody truck. Their marriage had nothing left in it for Lillian. It was as cold as the ashes that had once been their Buchan farm. Eric's good looks and stories about life in Australia had swept her off her feet in England, but his charms hadn't been for her alone. Memories of Cora crowded Lillian's mind; she pushed them aside.

If they lost Aunt Maggie's house because of Eric's conniving she'd tell Aunt Maggie about his philandering. She'd pull all the stops out to get her children back. She could look after Aunt Maggie without him. She'd work out a routine, spruce

Aunt Maggie up, make her good dinners, keep her healthy, be indispensable.

Aunt Maggie chewed on the stubs of her teeth as she escorted them to the truck to say goodbye. She walked to the front of the truck, her eyes sweeping over the rust, dents and wired down hood. "Will it get you back to the mill?"

"With a bit of luck," Eric said.

"Good. Lillian, make sure you come by bus next week. We don't want any breakdowns." Aunt Maggie gave Lillian's back a pat.

"Yes, Aunt Maggie."

"Eric. I'll lend you fifty pounds but it will come out of your inheritance." Aunt Maggie's tone was crisp. She tapped her chest and staggered. "I'd better lie down. Too much excitement for one day." She lifted her hand in farewell and left them standing by the truck.

"Inheritance! Did you hear? I'm in her will. Well, I'll be." Eric slapped his hat on his head and grinned at Lillian. "All aboard." He lifted Bubs into the truck and held the door for Lillian.

"You didn't even have to clean her house and she gave you bus money." Eric had to shout above the roar of the engine. "She doesn't like anyone. Hated my mother." He shook his head, his grin as wide as the dashboard. "How did you win her over?"

We don't like your mother, Lillian thought. "We love roses," she said. Tonight she'd write to her mother and arrange for Splinter's return. Writing to Mavis would be difficult though. She loved Johnny, wanted to adopt him and Johnny seemed happy there. His letters were full of fishing trips with his school friends and he never said he missed Lillian. Perhaps he thought he wasn't wanted because she hadn't sent for him when they moved to the sawmill, where there was a school, like she had promised? Perhaps he didn't want to come home?

4

Johnny's Story

Johnny wondered why his mother was crying and squeezing him so hard. It made him frightened.

"That's enough, now Lil," his Dad said, pulling her away. He ruffled Johnny's hair and cleared his throat. "We'll see you soon, sport. Be good for Aunty Mavis and Uncle Mank."

Johnny watched his family climb into the truck. He had never waved them off before. His insides squeezed. "I want to come with you," he yelled.

His mother leant out of the truck window. "I'll come and get you, Johnny. I promise. It's just until we find a place to live and a school for you."

Johnny frowned. Why wasn't Splinter staying with Aunty Mavis? Splinter had to go to school too. He watched his mother's arm wave until the truck was out of sight. Johnny kicked a stone.

Aunty Mavis put an arm around him. "How about we go to

the shop and buy an ice-cream?"

Ice-cream? He'd only had one from a shop once. It was delicious. Mr Fong had given it to him after their farm had burned down. He didn't want to think of the burned farm. He put his hand in Aunty Mavis's.

It was very silent in Aunty Mavis's house. For a moment Johnny thought he was all alone and that Aunty Mavis and Uncle Mank had gone away too. His heart sank. He jumped out of bed and rushed into the kitchen. Uncle Mank was sitting at the table reading the newspaper and eating his breakfast. The drum in Johnny's chest slowed. Aunty Mavis pecked him on the cheek with damp lips. He wiped the spot with his hand.

"Sit down. I'll get you some porridge," Aunty Mavis said. She put a bowl in front of him. Johnny stirred the porridge around with his spoon. He wasn't hungry. Uncle Mank folded his paper.

"Thought we might do a spot of fishing in the river," he said, smiling. "I'll show you how to make a fishing rod with bamboo and string." Johnny stopped stirring. Sometimes he went with his dad to the Buchan River and fished. They used hand lines. A rod sounded good.

"I'll make you some vegemite sandwiches and lemon drink to take," Aunty Mavis said.

"We'll have to dig up a few worms for bait," Uncle Mank said.

"I can do that, Uncle Mank." He was good at finding worms. He'd make the best bamboo fishing rod. The porridge tasted nice.

The bamboo shaft was the right thickness; it fitted in his hand just the way Uncle Mank showed him. All his fingers could close around it. He cut it down with the tomahawk Uncle Mank had brought and lopped off the thin end. He lay it on the ground, put his foot in the middle and bent one end up to test if it had enough spring the way Uncle Mank had done with his. Johnny trimmed off the shoots with his uncle's bowie knife. He made a split in the top of the pole, then picked up a ball of string and wedged one end of the string in the split. Then he wound string around the split and tied a double knot. He didn't cut the string until he had unwound enough to reach the centre of the river and a bit extra for the float, sinker and hook. He tied them on and held it up. It looked bonzer. Johnny handed it to Uncle Mank for inspection.

"Better than mine," Uncle Mank said, after flexing and casting it. "You'll be able to show the kids at your new school how to make a rod." Johnny didn't want to show any kids how to make a rod. He didn't want to think about going to school, it was too scary.

The school was huge and noisy. Johnny had never seen so many kids in one place in his life. There were classrooms for every age. Not just one room with little kids and big kids all in together like the bush school Johnny had been used to. He felt strange. At lunchtime Johnny watched the kids kick a footy around the school yard. He wanted to join in, but he was a new kid and the others hadn't asked him to play. The ball landed next to him. Johnny looked across at the kids and booted the ball back as hard as he could. He was a good kicker. The ball sailed over their heads and went right across the yard. Johnny waited to see what they would do.

A boy Johnny recognised from his class lifted his arm. "Come and play," he yelled. It didn't take Johnny long to make friends at his new school.

Cheeky had become his friend also. Cheeky was forty years old. A white cockatoo. He had a keen eye and a blue tongue. "Mank wants a beer," he squawked. Johnny gave his head a scratch.

"Good, boy, Cheeky." He grinned.

He wouldn't have taught Cheeky to say it if Aunty Mavis hadn't started making him go door knocking for Jehovah, with her. He hated going. People slammed doors and sent dogs out to bark at them. The Jehovah's men visited Aunty Mavis every week. Uncle Mank always did a bunk if he saw them coming. They hadn't come this week though and Aunty Mavis hadn't gone door knocking. It was because Cheeky had screeched, "bloody Jehovahs!" when Aunty Mavis had opened the door to them. Johnny had fallen on the floor laughing, he couldn't help it. Aunty Mavis didn't laugh. Johnny had gone to bed without his tea and Cheeky was moved to the back verandah. Johnny was sorry Uncle Mank got blamed.

"I'll let you go one day," Johnny said, scratching the cockatoo on the head.

"I want to go home." Cheeky squawked. He'd learned that in a week.

Johnny fiddled with his Meccano set. A big hole opened up inside him as Jingle Bells started playing on the wireless. Why had he been at Aunty Mavis's so long? His mum had said it was only going to be for a little while? He'd grown out of his shoes already. He didn't care if he had to walk five miles to school or sleep on a camp bed in the mill hut. Dad doesn't want me back, he thought. He knew it wasn't because he'd kicked his Dad when his Dad hit his mum. He'd asked Uncle Mank about that. Uncle Mank had gone silent for a while. Then Johnny had asked him if his dad was a bastard and Uncle Mank asked who told him that and Johnny told him Cora the slut's kids had said his dad was a bastard. Uncle Mank had coughed until his face was red. Then he told Johnny that his dad hadn't sent him to Aunty Mavis because he'd tried to help his mum, that Aunty Mavis had asked if he could come and stay until his dad found a house near a school. So Johnny was satisfied that it wasn't about the fight. Maybe his dad thinks he burnt the farm down. Had he? Johnny went back in his mind to that day.

They were all in their swimming togs. Johnny remembered

his father pumping up old tyres so he and Splinter could float on the river. Mum had made his favourite sandwiches, lamb and chutney. They had cake with hundreds and thousands on the top. Bottles of ginger beer. He had ridden on the back of the truck with the dogs and picnic basket all the way to the river. Dad had given him threepence for collecting the most mushrooms. He and Splinter had raced on inner tubes down the river. He'd helped Dad fetch wood to make a fire for the billy tea. Then when it was time to go home, his Dad had kicked over the fire and put some dirt on it. Johnny wished he hadn't stuck the stick in the glowing bit.

In the night it took off, starting as a small glow where they had picnicked. Dawn smoked into their house. Johnny was shaken awake by his father.

"Come on son, I need your help." It was the first time Johnny heard fear in his father's voice. His dad rattled off instructions. Johnny ran to the barn and collected buckets. Opened the gate for the cows and the horse. Helped his father wet down the chook pen and the house. His mother rolled her precious china in towels and sheets and packed it in tea chests and boxes. His father loaded the truck.

"Tell Mum I'm taking the tractor down the hill to have a look," his dad yelled. Johnny rushed inside, heart thumping.

By midday the fire had increased, helped by a strong wind. The oil in the eucalyptus leaves ignited, formed into fireballs and jumped the creek. A red haze and thick smoke blocked the view of the town. With his mum and Splinter, he ran around the house pulling clothes from cupboards and gathering precious possessions.

The windows in the house rattled from the constant drum of passing kangaroos. The cows bellowed.

Johnny remembered the look on his father's face as he burst through the door. His eyes were red and streaming. His hair full of ash. "Everyone get in the truck," he yelled. "We'll have to get out of here." His voice got lost in the shriek of the barn roof, as it burnt loose from its supports and lifted in the wind. They piled in the truck and raced towards town.

When they arrived at the local hotel in Buchan people cheered. Johnny felt like a hero.

"By God, we thought you were done for," said Plum the publican.

"It got everything else." His father hung his head and sobbed. Seeing his Dad cry made Johnny cry too.

"You can have the bungalow out back. It's only small: a double bed and three stretchers, but it will do for tonight. Got some tucker for you. Poor buggers. You look right done in," said Plum. Mr Fong gave Johnny, Splinter and Bubs each an ice-cream in a cone.

It was all my fault, Johnny thought. He loved Aunty Mavis and Uncle Mank, but he didn't want to stay here forever. A small sob escaped him.

The next day the letter from his mother came. Aunty Mavis cried when she read it. "I'm going home!" Johnny yelled.

5

A Broken Leg

Johnny's return was delayed. They were still in the mill hut. Four months had passed since their first visit to Aunt Maggie's. The whine of mill saws slicing through centuries old trees echoed Lillian's frustration as she cooked her family's dinner on the two-burner kerosene camp stove. She looked at Splinter's red eyes and Eric's I-told-you-so face.

She knew she shouldn't have insisted on bringing Splinter back before they moved, but Bubs had just turned five and Lillian didn't want her to start school without her sister as support. The local kids were a rough lot. The plaster cast on Bubs's leg was proof of that. She put the lid on the pot of stew and turned the flame down. Lillian's mouth tightened as her thoughts went back to the day Bubs's screams had made her rush from the hut.

"For God's sake, what's happened?" she had yelled, as Splinter stumbled towards her, red faced, panting, carrying Bubs.

Bubs had screamed when Lillian lifted her off Splinter's back. She was covered in vomit. Lillian tore inside and laid Bubs on the bed. She started pulling off Bubs's vomit-sodden clothes. Bubs shrieked and tried to push Lillian away.

"What's wrong sweetheart?"

"My leg!" screamed Bubs. "It's hurted." She groaned and tossed her head from side to side on the pillow.

"Barry Barlow let the rodeo cattle out of the paddock next to the school, when we were on our way home," Splinter wheezed, still panting from the effort of carrying Bubs. "Bubs was frightened and ran. Valerie Wallace, the policeman's daughter, saw her running and chased her. She caught Bubs and threw her on the ground near the cattle. Bubs tried to crawl away and Valerie jumped on her legs. Bubs was screaming and rolling on the ground. Valerie said she was shamming and tried to make her stand up. Bubs sicked on herself and went all limp and fell over. Her eyes were closed and she wouldn't talk to me. I think she fainted. The kids helped me put her on my back," Splinter said. It had all come out in a gulping rush.

That had happened three weeks ago and it was the straw that broke the camel's back for Lillian. It was time she got Aunt Maggie to move her tenants out. Her face hardened. She didn't blame Bubs and Splinter for refusing to go back to school. A spasm of coughing from Splinter broke into Lillian's thoughts. From the corner of her eye she watched Eric fetch Splinter a glass of water and pat her on the back. Guilt flooded Lillian – if only she hadn't insisted Splinter come back to the mill. It wouldn't have mattered if Bubs had started school late. How was she to know Aunt Maggie would take so long to move her tenants out? Her head started to pound and she felt a rise of nausea. Another migraine on its way. She rubbed her temple and looked at Eric. He wasn't sympathetic towards her migraine attacks. He said she brought them on herself. She saw his eyes narrow.

"Maybe Aunt Maggie's had a rethink, or you've said something that's put her off. You've been visiting her once a month and haven't made any progress," he accused.

Lillian's chin went up. "That's unfair. It's nothing I've said or done. I've bent over backwards for her. She's not going to be in a hurry while she has paying tenants." Perhaps she had made herself too convenient for Aunt Maggie? Travelling up every three weeks to clean her house, keeping her up to date with the family's goings on had served Aunt Maggie's purpose without Lillian living next door. Lillian had dropped many hints on needing a date to move her family next door, but Aunt Maggie had fobbed her off each time. If her tenants decided to take longer to build their new house it could be ages before they moved. Lillian couldn't bear the thought. It wasn't going to happen, she determined. The next visit Lillian would insist on a date. Bubs's leg would do the trick.

On her last visit to Eden Lillian had left Aunt Maggie early and taken a walk down Eden's main street, rejoicing in the sea air, her feet light as she passed the butcher shop, general store, milk bar, two hotels, bakery, drapery and the Fishermen's Club. Eden had a chemist and a doctor. Civilisation. The biggest thrill was the library. Lillian had envisaged all the books she would read. Agatha Christie was her favourite author. She'd discussed books with a woman in the library, who had introduced herself as Ingrid Kasbauer. Ingrid had invited her to afternoon tea when she moved to Eden. Lillian had been starved of female company and now she had a friend. Eden was going to change her luck. Lillian could feel it in her bones. Trouble was, the waiting to move was making her anxious and brought on her migraines. The next visit was going to be do or die with Aunt Maggie, Lillian resolved. She would get on her knees if she had too. She couldn't wait any longer. But she needed Eric to pay her bus fare – Aunt Maggie had forgotten to give her the money on her last visit. She turned to Eric.

"I was thinking of visiting Aunt Maggie tomorrow now Bubs can get around. I could take her with me so Aunt Maggie can see the cast on her leg. It might force her to give us a moving in date. What do you think?"

Eric sucked air through his teeth and gazed at the pot of stew on the burner. He was taking his time to answer, stringing her out, enjoying his power. She knew his game.

"Can we go to the beach when we go to Eden, Dad?" Splinter prompted, full of excitement.

"No. Bubs can't get her cast wet," Lillian said. Splinter's face fell. "You must be on your best behaviour if I take you," Lillian warned. "Cross your hearts." They nodded and crossed their hearts. "Splinter, go and read to Bubs, and get her to write the alphabet while I talk to Dad." As they walked away, Lillian continued, "I'll make a cake, butter Aunt Maggie up. We'll need money for the bus though. Unless you can take us, Eric?" Lillian searched his face for approval.

He fingered the cleft in his chin and nodded. "I suppose I can swap a shift. The truck needs a grease and oil change. I might even take some fishing tackle and drop a line in." The tightness in Lillian's chest eased.

Eric left them at the front of Aunt Maggie's house and headed for the wharf. Lillian knocked on the door. Aunt Maggie opened the door and beamed at Lillian. The smile became fixed when she saw Splinter and Bubs. Splinter coughed. Aunt Maggie stepped back.

"Cover your mouth, Splinter. It's not catching, Aunt Maggie," Lillian reassured.

"Mum's got cake," Bubs said. Aunt Maggie's eyes shot towards the basket Lillian was carrying.

"Help Bubs up the steps," Lillian said to Splinter, drawing

Aunt Maggie's attention to Bubs's plastered leg. Aunt Maggie gave Bubs a quick glance then her hand went out to the basket.

"Let me help you with that," she said.

Lillian snatched it away, annoyed at Aunt Maggie's indifference. "I'll just pop it on the table for now and get to the cleaning," she said briskly. "Then we'll have afternoon tea and a talk."

"Valerie broked my leg," Bubs said. Aunt Maggie's eyebrows went up.

"You can tell Aunty after Splinter and I finish the cleaning. We're going to do the windows today." Make her wait, Lillian thought.

The freshly scrubbed floor revealed a pattern on the linoleum that hadn't been visible before. Lillian tossed a bucket of dirty water out the back door and dropped a sodden mass of newspaper into the empty bucket. She stood back and surveyed the vinegar sheen on the windows, which now allowed a clear view of the sea, instead of the normal spotted haze that had every visitor running for an eye test. Lillian wiped her hands on her apron. It was time to get down to business. Hopefully, Aunt Maggie was champing at the bit to find out what happened to Bubs. Lillian went into the kitchen and fetched the cake. The smack of Aunt Maggie's lips was louder than the brave blowfly that hadn't seen the flypapers dangling from the ceiling. Lillian cut three small pieces of cake and one extra large piece. She put them on plates. Splinter and Bubs observed their mother with disciplined silence from two kitchen chairs in the corner of the sunroom and didn't protest at the small slices of cake she passed them. The large slice Lillian held out to Aunt Maggie. When Aunt Maggie made a grab for it Lillian removed the plate from her reach, not enough to be obvious, but enough to get Aunt Maggie's attention. The old lady's eyes shot from the cake to Lillian. "We've had trouble with the children's school, Aunt Maggie. We need to talk after tea." She put the cake in Aunt Maggie's outstretched hand.

Lying back on the chaise longue with her feet up, Aunt Maggie held her plate high and out of reach of the cat ensconced between her thighs. Her black dress was covered in cat hair. Puss purred as he kneaded Aunt Maggie's crotch. "Can I pat Puss, Aunt Maggie?" Splinter asked.

"Of course you can. He likes a scratch behind the ears best." Aunt Maggie smiled approvingly at Splinter. The child had worked as hard as her mother cleaning the windows. It was lovely to be able to see the fishing boats in the distance. Puss gave Splinter's hand a lick. "He likes you," Aunt Maggie said with approval. "So what's the problem with the school? I never liked school myself." Eric's father had caught Aunt Maggie kissing a girl behind the weather shed. He'd told everyone at school and her friends had all shunned her.

Splinter looked at Aunt Maggie with solemn eyes, "Bubs got the cane because she wet her pants. She's scared of the kids and won't go to the lavatory. They hold the door open and watch us do our business. They're mean to us. They say our mother's a pommy." Lillian frowned, it wasn't the story she wanted Splinter to tell.

"What do their parents sound like? I bet there are a few pommies amongst them." Aunt Maggie's forehead creased, "They're everywhere." She shook her head in despair. Lillian sighed. Who would have thought they'd all been allies during the war?

"What did your mother say to the teacher?" Aunt Maggie said.

"Their teacher was rude and patronising." Lillian said before Splinter could answer. "He told me Australian children were potty trained when they started school, that English children obviously weren't and I should bring my children up like Australians. They are Australians, born here, damn the man. He stood over me. I felt like I was holding my hands out for a caning." She studied

40

her hands and thought about the many canings she'd received in the orphanage. "I had a headmistress who was vicious." Splinter and Bubs looked at their mother with big eyes.

"Tch!" frowned Aunt Maggie. A piece of chewed cake dribbled onto the front of her dress. Puss craned his neck and licked it off then rubbed against Aunt Maggie.

"The teacher's clothes smelled of chalk," Lillian said, voicing her thoughts out loud. "It's a bit like brick dust. My throat closes over and I gag when I smell brick dust. I think it's to do with being buried under our bombed house for two days, during the First World War. I hate being closed in." Aunt Maggie, nodded. Her greatest fear was being buried alive and waking up in a coffin.

"Lightning struck a tree and it fell on my brother," Aunt Maggie stroked the cat lying beside her. "We were penning the sheep. I told him to get under the tree out of the rain. My father had to cut the tree up to get him out." She looked past Lillian. "He was a nice boy. I don't like storms."

The story watered a parched seed inside Lillian. It pushed its way upwards, finding cracks between the layers that had kept it dormant for years. Lillian understood loss and reached for the same understanding in the old woman opposite her. "My father was drowned in a diving bell when his ship hit a mine. It happened a few weeks before our house was bombed." A heaviness settled on Lillian.

"Was that our Grandpa?" Splinter said, interrupting Lillian's thoughts. Lillian looked at the attentive faces of her children. Talking about such things wasn't good for them. She cleared her throat and tried to make her voice light.

"How about we have another piece of cake?" Lillian said. Aunt Maggie swung her legs off the chaise and reached for her plate. "Stay there, Aunt Maggie, I know where everything is. Aunt Maggie smiled her pleasure and handed Lillian her plate.

Things are going well, Lillian thought. They were sharing their experiences and establishing a deeper connection. Lillian was feeling more confident. Soon she would steer the conversation towards Bubs's leg and insist on a moving in date.

"What did Eric say when you told him?" Aunt Maggie, asked.

Lillian hesitated. "He was understanding, but then he'd lost his own father when he was young." She picked up the bread knife and cut a piece of cake.

Aunt Maggie double blinked. "I meant the teacher, what did he say about the teacher?"

"Oh, the teacher." It was hard keeping up with Aunt Maggie. An image of Eric's face floated in front of her. The look of disgust he'd given her, when he'd asked what she'd said to the teacher. And Splinter had replied, "Mum didn't say anything, she ran home." Lillian looked across at Splinter. She was all ears. "Splinter, I want you to take Bubs outside for a while. You can hunt for snails in the garden while I talk to Aunty in private." Splinter frowned. Bubs tried to stand up, eager to go outside, and toppled sideways. Lillian jumped up and managed to catch her before she fell. "Help Bubs outside and mind the steps," Lillian said, leading Bubs to the door. Lillian watched them go down the steps and then closed the door. She returned to her chair. "Sorry about that, but it's better the children don't hear this. You never know where they might repeat things," Lillian said. Aunt Maggie sat forward, nodding with anticipation.

"Eric was furious when I told him what had happened. Of course he went to see the teacher. He said the teacher greeted him like a smelly sock, told Eric he didn't attend to school matters on Sundays and tried to shut the door on him. Eric grabbed the front of the teacher's shirt and hauled him outside. He gave the teacher a black eye." Lillian had thought it extreme at the time. Obviously Aunt Maggie didn't; she was looking positively thrilled. It wouldn't have gone that far if Lillian had spoken up for Bubs.

"Well done Eric," Aunt Maggie bristled. Her indignation postmarked Lillian's success. "And what happened to the girlie's leg?"

6

Convincing Aunt Maggie

At last Aunt Maggie was showing some interest in the children. Lillian wished she had a Bex powder to settle her nerves before she got onto the subject of Bubs. It needed all her attention if she was going to clinch the early removal of Aunt Maggie's tenants. "Another slice of cake, Aunt Maggie?" Aunt Maggie's crevassed tongue wiped the crumbs off her lip like a windscreen wiper. She nodded and passed Lillian her plate. Less than half the cake remained, so Lillian put a slice aside for Eric. She poured herself a cup of tepid tea, the colour of dark chocolate and added some powdered milk. It clogged on the top. She should have mixed it with cold water first then poured the tea. She scooped the lumps of milk off the top and returned to her chair with Aunt Maggie's second helping of cake.

"The mill is a rough area and the local children do much as they please," Lillian began. By the time Lillian finished her story

Aunt Maggie was jumping with indignation and Lillian was congratulating herself.

"I hope that girl got a whipping?" Aunt Maggie said. Lillian's lips set in a thin line; neither the child nor her father had apologised.

"We didn't get Bubs to hospital for a week because the bush nurse said her leg was only bruised."

Aunt Maggie's head wobbled with fury. "What an idiot, I'd have known it was broken. Fixed my brother up once when he came off a horse. I put his leg between two fence palings and wound it up with wire. The doctor said I did a fine job."

"I told the nurse I thought it was broken, but she wasn't having it," Lillian said. The blue uniform had stiffened and listed her qualifications while Lillian wilted in front of her. "She told me she would be back in a week to check on Bubs, that there were sick people in other towns she had to attend. She said Australians understood about waiting their turn." Lillian's nostrils flared. Aunt Maggie nodded, agreeing with the nurse. Lillian sat back and jiggled her foot. "I kept Bubs in bed and put hot poultices on her leg. I gave her a crushed aspro and mixed it with hot milk, sugar and a tablespoon of brandy." It was important she show Aunt Maggie how well she could look after an invalid. A flash of worn brown teeth rewarded Lillian's nursing skills.

"Did you give the nurse a piece of your mind?" Aunt Maggie loved a battle.

Lillian's foot went still. Damn! Why had she mentioned the nurse problem? She examined the back of her hand. "Um, yes I did."

Aunt Maggie's eyes narrowed, "What did Eric say?" He was becoming her hero.

"He was away working at the time, only came home when the nurse returned from her rounds, five days later. Bubs leg was blue by then." Lillian recalled Eric's fury.

"Call yourself a nurse," he had yelled, white faced at the sight of Bubs's leg. "Get a camp bed to carry her on. She's going to hospital. I'll borrow Toby's ute." Eric in his fury turned on Lillian. "Any fool can see this leg is broken. You should have stood up to this imbecile. You're bloody gutless," he snarled. She knew he was right; people in authority scared Lillian. There had been too many disciplinarians in the orphanage. Eric had also disciplined her when she had stood up to him. She knew better now.

"He reported the nurse for incompetence and paid the bully's father a visit," Lillian said. Aunt Maggie looked pleased. Lillian didn't mention Eric spent a week in gaol and the policeman a night in hospital.

"Well done, Eric." She stroked the cat in her lap.

"The children are too frightened to go to school. I've let Bubs stay home because her leg's in plaster. Splinter won't go to school without her. We really need to move." There was a pleading edge to her voice.

"Teach them yourself. I had to learn at home. Now come and help me plant some roses. They arrived yesterday." She thrust a Yates catalogue into Lillian's hand.

Devastated, Lillian gazed at the catalogue without seeing. All her cleaning, her stories, and she'd failed to make any headway. Didn't Aunt Maggie have a heart? What would she tell Eric? What else could she do? If only she had the money to move to Melbourne with the children. Damn, damn, Lillian swore under her breath, as she followed Aunt Maggie into the garden.

The earth was soft. Lillian held back tears as she dug a row of holes near the back door for Aunt Maggie to plant the small bushes. "We had those in England," Lillian said, reading the label and trying to sound interested but feeling despairing. "They're going to fill your house with perfume when you open the door."

"Can't leave the door open. The flies get in." Aunt Maggie sat on her haunches. "They'll make a lovely show though."

"What's the garden like next door?" Lillian said, longing in her voice. She stood on Aunt Maggie's step to see over the fence. "God, it looks like they're growing cars." Three vehicles at various stages of decay lay amongst over-grown grass.

Aunt Maggie craned next to Lillian. "I've never really noticed," she said, frowning.

"When I move in I'll make a lovely garden for you to look out on. I won't be able to afford roses, but geraniums should grow well."

"Geraniums attract flies; you could strike some rose cuttings? I know a few gardens around town we could visit with my new secateurs. They came with the last mail order." Aunt Maggie turned shining eyes on Lillian. "Why don't you move in while it's rose planting season? I'll get the tenants out in two weeks and then we can visit some gardens together. We'd have to do it when no one's at home." She gave Lillian a quick look.

Lillian's knees sagged. "Two weeks?" her voice was a squeak. "Of course, yes, that would be wonderful. In two weeks," she said again, to make sure she had heard correctly.

Aunt Maggie nodded. "Two weeks," she said.

Lillian held her breath and pulled Aunt Maggie into a hug. Her heart was in full flight. "I think we should make a toast to rose gardens with another cup of tea before Eric gets back from the seaside."

"Maybe a spot of brandy," Aunt Maggie suggested, catching Lillian's enthusiasm. "And it's beach, not seaside," Aunt Maggie corrected. When Eric arrived to pick Lillian up she was playing Aunt Maggie's piano accompanying the voices of Splinter, Bubs and Aunt Maggie singing *I'm looking over a four-leaf clover.*

7

The Move

The sound of seagulls replaced the whine of saws. The house Aunt Maggie gave them was big. The three bedrooms down one side had French doors that opened onto a wide verandah with sea views. The first bedroom was Johnny's.

"What do you think, Johnny? Nice, isn't it?" Lillian looked for a sign of interest.

"It's alright, I suppose." He looked at the green painted walls. "I had wallpaper with cars on it at Aunty Mavis's."

Lillian's excitement dulled. She understood Johnny's lack of enthusiasm – it was his way of paying them back for sending him away. She would get Eric to spend time with him in the shed, make a billy cart maybe. It had been difficult for her when she returned home after living in the orphanage. Timid and shy, Lillian had hidden her feelings, worried that she might be sent back if she said or did something wrong. As an adult, she understood the difficulties her mother had faced with three children, no husband, home or income and forgave her mother for those years she had spent in the orphanage. It hadn't been as bad for Johnny – Mavis loved him. Lillian gave his hair a rub. "You can put pictures up on the wall and I'll buy some fish and chips for tea. Would you like that?" Johnny's scowl was replaced by a smile. It won't take him long to find his feet, she thought. "Come on there's more to see." The family followed Lillian into the next room. "You're in here, Bubs."

"Alone?" Bubs looked at the French doors opening onto the verandah and the clump of bushes at its edge. There wasn't a key in the lock. She was afraid of bushes, bogeymen and the dark.

"Yes, but you can have tea parties in here with your friends." Lillian reassured.

Friends! Bubs face lit up. There would be no broken legs here. The children in the street were scared of Aunt Maggie. Bubs had learned that from the kid next door who hung over the fence and watched them move in. The kid-next-door's name was Sandra and she said Aunt Maggie was a witch. Her mother had said so, because Aunt Maggie stood outside their house and yelled at her parents if there was a falling out. All the kids in the street knew better than to get the old witch's dander up. "I'll ask Sandra to a tea party," Bubs said, pulling her thumb out of her mouth.

The bedroom next to Bubs's was at the top of the hall, near the front door. Lillian opened it. "And this is your room, Splinter."

Splinter squealed, "It's lovely Mum!" As well as French doors that opened onto the verandah it had a small window that looked onto the street at the front of the house. "I'm going to have pink curtains with flowers on them."

Lillian laughed and moved to the door opposite, opening it with a flourish. "And in here we have the drawing room." She felt like a museum attendant showing off a treasure. They crowded into the large room.

Splinter pirouetted across the dark polished floor to a big bay window, turned and bowed. "I'm going to hold plays and ballets in here. I'll need a long mirror so I can practise my ballet. It can go there." She pointed to the cream-plastered wall between two windows. At the end of the room was a formal fireplace with colourful pottery tiles. A black mantelpiece sat above it. "I can have puppet shows in the fireplace and my dolls can sit on the mantelpiece." She twirled with excitement. "It's bigger than two bedrooms."

Splinter's enthusiasm made Lillian want to cry. She couldn't remember when she had felt so happy. They were all laughing. "Sorry, young lady, this is our bedroom." Lillian put her hand on Eric's arm. They would have a new bed with no lumps in the mattress. She would have a desk to write at and a bookcase.

They moved down the hall into the sitting room. The large brick fireplace was big enough to burn a tree stump. Eric tapped the bowl of his pipe against a brick and filled it with tobacco. He loved a good fire on nights when a southerly howled like the sinners in hell, making toast in its embers and watching the wood burn. He knew just where to put his armchair. He grinned at Lillian. She could smell the chestnuts roasting.

"Are you happy, Dad?" Splinter hadn't seen her parents smile at each other in a long time.

"Sure am, Splinter." Eric was thinking that when Aunt Maggie died he'd sell the house and buy a farm.

"And you, Mum?"

"Yes, my girl, I have you and Johnny home." She pulled them to her. "And I'll have neighbours and shops I can walk to. I'll have a rose garden." A sob caught in her throat and she found herself crying, unable to stop.

Organising the house had taken a couple of weeks and Lillian was grateful that Aunt Maggie had left her alone to unpack and settle in. She straightened the tablecloth in preparation for her first visit and heard a bark from Jess, the stray kelpie from the mill that had attached itself to Eric. Lillian went to the window and saw Aunt Maggie coming through the gate in the fence that Eric had made and now joined their two yards. It saved Lillian having to walk down the driveway and onto the street carrying food trays and Aunt Maggie's washing. She filled the teapot with boiling water.

"There's a nip in the air this morning," Aunt Maggie said as she rocked through the door and moored herself at the table. "A small welcome present." She pulled the newspaper wrapping off a boiled fruitcake and placed it on the table.

"That's lovely, Aunt Maggie. I'll get a plate."

"You'll need a knife. I find a bread knife the best." Aunt Maggie patted the cake. The lace at her wrist, grubby and frayed, tickled the patchy grey icing.

An attack of reflux burned up Lillian's oesophagus when she saw the dirt under Aunt Maggie's nails. She put the cake on a plate and the breadknife next to it. "Would you like to cut it, Aunt Maggie?" As soon as she'd said it, Lillian kicked herself. Aunt Maggie mauled the cake into position and sawed off two slices. Glace cherries pungent with brandy glistened like eyeballs amongst the pressed fruit. Lillian broke off a portion of her slice and nibbled. It was tasty. She tried not to look at Aunt Maggie's hands. "Delicious, you must give me the recipe."

"Don't have one." Aunt Maggie shifted in her seat and released a pocket of poisoned air.

The smell conjured images of derelicts, alleyways and urine-coated doorways. Lillian wiped at her nose with a serviette. "Would you like to see around the house, Aunt Maggie?"

Inquisitive eyes brightened. "Yes, I'd like to see how you've set it up. Someone died in this house, you know. In the drawing room."

Prickles surfaced on the back of Lillian's neck. She believed in spirits and dreams as well as tea leaf reading, her mother had instilled it in her as a child. "Really? Who? How?"

"My sister, Elizabeth, whose grave you cleaned. It was an agonising death, poor thing. They said something was eating her stomach. Her funeral wasn't much to talk about. It was winter and only the geraniums were in bloom." Missiles of cake punctured the air as she spoke. "I hope I don't die in winter." A worried frown moved a smudge of dirt as she slurped the last of her tea.

At that moment Lillian connected with Aunt Maggie's need. "Daphne is lovely in winter, smells heavenly, polyanthus also blooms in winter and there's hellebores. Its nickname is Winter Rose. They grew near a stream on the farm we lost."

"Creek," Aunt Maggie said.

"Creek?"

"You should call it a creek if you don't want to sound like a pommy."

Old Biddy! "Would you like me to pour you another cup of tea, Aunt Maggie?"

"Hellebores? I'll keep an eye out for that." She covered her cup as Lillian lifted the pot to give her a top-up. "No thank you, I'll have a quick look around and then I think I'll go and do some gardening. Come over for a cup of tea tomorrow and I'll show you the Yates catalogue, see if you can find that helle … something rose for me, I'll show you my burial clothes too. You can be in charge of my funeral, see to the flowers, dress me." No man was going to put his hands on her or the children of the town gossips who had made innuendos about her single status. Lillian was in her debt.

Lillian gaped. "I don't know what to say, Aunt Maggie."

Aunt Maggie waved her hand in the air. "There's no need to thank me. We might go for a walk after our tea and visit some rose bushes." She winked at Lillian. "We might need the secateurs."

"Oh! Yes, righto." God, Lillian thought, I'm about to become Aunt Maggie's undertaker and rose thief. She felt a flood of warmth for the old lady.

The chair scraped as Aunt Maggie pushed it back and struggled to her feet. "Welcome to your new home."

"Thank you. I'm sure we're going to be good friends," Lillian said, leading her to the door and giving her a peck on the cheek.

Aunt Maggie's eyes danced away from Lillian. "Tomorrow, then." As soon as she was out of sight, Lillian opened the window and waved a tea towel around the room.

"What are you doing?" Eric asked, entering the kitchen.

"God almighty! Your aunt smells like a bucket of old socks. You'll have to say something to her, Eric. She needs a bath."

"Don't look at me like that. I'm a man, I can't tell a woman to have a bath."

Lillian bit her lip. "She's your aunt."

"If I remember correctly, you're the one who said she'd be bliss to look after," he laughed. "Looking after oldies is women's work so it's over to you." He picked up a knife, cut a slice of boiled fruitcake and took a bite. "Nice cake, I could get drunk on this. Where did you get the brandy from?" A tinge of rebellion nudged Lillian as she watched him finish the slice.

"Aunt Maggie made it. Did you see the state of her nails?"

Eric's lips pulled away from his teeth. "Thanks."

"Sorry, I didn't mean to put you off, I was just thinking about how we could tell her about her hygiene."

"Well you think about it while I sort out the shed." He ran his tongue across his teeth to clean off the cake and grimaced.

"That's right, leave me with the problem." She glared at his departing back and shut the door. How on earth was she going to get Aunt Maggie to have a bath? She couldn't just tell her she stank. What would the old girl think of her? Lillian didn't want to ruin their relationship after all Aunt Maggie had done

53

for them. Taking care of her wasn't going to be easy. Deep in thought, Lillian went to the window and watched Aunt Maggie cross the yard.

The kitchen door flew open and Splinter entered. She dropped her school bag on the floor. "Phew! It pongs like the cannery in here," she said.

"Aunt Maggie brought a cake over to see how we've settled in. I think she needs a bath and I'm wondering how to tell her." Lillian smiled at the look of concern on Splinter's face.

"You can't make her have a bath, Mum," Splinter frowned. "She might tell us to move out."

"I don't think she'd do that. We'll work something out. So how was school?"

"There's another new girl in my class. She's the Presbyterian Reverend's daughter."

"Really? What's she like?"

"She talks a lot and has a loud voice. She said her mother said the last vicar left the parish house filthy."

"Did she now." Lillian pursed her lips in thought. Tomorrow she was going to morning tea at Ingrid Kasbauer's, maybe Ingrid would have some ideas on what she could do about Aunt Maggie. It would be Lillian's third visit to Ingrid's since she had moved to Eden. They shared a love of books and had become good friends. But Lillian wasn't going to mention to Eric that she was going to visit Ingrid or discuss Aunt Maggie with her because Eric had raised his arm in a 'Heil Hitler' salute when Lillian had told him Ingrid had invited her to morning tea the first time. "She's Austrian," Lillian had said in Ingrid's defence.

"So was Hitler," Eric replied. Rather than embarrass Ingrid, Lillian used Aunt Maggie as an excuse not to reciprocate with invitations to tea, saying the old lady was possessive of her, which wasn't entirely untrue as Aunt Maggie always came up with something she needed doing if Lillian said she was going anywhere.

The walk to Ingrid's was a killer. She lived on the lookout hill above the wharf. Lillian stopped for a breather and took in the view. The day sparkled, like the bay. Fishing boats lined up along the wharf, their masts dotted with seagulls waiting for a feed. Children were diving off the jetty and racing each other to the small beach. Lillian screwed up her eyes to see if she could see Splinter and Johnny, but she was too far away. She sighed with the relief of it all. Aunt Maggie was a fairy godmother even if she was stinky. Lillian hummed as she tackled the rest of the hill.

Ingrid was a large woman with a broad kindly face and eyes as blue as the bay on a sunny day. She handed Lillian a plate of strudel. "Perhaps you could talk to ze doctor and ask him what to do? Maybe he tell her she could get sickness, ya?"

Lillian wrinkled her brow. "Aunt Maggie would know I had said something if I did that. I was thinking about the new Reverend. Have you met him? Have the CWA ladies said anything to you?"

Ingrid lowered her head. "CWA ladies don't talk to me. Many husbands died in war."

A moment's silence sat between them. "My father died in the First World War," Lillian said, quietly. Ingrid stiffened.

"Mine too. He was good man. We starve. Beg for food."

The Zeppelin that bombed Lillian's house appeared in Lillian's mind's eye. Her skin prickled. What would hers and Ingrid's lives have been like if there hadn't been a war? It was 1950; the war was over. Lillian leant across and touched Ingrid's hand. "It's not our fault, Ingrid." They clutched hands and cried.

"I think more strudel, ya?" Ingrid said, wiping her eyes and smiling. "Now we think about Aunty. Why not Aunty have Reverend to her house for afternoon tea?"

8

The Bath

The plate of scones was empty. Aunt Maggie licked her chops and beamed at Splinter.

"Mum helped me make them," Splinter said.

"She's turning into a good little cook," Lillian said. "She's made a friend at school. The new Reverend's daughter." Splinter watched her mother for her cue.

"The new Reverend's arrived? What's he like?" Aunt Maggie asked. Lillian coughed and dabbed her mouth with her handkerchief. It was Splinter's cue.

"His daughter's ten, same age as me," said Splinter. "She said the last Reverend had left the house very dirty."

Aunt Maggie's eyes widened. "Did she, now?"

"Yes, and she said that her father was upset because no one had invited them to afternoon tea yet. He said the CWA women must be a slack lot." Splinter gave her mother a quick look and received a nod of approval. Splinter sat back.

Aunt Maggie's head wobbled with indignation. "That wouldn't have happened in my day when I was in charge. I always organised the CWA get-togethers to welcome the new Reverends."

"You know, I was just thinking, Aunt Maggie, why don't we ask him to afternoon tea here?" Lillian said.

"I could make scones." Splinter said.

Aunt Maggie's eyes swivelled around the room. She put her finger to her lips and squinted at the clean window. Lillian waited. Splinter watched.

"That's a good idea," she said. "I'll show that lot I'm still capable." The CWA women had retired Aunt Maggie with the excuse she was too old to participate. None of them had been game enough to tell her that the locals had complained about her picking the icing off the cakes on the cake stall. "Perhaps Splinter could polish the silver for me? The linen cloth will need a press."

"I'm sure Splinter would love to do that." Lillian sewed a stuffed toy smile on her face and gazed at Splinter, who nodded glum faced. "Splinter could also help me give you a bath to freshen you up." Lillian held her breath and her smile in place. Aunt Maggie's eyes shot from Lillian to Splinter. She licked her lips. "At the same time, I could give your dress a spruce. I think Puss must have gotten in the cupboard at some time and sprayed on it. It smells a bit … er, catty. And we could get your lace collar all starched up," Lillian purred.

Aunt Maggie crouched in her chair and pressed her chins into her neck and looked down at her food stained dress. Lillian gave Splinter a small nod.

"I can help you, Aunt Maggie. You can have some of my new bath salts. You'll smell lovely."

"I don't need a bath. I had a wash yesterday." Aunt Maggie hunkered down on guard.

"We could boil water on your stove and fill the tub. It wouldn't take long," Lillian said. "We haven't met the Reverend's wife yet and we wouldn't want her to make any derogatory remarks around the parish about us, would we?" Lillian turned to Splinter. "The Reverend's daughter obviously repeats everything she hears at home from what Splinter tells me."

"He's not her real father," Splinter said. "Her mother's divorced." She sat back looking pleased with herself. Aunt Maggie leant forward.

"Divorced!" She had forgotten she was a pretend widow; that she had left her own husband. She loathed to break her hymen. Had left him after six months of marriage, virginity still intact. The chaise lounge creaked.

Alarmed at Splinter's knowledge, but sensing a victory, Lillian stood up. "I'm going to make a fire and boil some water. Where's the tub?"

"In the spare room," Aunt Maggie muttered.

Lillian and Splinter carried the tub into the kitchen. Two kettles and four saucepans of water sputtered on the stove. Aunt Maggie, swaddled in a moth-eaten dressing gown, the colour of ageing putty, glowered from a kitchen chair. Lillian arranged the soap, face washer and towels on a chair next to the tub.

"You can put the bath salts in now, Splinter," Lillian said. Splinter sprinkled her precious bath salts in the tub. The first kettle of boiling water went in, then Lillian added some cold water. Splinter swished it around. The water frothed. Lillian put aside one saucepan of boiling water to rinse Aunt Maggie's hair and emptied the rest in the tub. "All ready," Lillian said, testing the water with her hand to make sure it was the right temperature. "Now you get one side of Aunt Maggie, Splinter and I'll get the other to make sure she doesn't slip." It was more to make sure Aunt Maggie didn't run away. Splinter's eyes swivelled around Aunt Maggie's big pink folds and the sparse grey beard between her legs as she stepped in the bath.

Aunt Maggie scowled, "I didn't expect this when you moved in." Her sour tone made Lillian feel uneasy.

"You'll look like the lady of the manor when we've finished. Just think of how impressed the Reverend will be." Lillian handed Aunt Maggie the face washer. "Put this over your face so you don't get soap in your eyes when I wash your hair." It wasn't much different to bathing her siblings when they were small, Lillian thought, as she soaped Aunt Maggie's back. It had suited Lillian's mother to keep her at home while she went out to work, and at the time it had suited the timid child Lillian had become, thanks to an orphanage where rules and the cane replaced love. It occurred to Lillian that if her mother had encouraged her to go out to work she might have had more confidence, stood up for herself, managed to handle Eric's mother and his temper better. Been an asset to him instead of the burden he thought she was. Lillian stopped the thought. If it wasn't for her effort they wouldn't be living next door to Aunt Maggie. It wasn't Eric on his knees giving the old lady a bath.

Lillian scooped up a saucepan full of water and poured it over Aunt Maggie's head. She spluttered and slapped the air with the wash cloth, soaking the front of Lillian's dress. The tub rocked as Aunt Maggie tried to stand. Water sloshed over the side and pooled on the floor.

"Sit down, Aunt Maggie, or you'll slip. Get the mop, Splinter. Stop that, you're soaking me." Lillian wrestled the cloth from Aunt Maggie and stood back, hands on hips. "Aunt Maggie, I'm very grateful to you for giving us a house and I agreed to take care of you as payment but you have to let me do this. If you don't keep clean, you might get polio and die."

"Polio!" Aunt Maggie's pulse quickened; Lillian had struck a hidden terror.

"Yes, there's an epidemic."

"We've never had polio in Australia." Aunt Maggie's jaw jutted. "The pommies must have brought it here." For a moment Lillian considered filling the saucepan with cold water.

Splinter sucked in her cheeks and looked important. "Two kids at school have polio and they have to live in an iron lung." Aunt Maggie went still.

"What's an iron lung?"

Splinter leant in and whispered. "It's like a coffin."

A look of terror flashed across Aunt Maggie's face. "Finish the job, then, and make sure you dry me properly. I am not going to die of a foreigner's disease."

9

The Reverend's Visit

The house was immaculate, silverware shone and Aunt
Maggie still smelt of lavender bath salts, four days on.
Lillian was proud of her effort. She heard the Reverend's car
pull up in the drive and alerted Aunt Maggie then melted into
the kitchen to observe the guests from the kitchen window.
She saw the appraising look Eric gave the Reverend's wife as he
held the car door open for her. Eric said something, which the
wife responded to with an affected giggle, and Lillian lost her
enthusiasm for Aunt Maggie's afternoon tea. Eric was flirting.
The last time she had witnessed it, was with a waitress in the
hotel where they were staying after the fire took their farm.
Lillian noted the Reverend's wife's blonde hair and large bosom.
Not unlike the waitress at the hotel. The waitress had leant over
Eric's shoulder. Her melon breasts visible between two buttons
that had taken flight. "What's your fancy tonight, handsome?

The meat pie is yum." She had giggled, parting lips coated with lipstick, displaying nicotine stained teeth. "You can tell me how you like the pie when you've finished," she'd batted her glug-filled eyelashes at Eric. Lillian's blood boiled from the memory. Eric had looked into her cleavage, "I'm a slow eater," he said and winked up at her. The waitress had laughed and her breasts had brushed his arm as she had straightened. Lillian could still feel the humiliation of it. So brazen in front of her and the children and just after she had lost her home.

In hindsight Lillian wished she hadn't created the scene that had followed. But her nerves were raw after the fire, she wasn't thinking straight. She remembered standing up and throwing her serviette on the table. "I've had enough of this," she'd said. "How dare you talk to my husband like that, you hussy." Eric was on his feet in a flash. He had looked around the dining room at the other diners, given an inane laugh and tapped the side of his head with his finger. The waitress had scuttled off. Plum, the hotel owner had come over and asked them to leave the dining room. Back in their bedroom Eric had given her a hiding. Lillian now eyed the Reverend's wife and wished the afternoon was over. She slipped into the sunroom and watched Aunt Maggie greet her guests with a winner's chuckle.

"Good of you to come, Reverend Parker." The Reverend gave a polite smile. Aunt Maggie beamed. Her excitement was palpable. She had put one over the CWA ladies. Shown them up. Lillian felt pleased for her. With a flounce of clean lace at her wrist, Aunt Maggie ushered the short, rotund, Reverend, with his thin receding hair and watery blue eyes, inside. She motioned to Lillian hovering by the kitchen door. "This is Eric's wife, Lillian." Lillian pegged the corners of her lips up and nodded. The Reverend's wife followed her husband in and gave her strawberry blond curls a pat. Her plump cheeks dimpled at Lillian and her doll-blue eyes swept up and around the room. "Charming," she said to Lillian. The glance she gave Lillian's dress and brown shoes made Lillian feel like a fashion hazard. Not that Lillian would wear a white dress with a gathered skirt covered in large red hibiscus if she had a backside that large. Or a heart shaped neckline that showed off her breasts if she was a Reverend's wife. Although Lillian did envy the white bag and matching patent leather high heels. Taking the role of host Eric dashed ahead of the visitors and held out a chair for the Reverend's wife.

"Please sit here, Mrs Parker." He ogled her large round bottom as she pushed it towards the seat.

"Thank you." The Reverend's wife gave him a coy smile. Eric took the chair opposite and grinned into her cleavage.

The purse of Aunt Maggie's lips didn't go unnoticed by Lillian. It wasn't Eric's job to show visitors to their chairs. He was always correcting her if she made a social faux pas. Lillian watched his lechery and wasn't fooled by the coy response of the Reverend's wife. The woman was eating it up. The gossip in town was that the wife, a divorcee with a child, had been the Reverend's housekeeper in his last parish. Their affair had caused a scandal, which was followed by a hasty wedding and a new appointment to the backwater parish of Eden. Lillian had heard about it in the butcher shop. She sneaked a look at Aunt Maggie to see what impression the Reverend's wife was making. Having studied Aunt Maggie's reactions to everything, Lillian could see she was observing the wife through hooded eyes to avoid detection. Good, Lillian thought, knowing Aunt Maggie would be disapproving of the thick layer of powder, and the bottle blonde hair that had spent a night in curlers. The Reverend's wife crossed her legs displaying a plump calf. Aunt Maggie frowned. "Ladies didn't cross their legs, only their ankles," she'd told Lillian on one occasion. Lillian hadn't crossed her legs in Aunt Maggie's company since. The Reverend's wife peeled off her gloves. Lillian saw Aunt Maggie's mouth open at the red nail polish. The wife has nice hands, Lillian thought, looking at her own work-worn hands.

"Now, how do you take your tea, Mrs errr...?" Aunt Maggie shot a quick look towards Lillian, but Lillian couldn't help her hesitation, she'd been too intent on Eric when the Reverend had introduced his wife.

"Parker, but you can call me Lenore. Weak, black and a slice of lemon," Lenore said, syrup-voiced. Pink lips parted in a smile revealing a large gap between her front teeth.

The only lemon Aunt Maggie had was the expression on her face. She raised the creases in her forehead at Lillian who gave a shrug and poured what looked like a urine sample through a silver strainer into a cup. A little deflated, Aunt Maggie turned to her next guest.

"And you, Reverend?"

"White with one sugar, please."

"That's easily fixed." Aunt Maggie regained her confidence. She turned to go and saw Eric lift his face expectantly. Her eyes became darts. "Tea for you, Eric?" Her words were clipped.

"Thank you, Aunt Maggie, I like mine strong, milk and two sugars, please." He smiled at Lenore Parker and leant towards her conspiratorially. "We navy men like our tea strong and sweet." He gave a shark grin.

Feeling the creep of humiliation as Eric fawned over the Reverend's wife, Lillian watered the tea, didn't use the strainer and only put in one sugar. "This is Eric's." She handed it to Aunt Maggie. They exchanged a look and Aunt Maggie smirked.

Tea sloshed into the saucer as Aunt Maggie's hand trembled towards Eric. "Oh!" Aunt Maggie gave a shallow gasp and her free hand went to her heart. Eric grabbed the cup. The Reverend started to rise. Aunt Maggie staggered slightly and thumped into her chair.

"That happens to me too when I get up too quickly." Lenore neighed loudly and tossed her hair.

"Here, Aunt Maggie, I've made a fresh pot, sit and have your tea. I'll manage everything." Lillian handed Aunt Maggie a cup of tea and received a blink of gratitude. She passed around the scones and then sat down. Her eyes flicked between Eric and Lenore Parker as they guffawed at each other.

The afternoon progressed with Lenore Parker enjoying being the centre of attention, entertaining the company with stories about their former parish. Eric was a rapt audience. His sensual lips smiled, laughed and pouted in response. Her ginger eyelashes fluttered in the light of his admiration. Lillian sat on the edge of her chair while the Reverend filled her unreceptive ear with the state of the parish funds. She murmured responses and nodded politely, her mind on Aunt Maggie, worried what she was thinking about Eric's behaviour, or if she had noticed. She rubbed her temples and glanced across at Aunt Maggie and saw her look of concern.

Aunt Maggie's lips twitched encouragement. Then she folded her arms and her face darkened. The effort that Lillian had gone to, to make the Reverend's visit a success, had pleased Aunt Maggie and she didn't want Lillian to get a migraine – which usually meant shrivelled sausages and lumpy mash for tea, cooked by Splinter. And Aunt Maggie had had enough of the strawberry blonde wife, whose name she could not remember, who had dismissed her heart turn with a patronising smile and turned her cannonball breasts towards Eric's devouring eyes. And she'd had enough of Eric who had acted like a slobbering buffoon all afternoon. The guild ladies were welcome to the new Reverend and his wife.

"So, when will you be giving a sermon on the ten commandments, Reverend?" Aunt Maggie's voice drowned the guffaws of

Eric and Lenore Parker. Lillian tore her eyes away from Eric and straightened in her chair.

The Reverend stirred his tea and considered the question. "We won't reach that reading for a few months, Mrs Stewart. Is that your favourite sermon, if I may ask?"

"No, but there're a few in the parish who should be reminded about the retributions of adultery." She gazed around the circle, then rested her eyes on Eric.

Oh, God, what's she up to? Lillian thought. She saw the cup in Eric's hand stop midway to his mouth and return to its saucer. He shot a pleading look towards Lillian. Lillian pretended ignorance. The situation was getting interesting and she wasn't going to distract Aunt Maggie by handing more cake around as a diversion for Eric's discomfort. Her lips parted in anticipation and her eyes egged Aunt Maggie on.

"Is that the truth, Mrs Stewart?" It was a polite question that didn't require an answer.

"What else would it be, Reverend?" Aunt Maggie's voice held a challenge. The Lord's instrument double blinked and looked to his wife for help.

Lenore Parker leant towards Aunt Maggie, proud of her ability to defuse awkward moments. "I noticed your rose garden when I came in, Mrs Stewart. My favourite flowers, such lovely perfume. What's the red one called?" Lillian held her breath.

"Jezebel!" Aunt Maggie's talons stretched in her lap. Her eyes held Lenore Parker's as the name hung in the space between them. "And I'm growing them for a funeral."

Lillian could have fainted with delight as she watched the crimson petals fall off the Jezebel rose and heard Eric clear his throat. A feeling of admiration filled Lillian – if she only had some of Aunt Maggie's courage. Feet shuffled in the silence. When Lillian managed to rearrange her face she looked across at Aunt Maggie whose eyes went to the cups and transported them to the sideboard with the slightest movement of her head. Lillian jumped up. "All finished?" she asked the red-faced wife whose mouth had closed for the first time that afternoon and could only nod a reply. Lillian hummed as she carried the crockery to the kitchen.

During the relief of goodbyes, Aunt Maggie pressed a thick envelope in the Reverend's hand. "A donation towards the church hall," she purred.

He felt the wad of notes with a practiced finger. "May our Lord bless your generosity, Mrs Stewart." His smile was beatific. Aunt Maggie felt a pang of guilt and wished she'd given him at least one note with its number intact. The snails were prolific this year and had eaten quite a bit of her money. Tomorrow she'd take her money out of the paper bags and put it in a cardboard box. She was also sorry she'd bothered to bath.

Lillian stood at Aunt Maggie's window and watched Eric help the Reverend's wife into the car. She turned, dejected, as Aunt Maggie entered the kitchen, bristling with indignation.

"That's that then," said Aunt Maggie. When Lillian didn't reply, Aunt Maggie gazed around the kitchen for something to rally her spirits. The secateurs sat on the stove so she picked them up. "The Reverend said he was going to the hospital to visit the sick so he won't be home for a while." She opened and closed the secateurs. It took a moment for Lillian to realise the implication.

"You want to prune their roses?" She looked at Aunt Maggie and felt a surge of gratitude. "I'll get a basket and my coat."

They scuttled behind the hedges, keeping out of sight of the neighbours, Lillian picking up cuttings while Aunt Maggie pruned. Each cutting Lillian dropped in the basket was a piece of Eric and Lenore Parker. On the way home Aunt Maggie hooked her arm through Lillian's. "You won't have anything to worry about, I'll look after you," she said. "Just make sure I have a good funeral."

Lillian looked at Maggie's shiny face, pink with health. "Tomorrow, I'll make you a lovely steak and kidney pie." Prompted by instinct she added, "Eric had a win at the races and bought some nice steak." The old body stiffened next to Lillian.

"He gambles?" The voice smacked with disapproval.

"A lot," Lillian said, with a glint in her eye.

"His father was a waster," Aunt Maggie replied. Lillian's ears pricked. "But I don't want to discuss him, maybe another time. We should plant the cuttings in the morning before it gets too hot." The smile on the old face was full of mischief. Lillian gave her arm a squeeze. She was feeling much better.

10

Cora

They knelt on sugar bags, side by side, planting the Reverend's cuttings next to the Jezebel rose, grinning like co-conspirators. When the planting was finished, Lillian pulled off her rubber gloves.

"Come on Aunt Maggie, we deserve a cup of tea and a scone. There's a gardening article I found in the *Women's Weekly*. It was wrapped around my meat. I thought we might read it." They passed a pleasant hour until they heard Eric's truck return. "He's back," Lillian said. Aunt Maggie's lips disappeared. Lillian stood, she already had her strategy worked out. "I'd better go and get dinner started."

The pastry toughened as Lillian thumped and rolled, wishing it was Eric under her rolling pin while she listened to his excuses. Again! She'd heard it all the night before: how he had only been helping Aunt Maggie entertain her guests. How she should have been grateful to him. How the wicked old bitch had a nerve embarrassing an innocent lady like the Reverend's wife. Lillian let his bluster bounce off her ears without commenting, the same as she had done the night before. She held him in her peripheral vision and caught his look of mistrust. She ignored it. Let him wonder what I tell Aunt Maggie, she thought. Lillian conjured up pictures of the Reverend's decimated rose bushes with feelings of malicious delight.

The room went quiet. Eric had stopped talking. Lillian continued to pound the pastry in silence. She heard him growl, then slam out of the kitchen and her body went limp with relief. It was the first time she hadn't cried, or said, "How could you do this to me." Her act of indifference had stumped him, robbed him of the opportunity to hit out and blame her for his own shortcomings. She congratulated herself, and inwardly thanked Aunt Maggie for her support, grinning at the memory of the Jezebel innuendo, and her fervour as she had reduced the height of the Reverend's rose bushes by three feet.

Lillian pulled at the pastry; it stretched like an old piece of bubble gum, tough as a boot. Aunt Maggie deserved her best pastry. She put the ruined pastry to the side for Eric's pie and started on a new lot. It wasn't that she was jealous of the Reverend's wife – her feelings for Eric didn't go deep enough for that. It was how humiliated, demeaned and worthless he made her feel. How would he feel if the shoe was on the other foot? Not that she'd be game or even interested. The Cora episode had taught her that. Lillian's thoughts went back to their farm before the fire and she wondered how Aunt Maggie would react if she told her what Eric had done.

The Cora thing happened four months before the fire took their farm. The farm Lillian had worked hard to turn into a home. Patchwork curtains made from second-hand clothes Mavis had sent her hung at the windows and cushion covers she'd embroidered and stuffed with chicken feathers adorned an old settee. The rough plank floor was covered in cow and sheepskins. There was a glass cabinet with Lillian's Wedgwood china and a sea chest full of her books. It was rough, but they had been happy. Lillian had three children and had worked alongside Eric, milking cows and growing produce. She had made a friend called Cora, her only friend. Farm life was solitary. Cora was a widow with four children. She owned the only taxi in town. She'd delivered Lillian's food supplies the day they moved onto the farm and had stayed for morning tea. A month on and Cora asked Eric if he'd be her back-up driver in case her children needed her on weekends. They'd welcomed the extra money, and to show her gratitude Lillian babysat Cora's children if she was called out at night. Cora's husband had been an English immigrant. He'd died in a tractor accident. She showed Lillian photographs of him in England; said she was saving up to take her children to meet their grandparents.

The morning of the church cake stall found Lillian dithering over which pots of her homemade jam she should donate. She wanted to put her best foot forward to show she could make jam as well as any Australian farmer's wife. Eric was her tester. She'd made some scones, clotted cream, and scooped a spoonful each of strawberry, apricot and plum jam onto a plate. She sat the morning tea in front of Eric, on a table made from three wood palings stretched between two trestles. A cross-stitched tablecloth, with a picture of a thatched cottage and a woman gathering flowers in the garden, covered the table. Lillian scanned Eric's face and was rewarded by his smile and the smack of his lips.

"Best jam in the district." He scraped the last of the jam off his plate and glued two broken pieces of scone together.

"Good," Lillian said, pleased. "I'm donating some jars to the church cake stall today. I'm also taking a couple for Cora. You can drop them off to her."

Eric took the cakes off Lillian as she climbed down from the truck and carried them to the church cake stall. Two women in paisley frocks – one blue, the other red – touched their hair and smiled at him.

"What a help you are, Eric."

He lifted his hat. "It's always a pleasure, ladies." His eyes crinkled and his generous lips curved back in a good-natured smile. They tittered and moved some plates on the table. Lillian smiled. Eric was such a charmer.

"Will you be joining the menfolk for a cup of tea?" The woman in red paisley motioned towards a group of men sitting at a small table by the church entrance.

Eric looked away. "Ah, no, I have to do a taxi run."

"Cora must keep you busy," said blue paisley, and smiled at her friend.

Eric reddened. "Well, see you later then." He tipped his hat and turned away. The smiles disappeared from the women's faces. Knowing eyes collided then rolled across to Lillian, leaving an imprint of suggestion in the dust between them.

The reaction of the women irritated Lillian. "Cora's unwell. Eric's helping out." Why did she feel she had to justify the situation?

The woman in red paisley patted Lillian's hand. "Of course she is, dear." The hand withdrew and arranged some cakes. Lillian frowned, what was she inferring?

An hour later, by the river, Eric was panting. "I'm about to cross the finish line," he gasped.

"No," Cora moaned, "I'm not ready." She dug her nails deep

72

into Eric's backside. He jolted, the sudden pain breaking his rhythm. He stopped pumping, felt her thrust up, heard her moan and then pushed into her. Cora bucked. His head hit the glass and he opened his eyes and stared straight into a kid's face pressed against the steaming window. "Jesus, we've been spotted." He untangled himself from Cora and caught his knee between the seats. "Shit!" Cora shot up and pulled her dress down. The kids took off. Eric started the car and chased after them but they left the road and ran through the trees. He stopped the car.

"Bloody hell, I'm in for it."

"Leave her. Move in with me." Cora had let Eric know she was available when he began driving her taxi. It was hard bringing up four kids and running a business on your own. They'd been having an affair for a while. Eric was handsome, fun. Lillian was shy, nervous: didn't swim, ride horses or want to learn to drive. She could read tea leaves, though, and told Cora she had a secret lover. It had unsettled Cora for a time. But Cora was right for Eric and Lillian wasn't.

"No fear, my mother wouldn't abide divorce. She'd cut me out of her will and I'd lose my share of the farm. My grandfather built that place and one day it'll be mine. Nothing is worth losing that."

Cora's eyes narrowed. "Thanks very much."

He didn't hear her, his mind busy on solutions. "How about lending me the car for a week? I've got a plan."

"And what do you expect me to live off?" Cora was hurt by his rejection. She had struggled to keep up with the needs of the town, fending off potential competition. A week without the taxi might give someone else ideas. Anyway, why should she help him cover his tracks at her expense? There had been plenty of Eric's scratching her itch on the back seat. She didn't care about protecting her reputation. She was single and men were fair game. "The answer is no."

Eric got out of the car and skimmed the bush for a stir of leaves or a flock of startled birds. He then turned to Cora. "We need to work out a good story."

Out of breath, one of Eric's witnesses raced towards the cake stall, his eyes as big as gobstoppers and fearing for his life. He stopped in front of his mother, panting. "Me and Douglas," he gulped, "was playin' hide-and-seek at the creek and saw the taxi jumpin' up and down. We took a look and the taxi lady was in the back seat with Johnny's dad. He was on top of her with his pants off and his head was bangin' on the window. He chased us in the car."

Red paisley's face went the colour of her dress. She dragged her son off to the side and scolded him. The child cast a furtive glance towards Lillian. He sunk his head into his shoulders and looked at his shoes.

A bayonet twisted in Lillian's gut. It couldn't be true. But she knew it was. Eric enjoyed the effect he had on women. Flirted with them. And made fun of them later if she commented. She had shrugged it off as harmless. What a fool she was. Her breath came in short gasps. She put her hands on the cake table for support. Tuts of sympathy receded down a tunnel and the day disappeared into night as Lillian folded to the ground.

"Here, drink this." Blue paisley thrust a cup of tea in Lillian's hand. Her voice was kind. Lillian took a sip without tasting and drew in a sob. "Don't fret. Think of the children. Eric isn't the first one that she-dog has dropped her pants for. My Bert's told me. We wanted to warn you but didn't know how, you being from England."

"I ... I've got to go." Lillian pushed the cup away. She wanted to hide from the pitying eyes.

"My Bert will give you and the kids a ride home. You wait

here and I'll get the children." She patted Lillian's hand and bustled off.

The girls were in bed asleep and Lillian was reading Johnny a story when Eric arrived home. He stood in Johnny's doorway. Lillian didn't look up.

"I'm glad you got a ride home. I sent Kate's kid to tell you I had to do a trip to Bairnsdale but she said you'd already gone." Lillian knew he was watching her face for a reaction, so he'd know where he stood. She stopped reading, not trusting her voice, coughed and continued reading without acknowledging his presence. It wasn't looking good for Eric.

"Cora twisted her ankle. It was quite a bad wrench. She had to lie on the back seat with her leg up." That might explain what the kids saw. He'd tell Cora to wear a bandage tomorrow. "It took a while at the hospital. Fancy a cuppa?" He stroked his chin.

That was a good one. He must have wrapped her leg in his trousers, Lillian thought. No doubt they had planned what to say. How could he betray her like that? Her voice faltered as she continued to read, not trusting herself to look at him and not wanting to make a scene in front of Johnny. A tear rolled down her cheek and she brushed it away.

Eric shuffled in the doorway. "I'll stick the kettle on, then." He decided to wait until Lillian said something. It was possible she wouldn't have the guts and it would all blow over. He headed towards the kitchen to look for something to eat. There was nothing in the oven. She hadn't cooked. That was a first. He made a honey sandwich and got another story ready.

"Go to sleep, Johnny." Lillian closed the book and took a deep breath. She put out the light and went into the kitchen. Her eyes were an aquarium as she looked at Eric.

He handed her a cup of tea. "So how did the cake stall go?" The aquarium burst.

"The children saw you with Cora." Tears washed her face.

He turned from the disappointment in her voice. He was a mongrel and knew it. He'd cheated on her before, but she hadn't found out. "I don't know what you're talking about. Cora hurt her ankle."

"That's bullshit! A ten-year-old told his mother, who was standing right next to me at the church cake stall. The bloody church cake stall, Eric!" She was shouting now, her eyes large black holes. "He told his mother that Johnny's bare-arsed dad was on top of the taxi lady and that his head was banging on the window. How could you? You did it to the only friend I have, in a public place, for everyone to see. Haven't you any shame? Any thought for me?"

"It was nothing."

"Nothing? Really? How long have you been doing it with her?" Lillian couldn't bring herself to mention her friend's name.

"Look, I only did it so I could borrow the car and take you to visit your mother in Melbourne. We can't get all the kids in the truck."

"You did it for me! Is that what you're saying?" Lillian's eyebrows shot into her widow's peak.

He had surprised her. "You're always going on about seeing your mother, right? I thought ..."

"I'm being blamed!" It was hard to fathom his reasoning and for a moment Lillian dropped anchor, until she saw that winner's look on his face. "You stick your dick in that woman and blame me?"

Her coarseness caught him off guard. Lillian had never challenged him before. He ground his teeth. "It just happened. I asked Cora if I could borrow the taxi for a week to take you to Melbourne, give you a surprise, and she asked me to get in the back seat and talk it over with her. Next thing she was on my lap. What's a man to do?"

"I'd rather have ridden a horse to Melbourne than have you riding her. You, you, rutting animal." Lillian clawed her fingers and flung herself at Eric. He caught her wrists and shook her hard. She bit her tongue. Blood filled her mouth. She didn't recognise the look in his eyes.

The vein in his temple bulged. "Don't talk to me like that, woman." He clasped both her hands in one of his and slapped her across the face.

The blow made her ears ring. He slapped the other side of her face. She staggered, mouth open in shock. He held her up, his fingers biting into her thin wrists. Hurt and fear filled her eyes. She gulped back sobs and tried to free her hands. Her wrists pained in his vice grip. She pulled and struggled against him. "You're hurting me, Eric." He shook her hard and her head banged against the wall. She cried out.

"Let Mummy go!" Johnny stood near the door white-faced, two small fists held out in front of him, facing his father.

"Get out of here." Eric snarled. Johnny aimed a boot at his father's leg and wrestled between them, pushing against his father's anger. Eric shoved him away. Johnny sprawled on his back and covered his head with his arms. He felt the floor move under his father's footsteps and heard the door slam. He took a peek. His father had gone. His mother was crumpled on the floor, sobbing.

Three days later Eric returned with a bunch of roses and a stuffed rabbit for Johnny. "I'm sorry, Lil." He hung his head at the sight of her black eye and bruised cheeks. He was glad she couldn't get into town. It was bad enough being caught with Cora without the gossips saying he beat his wife. He felt ashamed of himself. He hadn't meant to hit her but she'd attacked him and something inside him had snapped. "I didn't mean to hurt you. It's tough for us blokes with all the war widows. They come looking for it, you know. It won't happen again."

There was many an occasion Cora had told Lillian how lucky she was to have such a handsome husband. Why hadn't she seen through her? Even the woman in blue paisley had mentioned Eric wasn't her first conquest. It wasn't just his fault. And if she hadn't rushed at him and scratched him he wouldn't have hit her. The shock of what he'd done nudged aside her excuses. He had slept with her best friend. He had hit her many times. Left her with bruises and broken her trust. In his absence she had thought about what she should do. She knew he wouldn't give up their farm; that she would be the one expected to leave. There would be no money, and the children? That was what worried her the most, the thought that he might take them off her and leave them motherless. Lillian understood what that was like. She looked at the roses and the guilt in Eric's eyes and convinced herself he would never do it again.

What a fool I was, Lillian thought as she pressed Aunt Maggie's pastry into the pie tin and filled it with steak and kidney. If Eric starts his womanising again it will be his balls in a pie. Thinking about Cora was giving Lillian a headache.

11

Carpentry

Nothing had come of Eric and the Reverend's wife. That had been four baths ago, it was 1951. Aunt Maggie would only allow four baths a year. Lillian's stack of hidden *Women's* Weekly magazines was growing, a gift from Aunt Maggie. Bought without Eric's knowledge. He disapproved of women's magazines, said it put ideas in women's heads and was a waste of money and in Aunt Maggie's case, his inheritance. Lillian hid them under Splinter's mattress.

Not that Lillian found a lot of time to read them, she was too busy with cleaning two houses, washing, cooking and gardening and sometimes escorting Aunt Maggie up the street, usually to Mick the butcher for cat food. Lillian liked Mick, he was kind and always passed the time of day with her, even when he had other customers. Lillian had little time to socialise. Then Aunt Maggie came up with the idea of making her own coffin, which

Lillian thought might give her some respite from Aunt Maggie's constant demands.

"Not coffin practice again!" Lillian rolled tired brown eyes and tucked a maverick wave of hair behind her ear.

Eric shrugged. "We have to go."

She hung on the edge of a reply, wanting to say, "your family are bonkers," but thought better of it. It didn't take much to change the look in his eyes. Straining on tiptoe, she felt along the top of the fridge, between the torch and the wireless, until her fingers found the box of Bex headache powders.

"I'm not going," Johnny said, hauling at his Sunday best shorts that were now too small. The set in Eric's jaw said otherwise. "But why must we?" Johnny dug his toe into the linoleum, his bottom lip not far off his bootlaces. Splinter and Bubs hung back, watching and waiting.

Eric's teeth ground down on the stem of his pipe. He sucked and breathed puffs of smoke. "Because I said so." Johnny's face clamped and he looked at his mother for support. Lillian gave Johnny a warning frown, she could read the smoke signals from Eric's pipe. The last thing she wanted was Eric to end up in one of his moods.

What was she to do? Aunt Maggie called the shots. Lillian rubbed her temples, Johnny had as much chance as a dingo caught in a chook pen she thought, and inwardly smiled at her colloquialism. She cursed the day she had encouraged Aunt Maggie's coffin idea. Eric thought she was pulling his leg when she told him, but he'd happily obliged.

They'd given her their tea chests, helped her move an old bed into the shed and lent her tools. Building the coffin would keep Aunt Maggie occupied, stop her from bossing them around for a while. Lillian and Eric had complimented Aunt Maggie on her craftsmanship and laughed in the kitchen when her shed had rung with the sound of hammering. That's how it went until the coffin was near completion. Now she was holding coffin practices. And these the whole family were expected to attend.

"It's not healthy for the children," Lillian complained to Eric after the first two practices. "You'll have to speak to her."

"Kids play cowboys and Indians. Pretend they're dead. What's the difference?" He'd shrugged. Of course he was just pandering to Aunt Maggie for his share in the will. It galled Lillian, but for the sake of peace she had gone along with it believing the novelty would wear off. It didn't and coffin practice was now once a month.

"It's not fair, Mum," Johnny said, folding his arms. It wasn't, but unless she could convince Aunt Maggie otherwise, they all had to toe the line. And from the look on Eric's face, Johnny was heading for a clout.

"The quicker you get ready, the sooner it will be over," Lillian said, trying to ease the tension. She took a powder out of the Bex box, unfolded the paper wrapper and shook the contents into half a glass of water and stirred it with her finger. She swallowed the bitter concoction in one gulp. It was eleven in the morning and this was her second powder since breakfast. Eric raised an eyebrow at her. "What?" She said. "I'm getting a migraine."

He grimaced and turned back to Johnny.

"When is she going to die, Mum?" Johnny looked up at his mother, eyes like a seal pup.

A laugh jerked inside Lillian and she managed to contain it to a nervous giggle. It was a question she'd sometimes asked herself, on her knees scrubbing the old girl's floor, but then felt bad after the thought. Lillian frowned. "Don't talk like that."

"But I hate coffin practice," Johnny whined.

"Aunty's expecting us, love." Lillian said. How could she put a stop to this? Burn the old girl's shed down? She turned to the window. A cool breeze made sails out of the lace curtains, lifting them up to reveal an expanse of blue that married the sky on

81

the horizon line. She watched a ship move into the frame of the small window. It worked its way through white caps, like a sock poking up and down in the suds of her washtub. Her eyes took on a far off look as the Bex powder kicked in and made life tolerable. How different everything had turned out from what she had dreamed.

To confirm Lillian's thoughts a maggot-fat blowfly smacked into the window with a dry crunch and dropped onto the sill and whirred like an engine. Lillian turned from its efforts to right itself and watched Eric comb spit-dampened fingers through Johnny's dark hair to flatten the cockie's crest near his part line.

"Yuck, Dad." Johnny dodged the clout to his head a bit too late. His lip trembled. He stared at the floor, avoiding the steady green eyes that commanded total obedience, like the razor strop hanging on the wall.

"Blazes, I'm sick of this, I need a holiday." Lillian blurted. Surprised, Eric looked at her and laughed.

"Forget it," he said.

She wasn't going to. "I'll make you some custard for afterwards, Johnny, so don't make anymore fuss." The kids deserved a reward for putting up with the pantomime. Lillian rested her hand on the back of Johnny's neck.

Eric frowned. Johnny was a whinger, thanks to Mavis spoiling him and Lillian was making him into a ponce. He clenched his teeth, caught Johnny's eye and looked up at the razor strop. Eric didn't enjoy coffin practice either but he suffered the old girl because she slipped him a fiver, more if the kids behaved themselves. It was his horse betting money. He turned towards Splinter and Bubs. They stood up straight.

"Attention!" Eric gave them a salute.

The girls saluted back. Splinter flicked her ponytail and rubbed the toe of one patent leather shoe against the back of her sock to get a better shine. She did the same with the other one.

Lillian smiled to herself. Her girls looked lovely in their matching ribbons and white organza dresses. They were very alike: fair hair and turned up noses. They got a kick out of dressing up in their best frocks.

Bubs had learned how to manipulate her father from her older siblings' mistakes. "We've got new ribbons." Her gap-tooth grin made him laugh.

"Lovely. I'm sure Aunty will like them." Eric knocked his pipe on the sole of his shoe to get rid of the remaining tobacco and put it in his pocket. He checked his reflection in the window and smoothed his neatly parted brown hair. Then stroked his clean-shaven chin and smiled with satisfaction. People likened him to Clark Gable. Secretly, so did he. He held out his arm to Lillian. "Ready to go, my dear?"

She gave him a disdainful look and ignored the arm. Sometimes his vanity got on her nerves but she knew she was partly to blame for that. Early in their marriage she had hung on his every word, believed everything he said and told him he was handsome and that he had a body like Tarzan. Fool, she admonished. Coffin-practice days always made her crabby. She shook her irritation off. "Come on, kids, time to bow and scrape." Like your father, she wanted to add.

"Mind the washing," Lillian yelled, from the rear of her gaggle as they crossed the yard. A line of sheets stretched from the kitchen tank to an unpainted weatherboard dunny that leaned like a tired old man against the back fence, a lair of spiders: big fat black ones that found their way onto the washing. If Lillian could avoid the dunny she did, opting for the chamber pot that she emptied into a hole under the plum tree. So many times she had asked Eric to move the clothesline and he was always going to, or promising to build a new lavatory. The lavatory was peppered with bullet holes. When the sun streamed through they were like eyes. How no one had ever been shot sitting on the dunny was beyond Lillian. It would happen one day. She just prayed it wouldn't be a member of her family. When she mentioned her fears to Eric he just pooh-poohed her. "The kids want to learn how to shoot," he had said. It wasn't only his children who banged away in their backyard, any of the kid's friends could have a go. Eric always looked over the fence to check the neighbour wasn't collecting her washing before they started shooting. He was conscientious when it came to guns. "You can never be too careful," he'd say as he loaded his rifle.

When the lavatory collapses on him he'll build a new one, Lillian thought, smiling with anticipation.

They drew level with the shed and Jess rushed out, leaping with excitement, straining at the end of her rope. Knowing Aunt Maggie was waiting on the other side of the fence, Johnny ran over to Jess. She pawed her way up the front of his shirt and landed her big wet tongue across his face.

"Johnny, leave that damn dog alone and get over here or I'll give you what for."

"Sorry, Dad."

Lillian frowned. "And I'll give you what for if that dog's made your shirt dirty." Washing was the sigh in her week that left her once lovely hands looking like cooked lobster shells.

"Close the gate!" Aunt Maggie's voice was a snap of elastic. Johnny ambled through, pulling the gate hard behind him. The rickety fence shook. He smirked. Lillian gritted her teeth. It was going to be one of those days.

"Rascal," Aunt Maggie growled as Johnny passed just out of her reach. He wasn't going to get away with it.

12

Coffin Shed

Lillian determined that this was going to be the last coffin practice. They lined up for Aunt Maggie's nod of approval. Johnny made a fart noise with his armpit and the girls giggled. Aunt Maggie's eyes became frosted slits.

Lillian put her hand on Aunt Maggie's arm to distract her from Johnny. "You're looking well today, Aunt Maggie." It was the wrong thing to say. Aunt Maggie staggered and clutched her heart.

"I'm not the best. It's the heart." She did a sidewards two-step.

"Perhaps you're not well enough for coffin practise, Aunt Maggie?"

Was that hope or concern? Aunt Maggie wasn't sure. She regained her balance. "It comes and goes. I'll be alright." She patted the coiled plait at the back of her neck that added to her look of severity.

Lillian noticed the cameo brooch in the middle of a large food stain, and the grubby lace cuffs. She'd have to work out how to get that dress in the wash.

A cockatoo's claw with a big gold ring pointed towards the shed door. Coffin practise was the only time Aunt Maggie wore jewellery. "Open up Eric."

The shed door was stubborn with a trick to the bolt. Eric struggled with his foot beneath the corrugated tin doors to keep them level and tried to move the bolt. It wouldn't budge. He cursed under his breath. "I'll have to oil this bolt, Aunty."

"Move over, I'll do it." Aunt Maggie crowded Eric out of the way. Although short in stature, she was strong, thanks to Lillian's cooking. She heaved her body into the door, at the same time banging the bolt backwards with the heel of her hand.

Johnny crossed his fingers to stop the door opening. The billycart race was on today and he and Splinter had been practising for ages. Deep down he was convinced Aunt Maggie knew about the race and called the coffin practice on purpose. He might have been right. The shed door swung back and Johnny's shoulders slumped. Aunt Maggie quivered with importance.

"Everyone inside." She herded them through the door.

Bubs handed out the hymn books. The pages were marked. She enjoyed this monthly ritual and loved to stand in front of the class and give her report on coffin practice. Felt proud when her teacher gasped. The rapt looks on her classmates' faces made her feel special and popular. No one would break her leg in this school. Of course she didn't tell her father about her reports because he always said it was nobody else's business.

"Pull the door shut, we don't want flies in here."

Lillian pulled the door shut and sighed. "You'd think we were on a film set," she muttered to Eric.

In the centre of the shed, in a glow of broken sunrays that splashed through gaps in the walls, perched Aunt Maggie's coffin.

Lillian couldn't help smiling at the beam on Aunt Maggie's face. The coffin was ingenious. Made from a single iron bed Aunt Maggie had turned upside down and using its long legs as supports, she had attached broken down tea chests along the sides and ends. The wire-mesh base was covered with a horsehair mattress to ensure comfort. Her recent addition was a lid made from an old door, which she had secured to the bed legs on one side with wire she had threaded through the hinges. The doorknob had been polished with Brasso.

Being the appointed funeral director, Lillian arranged everyone in a semicircle around the coffin. This will be the last time, she reminded herself. Aunt Maggie lifted the lid and propped it open with a garden rake. She stood back, head to one side, hands on hips and surveyed her carpentry. Johnny nudged Splinter and pulled a face. Bubs giggled and stopped when she saw her father's eyes change from green to a slippery grey. Aunt Maggie hitched up her dress and lifted a sturdy leg.

Eric stepped forward. "Let me help you." He put his arm around her back to support her. She knocked it away.

"I can do it myself, thank you. Go back to your place." Eric's arse nipped the seam in his pants as he retreated. Lillian yawned to cover her grin. Aunt Maggie gripped the sides of the coffin and swung her leg over, like mounting a motorbike. She took a few seconds to get her balance and followed with the other leg. Then she squatted and eased herself onto her back. It was a tight fit and she wriggled into a more comfortable position, crossed her arms over her chest and closed her eyes. There were snorts and gasps and a blowfly. God, Aunt Maggie hated blowflies.

"Lillian, when I'm dead, shut my mouth so the flies don't get in."

The hymn book went up in front of Lillian's face. "Alright, Aunty."

"You're not singing." Aunt Maggie's ear extended to every voice.

"Swing low, sweet chariot," they sang amid coughs. Tone deaf and a confident baritone, Eric threw his shoulders back and drowned out his family. Johnny nudged Splinter to get her attention. She looked at him. He squeezed his eyes shut, opened his mouth wide, imitating his father. Splinter snorted which set Bubs into a fit of giggles. Eric glared at them.

"Behave yourselves."

"Sorry, Dad."

"Don't apologise to me, apologise to Aunt Maggie."

"Sorry, Aunt Maggie," they said in unison.

She opened one malevolent eye.

It had surprised Aunt Maggie that she'd lived to eighty-four. She had expected to follow her sister's early death. The extra years had given her time to organise a perfect funeral and to make sure she wouldn't be buried alive. She'd heard tales about scratch marks found on the insides of coffin lids. Those smart coffins made from mahogany, with their wasteful silver handles and big lids, were heavy and cumbersome. She didn't trust them. She wanted to make sure she could escape. It would be Lillian's duty to be in charge of the burial, and Lillian had better get it right!

"Lower the lid, Eric". Everyone went quiet as Eric carefully removed the rake and lowered the door. "Keep singing," yelled Aunt Maggie as the lid settled in place.

"Onward Christian soldiers! Marching as to war, with the cross of Jesus, going on before," shouted Johnny, stamping up and down. Eric picked up the tune and the girls joined in the chorus. Lillian did a jig. The lid of the box began to rattle. They stopped dancing, continued singing and watched. It lifted jerkily. Aunt Maggie's arms trembled under the strain. She brought her gartered knees up as extra support and pushed until the lid was a quarter way open. Then it slowly closed as her arms gave out crating her in darkness.

It was claustrophobic. Aunt Maggie tried again but only managed to open the lid an inch or two. Light bled through the crack like a leaking heart valve and then collapsed with her weakened wrists, enclosing her in the tomb she had built.

Everyone stopped singing, eyes on the lid. Lillian pressed her hand against her chest and took big breaths in empathy. Splinter thought about how she could make the event into a play for her parents. It would be as good as the Anzac Day Parade when she dressed in her nurse costume and wound Johnny up in tomato-sauce bandages. Bubs wondered if Aunt Maggie was going to have a heart attack. Johnny thought about the custard his mother had promised. It crossed Eric's mind that Aunt Maggie could be in a lot of trouble if she ever practiced without them present. He hoped she would. The family waited, not wanting to spoil Aunt Maggie's occasion. Then desperate knocks came from inside the coffin. Eric took out his pipe and began to fill it.

The deliberate action alarmed Lillian. "Help her out, Eric."

He took his time pocketing the pipe, then grabbed the doorknob. The lid came up and Eric propped it open with the rake. He squared his shoulders. "I'll oil the hinges for you tomorrow, Aunty."

Aunt Maggie rose from the dead. "It's no good, the door's too heavy. I'll have to make another lid, she gasped." Her throat was as dry as a worm on a gravel road. Disappointment looked for someone to blame. "Lillian, I want you to cut down on my dinner helpings. I've put on weight since our last practice. The coffin is too tight."

"Yes, Aunty." Lillian would add it to the list of promises she'd made to Aunt Maggie when she got home.

"Well, keep singing." Aunt Maggie's voice hammered into them like a rusty nail. They sang and Jess joined in from the end of her rope. Furious, Aunt Maggie wrestled to get out of the coffin and farted.

"Aunt Maggie farted." Johnny said. They all laughed.

In a spray of spittle Aunt Maggie whirled on Eric. "Coffins are expensive and if I have to pay for one it'll come out of your inheritance! Or maybe I should start charging you rent!"

Smarting from the threat of losing his inheritance, Eric glared at Lillian.

Her fault, again. Lillian stretched her hand out to Eric. "Give me your hymn book." Scowling, he handed her his book. The children felt the tension, came forward and placed their books on the shelf and waited. Aunt Maggie straightened the books, her lips a straight line. Lillian inclined her head towards the door. "You lot, go and get changed." Relieved, they rushed outside and raced each other to the gate.

"Let's teach Jess *Onward Christian Soldiers*," yelled Johnny.

Steely-eyed, Aunt Maggie pushed past Eric. Her bandy legs marched across the yard to the back door. When the door slammed behind her Lillian turned to Eric, her voice an appeal. "Poor old duck. It's awful to have phobias. You can't blame the kids. I find it hard not to laugh and I know you do too."

"I'm in her will and I'm not going to upset her. I've worked hard for it."

Lillian raised her eyebrows. "I'm the one who takes care of her. Come on, she can't help being old." She pushed away her feelings of revulsion as she looked at the sun-bathed coffin. "If only my mother could see this," she laughed.

Needled, Eric snapped back. "My family is none of her business. Your mother's an old tart. She's had three husbands and a paramour; she can't talk." He glowered with disapproval.

In a rare moment of defiance Lillian turned on Eric. "That was because my father died in the war and she was left with four children."

"What do you mean? She didn't look after you. She put you in an orphanage. I never told my family you were from an orphanage."

"I'm not. You know very well Mum got us out as soon as she could. That's why she married again."

"Yeah and she had the poor bastard put away, so don't tell me about your mother's virtues and don't go writing to her about my family." Eric often took a pencil to the impressions Lillian's pen had left on the writing pad to see what she'd written to her mother.

"He was gassed in the war and violent." Lillian's voice rose in a last effort to defend her mother. "And I don't have time to discuss it because I have to go to your Aunt's dress rehearsal. Unless you'd like to do it," she said, knowing full well Aunt Maggie wouldn't let him in her bedroom. Aunt Maggie was probably the only woman's bedroom Eric wasn't welcome in, Lillian thought, still seething over his scathing comments about her poor mother.

13

Dress Rehearsal

"Blast him, blast his whole bloody family," Lillian muttered. How dare he criticise her mother. She was a kind, loving woman not like his stone-hearted mother. None of them had gone through a war or starved. One day Eric would regret the way he treated her. Lillian lifted a hand and swiped at a blowfly as she reached Aunt Maggie's back door. "Bloody flies," she yelled.

She stood on the back step and took a deep breath to calm herself. The roses at the back door caressed the air with their perfume. It seeped into Lillian's body filling her with memories and a yearning for England. She looked at the colourful blooms in full maturity, picked a petal and put it in her mouth, cushioning it on her tongue. She needed a break from all of them. It would be nice to visit her mother and sister in Melbourne. Right now though, she could do with a Bex powder. Make it two. "Yoo hoo, Aunt Maggie, it's me." Lillian stepped inside.

A weak response came down the hall. "Come in the bedroom, I'm not feeling very well. And shut the back door." Lillian straightened her shoulders and wished the lid had worked on the coffin and the children hadn't laughed. It was going to cost her. She banged the door closed so Aunt Maggie could hear. The cool interior was a welcome relief from the hundred and one degrees outside. Blinds were drawn against the heat and Lillian fumbled down the hall as her eyes adjusted to the dark. The house smelt of mothballs and old clothes. She popped her head around Aunt Maggie's bedroom door. The room was large and bright. A slight sea breeze shifted the lace curtains at an open window that looked out to sea.

"Don't stand there gawping, come in." Aunt Maggie lifted out a long cream silk dress from a big Victorian wardrobe that hid most of the flower wallpaper, now yellow from age. She carefully laid the dress on an overstuffed bed and ran her hand lovingly down its folds. Then she reached for a hat box and removed a bonnet with long ribbons. She put the bonnet next to the dress.

"You'll look beautiful in it, Aunt Maggie." It was the same platitude as last month and Lillian had to force enthusiasm into her voice. A gnarled hand made a grab for the brass knob on the bedhead and a pair of eyes blinked up at Lillian. Lillian played her part. "I think you've had too much excitement, Aunt Maggie. It's not good for your heart. Why don't you sit down and let me get everything out for you?"

"No, I prefer to do it myself." She gave her chest a couple of whacks to steady her heartbeat.

Here we go, Lillian thought.

Aunt Maggie wobbled over to a big oak chest of drawers next to a small marble-topped table with a china jug and washbasin. Pulling open a drawer, she took out a pair of long cream gloves and silk stockings, placing them next to the dress. Lost in thought, Lillian gazed out the window past the flowering grevillia that was busy feeding the wattlebirds and watched some fishing boats bobbing on the sapphire sea. The rattle of a billy cart and the excited voices of Johnny and Splinter could be heard as they passed aunt Maggie's house.

"Pay attention."

"I am, Aunt Maggie, I was just waiting for you to get everything out." Lillian sighed.

"These are what you lay me out in and make sure the bonnet is tied under the chin. It will keep my mouth closed so the flies don't get in."

"I know, Aunt Maggie, we've been through this so many times. Why must you keep telling me?"

"You're a daydreamer, that's why." Daydreaming was Lillian's escape; she couldn't help it. Her eyes always glazed over when Aunt Maggie talked about her funeral preparations. "It's not going to be long before I die, you know. I can feel it coming and you're in charge of my funeral." She tottered and righted herself on the wash stand.

An intense tiredness seeped through Lillian. She was tired of Aunt Maggie's shenanigans and Eric's complaints about her extravagant food bills, that she read too much and that her friend was a Kraut. Lillian felt drained of energy. But there was no escape from the coffin clothes arranged like a corpse on the bed. Aunt Maggie's foot tapped with impatience. "Well?" she said.

In her head, Lillian was going through the tussle of squeezing Aunt Maggie into her dress. Readying herself for the complaints and spit missiles until she had Aunt Maggie trussed like a martyred virgin dressed for death. It was an exhausting charade. Lillian had had it. Feet shuffled and Aunt Maggie's head jerked back. Her eyelids developed a tremor. Lillian's fingers drummed the washstand. "It's time you stopped this nonsense, Aunt Maggie. You said you would die last year. You're a healthy old woman. I'm sick to death of your dying. It's morbid and what's more it's a bad example for the children."

Shocked, Aunt Maggie clutched her heart and staggered to the pillow end of the bed where she could flop down without disturbing her clothes. "I … I get these attacks much more often now." She collapsed on the bed.

It was submission. For the first time Lillian was in control. Lillian's five foot three inches grew into six foot eight. It was such a relief to speak her mind. She should have done this long ago. Ignoring the threat of Aunt Maggie's impending heart attack, she smiled like Bette Davis in *Dark Victory* and revealed her secret longing, to see how the old girl would take it.

"My mother wrote and asked me to come for a holiday."

This bit of news took Aunt Maggie completely by surprise. Her eyes shot open and she jerked to her feet. "What do you need a holiday for? You don't work!"

"I don't work?" Lillian was incredulous. Angry tears stung her eyes like they did when she chopped onions for Aunt Maggie's steak and kidney pie. If she had that pie right now she would dump it on the old girl's cream silk dress. When she spoke her voice was quiet and measured.

"What do I do all day?" She surveyed the bedroom and walked over to the washstand. Slowly, she wiped her finger along the surface then held it up and inspected it. She continued moving around the room in a quiet fury, wiping her finger across the cupboards, over the bedside table, the lamp, along the window ledge and in and out of the patterns on the iron bedhead. She put her finger under Aunt Maggie's nose and stared into her eyes.

"Clean," she said, waggling her finger, "bloody clean."

Aunt Maggie's head recoiled. Lillian had never used such strong language in her presence before. Heart attack forgotten, she paced the room unsure of what to do. Without thinking she trailed her hand over the washstand and checked the tips of her fingers to see if there was any dust on them. Her shoulders slumped. Lillian sensed a victory. The migraine that had been coming on since coffin practice eased and she felt a bit better. For the first time since they had known each other Lillian was telling Aunt Maggie just how she felt about being the obedient servant. Aunt Maggie was beginning to understand.

"You know what you need is a good tonic," Aunt Maggie said. "Tell me when that travelling salesman comes again." She rubbed her forehead trying to think of his name. "You know who I mean, the Rawleigh's man. When he comes next, I'll buy you a tonic. Maybe you need to open your bowels. Epsom salts will do the trick. Always works for me."

The fight went out of Lillian. She turned and gazed out the window. The sapphire blue sea had changed to a dull uninteresting grey. She remembered standing here in spring and seeing a passing whale blow a raspberry in the air. Taking a hanger from the cupboard, she hung up the cream silk dress with a sigh.

"I haven't tried that on yet," Aunt Maggie protested, moving towards the wardrobe. But Lillian didn't seem to hear her. She packed the bonnet into the hatbox and slid it on top of the wardrobe.

"You know what I really need?" Lillian said, turning to Aunt Maggie, "I need a washing machine. I saw a beauty in Pearson's shop and it had a really big mangle. Perhaps you could tell Eric." There was no punch in her request just a tired lifting of her eyebrows as she looked at Aunt Maggie.

Aunt Maggie chuckled. "He already owes me five pounds. I doubt he'll have money for a washing machine. He spends it all on the horses. That reminds me, I think my bed linen needs a wash." Aunt Maggie had become house proud since Lillian's arrival. She gave the pillow a pat.

A familiar pain began to throb behind Lillian's eye, removing all her resistance. She wilted onto the bed and pressed her forehead against the cool metal of the bedhead and wished her life could be different. Her mother had always told her she would never stand on her own two feet until she took control of her life, but how could she change things when she didn't have anything, no support and not a razoo to her name?

It was sad to see Lillian like this. Forgiving her previous outburst, Aunt Maggie wondered if she was coming down with something. Of course it was that demanding Eric. He only thought of himself. He was a waster, spent all his money on gambling. She had been giving Eric's gambling a lot of thought. She didn't want him to waste her money after she'd died and leave Lillian to struggle. Those rude children needed a firm hand too. Aunt Maggie rubbed her palm down her thigh. She would love to smack that cheeky Johnny. Poor Lillian, she had a lot to put up with. A candle of warmth filled Aunt Maggie and in a moment of great generosity she went to the wardrobe, took a five-pound note out of a shoe and tucked it into Lillian's hand, her chubby cheeks shining. "After I'm gone you'll have nothing to worry about," she said. Opening her hand, Lillian gazed at the note and gave a wan smile.

"Thank you, Aunt Maggie, I'll put it aside for the washing machine." The goodwill gesture heralded a softening in Aunt Maggie, something Lillian might be able to use to her advantage. She thought of the resolve she'd made when she entered the house and forgotten about when she'd dared to mention a holiday. There would be a compromise. "I won't be coming to any more coffin practices, Aunt Maggie, neither will the children. I saw death when I was a child and I want my children to respect it, not laugh at it. Besides, I don't want you to die. I would be sad." Lillian doubted Eric would be sad. With Aunt Maggie gone he could go back to chasing women again and gamble his inheritance, do what he wanted irrespective of what she would like.

It took Aunt Maggie a moment to realise what Lillian had said. No more coffin practice? Lillian would be sad if she died? Aunt Maggie coughed. "Well as long as you know what to do when I die. I want people to remember my funeral. It has to be perfect."

"I'll see you get the best funeral in Eden, Aunt Maggie. Now if you'll excuse me I have a migraine. I need to go home and lie down." Lillian had accomplished what she'd set out to do, but it didn't ease the pain in her head.

At home, Lillian made straight for the Bex. She shook a powder into a glass of water and unfolded another one then folded it up again. She still had to get tea and it wouldn't be fair leaving the children to fend for themselves. Especially after having to suffer coffin practice. Tonight they'd all have to put up with the leftovers. And she'd make some custard for Johnny because she had promised. It was all she could be bothered with.

14

Up in Smoke

The sea pounded the rocks. Spume filled the road outside Aunt Maggie's house. The wind roared. None of the fishing fleet had gone out. All the fishermen were in the Club betting on horses and playing poker. Eric was in the Club with them. Good for some, Lillian thought, ironing the collar of his shirt. A gust of wind rattled the windows. She looked over at Aunt Maggie's house and wondered if she was frightened. Better check, she thought. She heard Splinter's footsteps on the verandah.

"Splinter!" Lillian yelled.

Splinter bounced in the kitchen and flung her school bag on a chair. "I got blown into Spencer's fence on the way home."

"Well, I need you to go over to Aunt Maggie's and see she's alright."

"Can I have a cup of Milo first?" Splinter said.

"No. You only have to stick your head around the door."

Lillian put her hand in her apron pocket and pulled out her last piece of chocolate. "Here, now be a good girl and go and check on Aunty."

Splinter turned the handle and the door blew open pulling her with it. She pushed it closed behind her and looked around. The chaise longue was empty. A billow of smoke came out of the kitchen. Splinter went into the kitchen. Aunt Maggie was on her knees in front of the stove.

"Hello, Aunty Maggie. Mum sent me over to see if you were alright."

Aunt Maggie grunted and poked a piece of paper into the grate. Wind came down the chimney and blew the paper and a stream of ash towards Splinter. She bent down and picked the paper up. It was half burnt. "This is a five-pound note, Aunt Maggie!"

"I know child, give it here." Aunt Maggie held her hand out and Splinter gave it to her.

"Why are you burning money, Aunt Maggie?"

"The worms have eaten the numbers off, it's no good."

"Can I see?" Splinter picked two ten-pound notes off a small pile next to Aunt Maggie. She held them up. "They look pretty. A bit like lace." She put her finger through one of the wormholes in the ten-pound note and held her hand out. "Look I have a ten-pound note ring," she said. "How did the worms get inside the house?"

"They didn't. I hid the money in the garden and you mustn't tell. Your father might dig my yard up," she said.

"Why do you hide your money in the garden?"

"In case my house burns down like your farm did. Lightning can do that you know."

"Is that what you buried your money in?" Splinter asked, pointing to a brown paper bag covered in mud. Aunt Maggie pursed her lips and nodded. "I keep my pencils in a biscuit tin.

It's got a lid. You can have that," Splinter said. Aunt Maggie's eyes widened. Splinter pushed the notes around. "I could cut the bad bits off the ends and stick the good bits together?"

"The numbers would be different each end and the bank would know," Aunt Maggie said.

Splinter considered the notes. "A shop mightn't know," she said.

Aunt Maggie gave her an appraising look. "You're a clever girlie. If you want to try you can."

"Thanks, Aunt Maggie." Splinter stretched her hand out to pick up the rest of the notes.

Aunt Maggie pushed her hand away. "Just try those two, if it works tell me." She wouldn't burn any more.

"She what?" Lillian shrieked. She plopped onto Splinter's bed, the sticky taped note in her hand.

"She said I wasn't to tell," moaned Splinter. "I promised I wouldn't. You mustn't say I told you, Mum."

"Has she gone bonkers? What will she bloody do next? How much did she burn for God's sake?" Lillian felt like crying.

Splinter's eyes widened at her mother's swearing. "I don't know. She was doing it when I went in."

"Wait 'til your father hears this."

Splinter's face puckered with concern. "You can't tell Dad, Mum. Aunty said he'd dig up her yard if he knew."

Lillian stared at Splinter. A hysterical giggle escaped her. She could see Eric digging up the yard. Aunt Maggie wasn't stupid. She turned the note over in her hand. Splinter had done a good job. Telling Eric would only benefit him. It wouldn't help her or the kids, she thought. They had lived in Eden two years and Eric had never been out of work. He did contract work for the

Department of Main Roads and repaired motors in his shed. He often boasted how much he'd been paid for fixing a motor. They didn't pay rent, so where did the money go? Lillian didn't get any, there was no housekeeping money, everything was put on account which Eric went through with a keen eye and paid when he felt like it, keeping desperate shopkeepers waiting, caring nothing for Lillian's mortification. The occasional block of chocolate and milkshakes for the kids came from coins she rescued in the bottom of the copper. Lillian still resurrected Mavis's hand-me-downs with a piece of lace, a pocket or some bias binding. She was thinking about the burnt money when Eric came back from the Fishermen's Club.

"Guess what?" he said, all grin and smelling of beer.

"You've won the lottery?" Whatever it was it had to be better than Aunt Maggie burning her money.

"I've leased a farm on the Towamba River," he said. Lillian's heart skipped a beat.

"Whatever for?" Apprehension gripped her. The worst thing that could happen was to be stranded on a farm again. He'd never mentioned a farm. She saw his face darken.

"It was a great offer, two hundred and fifty acres. It has a small bungalow by the river. I can grow potatoes for the market. We can have our own butter, cheese, fruit."

"I have to take care of Aunt Maggie," Lillian said, panic rising.

"You still can."

"What? You're going to live on the farm by yourself?" The idea appealed to Lillian. She could stay in the house in Eden and care for Aunt Maggie and Eric could bugger off. The frown on Eric's face said that wasn't the plan.

"No, I'll run it on weekends. The kids will love it. They can swim in the river. There's an orchard.

"How much did it cost?" Lillian asked. Why didn't he consult her before he did things? Think about what would make her life easier? She would like a washing machine, an electric stove, and a hot water tap in the kitchen, hot water in the laundry and to visit her mother in Melbourne. Anxiety and anger threaded through her. Eric always said he didn't have any money when she asked him for anything. Where had the money for the farm come from? From Aunt Maggie? Had he found some in her garden? Lillian chewed her lip. She decided not to mention Aunt Maggie burning her money.

"I had a small bet today and won enough to lease Willy Giles's place. He wants to buy another trawler and won't have time to work the farm. Said I could have it for five years. Paid him there and then." Eric laughed. He had calculated that Aunt Maggie would be dead by the time the lease was up and with his inheritance and the sale of the Eden house, he'd be able to buy the farm outright. He wasn't going to tell Lillian his plan yet, might wait until Aunt Maggie died. He didn't want any opposition. "I'll take you and the kids to see it on the weekend."

The track to the farm was a boneshaker. A sense of foreboding filled Lillian as the forlorn timber house with its sagging roof came into view.

"See, isn't it a beauty?" Eric said. "The kids can pick blackberries. There's masses by the river. You can bake those delicious tarts of yours." Lillian didn't share his excitement. All she could think of was how remote it was.

While Eric and the kids were having a swim, Lillian sat on the verandah, a book in her lap. She had needed a break from Aunt Maggie, some peace and quiet. It's alright for an occasional weekend, she thought, but I'm never going to move here. Putting up with Aunt Maggie's eccentricities was better than the loneliness of farm life. But Aunt Maggie wouldn't be around forever and what then?

The farm was already paying for itself due to Eric's underhanded tactics. He hadn't done much to it, sewn a few potatoes, made a vegetable garden, bought a couple of sheep. Then the drought happened. A blessing as it turned out. The local farmers were struggling to feed their stock, driving their cattle down the main roads to eat the grass that grew on the sides. Eric's pasture had hardly been touched. His neighbour, McKenna, had started driving his cattle over the river onto Eric's property, during the week, when Eric wasn't there. The telltale piles of manure and hoof prints by the river told Eric what was going on. He paid McKenna a visit. They had a cuppa and then Eric got down to business.

"I'll graze your cattle for fifteen quid a week," Eric said.

"You've gotta be kidding, mate," McKenna laughed. Eric's eyes went hard. He took some short puffs on his pipe. McKenna had dough but he never paid for his round in the Fishermen's Club. "I buy hay," McKenna said.

"I think you're telling a porky pie," Eric said. "I know you've been sending your cattle over to my place. I think you're a bit of a sneaky bastard."

"Think what you like. I'm not paying you fifteen quid a week." McKenna pushed his chair back. "I've got things to do, mate."

Eric bashed his pipe on the sole of his shoe, pocketed it and stood up. "You might regret that decision," he said. All the way back to Eden, Eric thought of ways he could get back at McKenna. The engine was smoking by the time he pulled into his driveway.

The truck door slammed. Lillian went to the kitchen window and saw Eric storming across the yard. Her pulse quickened. She busied herself at the stove.

104

Eric entered the kitchen, hung his jacket behind the door and flung himself into a chair.

"Cup of tea?" She said. He wasn't ranting, so it was nothing she had done. Eric shook his head. "Anything wrong?"

"McKenna reckons his cattle aren't eating my grass, says he buys them feed. Lying mongrel."

Farm problems. Lillian perked up. "Really? Poor animals must be starving. Glad we're not relying on a farm."

Eric slammed his fist on the table. Lillian jumped. "He's not stealing my bloody grass."

"No, of course not, I was just saying, poor cows."

"I'll shoot his bloody cows if I see them on my property," Eric said. Lillian's insides tightened.

"Don't forget his brother-in-law is Constable Sluggo," Lillian said. Constable Sluggo's real name was Patrick O'Day. He was a big man and an ex-boxer.

"He'd have to prove I did it", Eric said. "I could have been roo shooting and made a mistake. Plenty of roos on my land."

"You can't do that. What would Aunt Maggie say if you ended up in a court case?"

"Too bad. We can always move to the farm if she doesn't like it."

Lillian's mind raced. "The other day you mentioned the truck was between contracts, so why don't you stay at the farm next week? Let McKenna think you've moved in. Come home on the weekend and fix motors? Don't be so predictable with your days at the farm." Eric lit his pipe, smoke curled from the bowl as he gazed towards the window and smiled. It was a good idea. Lillian congratulated herself.

The heifer's udders were the size of inflated bagpipes. Encouraged by Eric she ate the grass behind the house, her poddy calf munching beside her. Eric made soothing noises and approached the heifer with a saucepan. Half an hour later he sat on the verandah of his farm enjoying a cup of tea and McKenna's milk. He'd shot a couple of roos so McKenna would hear the gun and know he was in residence. On the weekend, when he was back home, he'd sort the truck out.

Lillian watched Eric from the window as he erected sides to the back of the truck. "At least he's not in a bad mood," she thought. She saw him straighten and look towards the back fence. He lifted his arm in greeting. Lillian's lip curled. The headmaster's wife. They were always chatting over the fence. Usually the headmaster's wife caught Eric when he was coming out of the dunny. She wasn't Lillian's main interest, though. There was a cunning look about Eric. He'd had it since he'd come home from the farm. It worried her. When she'd asked him about McKenna's cattle, Eric had shrugged and talked about ploughing and sewing potatoes. Whatever he was up to, Lillian hoped Aunt Maggie wouldn't find out.

The kids were down at the beach, Lillian grabbed her hat and some empty jars. She liked to collect beach glass and make borders around her rose beds with it. It was calming walking along the beach, sand squeaking underfoot. The patterns at the water's edge when the surf rolled back. The tiny holes it left that bubbled and popped. The tickle of seaweed against her legs when she paddled in rock pools. At the beach she didn't feel all squeezed together. At the beach she'd forget Eric and the farm.

Lillian emptied the beach glass she had collected, sat on her haunches in the garden and continued to make a lovely edge around the rose bed. She turned at Eric's approach.

"Looks nice," he said, smiling. He was buttering her up. When she'd first started her hobby he'd said it was childish.

"I'll be away for a couple of days, Lil. The tractor needs a spare part. I'll have to go to Sydney."

Lillian's hackles rose. So that was it. He'd bought the tractor a month ago, another one of his bargains for the farm and now it wasn't working. Her younger sister was getting married in Melbourne and Eric had said he couldn't afford for Lillian to go to the wedding. There was fifteen years in age between her and her sister. In England, Lillian had looked after her while her mother worked. She rubbed the palm of her hand over the glass.

"Costing you money already is it?" she said.

Eric's face darkened. Lillian had gotten a bit too big for her boots since they had moved next door to Aunt Maggie. She had better watch it; Aunt Maggie wouldn't be around forever. "The tractor is going to make the farm successful. We'll make good money from a potato crop."

You will, she thought. Her leg cramped as she tried to stand. Eric put his arm under hers and helped her to her feet. She looked at him, surprised.

"We need the tractor. It was a good buy," he said. He sounded apologetic.

She sighed. "I hope you have a good journey." She shouldn't have been mean to him even if she didn't want the farm to work.

Eric loaded the heifer and her calf onto the back of the truck. The drive to Sydney would take eleven hours; he should arrive in time. He had entered them in the Sydney show.

The poddy calf and mother wore a blue ribbon around their necks. Eric stood between them, grinning. The camera flashed. The picture made the paper. He got a good price for the poddy and heifer. He was going to buy presents for the family. A washing machine for Lillian, second-hand bike for Johnny and a pair of shoes each for the girls. It was a shame the horse he backed before he left Sydney hadn't come in.

15

Aunt Maggie's Flu

"The funeral is in Wollongong." Lillian handed Eric the telegram. She couldn't force a tear from her eye. "You will have to go on your own. The kids have to go to school." She rubbed Eric's back as he sat at the table with his head in his hands.

"At least it was sudden. She didn't suffer." Eric wiped a hand across his eyes. "Poor mother, she didn't have a happy life. I guess we'll have to discuss what to do with River Bend." Lillian didn't want to think about River Bend.

"I'll pack your bag and then you'd better get going." Lillian clucked her tongue, "I can't believe Mavis didn't delay the funeral another day to give you plenty of time to get there." She gave Eric a squeeze. "Come on. Get out of those overalls and have a wash. I'll put some clothes out for you and pack you a lunch."

"I would like to have seen her before she died, cleared the

air between us." Eric said. It wouldn't have happened, Lillian thought. A saint couldn't reason with her.

An hour later Lillian waved goodbye to Eric and went to see Aunt Maggie who had the flu.

Aunt Maggie lay on the chaise longue wrapped in a dressing gown. A thermometer protruded from her mouth. Her nose was red, eyes streaming. Lillian removed the thermometer and checked the result, "It's normal," she said. She filled a spoon with Irish Moss cough mixture and fed it to Aunt Maggie. "I'll get some water and give you a couple of aspros."

"My heart is beating so fast," Aunt Maggie rasped, after swallowing the aspros.

"The aspro will settle it."

"You're a good girl," Aunt Maggie said, patting Lillian's hand.

The gratitude pleased Lillian. She wasn't thanked very often. She took the old hand in hers. "There's something I have to tell you, Aunt Maggie." Aunt Maggie paled.

"I'm dying?"

"Of course not. I just wanted to tell you that Eric's mother died yesterday. We received a telegram this morning. They're burying her in Wollongong, in the cemetery where her mother is buried. Eric's left for Wollongong already."

Aunt Maggie relaxed and her eyes brightened. "Dead? What did she die from, a heart attack?"

"She had a stroke," Lillian said. Aunt Maggie looked pleased.

"We should celebrate, give her a send off. Fill the brandy glasses," she said.

Aunt Maggie was into her third glass and Lillian was desperate to get away. Triggered by Eric's mother's death, Aunt Maggie had been reminiscing about her childhood for an hour and Lillian was bored out of her mind. She'd heard the same stories many times. Thoughts of how she could get away were going through Lillian's head.

"You know she's gone to hell," Aunt Maggie said suddenly.

"Pardon?" Lillian frowned. "You shouldn't say things like that, Aunt Maggie. It's not good to speak ill of the dead. Let bygones be bygones."

"She killed my brother."

"What?" The old girl was hallucinating. She should check Aunt Maggie's temperature again.

"She did," Aunt Maggie nodded. "He didn't drown. He ran off to New Zealand. He had a floozy over there. Someone saw them at the races and wrote to Eric's mother, sent her a photo of them. My brother gambled every cent he had. The floozy kicked him out and he had to work his passage on a ship to get back to Australia. He came here asking me for money. He went back to River Bend. Arrived at night. There was a terrible argument. Howard, Grahame and Eric saw it. It was poor Howard who told me. The lad was in an awful state, terrified he'd go to prison." Aunt Maggie drained the rest of her brandy and licked her lips. "She hit Eric's father with a crowbar. Killed him outright. The boys buried him next to his headstone by the river. Eric ran away the next day. We decided to keep it a secret." Aunt Maggie's head fell back and she started to snore.

Lillian sat motionless. Eric's mother murdered his father? It was unbelievable! Lillian went over her encounters with Eric's mother. When she had just arrived in Australia, Eric had taken her to River Bend, where they were to live with his mother and brother Howard. That first meeting. How fraught it was. She had given her new mother-in-law a hug and the woman had stood like a fence post. She'd gazed at Lillian with cool eyes and a set to her mouth. It had confused Lillian, made her wary. She had pictured Eric's family as happy, easygoing farm people, like in the novels she'd read about Australians. Instead she'd met a silent wall of opposition. They had wanted Eric to marry locally

111

in order to strengthen their farm and influence. Lillian was a disappointment, a burden. English. The realisation had come to Lillian when his mother had locked her in her bedroom for two weeks.

Eric was away, finishing his service in the navy. Lillian had to stay with his mother and brother Howard on the farm. The Second World War had started. Eric had been exempted from serving in the war because Australia needed farmers. Sitting in Aunt Maggie's sunroom, listening to Aunt Maggie snore and the surf in the distance, she remembered how lonely she had felt on his mother's farm. Not a soul for miles, no houses to be seen. The wireless controlled by Eric's mother, only switched on for an hour at night to listen to the news. The mail delivered once a week and no news from Eric in two months. How she had worried about him, about her family facing war in England. A black cloud had engulfed her. She remembered clutching Howard's hand and begging him for money so she could go back to England. How desperate and mad she'd been.

It still filled her with shame when she thought of what she had looked like when Eric returned to the farm, back from the navy. He had stood in the doorway of their bedroom. "Lillian!" His cry had wrenched her heart. The room stank of sweat, vomit, urine and stale air. She had looked at him with dull eyes. Her hair was matted on the pillow and a stained satin petticoat bagged around her thin body. He whirled, facing his mother and his brother who hovered in the hallway. "What in God's name have you done?"

"I told you she wasn't cut out to be a farmer's wife. You should have listened to me." His mother's face was rigid. Howard chewed his lip and hung his head.

"What were you thinking, locking her up like that?" Eric's voice shook with rage.

"And what would you have us do? Let her run away? Leave the farm to go to ruin while you chased around the country looking for her? How do you think that would make us look?" his mother said.

Howard shuffled from foot to foot and rubbed a hand across his eyes. "I told Mother we should get the doctor or ask the vicar to come and talk to Lillian."

"What did you expect marrying a weakling? She's English, she'll never be any good on a farm. If I'd known you were going to react like this, I would have packed her off to your sister in Sydney," his mother had said.

Eric's face had been pale, a vein had throbbed in his temple. "We won't be staying here. I'll find another farm, rent one if I have too. Now get out and leave the key to the door."

He had carried Lillian out to the verandah and laid her on the old settee in the late afternoon sun then emptied the commode in the garden. He changed the sheets on the bed, poured hot water in a basin, and taken a towel and soap into the bedroom. He carried her back to the room and wiped away her loneliness with a soft damp cloth. And all she could do was gaze at him in silence.

The next day they drove down the long driveway past the giant fir trees that his grandfather had planted, with his mother's voice screaming behind them. "She will be your downfall; you mark my words." There had been eight years of silence between Eric and his mother after that. Until the fire took their farm and Eric and Lillian were forced to go back to River Bend. Then Grahame had turned up. Now Eric's mother was dead, Lillian wondered what they would do with the farm? She was glad Eric didn't have enough money to buy his siblings out. Nothing would make her go back there – too many bad memories. And especially with a murdered man buried on the property. She shuddered. It was all so hard to believe. Lillian covered Aunt

Maggie with a rug and took their glasses into the kitchen and rinsed them in the bowl of cold water on the table. She dried them and put them back in the sideboard and then quietly closed the door and made her way home.

"How was the trip?" Lillian asked as Eric walked in the kitchen. It felt awkward greeting Eric and knowing about his mother. He took his hat off, hung it behind the door and flopped in a chair. He looks tired, Lillian thought. She put a strong cup of tea in front of him and cut him a slice of the cake she'd just made and waited for him to give her his news.

He filled his mouth with cake and had a sip of tea and gazed out the window towards Aunt Maggie's. "How's the old girl?" he said.

"She's getting better, poor old thing." Lillian replied. Fortunately, Aunt Maggie hadn't mentioned their conversation about Eric's father. Either she had been too sick or hadn't remembered past her first glass of brandy when they farewelled Eric's mother. It was a relief as far as Lillian was concerned. She didn't want Eric to know she knew. Best let sleeping dogs lie, as her mother would say.

"She's our only hope now," he said in a subdued voice.

Lillian frowned, "What do you mean?"

"Mother had nothing to leave. She signed the farm over to Howard after she'd had her first stroke, before we were married." His voice caught and he turned his head away so Lillian couldn't see his face. "All the money I put in that farm." He shook his head.

Howard did that to them? Meek, Howard? "Can you get any of it back?" Lillian was furious. Howard knew how hard they had struggled. They had three children to support. He'd taken money from them after they lost their farm in a fire. How could he? If it hadn't been for Eric carting logs for the mill during week days, the farm would have gone bankrupt. Howard didn't even like farming; Eric was the farmer in the family. It was hard to get her head around what Eric's family was capable of.

"He sold it the day after Mother died. It seems he'd had someone in the pipeline for a while," Eric said. "The treacherous bastard wasn't at the funeral. Too scared to face me. The others missed out as well, of course. On the farm that is. Mavis and Patricia got Mother's jewellery. "I'll make sure Aunt Maggie knows what he did so she doesn't leave him anything. If I ever get my hands on him ..." Eric gritted his teeth. What a family, Lillian thought.

"Turn the wireless on, Lil, I haven't heard the news for a couple of days."

"I took it over to Aunt Maggie so she could have some company while she was in bed with the flu."

"Struth, Lillian. Don't overdo it, she'll never kick the bucket at this rate."

"Don't say that. I don't want her to die." Aunt Maggie had been a good patient, hadn't complained or demanded anything from Lillian. There had been nothing but smiles and gratitude all through her flu bout.

16

Melbourne

Lillian was pleased to see Aunt Maggie looking better. She collected the handkerchiefs on the floor and dropped them in a bucket of Dettol water. Rubber gloves covered her hands and a small block of camphor, in a muslin bag, hung around her neck. "I'll just put these on to boil," she said. She carried the bucket to the kitchen and put it on the stove, gave the fire a poke and added a block of wood, then returned to the bedroom. "Eric came home late last night. I'll get him to tell you all about the funeral." Aunt Maggie's eyes opened. Lillian pulled up the blind; the sea was serene and blue. "It's a lovely day. If you feel well enough I can get a chair and you can sit on the verandah? I'll bring my knitting over and make a cup of tea. It will do you good to get some fresh air."

Lillian unlatched the bedroom window and opened it. "We need to air your room so we can get rid of the germs. No one will come near here now Eric's home." Aunt Maggie had refused to have the window opened during her illness. She had heard someone on her verandah, a prowler. Lillian thought she must have had a temperature, but latched the window to give her peace of mind.

"Now let's get you dressed." Lillian pulled the cupboard drawer open and removed a pair of well darned black woollen stockings, a long petticoat and a pair of knee-length orange bloomers. "It's warm outside but there's a sea breeze and I don't want you getting cold." She helped Aunt Maggie into her underwear and slipped a black chenille dress over her head. Aunt Maggie sat like a lamb while Lillian brushed and plaited her hair. "All done," Lillian said. "You go and sit on the verandah in the sun while I take the wireless back to Eric and fetch my knitting."

"I like the wireless."

"I have to take it back, it's Eric's," Lillian said. Aunt Maggie's bottom lip pushed out. "Why don't you buy yourself one? The batteries last for ages. When you're feeling well enough to go up the street we can see how much they cost?" If only Lillian had thought of getting Aunt Maggie a wireless earlier, it might have been the solution to coffin practices. It would have given her more time to visit Ingrid and the library.

Aunt Maggie looked thoughtful. "I'll count my finances." She had been checking her money every few days since the worms had eaten so much and she'd had to burn it, although she did manage to pass a few mended notes to the shops. Splinter's pencil tin was proving itself, there hadn't been any more damaged notes since she'd started using it, but she checked every week just in case.

"It's a shame we don't live in the city; wirelesses are much cheaper there," Lillian felt a tug of longing; it was eight years since she had visited her mother in Melbourne. What if something happened to her before she saw her again? Her chest tightened. It had upset Eric that he hadn't seen his mother before she died.

117

Suddenly, it was imperative that Lillian visit her mother. She would put the hard word on him. Insist. Mavis might come down and look after Aunt Maggie and the kids. Lillian knew she would love to see Johnny. Maybe she could get a lift to Melbourne with one of the log trucks if Eric couldn't afford her bus fare? Lillian picked up the wireless. "See you later, Aunt Maggie." On the way back to her house her head was full of strategies.

Eric put the wireless on top of the fridge and turned it on, fiddling with the tuner, pleased to have it back.

"Aunt Maggie is going to buy herself a wireless," Lillian said. Eric looked at her, surprised. "I said I'd take her up the street to see what they cost. Of course, they charge an arm and a leg in Eden." She put the finishing touches to the shepherd's pie and slid it into the oven.

Eric frowned. "A waste of money at her age, she could drop dead anytime."

"Yes, I've been thinking about that a lot lately, especially since you said how much it hurt you not seeing your mother before she died. It made me think of my mum. I couldn't bear it if anything happened to her, having not seen her in so long." Lillian rested her hand on Eric's shoulder. Eric went quiet. "I was even thinking I could get a lift with one of the log trucks. I know it would take an extra day to get to Melbourne but it wouldn't cost us anything."

Eric's mouth dropped open. "Are you mad? Do you realise you would have to sleep in the log truck with a logger? No respectable woman would do that." He shook his head. Eric knew the loggers. They were drinkers and womanisers; pub gossips. Lillian was out of her mind if she thought he would allow his wife to do such a thing. She'd be talked about like Pixie Taggart, the barmaid at the Fishermen's Club, a divorced woman who lived on her own. Most of the loggers boasted they had been through Pixie. Eric chatted to her a lot. He wouldn't mind a bit of Pixie, she was a flirt and had given him the come on more than once. He filled his pipe and looked across at Aunt Maggie's window. If Lillian went away who would look after Aunt Maggie? He grinned. "Haven't you forgotten something?" he said, lighting his pipe. Lillian raised an eyebrow. "Who's going to look after Aunt Maggie?" He could just see Aunt Maggie's outrage at the thought of Lillian going away.

"Aunt Maggie would never let you go," he said.

"What about your sister? Mavis would love to see Johnny again." Eric's face went still, he sucked on his pipe.

"I don't want her snooping around Aunt Maggie's for a week," he said. Mavis was avaricious, she'd wheedled money out of a wealthy uncle and the rest of her siblings had missed out.

Lillian put Mavis on the back burner. Eric hadn't said no outright to her going to Melbourne, just to going in the log truck. She would have hated to go in a log truck anyway, all those hours on the road with a logger, what would she have talked about? Of course she wouldn't sleep in the truck with a man. Ingrid had a swag her husband used to use, Lillian could have borrowed that. She had only come up with the truck idea to show Eric how serious she was. But she could enquire around town and find out if any family was travelling to Melbourne and ask for a lift. The next time she was in the butcher's she'd ask Mick if he knew of anyone going to Melbourne. It wouldn't hurt to check the bus fare either. Maybe one of the kids would lend her their savings? Lillian was determined to overcome Eric's obstacles. She opened up her recipe scrapbook and looked for the rainbow cake recipe, it was the one she made for the children's birthdays. Aunt Maggie would love it.

Aunt Maggie was sitting in the kitchen with Splinter's pencil tin open on the table when Lillian came in with a thermos of tea and a slab of rainbow cake. She put a rubber band around some notes and caught sight of the cake. A smile split her face. Lillian tried to do a quick calculation over Aunt Maggie's shoulder at how much money was in the tin, but the notes were in bundles and different denominations. A piece of paper with pencilled numbers lay next to the notes. Aunt Maggie put the lid on the tin and held up the notes she had banded. "There's ten pounds there for a wireless."

The only wireless you'll get for that is from a pawn shop, Lillian thought. She didn't say so because she wanted Aunt Maggie in a good mood. "We'll take a walk up the street tomorrow and see how much they are. Look, I've brought us cake for afternoon tea." A lick of the lips rewarded Lillian.

When Aunt Maggie was settled on the chaise longue in the sunroom, Lillian moved a chair next to her for the tea and cake and pulled a chair over for herself. Then she went into the kitchen, poured tea from the thermos flask into two cups and put one small and one large piece of cake on two plates. She carried the tray into the sunroom and put it on the chair beside Aunt Maggie and then sat down.

"I've had a telegram from my youngest sister, Lucille, in Melbourne. She's the ballet dancer," Lillian said proudly. "She said my mother has been ill and is in hospital. She is recovering though." Lillian crossed her fingers at the lie; she didn't want to jinx her mother. "Lucille is going on tour with the ballet company and won't be back until after Mum gets out of hospital. She's asked me if I could stay with Mum for a few days until she returns from the tour. It's probably for a week." It came out in a gabble. Aunt Maggie's eyelids lowered as she absorbed the news.

"Did she have a heart attack?"

Lillian had bite of cake. She hadn't thought to name an illness. Why had she said hospital? She could have said a twisted ankle or something. Aunt Maggie would be jealous if she said heart attack. A list of diseases flashed through Lillian's mind. She finished her mouth full and wiped the corners of her mouth with her fingers. "She has pneumonia," Lillian said. She gazed just above Aunt Maggie's nose so she could hold her ground and not look away.

"Teddy Edwards died of pneumonia. Coughed his lungs up, his mother said." Aunt Maggie settled back on the chaise longue. "What about my dinners?"

"Splinter is very good at sausages and Eric makes a good stew. Johnny can do your shopping." Lillian noticed Aunt Maggie's lip curl at the mention of Johnny. She would have to have a word with Johnny and make sure he didn't antagonise Aunt Maggie while she was away. "You won't want for anything. I'll leave everyone instructions."

"You had better get me another bottle of brandy before you go. I never know when I'm going to have a heart turn." Last night her heart had nearly marched out of her chest. The prowler she had heard when she was sick with the flu was back. The boards had creaked outside her bedroom window and she'd heard footsteps. Perhaps he had been watching her counting her money? "I hope I won't die before you get back."

Lillian sucked in her cheeks to stop a smile. "You won't, Aunt Maggie, it's only for a week."

On her way home, Lillian had an urge to skip across the yard. It was quelled by the thought that Aunt Maggie might be watching from the window. Now she only had Eric to conquer. She'd pick some beans and a cauliflower from the garden, roast a leg of lamb and have rhubarb and custard for desert. It was one of Eric's favourite meals.

Lillian opened the oven door, removed the roast and set it to the side of the stove. She stirred beaten egg yolks, sugar, vanilla and milk until they turned into a thick cream and planned what she would say to Eric. He wouldn't have expected Aunt Maggie to allow her to go to Melbourne. It was only the bus fare holding her back now and she'd need that soon or Aunt Maggie might wonder why her sister wasn't back from the ballet tour to look after their mother. Lillian would tell Eric during dinner, it would be easier in front of the kids. They knew how much she wanted to visit their Nanna. They would tell their father that they could look after themselves if he tried to use them as an excuse. Splinter's voice broke into her thoughts.

"Mum, Johnny's just picked his nose and flicked it at me. He's jealous because I'm winning at drafts." Johnny leaned towards Splinter and wriggled his nose-picker finger at her. "Mum, Johnny's being disgusting."

"Johnny!" Lillian didn't want any fights to muck up her plans. "You'll have to pack that game up in a minute. Tea will be ready soon." Lillian poured the custard into a large jug. The sweet smell filled the kitchen.

"Can I scrape the custard pot, Mum?" Splinter asked.

"I suppose." Lillian passed the pot to Splinter. The bottom of the saucepan was toffee brown where the custard had begun to burn. Splinter ringed the inside of the pot with her finger and sucked noisily.

"Don't use your finger. Get a spoon."

Keeping her prize in hand, Splinter fetched a spoon from the cupboard drawer. Johnny and Bubs ran for their spoons. Splinter held the saucepan above her head and lashed at Johnny with her foot. "I'm not in the mood for this," Lillian yelled. "Splinter asked first, your turns will come." Johnny slumped into his chair and scowled at Splinter. She scraped the pot and licked the spoon, smacking her lips at him. He gave her chair a vicious kick under the table and swept the drafts off the board. Lillian's jaw set. She lifted a bowl of rhubarb out of the refrigerator and put it on the table. She filled a dessert bowl with rhubarb and spooned custard on top. The dessert was put on a tray for Aunt Maggie. "When I've carved the lamb you can take Aunt Maggie's dinner over, Johnny."

"It's not my turn."

"Tis so," said Splinter.

"Not! I did your turn when you went to the dentist. You owe me. She owes me, doesn't she, Mum?"

"Stop arguing, I'm not changing the roster. It's your turn. When you go to the dentist, Splinter will do it."

"It isn't fair. I get all the jobs. Why can't Bubs take it?" Johnny scowled at Bubs.

Lillian tucked a piece of damp hair behind her ear. It was hot in the kitchen. She didn't want any arguments. When the kids argued Eric got into a mood and if that happened she'd have no hope of talking to him about Aunt Maggie. Apprehension was making her jittery. After tea she'd take a Bex and go to bed early. She gave Johnny a cold look. "Bubs doesn't take Aunt Maggie's dinner over because she's too little and you will do as your told or I'll get your father to deal with you."

Johnny kicked the leg of the table. He didn't see his father come through the door, but rocked sideways as the rolled up newspaper smacked his head. Johnny covered his red ear and blinked back tears.

"Don't kick the furniture," Eric growled, pipe clenched between his teeth. He walked to the fridge, reached up and switched on the wireless. "No talking while the rugby's on." He positioned himself next to the wireless and reached for his pipe.

Lillian put her finger to her lips. "You girls go and wash your hands."

The rugby commentator's voice went up an octave. Eric threw his arms in the air and did a jig. "It's a try, we've got another try, they can't catch us now. You beauty."

Lillian smiled pretending to show an interest as she set

the table. Eric had tried out for the Australian rugby team but missed selection because of his ingrown toenail. His sporting achievements were in all the letters he'd written when they were courting. They were in the back of her wardrobe, tied with blue ribbon. He hadn't kept her letters. He told her after they were married that her backhand writing style showed a lack of character. Lillian wrote perpendicular now.

It occurred to Lillian that the Wallabies' winning streak might be hers as well. She spread out six plates and put the lamb on the carving board. Her lips thinned as she saw Eric open the paper to the horse racing results. There was always enough money for a bet. She shoved a fork into the lamb, cut off some slices and put them on a plate, arranged vegetables around the lamb and poured gravy over the top. Aunt Maggie will enjoy that Lillian thought. She put it on the tray next to the rhubarb and covered both dishes with saucepan lids.

"Looks tasty," Eric said eyeing Aunt Maggie's dinner. His appreciation was a good sign. Lillian pushed the tray towards Johnny.

"Off you go." She gave him her no nonsense look. Johnny snatched the tray and clomped outside. Normally Lillian would have told him off but she stayed silent to keep the peace.

After Johnny had gone Lillian carved the rest of the lamb. She filled Eric's plate with the best slices and added the end of the leg bone. A small round cluster of tiny white things, like plum blossom, caught her attention. They were wriggling on the leg bone. Lillian peered closer. Maggot lava! Bloody hell. The dinner was ruined. She inspected the rest of the leg, it was clear, only one spot had been blown. She gnawed her cheek. It was a bugger that it had to be on the leg bone, it was Eric's favourite part. No one else ever got the bone. She looked at Eric. He was intent on the wireless and filling his pipe. Her dinner plan was too important to spoil. She scraped the maggots off the bone and ladled gravy over the top. It looked fine. Relieved, Lillian loaded the plate with roast potatoes and vegetables and put it in front of Eric. Then she served the children and herself.

17

Lamb with Extras

On the way over to Aunt Maggie's, Johnny ducked behind the tank stand and lifted the cover off the dessert. Some custard came away on the saucepan lid. He licked it clean. Aunt Maggie wouldn't miss a couple of spoonfuls. He dipped his fingers into the dessert, took several scoops, sucked his fingers clean then patted the top flat and replaced the lid.

"Got your dinner, Aunt Maggie." His smile was beatific as he entered Aunt Maggie's house.

"Wipe your feet and don't step on the carpet." Aunt Maggie's voice stung him like a stick around the legs. She hadn't forgiven him for laughing at coffin practice. Johnny negotiated the perimeter of the faded Persian carpet and headed for the kitchen door at the same time as Aunt Maggie's cat was making his exit from the kitchen. Puss curled through Johnny's feet, tripping him up. His shin collided with the corner of the sideboard.

Photos fell and the decanter rocked. Johnny winced and steadied the tray. His eyes accused the departing cat.

More concerned about spillage than shins that deserved bruises, Aunt Maggie rescued the decanter. "Watch where you're going, boy." She picked Puss up and checked a big lump on his face. She gave it a poke and squeeze. Puss yowled and clawed his way out of her arms.

Johnny limped into the gloom, dodged the flypaper hanging from the ceiling and clattered the tray onto the kitchen table. He rubbed his shin and glared at Aunt Maggie, but she was too busy spitting on a scratch to notice. "Tell your mother Puss has an abscess and I need her to help me lance it."

Johnny scowled at Aunt Maggie and scuffed his feet on the Persian carpet as he limped out the door.

"If we wait for Johnny the food will go cold," Lillian said, pulling out a chair and sitting down. She watched Eric from the corner of her eye as he swamped his plate in gravy and went through the ritual of dipping the point of his knife into the salt cellar then tapping it over his food with a fork to distribute the salt across his plate. A ritual she found irritating, along with the deliberate buttering of his bread. None of them were allowed to start eating until he took his first bite. Most nights Lillian ate in the other room to avoid the tension he created at the table, but tonight was different. Tonight she was going to tell Eric that Aunt Maggie had agreed to her going to Melbourne for a week. The best time to bring it up was between mains and dessert. It was Eric's most mellow time. Lillian waited for Eric to start eating and then filled her mouth with baked potato. Johnny limped into the kitchen.

"I've hurt my leg." He went around the table and lifted his leg up for his mother to see. "Puss did it and Aunt Maggie liked me getting hurt." Lillian gave it a glance.

"It's just a small bruise," she said.

Johnny frowned. He thumped into his chair. "She wants you to lance Puss's abscess." Eric dropped his fork and pushed his chair back. Johnny smirked. Lillian could see the change in Eric's mood. The little bugger was going to ruin her plans.

"Don't talk about things like that at the meal table," she snapped. The atmosphere in the room tensed. "Get your dinner off the stove and any more talk like that and you'll go to bed." She put a slice of lamb in her mouth and looked up at Eric. "Mmmm, delicious." He picked up his fork. Lillian relaxed.

"Is it your birthday, Mum?" Johnny asked, trying to get back in his mother's good books.

"No, Johnny."

"Why are you sitting with us then?" All eyes turned to her.

"Good grief! Can't I sit here if I want?" She hadn't expected her presence to cause a fuss. "My food usually goes cold while I serve everyone else's and I wanted to sit with you all. Is that alright?"

"No talking at the table, or speaking with your mouths full," Eric said, frowning around the table. Lillian's presence at the table had even surprised him. The habit she had of always taking her food into the other room irked him. The wireless blurted out the weather report filling the silence while Eric chewed. Tomorrow was going to be hot and sunny; he might take the kids for a swim. His fork went into the lamb. Lillian kept her eyes on her plate.

"Tasty bit of lamb, that," Eric said.

Lillian tried not to show her revulsion. She should tell him. The bone went into his mouth, gravy dripped onto the plate. He sucked the bone and picked some meat out of his teeth with a fingernail. Bubs leaned forward and pointed at her father's plate.

"What's that, Dad?" Lillian's eyes followed Bubs's finger. She saw a tiny movement on Eric's plate. Oh hell!

"Don't talk unless you're spoken to and don't hang your head over my food. It's rude."

"But something's crawling on your plate, Dad."

"Eh?" Eric jolted forward, picked up his plate and peered. "Stone the crows! It's bloody maggots. My food's been blown." His cheeks expanded. He pushed his chair back and dashed from the kitchen. The children followed him outside and watched in awe as he vomited onto the ground. Lillian glared at a dead blowfly on the window sill.

Recovered, Eric stomped into the kitchen, the children in tow. "How could that have happened?" His eyes hunted the room for a culprit.

"Johnny left the door open when he was carrying Aunt Maggie's tray," Splinter offered. Eric burped and wiped his mouth on his sleeve.

"Blowed if I know," Lillian said, not wanting the blame to rest on Johnny. Eric gave her a sharp look. She hadn't meant it as a pun. "I'll make you a cup of tea to wash it down." All the effort she had gone to. What a disappointment.

"Yours could've been blown too?" Eric said. He was surprised Lillian wasn't making a fuss; most things made her squeamish; she hated finding worms in her fruit. He'd often given her an apple or peach he knew had codling moth in it, just to watch her reaction.

He belched. Lillian burped in sympathy. She would like to disappear into her bedroom.

"Maybe Aunt Maggie's dinner has worms," Bub said.

Lillian whirled on Bubs. "Don't you say anything to her." Bubs's shoulders slumped. It would have made a good story at school. Lillian handed Eric a cup of tea. "Why don't you play a game of cards with Splinter? It will take your mind off what you've eaten." Discussing her holiday was definitely off the cards right now. What could she do to make up for the disaster? Lillian fetched the cards and put them on the table. A pile of ironing sat in the basket. She didn't feel like doing it, but she had a lot to do if she was going to Melbourne. She put the iron on the stove to heat and emptied the basket on the floor.

Splinter dealt two hands and Bubs picked one up. "You don't know how to play poker, Bubs. It's only Dad and me."

"I do know how to play."

"I'll play a game with you tomorrow," Eric said.

Bubs's face darkened. She pulled her chair next to the ironing board. "Mum, did you know that people with 'arsitus' or something, were cured of their pain if they stood inside a whale?

"Arthritis, Bubs and I didn't know."

"Old Tommy told me when I was fishing at the wharf. He said his mother did it. He said they made holes in the whale carcasses." She looked over her shoulder at her father. "He said sometimes the holes were full of maggots but people still climbed into them." Lillian sucked her cheeks in and lowered her head. Eric's chair scraped behind her.

"Ah, for Christ's sake," he said, rushing from the room.

Lillian snorted, she couldn't help herself. At least Eric wasn't in a bad mood and accusing her of causing the lamb to be blown. It was odd that he wasn't ranting at her.

"The people weren't allowed to wash for a week after they did that, so they must have been very stinky," Bubs said.

"They would have had to throw their clothes away," Lillian replied.

"No, they didn't wear clothes." Bubs said.

Lillian put on a stern face. "I think that's enough talk about whales and maggots, Bubs. It's time you got ready for bed." Lillian picked up her white lace nightie out of the pile of ironing. There was still sex as a last resort. The white lace nightie was a gift from her mother. She had given it to Lillian the last time she had seen her. Told Lillian to pretty herself up more, said she'd let herself go. It was her mother's way of excusing Eric's wandering eye.

The nightie looked good. Its thin straps and low neckline enhanced her décolletage, which was smooth and unblemished. Lillian sprinkled some eau de cologne on her hairbrush and pulled it through her thick auburn hair. She would show more interest in sex tonight. Sex was an expectation for Eric, a jar of Vaseline his foreplay, not the romantic journey Lillian liked. She thought about when romance had been a part of their marriage, before the children. A time when Eric put bars of chocolate on her pillow and greeted her with a bunch of wild flowers after a day farming. She remembered the time they sat side by side milking cows and had had a milk fight with the cow's teats, soaking each other's faces. They had collapsed with laughter. Then Eric had picked her up and dumped her in the hay. They'd begun to make love and Lillian complained about the hay's roughness on her skin. Eric had pulled his trousers off, laid them on the hay and swept his arm towards them, bowing like Sir Walter Raleigh had done with his coat over a puddle for the Queen to step on.

In those days she'd adored him, enjoyed the sex. But then the children came along and Cora came on the scene and Eric became a bully. Lillian patted her hair and bent towards the mirror. Her eyelashes were still thick and black, but the crow's feet around her eyes had deepened. The bags under her eyes were permanent and made her look tired. The skin over her high cheekbones was still smooth and unlined. She dabbed some rouge on her cheeks with a piece of cotton wool, then licked her finger and ran it over her arched eyebrows. "You'll do," she said to the mirror. She pulled the covers back from the bed and lay down. Minutes later Eric walked in. Lillian rolled over and looked up at him. His eyes widened. "How are you feeling?" she said. His eyes swept her body and he grinned.

"I could do with a stomach rub."

Lillian patted the bed, "I can do that."

Eric was still snoring when Lillian got up. They'd had sex twice before they'd fallen asleep. He'd gasped, when she had cranked him up the second time. "I feel sexy," she had breathed in his ear. "I think it must be the oysters that I ate off the rocks when I was glass hunting on the beach." Lillian wondered what she would do if he started bringing home platters of oysters. She put on her dressing gown and slippers and tiptoed down the hall to the kitchen. She wanted to wake Eric with a cup of tea before the kids got up. Start him off in a good mood and then tell him about Aunt Maggie.

"What's this?" Eric said, when Lillian put the tea on his bedside table.

"I thought you might like a cuppa in bed for a change. I've made porridge and there's bacon and egg if you like?"

"Lovely," Eric said. "Have you spoken to Aunt Maggie about going away for a few days? I've been thinking the kids and I can manage her for a week. I don't want Mavis ferreting around Aunt Maggie's things when she hasn't done the hard yards taking care of her. I tried to buy you a bus ticket yesterday, but the paper shop had closed early. I was going to tell you last night and then you put it out of my mind." He grinned. "You can buy it yourself today."

18

Pixie

There were a lot of people waiting for the passengers on the bus. Lillian gazed anxiously around for her mother. A white handkerchief fluttered at the back of the crowd. Lillian's heart leaped.

"Mum," she shouted, grabbing her suitcase and rushing towards her mother. They clasped each other, hugging the years away.

"You look thin," Louise said, holding Lillian at arms length. It shocked her to see how gaunt her daughter looked and how poor her clothes were. Lillian's coat was frayed at the sleeves.

"I was a bit carsick. All those windy roads. You look marvellous, though." Her mother had always had an eye for fashion, could copy a dress from a picture in a magazine. "You can help me buy a piece of material and make me a dress before I go home." She laughed, "I can't believe I'm in Melbourne."

On the tram, tucked against her mother, Lillian listened to the chatter around her and drank in the city lights. All the clamour should have jangled her nerves. Instead she felt calm, like she had just slotted into a space that had been waiting for her.

The following day they went to Myer and Lillian gaped at clothes she could never afford. Eric had only given her ten pounds. Aunt Maggie had also given her ten pounds. Eric didn't know about that. Lillian was going to buy material and patterns with her money. They chose an assortment of sandwiches and a cake each for lunch. Lillian was in heaven.

"I still pinch myself I'm here," she said, looking around at the tables full of people. "Aunt Maggie didn't put up much opposition to my leaving her for a week. She's a bit of a handful. Likes to run my life. I'd hate her to die, though." Lillian rested her chin on her hands. "She keeps Eric on his toes." Lillian laughed. "I think Eric would cheerfully kill her off if he could. He wants his inheritance and I fear it's to buy that farm. I'm sick of farming. I want people around me. I couldn't face that isolation again."

"The old girl might be a handful," her mother said, "but she's in your corner and don't forget it."

"What makes you so sure of that?"

"She's a miser and she gave you ten pounds."

Lillian threw her head back and laughed. "It was a mended one. She told me city shopkeepers would be too busy to notice." Lillian filled her mother in on the note burning and Splinter's sticky tape repairs. She took the note from her purse and passed it to her mother.

"Good Lord! I don't believe it." Her mother inspected the note. "It might pass. I say we try it in the material section, they're always busy in there." She handed the note back to Lillian. "Tomorrow we're going to the ballet matinee, Lucille left us two tickets. Then I thought we might visit the Botanical Gardens."

They finished their lunch and headed for the dress materials. The week flew by.

Lillian heard the bellbirds before she caught her first sight of Eden through the bus window. The sea was so blue. It's lovely, she thought. If only she could live half a year in Eden and half a year in Melbourne. Lillian had put on weight, her hair was styled and she was wearing one of the two dresses her mother had made for her. The russet colours in her dress showed up the auburn lights in her hair, adding colour to her cream skin, deepening the colour in her eyes. She looked pretty, felt good.

"Mum!" shrieked Bubs. The children rushed at her. Lillian hugged them in close, she'd missed them. Eric grinned and gave her an appraising look.

"How's Aunt Maggie?"

"Guess what, Mum?" Bubs beamed, "I caught some fish and Aunt Maggie said Puss loved fish and she gave me sixpence for them. I'm going to fish for Puss and save up for a pony."

"Well, aren't you a lucky duck! Good on Aunt Maggie." Lillian gave Bubs a squeeze.

"She was over here this morning to see when you'd be back. I told her the bus gets in late at night. She said to make sure you came over in the morning."

The next morning Lillian opened Aunt Maggie's back door and called out. "I'm back, Aunt Maggie."

A faint voice came from the direction of the chaise. "Come in, I've had a bit of a heart turn." Lillian smiled to herself. Aunt Maggie had obviously missed her. She rested her mop and bucket by the door and went over to Aunt Maggie.

"How is your mother? Better than me I hope. I haven't been well since you left."

135

"I'm back now so I'll have you well in no time, and my mother is much better, thank you. I don't know what she would have done if I hadn't been there. I told her how generous you were letting me go to Melbourne when you hadn't been well yourself. As a matter of fact, she gave me a present to give you." Lillian went over to the bucket and took out a bottle of brandy. Her mother didn't drink brandy. It was Martell brandy, a gift to Lucille. Her mother had had it in the cupboard for years. Aunt Maggie's heart made a rapid recovery. She shot up into a sitting position, grabbed the bottle and read the label. She beamed at Lillian.

"How thoughtful of your mother. Fetch two glasses and you can tell me about Melbourne." It was eleven o'clock in the morning. If Lillian had a brandy this early she wouldn't be able to cook dinner. She put a measure of brandy in Aunt Maggie's glass and added water. Then she filled her own glass with water and splashed in just enough brandy to colour the water.

"You're not to worry about cleaning today, I want you to tell me about Melbourne." Her eyes twinkled. "Did you manage to spend the ten-pound note?"

"I did. Bought myself some nice material and made a dress." The rest of the morning Lillian entertained her with stories about her time in Melbourne.

It was Saturday. Eric was at the farm for the weekend, the kids had gone to the beach and Aunt Maggie was listening to her new wireless. She'd bought it when Lillian was in Melbourne. Lillian could put her feet up. She had only just sat down and opened her book when there was a knock on the front door. She closed the book and went to the door expecting to find one of the children's friends.

"Ingrid! What a nice surprise. Come in."

"Eric's at the farm, No?"

Lillian nodded. "You look hot."

136

"Ya, it is devil day," Ingrid said.

"We can sit in the lounge where it's cooler." The house was dark, blinds drawn against the heat. Ingrid put her hands out to feel her way down the passage.

"I can see nothing," she said as her eyes tried to adjust to the change in light. Lillian took her hand and guided her to a chair.

"I'll fetch us some lemonade," Lillian said. She was surprised at the visit. Ingrid didn't like Eric, he'd been rude to her a number of times, clicking his heels together or making a comment about Hitler in her company. Usually, Lillian met Ingrid in the library or visited her when she needed a break from Aunt Maggie. The jug of lemonade was cold from the fridge. Lillian had made it yesterday. She poured two tall glasses and put some biscuits on a plate and joined Ingrid in the lounge.

"I have somezing to tell you and it does not make me feel good," Ingrid said.

Lillian was instantly concerned. "What is it?" Are you ill?"

"No." Ingrid tapped her fingers together, her face serious. "I tell you this before you hear elsewhere."

"Go on." Goose flesh crept up Lillian's arms.

"It is Eric. I see his truck three times in Pixie Taggart's house when you were away." Ingrid put her hand on her heart. "I am your friend. It hurts my heart to tell you this."

"Couldn't he have been helping her with something, fixing her car maybe?" Lillian wanted to believe Eric was innocent. Ingrid shook her head.

"She boast about it in the Fishermen's Club when she drink too much." Ingrid looked at her hands. "I go there sometimes when I am lonely. I hear her." Lillian's face paled.

"Oh, God! You're telling me the whole town knows?"

"Soon, yes."

Lillian sat stunned, staring at Ingrid. She wished Ingrid hadn't come, although it was better to hear it from a friend. She knew

137

what it felt like to be whispered about, the stares and knowing looks. She'd had that when Eric had the affair with Cora. Lillian put her face in her hands. "Thanks for telling me, Ingrid. I'd like to be alone now so I can think about this."

"Ya, I go now. I wait for you to visit me." She stood up and gave Lillian an awkward hug. "I see myself out." Lillian nodded. She was going to take two Bex and lie on her bed.

Rage took over Lillian's senses. It was fortunate that Eric wasn't home or she would have attacked him and then he would have beaten her. How could he do this to her and with Pixie Taggart, that two beers slut! What would Aunt Maggie think if she found out? Perhaps she would evict them? Lillian had to calm herself. Think. Not rush at Eric with accusations like she'd done in the past. There was too much at stake. She needed time to think. Tonight, the kids would have to fend for themselves. Lillian just wanted to be on her own. Tomorrow, Eric would be home by lunchtime.

It wasn't the birds that woke Aunt Maggie the following morning. It was the grumble of her empty stomach; she'd gone to bed without any dinner. Shoving her feet into a pair of old tartan slippers she went into the kitchen, lit the fire and burnt her toast, muttering to herself as she wiped a generous helping of rancid butter over its charred surface. It was very remiss of Lillian to treat her with such disregard. Not even a message from the children. She was carrying her breakfast into the sunroom when Lillian tapped on her door.

"It's me, Aunt Maggie."

Aunt Maggie set her tray down and strode to the door, prepared to give Lillian a piece of her mind. The swollen red eyes and pale face that greeted her dissolved the lecture. Lillian fell onto Aunt Maggie with a guttural sob.

"The devil," she said for the third time as Lillian poured out her unhappiness on the chaise longue.

138

"I feel so humiliated, Aunty." She wiped her eyes with her hankie. Two soft old arms went around Lillian. She rested her head on Aunt Maggie's clean, lavender smelling dress. "I'm sorry you didn't get any dinner last night. I was too sick with shock to cook." A hand patted Lillian's back and she felt a pang of guilt. "I'll make you something special tonight."

"Have you had it out with that devil?"

"No, he's at the farm and won't be home until lunchtime. I don't even want to look at him. He makes me sick." Lillian studied her hands. "He beats me, you know. He's done this before." Aunt Maggie went rigid. It was a huge gamble Lillian was taking, she'd spent the whole night thinking about it. "I thought moving next door to you he would be different, more respectful."

"He fornicated and hit you?" Aunt Maggie's top lip disappeared behind her bottom teeth. "I want to know about the other time the brute fornicated." Her outrage was a comfort to Lillian.

"It was with my best friend. I don't really want to talk about it."

"Nonsense!" Aunt Maggie got to her feet. "What you need is a pick-me-up." She went to the sideboard and poured Lillian a generous brandy and a small one for herself. "It's good for shock," she said, pushing the glass into Lillian's hand. The brandy scorched its way down Lillian's throat. "Lie on the chaise and put your feet up." Aunt Maggie plumped a pillow under Lillian's head and tucked a blanket around her feet. "Now tell me about the other times."

Under Aunt Maggie's sympathetic gaze and the dulling effect of the brandy Lillian quietly obliged.

"The first time he did it was in Buchan before our farm was burnt." Lillian could pinpoint the moment Eric had killed her love for him and now she was about to demolish Aunt Maggie's hero. "He had an affair with my best friend. They were seen in a taxi, down by the river in broad daylight, by two children. We had a row over it and Eric beat me." The legs of Aunt Maggie's chair scraped the floor as she jumped to her feet. The decanter shone like a diamond above Lillian's glass as Aunt Maggie topped her up. A dull floating feeling inside Lillian's head had replaced the turmoil of her night. It was such a relief to purge herself of Eric's treachery. Apart from her mother, Lillian hadn't told anyone about Cora. She had another gulp of brandy. There was a pain in her stomach, she needed some food to soak up the alcohol, she hadn't eaten breakfast. She tried to stand up and fell back on the chaise. "I'm feeling a bit woozy. I think I need something to eat to soak up the brandy."

"Stay there, I'll get some biscuits and cheese." Aunt Maggie marched into the kitchen. Lillian lay back on the chaise, grateful for Aunt Maggie's concern. Her mother had been right. Aunt Maggie was in her corner. They looked out for each other. The packet of biscuits hadn't been opened, they weren't broken and full of webs, but the cheese was covered in mould. She ate it anyway. "He's such a womaniser, so vain. Two weeks after we lost our farm we had a row over a waitress he flirted with. Did it in front of me and the children in a hotel dining room." Aunt Maggie clucked her tongue. "He beat me that time too. I don't know how many more women he's played up with. They probably had husbands so Eric was more discreet. He must have thought it was Christmas with me out of the way in Melbourne. I guess he didn't consider he'd be seen by my friend. And didn't think Pixie Taggart would boast about it in the Fishermen's Club."

"The fornicator," Aunt Maggie growled.

"I'm not going to say anything to him just yet. He has a terrible temper. I'll give it a few weeks and when my pain and humiliation has blunted I'll have it out with him." Lillian felt her eyes closing. "I should go home and lie down, sleep the brandy off. I'm feeling so tired."

"You can close your eyes here, for five minutes," Aunt Maggie said. Lillian slept while Aunt Maggie attended her rose garden.

"The devil is back." Aunt Maggie said, shaking Lillian awake. "Come on."

"Come on where?" Lillian said, blinking.

"We're going to see to that fornicator." Aunt Maggie snorted.

Lillian's hand went to her mouth. She was fully awake and terrified. "No, we can't. He must not know I told you." Lillian looked at Aunt Maggie and saw the clench of her jaw, the matting eyebrows and quiver of outrage. The unknown was about to reveal itself. Why hadn't she kept her mouth shut?

"I'll get my umbrella. How dare he treat us like that." Aunt Maggie strode to the umbrella stand and took out a black umbrella with a steel point and leather handle.

Bugger! What was the old girl going to do? "Don't do anything, Aunt Maggie, it'll only make matters worse. Let's leave it for a week and then say we both heard it from a neighbour. And then maybe you could just have a word with him, sort of suggest you don't like scandals." Lillian bit her lip. "Tell him if he doesn't behave you will reconsider keeping him in your will." God, Eric would kill her if he knew what she'd done. Lillian put a restraining hand on Aunt Maggie's arm but Aunt Maggie shook her off and turned a disdainful face.

"Get some backbone, girl. I'm not letting him do this to us. It's going to be the talk of the town. He's got too many cows in his pasture. Needs to be knackered."

Bile filled Lillian's throat and her head began to pound. She wished she hadn't had the brandy. This couldn't have a good outcome. Aunt Maggie charged out the door, umbrella poised like an angry rhino. Lillian had to trot to keep up. "We should talk about this, Aunt Maggie, there's no knowing what Eric will do."

"Pull yourself together, girl. He's my nephew and he'll do as I say, or else."

Eric was having a quiet smoke on the verandah and reading the paper when the umbrella came down on his head. Lillian hid behind the door but stayed where she could hear every word.

"Fuck!" Eric whirled around and made a grab for the brolly and stopped dead, mouth open. Aunt Maggie's eyes bored into his. The umbrella point jammed into his chest.

"You're a devil, Eric, fornicating and shaming the family. If you do it again, I'll have you out of the will. And don't let me hear that you would raise your hand to a good wife. Do you hear me?" She jammed the umbrella into him one more time, punctuating her sentence. It hurt like hell.

"Yes, Aunty." He looked at the ground, eyes smouldering, face flushed as Aunt Maggie stormed home. Who had told her about Pixie? Had the kids ever mentioned he'd hit Lillian?

Hearing Eric's meek reply, Lillian made herself scarce, donning her hat and gardening gloves and creeping around the house to her rose garden. She was a jangle of nerves as she pulled out weeds. He stomped around the corner and came up behind her. She turned. "You're back early. I didn't hear the truck." She forced an innocent smile. Eric looked sheepish.

"Aunt Maggie was just here."

"Does she want me?" Lillian stood up and stretched.

"Just now," he said. He shuffled, waiting for her to say something. Lillian let him stew.

"I'll be in the shed if you need anything," he said.

"Right," she said, turning back to the rose bed. "I don't suppose you could make a sandwich for the kids when they get home? They're at the beach. I'd like to visit Ingrid. I haven't seen her since I got back from Melbourne."

"I can do that." Eric was quick to oblige. Guilty, thought Lillian. She would have to be ill before he'd make the kids a sandwich. And he hated her going to Ingrid's. Lillian avoided the town and kept her sunshade up to hide her face. It was a fair walk to Ingrid's using the back streets. The new shoes she had bought in Melbourne had given her blisters and her feet were hot. She took her shoes off and went down the wharf steps and dangled her feet in the water. A couple of fishing boats nudged the wharf. There wasn't much activity about, most of the fishing boats were out. If only life could be this tranquil she thought, looking across the flat blue surface to the other side of the bay. How long should she put the confrontation with Eric off for? What would she say? This time though it would be different, Lillian had Aunt Maggie in her corner. And Aunt Maggie hadn't told Eric who had told her about Pixie, so Lillian could tell him that she had learned about Pixie from Aunt Maggie. Tomorrow she would sort it out with Aunt Maggie. Lillian wiped her feet on the hem of her dress and put her shoes back on. Then started up the lookout hill to Ingrid's.

19

Blue Box

The wharf hill was a killer and Lillian was panting by the time she reached Ingrid's door.

"It is good to see you," Ingrid said.

"I hope you're not going out?"

"No, I have just made a strudel. It is good timing."

"I have lots to tell you," Lillian said, following Ingrid into her neat little kitchen. She sat at the kitchen table facing the view of the bay. Ingrid cut the strudel and put it on two plates, then skimmed the thick cream off the top of the milk and put it in a bowl with a spoon.

"You start. I make a cup of tea." The strudel was warm and comforting. All the more delicious because someone else had made it. Lillian let out a sigh. Ingrid's house was so peaceful, not full of drama like hers.

Ingrid sat opposite Lillian and poured two cups of tea.

She passed one to Lillian and leant forward. "Tell me what is happened now?" The solemn look on Ingrid's face triggered something inside Lillian. Her morning with Aunt Maggie and Eric suddenly seemed so absurd.

Lillian grinned. Then started to laugh. Tears ran down her face. Ingrid was looking at her as though she had gone mad. "Oh, God, I'm sorry," Lillian said, mopping her eyes. "After you left yesterday, I was so upset. I dosed myself up with Bex powders and went to bed. The kids had to get their own dinner and I forgot about Aunt Maggie. I had a dreadful night. First thing this morning I went over and apologised to the old girl. She was marvellous, filled me up with brandy and called Eric a fornicator. I fell asleep on her chaise longue for an hour. Then Eric came home and she ..." Lillian snorted, and had to turn her head away from Ingrid's amazed gaze to compose herself. "She clobbered Eric with her umbrella and stuck the pointy end in for a good measure."

"Mein Got! I would like to see that."

Lillian wiped her eyes and became serious. "I walked here the back way. I didn't want anyone thinking, 'There goes the Pom, her husband was up to no good with Pixie Taggart'."

"Take Aunt Maggie vis you next time you go up town. They vill be too scared of her to look at you. I hope her umbrella gives Eric a big headache."

"I hope he never finds out I was the instigator," Lillian said, chewing her lip.

"Good for you, he deserve it." Having Ingrid's support was a comfort. They sat with their thoughts, eating the strudel.

"It's going to be difficult with Eric and Aunt Maggie not talking to each other," Lillian said, breaking the silence.

"Just ignore."

"When I was in Melbourne I took a ticket in the lottery. If I win, I'll go to England for a holiday and I'll treat you to a holiday in Austria." Ingrid gave her the thumbs up. "It's funny but I only think of going to England for a holiday, never to live." Lillian looked out the window at a seagull-filled sky and the beaches tucked in coves around the bay. "It's beautiful here. Where in England could you have a beach all to yourself or boil a billy in the bush to a serenade of bellbirds?" Crowds of houses in cobbled streets filled Lillian's mind. "What I miss about England is eating scampi and chips on Friday nights and going to the local on Sundays for a beer with the neighbours. Could you imagine us going into a bar here? We would be arrested."

"I don't want to go in the bar. Men do pissing and sick – they have sawdust on floors!"

Lillian laughed. "Australia is still stuck in the England of their grandfathers."

"At home ve sing in the pub."

"I went to shows in Soho and to the pictures with my sisters."

"Why did you marry, Eric?"

"He was so handsome, like a hero in a novel. He told me stories about his dog rounding up the sheep and a horse that knew its way home when he fell asleep in the saddle. Eric did things I only read about in books, and life on a sheep station sounded fantastic. It was a long way from wars."

"Ah," Ingrid gave a sage nod. "It is always the handsome sailor or the wounded hero. My husband was wounded hero. He bring me here and run away." Like Lillian, there was no money for Ingrid's return.

Lillian sighed. "Nobody ever asks me anything about England or my life there. You'd think I never existed before I came here. I remember telling one of the CWA women about a Noel Coward play I saw in London and she put on this toffee accent and said, 'Oh, we saw a play in London, did we?' I didn't talk about myself after that."

"Jealous," Ingrid said.

"Did you know at the last CWA meeting they gave me back two cardigans I knitted for the church fete? I was so embarrassed. They measured the arms and one was an inch longer than the other. I pulled them undone and knitted one for Aunt Maggie. She wore it every day until it was covered in food. I had to wrestle it off her to wash. If it hadn't been for Aunt Maggie pressuring me, I wouldn't have joined the damn CWA.

"Aunt Maggie had been on their committee for years. I heard they retired her because she handled the cakes and picked the icing off them at the cake stalls. They didn't tell her that though. She thought they'd kicked her out because she was too old. None of them visited her after her retirement. Poor old duck, so much for Christian ladies. She wanted me to join so she could keep up with their doings. Apparently I was only accepted as a member because Aunt Maggie gave them a donation. I am Church of England but I attend the Presbyterian church for Aunt Maggie's sake. I know they think I'm a stuck up pommy." Most of the local women believed Lillian only looked after her husband's wealthy aunt because she wanted to inherit her money. They had never bothered to get to know her. The friends Lillian made were transitory like the bank manager's wife or viewed with suspicion like the draper's wife, who townsfolk thought was a witch because she practiced meditation and held the occasional séance, which Lillian and Ingrid attended.

"I cannot be a member. They tell me their husbands die in the war." Ingrid looked sad. "Come we forget those ladies," she said, pushing her empty cup in front of Lillian. "You read the leaves for me." Ingrid had faith in Lillian's tea leaf reading. Once Lillian had told Ingrid to hide her valuables because someone she thought of as a friend would try and steal them. Not long after Ingrid had come home to find her boarder of six months gone and her house ransacked.

Lillian looked into the cup. "You are going on a journey." She turned the cup around, "but you will return." Lillian felt relieved. She didn't want to lose her friend.

"Maybe it is the lottery ticket you win?" laughed Ingrid. Lillian put her chin on her hand and gazed at Ingrid.

"Ingrid, I came to see you today because I need your advice. I don't know when I should tackle Eric about his affair with Pixie. I'm not sure how to go about it. At the moment, he's pussyfooting around me, unsure what I know, or if Aunt Maggie told me. I know as soon as I say something he will come up with some baloney to defend himself. Then he'll accuse me of listening to gossip and having a suspicious mind. This isn't the first time he's done this to me. He's had other affairs."

"Nein! That is terrible."

"Yes, and he's raised a hand to me in the past. What he's done is festering inside me yet part of me wants to let it go now Aunt Maggie has stood up to him. What do you think?"

"You must not let him get away wiz this, Lillian. He has no respect for you. Aunt Maggie have no respect. You must talk to him tonight, sooner better. Not good for you to carry inside you. Tell him you hear in shop. He vill not ask who said. What you must do is give ultimatum."

Lillian turned her wedding ring around her finger. What ultimatum could she give him? She couldn't move to Melbourne without money. Her mother only had two bedrooms, not enough for her sister, Lillian and three children. Lillian would have to find a job. Aunt Maggie wouldn't help her move to Melbourne because she had become used to Lillian taking care of her. "What ultimatum can I give Eric? I have no money."

"You move girls in one room together and you take other bedroom. Don't do his washing, don't speak. Steal his money. Tell him Aunt Maggie say to you that if you unhappy she cut him from her will. You have lots of ultimatums, Lillian. He must beg your forgiveness. Do kind things for you, promise no more women. Tell him Aunt Maggie will help you wiz money. He not brave enough to ask her if true."

It was good sense, Lillian's head cleared. She looked in admiration at her friend. Ingrid had given her strength. In the past Lillian had given in to Eric's bullying, taken on the guilt for his actions, fearing his temper and his fists. "Thank you, Ingrid." Lillian had two women in her corner now.

On the way home from Ingrid's Lillian passed the Eden whaling museum. She felt an affinity with the whales on display. They had been the unsuspecting victims of a pack of killer whales. Lillian knew what it felt like to be trapped.

After the children had gone to bed, Lillian faced Eric. "I know about you and Pixie. Two women I won't name, were talking about you in the shop."

Eric dropped the pipe he was filling on the floor. "What are you talking about?" he blustered.

"You couldn't wait to send me to Melbourne could you? According to witnesses your truck was seen parked in Pixie Taggart's place quite late at night on three occasions. This is a small town. Everyone knows everyone's business. No different to Buchan and Cora."

"It's bullshit. Her car broke down at the club. I gave her a lift home in the truck and the following night I fixed her motor."

"That's not what Pixie said in the bar," Lillian said quietly, her eyes hard. Eric looked around the room. He stepped towards her, menacing.

"I wouldn't do anything you might regret. Aunt Maggie doesn't like men who beat their wives. She said she'd give me whatever money I needed to help me start a new life in Melbourne if you ever laid a hand on me." Although Lillian's insides shook, her eyes didn't waver. Eric looked away. Lillian could have heard a cockroach crawl. "How dare you humiliate

149

me with that two beers slut, Pixie Taggart, Eric? It's not only me you've humiliated. Aunt Maggie is seething."

"What do you expect me to do when I need sex and you're gallivanting in Melbourne?" Eric said.

"The same as other husbands do, Eric. Practice self-control. You went without sex for more than a week when I gave birth. Lillian frowned. She was feeling strong. He was squirming in front of her. The worm. "I'll let you practice your self control. I'll sleep in Splinter's room until I can forgive you."

The kitchen door slammed as Eric stormed out. Lillian collapsed in a heap on the chair. Why hadn't she stood her ground years ago?

Two weeks had passed and Eric had hardly spoken a word to her. He was punishing her for standing up to him. Lillian was sleeping in Splinter's room. Eric was still going to the Fishermen's Club, but according to Ingrid he wasn't speaking to Pixie. Ingrid had heard that Eric had told Pixie off for boasting about their affair. It was good news for Lillian, although she still burned at his deceit. Which was why she made the decision about her engagement ring.

The small blue velvet box sat on Lillian's dressing table. She opened it and gazed at the bridge of sapphires and opals. Eric had bought the ring in London. Bent his knee in Kew Gardens under a eucalyptus tree and slipped it on her finger. She remembered how posh she had felt. None of her married friends had had engagement rings. It had been so romantic. Lillian snapped the lid shut. The ring had sat in her drawer for years. They never went anywhere for her to wear it and at home her hands were either in rubber gloves or covered in flour. She dropped the box in her handbag.

The young butcher's apprentice ducked his head around the sheep carcass and smiled shyly as Lillian entered the shop. Lillian felt a rush of remorse. It wasn't too late to change her mind.

On her last visit to the butcher shop Mick had told her the young lad wanted to get engaged but hadn't time to drive to Sydney to buy a ring. On an impulse, Lillian had offered him her ring. "I'll sell you my engagement ring if you are interested?" She swore the apprentice and Mick to secrecy. Said she didn't want to embarrass Eric, but the truck needed new parts. The lie had made her face burn. Mick had rushed to her rescue and promised he and the lad wouldn't tell a soul. It was a done deal. The lad would bring the money at the end of the week and she would give him the ring.

Lillian took the box from her handbag. "I hope it brings you luck," she said, putting it on the counter. The lad wiped his hands on his apron and went over to his jacket and removed an envelope.

"Thank you," he stammered, handing her the envelope. Lillian nodded, she couldn't speak. Mick trimmed a leg of lamb and wrapped it in paper.

"On the house," he said, pushing it towards her.

"You needn't," she said, not looking up in case he saw the tears in her eyes.

"I insist." Mick squeezed her hand.

Flustered, Lillian grabbed the meat. "That's kind of you," she said. "I'd better go. I'm expecting a visitor." Lillian hurried from the shop. She'd have to think where she could hide the money.

20

Blackberry Tarts

The cow bell clanged. "Shit! What does she want now?" Eric growled. He slammed the kitchen door behind him. Lillian watched him stride across the yard to Aunt Maggie's house. Things had to be sorted between him and Aunt Maggie. He was still in her bad books since the umbrella incident and she had taken to summonsing Eric with a cow bell when she wanted something. The small handouts for the odd jobs he did for Aunt Maggie, which he relied on for betting money, had been replaced by half-mast eyes and a stiff nod of thanks. It was loyalty to Lillian, and she appreciated it, but it wasn't helping the tension in the family. For the kids' sake, Lillian had to get things back on an even keel. She hadn't forgiven Eric, but like it or lump it she was stuck. Today, she would move back into her own room and sleep with Eric again.

The sex was like a magic switch. Eric put a cup of tea next

to Lillian. "I've made porridge if you want some. How about you and the kids come to the farm with me on Saturday and we'll have a picnic. We'll just make it a day trip as I have a motor to fix on Sunday. The blackberries are ripe and I thought we'd pick them before I burn them out. They've become a pest. You could make some of those lovely blackberry tarts of yours?" He grinned, looked boyish. Lillian didn't want to go to the farm. She enjoyed her weekends without Eric, but their relationship was on the mend and if a day at the farm would help, she'd go.

"Lovely idea. I'll let Aunt Maggie know we won't be here for the day and pack a picnic." A thought crossed Lillian's mind as she sipped her tea. They had never taken Aunt Maggie for an outing before and it might be a good way for Eric to bury the hatchet if she came with them. She voiced her thoughts over breakfast.

"Are you mad?" Eric said. "How would I get her in the truck? I'd need a hoist."

"What if you just asked her? If she says yes and you can't get her in the truck at least you've shown you're willing and it might improve her attitude towards you." Lillian reasoned. Eric scratched his head. He was sick of the cow bell. It could be worth a try.

The two crates Eric had put down creaked as Aunt Maggie clambered up. Eric stood behind her supporting her bottom with his shoulder. Inside the truck Lillian kneeled on the seat facing the open passenger door and clasped Aunt Maggie's hands.

"One, two and three," Eric grunted. Aunt Maggie landed on the seat and righted herself. Eric stood back red faced. "Johnny and Splinter, hop on the back and hang on tight," Eric said. Aunt Maggie moved into the middle of the seat and Lillian climbed in beside her. Bubs sat on her knee. Eric got behind the wheel. "Off we go," he said in a jovial voice, his face fixed in a smile, eyes a bit maniacal. Lillian kept her face to the window desperate not to laugh. They drove with their windows down while Aunt Maggie farted all the way to the farm.

After they had picnicked on the verandah, Lillian and Eric left Aunt Maggie lying on an old couch with the newspaper and went to pick blackberries. Aunt Maggie was happy to wave them off and quite sentimental at being invited out for the day. She loved the birds and the trees and looking out over the river and hills. It reminded her of her youth. She would consider doing it again.

While they picked blackberries Lillian and Eric snorted with laughter. The tension had been broken at last. They filled the bucket and sat in the shade of a gum tree and watched the children swimming. It was peaceful. Lillian felt relaxed, she was enjoying herself, it was such a relief to be back to normal.

Eric picked a piece of grass and tickled her face. She grabbed it and the seeds came away in her hand. Eric looked at her hands. They were red and cracked. "We'll have to think about getting a washing machine," he said. Lillian's eyes widened.

The truck was parked next to the verandah and easy for Aunt Maggie to step into it. Once they were all in, she put her head on Lillian's shoulder and went straight to sleep.

They didn't get back until late. Lillian and Eric got out of the truck and Lillian went around to the driver's side and climbed back in to get on the other side of Aunt Maggie. Eric fetched the crates and put them next to the truck door for Aunt Maggie to step onto. "We're home, Aunt Maggie." Lillian said, giving her a shake. Aunt Maggie's mouth snapped shut and her eyes flew open. "You slide over and Eric will help you out." Aunt Maggie managed it with ease. Lillian saw her to bed and then went home. It had been a relaxing day and Eric was in a good mood. Tomorrow she would make some blackberry tarts.

In the morning Lillian woke up feeling nauseous. It went away after she had a cup of tea. She baked two blackberry tarts and put the rest of the blackberries in a saucepan to make jam. When the tarts had cooled, Lillian carried one over to Aunt Maggie's. She was still feeling off colour. Her breasts felt sore. Her brow creased. She counted back to her last period. It was late. Oh, God! She didn't want another child. She was forty-one years old and had her hands full with Aunt Maggie. When had it happened? It must have been the night when she moved back into Eric's bed. The condom had broken. She'd douched afterwards but the douche was old and the hose perished in places. She'd asked Eric for money to buy a new one, but he'd said it was still alright.

"You look peaky," Aunt Maggie said, noticing Lillian's white face as she took the tart from her. "Would you like some Epsom Salts?" Lillian had a bout of reflux.

"No thanks, I'll go home and lie down. It could be a touch of the flu. I'll come over and clean for you tomorrow. Enjoy your tart," Lillian said and hurried down the steps before Aunt Maggie could ask her to stay for tea. When she reached the gate in the fence she saw Eric busy in the shed working on a motor. She closed the gate and went over to the shed. "Got a minute?" she said. Eric put the screwdriver down and turned.

"What's up?"

"We need to have a word while the kids are at the beach. I'll make a cup of tea." She rushed off. Eric picked up a rag and wiped the grease off his hands. Lillian stoked the stove and put the kettle on. She set out the cups and saucers and put tealeaves in the teapot. Her heart was racing. Eric came in the kitchen and took his pipe from his pocket.

"I think I'm pregnant," she said, not looking at him. The pipe stopped halfway to his mouth.

"Stone the crows! How did that happen?"

"You tell me," she said.

"You couldn't have douched properly," he said. Water spat

from the spout of the kettle and sizzled on the stove. Lillian sat down and folded her arms. Eric made the tea.

"What can you do?" he said.

"I could have an abortion," she said quietly. It wasn't new in her family. Her mother had had two abortions in England. Lillian had cared for her at the time. An abortion wasn't something she looked forward to.

"You'll be the talk of the town," Eric said, frowning. Lillian raised her eyebrows.

"I mean, the young girls that get into trouble and go to Sydney have all been found out," Eric said, quickly.

"Not if I go to Melbourne and visit Mum. I could ask her to find a doctor for me. I should only be gone a week." The thought of seeing her mother again picked up Lillian's spirits. "I'll write to Mum tonight, ask her the cost." Eric chewed the stem of his pipe. Abortions were expensive. Another bus ticket to Melbourne. A week looking after Aunt Maggie. He shuddered.

"We'll have to put buying the washing machine off," he said. He'd already done that when he had bought timber and cement to build a milking shed on his farm for McKenna's strays. "Maybe Aunt Maggie would lend you the money?"

"What! I'm not telling Aunt Maggie I'm going to have an abortion. What would she think of us?" Borrowing from Aunt Maggie would mean Lillian would be more obligated, feel she should spend more time with her. Lillian didn't mind Aunt Maggie's company, but she also liked to visit Ingrid and the library and collect glass on the beach. Lillian had to make excuses to get some time on her own. Anyway Aunt Maggie would probably be horrified at Lillian having an abortion.

"It might be easier to have the baby," Eric said. He liked kids.

"I was advised not to have any more children. Remember?" The doctor had told her it would be a risk to have any more children after Bubs was born. Her recovery had been slow, she'd fallen into the doldrums and hadn't wanted to get out of bed in the morning. Anyway, when would she get the time to care for a baby? And what if she was too sick afterwards to care for Aunt Maggie and the kids? "I'll have a talk with Ingrid." Eric grimaced. "She's the only one I can trust," Lillian said.

Eric shrugged. "Beggars can't be choosers, I guess." Eric could make some discreet enquiries of his own around the Fishermen's Club, but he wasn't well liked and they might think he had gotten someone other than Lillian into trouble and start a rumour. It was better if Lillian handled it.

"Two heads are better than one," Lillian said, when Ingrid opened the door. Ingrid motioned her to an armchair and Lillian flopped into it. "I bring you another problem to help me with. You should start an advice column in the *Women's Weekly*," she smiled.

They discussed Lillian's problem over a sherry. Ingrid rummaged through a drawer in her sideboard and withdrew a small address book. She opened it at the back and found a pen and an old envelope and wrote down a name and address. Then passed the envelope to Lillian. "Here is name. I will write to him and get you a visit time."

Lillian looked at the envelope and read the neat print. "Rudolph Wagner," she said. "Fitzroy? Is that in the city?"

"Ya, and he was doctor in Austria but never a doctor in Australia. I was taking care of his children. It was ten years ago, but he is still there." She pointed to the address. "We send Christmas cards."

"I can't thank you enough, Ingrid."

Ingrid shrugged. "Psh. If we women don't look after each other who vill?" Lillian nodded, it was true.

In bed that night, Lillian told Eric, "I have the name of a doctor in Melbourne who will do it."

"Alright. I'll have to rustle up the money. It is early days isn't it? You can wait another month?" Lillian nodded. "Ingrid's writing to the doctor and he will get in touch with Mum about dates. I should hear from Mum by the end of next week."

21

Johnny's Late Delivery

The clock said six thirty. Aunt Maggie would be going to bed soon and Lillian had only just finished ironing her sheets. She slapped at a mosquito on her neck, put the iron on the stove to heat and stoked the fire. Damp curls stuck to her forehead. It had been a scorcher of a day: too hot for the violets on the window sill. Their flowers hung like dead flies attached to strings of cotton over the side of the red clay pot. Lillian tapped the thermometer and the needle didn't move off eighty-five degrees, five degrees higher than outside. She wouldn't mind catching a virus so she could have a rest. She was still waiting for her mother's letter so she could plan her trip to Melbourne.

Splinter dropped her schoolbag on the porch and pushed open the kitchen door, "Sorry I'm late, Mum," she puffed. "We had tunnel-ball practice. It's school sports next week." Lillian removed a plate covered with a saucepan lid from the oven and put it in front of Splinter. "Bangers and mash, goodie!" Tomato sauce haemorrhaged over the plate as Splinter whacked the bottom of the bottle. "What's for dessert?"

"Apple pie," Bubs said from her end of the table.

"Yum!" Splinter folded her sausage in a piece of bread and took a bite.

"Aunt Maggie got cream with hers. We didn't get cream," Bubs said.

"There was only enough cream for your father and Aunt Maggie. The milkman's been skimming the milk."

Splinter frowned. "It's not fair. Aunty always gets the cream. She'll be too fat for her coffin."

Bubs stuck her lip out. "She's mean. I had to get up at five o'clock to catch fish for her old cat and she only gave me threepence. She shouldn't get any dessert."

Lillian laughed. "Oh dear, thank your lucky stars you've got food." She stopped smiling. "There are plenty of children in England who are starving."

"The fish were worth sixpence and she only gave me threepence. I'll never save enough to buy a pony," Bubs whined.

"Don't go on about it." Lillian folded the sheets and put them in a wicker basket. "It's nearly Aunt Maggie's bedtime. Bubs, I want you to run over to the shed and get Johnny. He'll have to take the sheets over and help her make her bed. I haven't got time." Lillian's serial was about to start on the wireless.

"I'm not going to fish for Puss ever again."

"Call Johnny now or Aunt Maggie will have to sleep without sheets."

"Good."

Lillian looked at her glowering child. She didn't blame Bubs for being angry. How could Aunt Maggie diddle a kid out of threepence? But what else could they expect from someone who only owned one set of sheets and wouldn't have electricity? "You should have taken the fish over before school and not left it in a bucket all day under the kitchen window. The house was full of flies. Now go and get Johnny."

Bubs knew Johnny was going to hate her news and she gave a tight smile. He had borrowed her savings to buy a bicycle pump and hadn't paid her back. "Johnny, you've got to take Aunt Maggie's ironing over." She said as she entered the shed.

"Bloody hell!" The swear word slipped out and his head whipped towards his father who was about to throw a rope over a beam and hoist a motor. The snaking rope nipped the back of Johnny's shirt as he made his exit.

"You want me, Mum?" It might be wise to keep on his mother's good side. She'd sneak him a sandwich if his father sent him to bed for swearing.

"Take these sheets over to Aunt Maggie and give her a hand making her bed. You'll have to hurry, it's getting dark."

"You want me to make her bed?" His eyebrows climbed as high as his voice. "I don't know how to do that. Splinter does."

"Splinter hasn't eaten her dinner. She had tunnel-ball practice."

"Who took Aunty's dinner over? It was Splinter's turn."

"I did. Now go. If you don't make a fuss I'll give you some extra dessert. And you'd better apologise to Aunt Maggie. She complained about your fingerprints in her custard. Do that again and you won't get any dessert for a month." Johnny's cheeks blotched. He picked up the basket and left.

The basket sat on the back step while Johnny tapped on Aunt Maggie's door. He moved from one foot to the other, impatient for the new Dick Tracy comic in his school bag. He put his mouth to the keyhole. "Hello, Aunt Maggie, I've got your 'shits'." He grinned and listened, but there was no response. Maybe she had gone to bed without her 'shits'. He giggled, then thought he'd better look through the kitchen window to see if she was there. He left the basket on the step and went around to the kitchen window. Yellow light flickered in the gap beneath the blind. He stepped over the garden bed and stood on tiptoes, squinting into the light. Aunt Maggie was sitting at the table. On it was a bucket, two biscuit tins and a cardboard box. She pulled a note from the box and held it up to the lamp, gave it a close scrutiny and put the note on one of two small piles in front of her. She repeated the process, frowning and muttering.

Johnny pressed his face harder against the dirty glass and his eyes narrowed. She's counting her money? He'd heard his father telling his mother in hushed tones about Aunt Maggie's nocturnal habits. He decided to play a game. If she put the next note on the left pile, he would tap on the window. If she put it on the right one, he would bang on the door. She smoothed the note and put it on top of the left pile. Johnny's fingernails danced across the windowpane. Aunt Maggie's head snapped up. Rising from the chair she peered at the window. Her hand went to her heart. Johnny stifled a giggle, sure she had pooped her pants. Snorting, he left the window and stamped around to the back door.

The tap on the glass startled Aunt Maggie and so did the flattened nose and gopher lips. Could it be the same person who stumbled on her verandah a few nights ago? A vein pulsed in her throat and her heart drummed against her ribs. The face disappeared and she heard the crunch of heavy footsteps around the house. She swept the notes into the bucket, put it behind a flowerpot on the stove and crept up the hall to her bedroom. The wardrobe door squeaked as she pulled it open. Eric would have to oil it. Her hand patted over the funeral dress and in between coats to the back of the wardrobe until she touched a shaft of cold steel. She eased the loaded .410 single-barrel orchard gun out of the cupboard. If someone was coming after her money they were in for a shock. The grandfather clock in the hall was silenced by the beat of her heart as she tiptoed towards the back door.

Johnny held the basket of ironing and it was starting to get heavy. He rested it on his knee. Maybe she hadn't seen him. He was about to put the basket down and knock again, when the door suddenly jerked open. His mouth opened in greeting and then he saw the gun. It was pointing straight at him. The greeting died. "Don't shoo…" His words were lost in a roar. Air exploded in his ears and the basket of sheets landed on top of him as he hit the ground.

The gun kicked against Aunt Maggie's shoulder, knocking her backwards. Johnny's scream followed her to the floor. She lay on her back and gasped like a suffocating fish, the gun clasped in her arms. Long red bloomers glared beneath the raised hem of her black dress. She shifted her body a fraction and a pain shot through her right shoulder. Was it broken? She drew a shuddering breath and winced. Her mind buzzed like the post-office switchboard in an electric storm. Was that Johnny screaming? Was he dead? Dazed, Aunt Maggie lifted her head and looked around but the effort was too much and her head banged back on the floor.

Not far away in his garage, Eric turned the nut one more time then put the spanner on the bench and wiped his hands on a rag, his mind on the headmaster's wife. She had caught him coming out of the dunny and voiced her concerns about him shooting bottles off their dividing fence. Then she asked if he'd look at her mower, preferably when her husband wasn't at home. Thinking about her made his penis stick up. He gave it a stroke. The blast from a shotgun and Johnny's scream killed his hard-on.

In the kitchen, Lillian glared at the iron on the stove. She examined the burn on her hand. The gunshot obliterated Lillian's thoughts. She pressed her hand against her womb. "Christ, what was that?" Splinter and Bubs looked up, eyes wide. "It came from Aunty's." Lillian tore out the door and across the yard with Splinter and Bubs close behind.

Eric arrived first. "God Almighty!" His eyes bugged as he looked from Aunt Maggie spread-eagled in the doorway to Johnny lying at the foot of the steps under the pile of sheets. Eric dropped to his knees next to Johnny, his heart racing, belly sick with fear. "Oh God! Oh God!" He pulled the sheet off Johnny's face. "Are you alright, boy?"

Johnny opened his eyes, his ears felt full of water. He could hardly hear his father. "I don't know." The words were a squeak and he began to twitch.

Panic gripped Lillian as she reached the gate and saw Eric on his knees next to Johnny's sheet-covered figure. The thud of her heart grew louder. Everything slowed, her limbs felt leaden and she seemed to be inching forward. When she reached Johnny her legs folded and she landed on her knees beside him. Eric stood up in slow motion, moved away from her like someone in a dream. She lifted Johnny's head into her lap. He moaned. The sound jolted Lillian out of her dream state. The pungent odour of hair left in curling tongs too long, filled her nostrils. She saw Splinter and Bubs standing beside her, clinging to each other, mouths open. Bubs was crying and Johnny breathing. He wasn't dead.

"Is he alright, Mum?"

"Johnny love, are you alright? What happened?" Lillian felt him press into her.

He lifted a hand to the top of his head. It felt like the stubble on his father's chin. His scalp felt sticky. Had it melted?

Lillian rocked him. "What happened, speak to me?' She choked.

"Aunt Maggie shot me." His voice muffled in the front of her blouse.

Lillian gasped. "She did what?" She tore off Johnny's shirt, looked at his chest, back, legs and arms.

"My head hurts," he moaned.

Lillian grabbed his head and pulled it down. "Good Lord, the parting in Johnny's hair is wide enough to land a toy plane." She looked across at Eric. "His scalp is fried."

Johnny howled with terror, "Am I going to be bald?"

Eric stood at Aunt Maggie's feet, white-faced, eyes as cold as an arctic wind. He shook his head in disbelief. He didn't bend to examine her. She lay there looking up at him with shocked eyes. A pulse ticked in Eric's temple. He looked down at Aunt Maggie spread eagled on the floor. "You stupid old bugger." Aunt Maggie suddenly went into a fit. Her legs jerked, bubbles popped from her mouth and a noise like a strangled crow emanated from her throat.

"I hope you are having a heart attack, you mad old cow." Eric's eyes were slits. He leant over and snatched the gun from her arms. "You could've killed him. What were you thinking? They can put you away for this." Sweat glued his shirt to his back.

Aunt Maggie gave up on a curtain call; no one cared about her. They were all huddled over Johnny, except Eric who was looking at her as though he wished she were dead. She rolled onto her stomach and pushed herself up on her knees. Her arms shook so much she belly-flopped on the floor and had to scrabble towards the chaise longue. Eric grabbed her under the arms and dragged her to her feet. A hot pain shot through her shoulder. She moaned and leant against the wall to steady herself.

Lillian helped Johnny up. "Come on, pet, we'll go home and I'll make you a nice cup of Milo." She glanced at the scattered ironing and turned to Splinter and Bubs still clinging together. "You two pack those sheets in the basket and put them in Aunt Maggie's bedroom. She can make her own bed." Lillian put her arm around Johnny and led him through the gate in the fence.

Johnny shivered as he walked next to his mother. Aunt Maggie had tried to kill him, the old cow. He'd get her back. He'd report her to the police. He had to get the gun and dust it for fingerprints. That's what Dick Tracy would do. From now on he was going to carry his catapults and save plum pips. Johnny made the best cattys in school and traded them for the latest comics. They were made from old bicycle tubes that he cut into six-inch lengths and tied onto forked sticks collected from the branches of strong saplings. The fork had to be wide enough to shoot a large stone through, and strong, with good hand grips. The pouches that held the ammo were made with leather cut from an old car seat. After he'd killed a crow using an apricot pip, the orders for his catapults flowed in. Aunt Maggie had better watch out. His legs went rubbery and he tottered against his mother, tucking into her warmth, enjoying her closeness. She felt soft and smelled of cooked apples and pastry just out of the oven. If his mates saw him now they would call him a sissy for walking with his arm around his mother.

Eric prodded Aunt Maggie towards the chaise longue with the barrel of the gun. She tottered from sideboard to chair. The pain in her shoulder ran across her chest and down her arm. The intensity of it made her pant. Beads of perspiration popped through her pores and her body was clammy. Could she be having a heart attack?

"I'm taking the gun." He watched her crumple on the couch then turned and stormed out.

After he had gone Aunt Maggie lay on the chaise, awash with guilt. How could she have known it was one of the children? They never came after dinnertime. It was getting dark. She couldn't see very well in the dark. How could they think she shot Johnny on purpose? It might be time to get new tenants. Her lips pinned together. She was glad it was Johnny and not Splinter. She would have to keep a close eye on him from now on. Sneaky, that's what he was. Her face relaxed and her eyes looked into the distance. But what if it had been Splinter? That would have been awful. Such a willing child, she did Aunt Maggie's shopping, packed it away. Better behaved than the other two; a kind girl. She pictured the full glass of brandy Splinter always gave her and realised her throat was dry. She needed a glass now. The walk to the sideboard was painful and made her feel weak in the knees. A gust of wind rattled the window. Aunt Maggie cast a wary eye at the dark clouds blowing in from the sea. Would Lillian come over if there were a storm? Aunt Maggie tottered back to the chaise with a glass full of brandy and her head full of memories.

It was a thunderstorm that had endeared Lillian to Aunt Maggie. Lillian had been sweeping the kitchen floor when a blast of thunder burst above the house. It had given Aunt Maggie such a fright, she had run screaming into her bedroom and clambered in the wardrobe. Lillian had followed her.

"It's alright, Aunty, it won't hurt you. It's just thunder."

"You promise you won't tell anyone I'm afraid of storms?" Lillian had promised. There was another huge bang of thunder. The windows rattled and sheet lightning had lit up the room. Aunt Maggie had buried her head in her funeral dress and moaned. Then Lillian had begun reading the gardening section from the newspaper to her and she had forgotten all about the storm.

Thinking about Lillian's kindness took the edge off Aunt Maggie's anger. But Lillian should apologise for leaving her lying on the floor at Eric's mercy. It wasn't as though she had shot at Johnny on purpose. She had missed. In a moment of self-pity Aunt Maggie decided to cancel the subscription to the *Women's Weekly*.

22

A Robber and Doctor

The cup shook, spilling Milo into the saucer, Lillian put it in front of Johnny. A migraine was kicking the base of her skull. She swallowed a Bex powder to dull the pain and steady her nerves, then put the kettle on the stove for a pot of tea.

Eric thundered into the kitchen and dropped the gun on the table. He bent over Johnny and examined his head. "Crikey Moses, he reeks of cordite! Another inch and he'd be a goner. I should report the old fool."

"She wants me dead. We have to report her to the police," Johnny cried. He could see himself lying in Aunt Maggie's coffin, blood seeping from a big hole in his head.

Lillian put her arm around him. "Aunty didn't know it was you. She's an old lady and she was frightened. I'll buy you a comic." She looked up at Eric. "You're frightening him. Don't make an issue out of it or the authorities might say Aunt Maggie's unfit to live on her own." She lowered her chin and peered over the top of her glasses. "That would mean Aunt Maggie might have to move in here." The room resonated with the beating of their hearts. Lillian knew if Aunt Maggie was put in an institution, Eric's siblings might insist they pay rent or tell them to move out. Lillian couldn't face moving again; this was her home. There was also the other thing – she would lose her protector.

Eric's lips tightened over clenched teeth. He could hear Aunt Maggie shouting her demands down his hall, insisting her piss-pot wasn't full enough to empty, see her spitting her dinner down her dress and squashing flies on the window with her fingers. God, he couldn't bear the thought. He shook the images off and turned his attention to Johnny's head. "Lillian, bring me some warm water and the iodine, please." He spoke to her nicely. Johnny's eyes widened with alarm. Eric patted him. "Don't worry mate, it doesn't sting for long."

"No, butter is better for burns and it won't hurt." Lillian poured some Dettol in a bowl of warm water and tore off a wad of cotton from a roll of cotton wool and handed them to Eric. Then she took the butter out of the fridge and put it next to him. Their eyes connected and he gave her a small smile. Lillian felt a twinge in her stomach and massaged the sore spot, remembering the doctor had told her not to take so many Bex powders. Eric soaked the cotton wool in the water and bathed Johnny's head.

It hurt. Johnny gritted his teeth, trying to be a man and focused his thoughts on Aunt Maggie. He would run away from home if she moved in with them. He stared up at his mother. "Aunt Maggie can't live with us. She's a murderer."

Splinter walked in carrying the basket. "Who did she murder?"

"Did Aunt Maggie kill someone?" Bubs crowded through the door behind Splinter and jostled for a position next to Johnny.

Lillian sucked in her breath and frowned at the children. "She hasn't killed anyone." She could see this was going to end up in another scandal for the town. "For God's sake, Eric, we'll have to talk about this later. You kids aren't to tell anyone." She eyed Bubs. "Do you hear me? Not a word to your teacher." They all nodded, including Eric.

The reality of what his mother had said suddenly struck Johnny. If he couldn't tell anyone, then the kids at school would never find out how close to death he'd been. How could he explain his sizzled head? The kids would make fun of him and he'd have to wear a hat. Aunt Maggie would get away with attempted murder. It wasn't fair.

"She must have thought I was a robber, cos she saw me looking through the window when she was inspecting her money. I gave her a fright. She looked like she'd sat on a tack." He giggled. Remembering the fear on Aunt Maggie's face made him feel better.

Inspecting her money? Bubs's ears tingled. No one told her not to share that with her class.

"Poor Aunt Maggie's scared of lots of things. I wouldn't like living in that dark old place on my own," said Splinter.

"What do you mean inspecting her money?" Eric said, frowning.

"She buries it and the worms eat it," Splinter said. Eric looked at her astounded.

"Buries her money?"

"Yes, she told me," Splinter said looking guilty.

"The daft old bugger." Eric chewed on his pipe. What would happen if Aunt Maggie dropped dead? Nobody would know where to find the money. The map was in her head. He would have to have a look around her garden, tell her he saw a snake or a bandicoot so he could have a dig. He tipped his chair back and stared at the ceiling.

A deep sigh escaped Lillian. "Splinter caught her burning a handful of money in the stove a few weeks ago. She said worms had eaten the numbers and the notes weren't any good." Her voice trailed and she looked at Johnny. Imagine being killed for a few worm-eaten notes.

The pipe teetered on the edge of Eric's lip. "What?" He started up from his chair. "Why didn't you tell me?" Eric had forgotten they hadn't been speaking at the time. Burnt her money? "For Christ's sake, Lillian!" The pipe between his lips got the same treatment as a lamb bone. "Fancy letting her do it; what were you thinking of?" He banged his fist on the table. The children jumped and turned big eyes towards Lillian. "Bookie Jim might have taken the money." He looked at Lillian and shook his head, appalled at her stupidity.

The curl of Eric's lip brought Lillian to her feet. She gripped the table and leant towards him, her face inches from his. "Firstly, I didn't let her do it. Splinter saw her, not me. And do you think for a minute that I was happy to hear all that money went up in smoke? God knows, I could have put it to good use. Splinter needs new shoes and I would like a washing machine and a steam iron." At the time Lillian had been preoccupied with going to Melbourne. Also, she had promised Splinter she wouldn't tell. "I didn't tell you because you were engaged in another affair at the time." Her eyes bored into Eric's. He stepped back, her vehemence catching him off guard and remembered she was pregnant.

"Furthermore," she said. "I'd like to know what you expected me to do? Should I have charged over there and told Aunt Maggie what she should do with her own money? If you had got your hands on it, you would have wasted it on an old nag that took two minutes to cross a finishing line. That's no different to Aunt Maggie sticking it in the fire." Lillian saw the pinched looks on the children's faces as their eyes darted from one parent to the other. She calmed and lowered her voice. "You said you weren't going to bet anymore." That was a promise he had made when they couldn't pay the grocer and Lillian had to beg Aunt Maggie for a loan.

Eric looked around for a lifeboat. Took his pipe from his mouth and tapped it on his shoe to get rid of the ash and avoid the reproach in Lillian's eyes. He'd lost a packet on the horses recently and owed Bookie Jim. The cicadas outside increased their roar.

"My head's hurting," Johnny said, breaking the tension.

"I'll get you a Bex. "Lillian said. She'd flummoxed Eric for the first time in her life and wanted to maintain her winning streak. Lillian mixed a Bex in a glass of water and gave it to Johnny. He had a sip and screwed up his face. "Just drink it down, quickly," she said.

Eric packed his pipe and stared into the distance, "I'll have a talk with Aunt Maggie tomorrow and convince her to put her money in the bank. Can't understand why she thinks a bank will steal her money. Silly old buggar."

Bubs eyes widened. "The Post Office doesn't steal my money. They write what I give them in my savings book. I can always see how much I've got."

Lillian looked at her with interest, she'd never thought of opening a post office account, maybe a postal account wouldn't require Eric's signature. If that was the case she could invest the money she got for the ring. It had been burning a hole in the back of her drawer. The tide went out on her anger. Johnny's near death had given them all a shock. Fighting with Eric wasn't going to solve the problem.

Johnny felt the burn on his head.

Lillian slapped his hand. "Leave your head alone, Johnny."

"It hurts," he whined. It was red and weeping.

"First thing tomorrow, I'll take you to see Doc Smith." Lillian chewed her lip and looked at Eric. "If we tell the doctor about

Aunt Maggie shooting Johnny, he might have her declared insane. What if we say Johnny was loading your gun and it went off?"

"Good idea." Eric nodded.

"Nobody tell. Cross hearts," Lillian said. They did. Lillian poured Eric a cup of tea, relieved they were talking to each other again and sharing a problem. "We should also get the doctor to check on Aunt Maggie. She's had a shock. Probably needs a sedative."

"Serves her bloody right," Eric's shoulders hunched and he frowned into his teacup. Lillian had a sudden urge to giggle, more from nerves than humour. The same as she did in church when Eric glowered at her if she whispered to the children. It burst to the surface. Her family looked at her amazed.

"What are you laughing about?" Eric said.

All Lillian's pent up emotions erupted. She doubled with laughter. "Oh, dear. Oh, Lord." She took her glasses off and mopped her eyes on the hem of her apron. "You called her a stupid old fool. She'll probably cut you out of the will." Sometimes Lillian wished she would. Living with Eric's inheritance expectations had rested on her shoulders and she was blamed for all their bad luck. He didn't have to say it outright – it was in his eyes when he looked at her with resigned distaste.

Eric tapped his teeth with his pipe, deep in thought. Telling Aunt Maggie off had made him feel good. He was sick of her giving him a hard time. There had been hours he'd spent trying to think of ways he could kill her off. Now he had something over her, Aunt Maggie would have to pull her head in. She wouldn't dare cut him out of her will. Tomorrow he would drop a word in Doc Smith's ear about the old girl going a bit peculiar, suggest she might need someone to make decisions for her and get Power of Attorney. The Doc was a good bloke. "You check on Aunt Maggie tomorrow and I'll take Johnny to see Doc Smith," Eric said.

The following morning Lillian stood on Aunt Maggie's doorstep. "The doctor's coming to give you a check up."

"I don't need a doctor," Aunt Maggie leant against the doorframe, a tea-towel sling supporting her arm.

"You do, and he's on his way." Lillian stared Aunt Maggie down in the same way she did Johnny when he defied her. Aunt Maggie lowered her eyes and shuffled. "What you did was terrible, Aunt Maggie, you could have killed Johnny and I want you to tell him you're sorry." Aunt Maggie's chin jutted. Her relationship with Johnny had always been fraught. Lillian's eyes narrowed. "I'll bring your dinner over tonight. The children don't feel safe." That's how it would be until Doc Smith reported back to Lillian.

When the doctor knocked, Aunt Maggie opened the door and kept him on the top step, her bulk barring the way inside. "I'm just here to give you a once over." The crow's feet at the corners of Doc Smith's kind eyes deepened with his smile. Eric had already worded him up about her drinking and, like the confessional, Doc Smith was sworn to silence.

"How much do you charge?"

"The same as I charge everyone else in town." Aunt Maggie moved back just enough for Doc Smith to squeeze past and catch the smell of alcohol on her breath. He gave the room a quick survey and noticed the brandy in the decanter on the sideboard. Aunt Maggie held her shoulder and grimaced as she lowered herself onto the chaise longue.

"You look like you're in a bit of pain, Mrs Stewart. I'd like to examine you if you don't mind."

The sympathy in his voice unravelled Aunt Maggie like a caught thread in a wool jumper. She began to cry. "They won't put me away, will they?" She looked at him from the corner of her eye, unsure of how much he knew. A string of snot leaked from her nose and she caught it between her fingers and wiped it on her dress.

Doc Smith looked surprised, eyes widening behind his rimless glasses. "Whatever for? I understand you had a spot too much brandy when you had heart flutters and misjudged the door. That's not a cause to declare you incapable of looking after yourself."

Aunt Maggie's face collapsed with relief. "Did Eric tell you that?"

"He did." Doc Smith didn't mention that Eric was concerned about her financial competency. Doc Smith had asked Lillian what she thought, and Lillian had said Aunt Maggie was more than capable of managing her own affairs. "You're lucky to have people who care for you so well."

Aunt Maggie nodded and decided she wouldn't cut Eric out of her will for taking her gun and treating her as though she was senile.

"Just go easy on the brandy. It doesn't cure everything." He felt her arm. "Nothing broken, just badly bruised. Keep it in a sling and take Aspro for the pain." He put a sling on her arm and closed his bag. "I can see myself out."

The plum pudding had taken most of the morning to make and Aunt Maggie's last shot of brandy. It was Johnny's peace offering. Wrapped in an old tea towel and tied with string, it hung off her door handle like a testicle. Easing the blind aside Aunt Maggie peaked across the yard. Eric was reading his paper on the front verandah. Her lips twitched with annoyance. If she went up the street she'd have to walk past him. The last thing she wanted was to see Eric's accusing face. She let the blind go and made her way into the sunroom.

There was a knock on the door. Aunt Maggie opened it and Lillian entered with a mop and squeeze bucket. They gazed at each other. Lillian's eyes were as distant as Tasmania. Aunt

Maggie rail-tracked her lips shut and made for the couch. The mop banged into walls, slapped the floor and then marched towards the door over Lillian's shoulder. As she reached for the door handle, Lillian saw Johnny's 'sorry pudding.' A strong smell of brandy emanated from the pudding. She slid a look towards the empty decanter on the sideboard. It was an interesting situation. Who would Aunt Maggie get to buy her a bottle of brandy? It wouldn't be Lillian. Serves her right thought Lillian, although deep down she felt a pang of sympathy. She knew what it was like to be alone. She turned to Aunt Maggie. "Johnny is a child. He thinks you wanted to kill him. You need to say you're sorry, then everything will be back to normal." Aunt Maggie's eyes semi-closed and she didn't answer. Lillian shrugged and pulled the door open. A sign fell off that read, KNOCK LOUDLY AND LEAVE TRAY ON STEP.

After Lillian had gone, Aunt Maggie picked the sign up and put it in the kitchen stove. The day before, her dinner had been left on the step with the lid half off. Lillian had been too busy to take it over and Bubs had started doing Johnny's duty and there had been paw prints in the mash. It wasn't so much the thought of Puss eating off her plate that bothered Aunt Maggie. The abscess on Puss's face had grown bigger and she was scared it might be catching. She wanted to ask Lillian to look at it but they weren't speaking. Lifting the blind, she had another peek out the kitchen window. Eric didn't look as though he was going to move. Blast the beggar! Aunt Maggie paced the kitchen. She needed some brandy and some mince for Puss. Also, she wanted to know if she was being gossiped about in the town. She threw her purse in the string bag.

23

Aunt Maggie's Lift Home

Between the top of his newspaper and the brim of his hat, Eric watched Aunt Maggie draw level with his front gate. He put the paper down and reached into his pocket for a plug of tobacco. He shaved off a few pieces with a pocket knife and pressed them into the pipe's bowl with his thumbs, struck a match and sucked, all the while pretending he hadn't seen her. He could tell she was aware of him by the way she looked straight ahead, shoulders back, chin in the air and bandy legs rocking like a sailor. She swished a string bag over her shoulder to flick the flies off the back of her black dress. Fit as a fiddle, he thought. He hadn't seen her since the shooting. Halfway up the street she gave a slight stagger for his benefit. His eyes pushed her up the hill. When Aunt Maggie kicked the bucket he was going to buy the farm. After all the grovelling and fawning he'd had to do to inveigle his way into her good books, he deserved it.

He watched her disappear over the hill and thought how much she'd changed. No longer the sallow-cheeked, grubby old woman she was when they first moved in. She was a picture of health: clean, pink-cheeked and chubby. Lillian was looking after her a little too well and the old bugger looked like she'd never fill her coffin.

Smoke curled from Eric's pipe. He watched it drift towards the block of blue that stretched as uninterrupted as the placid ocean beneath it. The hot sun stopped at the edge of the verandah. He gazed up the road to see if Aunt Maggie was on her way back but nothing moved in the street. The weekend would be perfect for planting a crop of potatoes. He had another look up the street to see if Aunt Maggie was in sight and made a mental note to make some adjustments to her gun.

The hoot of a passing car broke into Eric's thoughts. He checked the street for Aunt Maggie again and looked at his watch. She was taking her time.

The pittosporum trees that flung their shade down the wide street were in full bloom. Aunt Maggie's nostrils sucked up the heavy perfume. It was a nice relief from the stench of cooked tuna that came from the cannery and suffocated the town on breezeless days. Aunt Maggie nodded at the proprietor on the steps of the general store, her mind preoccupied with thoughts of Lillian and a solution to the bad feeling between them.

"Lovely day, Mrs Stewart, good to be alive." He lifted his cap.

"It is for some, Horace." She flicked the string bag over her shoulder like a penitent, unsettling the flies that hitchhiked on the back of her dress. Horace backed up the steps and retreated indoors. After a quick reconnaissance of the street, Aunt Maggie disappeared into the pub, then next door to the drapery shop's mothball interior. The string bag was full by the time she crossed the road to Mick, the butcher.

Pushing his paperwork aside, Mick looked over the top of

his glasses and raised his eyebrows. The old lady hadn't been in his shop for a while and when she did come Lillian usually accompanied her. He wondered how Lillian was going. She had been sending her kids to buy the meat. He missed her visits and truth be told he was a bit sweet on Lillian. Mick pushed his chair back and stood up, knives scraped together at his tool belt. The ties on his clean black and white striped apron wrapped around his small frame twice and his wellington boots made trails in the sawdust-covered floor as he clanged towards the counter. His voice was deep and pleasant. "It's a while since I've seen you, Mrs Stewart. You're looking well. What can I do for you today?"

"Hello, Mick, I'll have one and sixpence worth of mince please and make sure it's not fatty. I haven't long to go, you know. Bad heart." She gave her chest a tap.

"Sorry to hear that, Mrs Stewart, but I'm sure you have a lot of years left with the way Lillian looks after you." He gave her a beguiling smile.

"Well I haven't." She skewered him with her voice. Mick jiggled the knife sharpener on his tool belt and his left eye twitched. Aunt Maggie sagged. "The heart's been playing up a lot lately." She snatched a look at Mick. "If you hear of anyone who wants to rent a house, the house next door to me might become vacant."

Mick gaped. "What? Lillian's house? Are they moving?" He'd seen Eric in the Fishermen's Club and he hadn't mentioned moving.

"If I find someone who wants to live rent-free and keep an eye on me, I'll consider it. My family don't care about me." There was a faux catch in her voice. "I'm a sick old woman." That should get around town pretty smart, she thought. She watched Mick put a handful of mince on the scales. "You're a good boy, Mick. So was your father. I remember him well. Always added some extra meat after he'd weighed it."

179

Mick parcelled up the mince and put it on the counter. "That's one and six, Mrs Stewart."

She weighed the mince in her hand and pinched her lips. The mince disappeared into the string bag. Aunt Maggie rummaged for her purse. Suddenly she winced, clutched her heart and fell towards the counter. Mick's arm shot out to catch her head but fortunately Aunt Maggie had managed to shield her face with her hand before it came in contact with the hard surface.

"Are you okay, Mrs Stewart? Would you like me to call the doctor?"

"No, Lillian sent him to visit me, he can't do anything, I'm beyond help. He charges too much, anyway." She stood with her head resting on the counter, looking up at him. "But you could let Lillian know I had a turn in your shop."

Aunt Maggie's cunning wasn't lost on Mick. He wasn't short of it himself. This would be a good chance to see Lillian. "I can help you home if you want?" Mick pulled at his ear – the van was doing deliveries and she was too heavy for him to lug. He noticed the wheelbarrow. He'd carried a few sheep in that. "The van's out, but I could take you in the wheelbarrow?"

Assisted home! That would prick Lillian's conscience, make them all sit up, and a wheelbarrow would be like a stretcher. Aunt Maggie smiled her agreement.

Mick lined the barrow up. Aunt Maggie gripped him around the neck and he walked her backwards between the handles. "Righto, now sit." She dropped into the barrow, her grip still tight around his neck. His eyes bulged just before his face disappeared between her thighs. Mould, mothballs and the smell of cat's piss pressed into his nostrils. He screwed his head to the side and gasped for air. Mick blew his nose and gargled before he left the shop.

Knees up and spread wide, Aunt Maggie's once white bloomers winked a yellow-stained crotch as she jostled along.

Mick kept his eyes averted, his stomach already weakened. When he reached the top of the hill he was buggered. He took a breather. "It's all downhill from here, Mrs Stewart." He wiped his brow on his sleeve.

The descent was steep and the wheelbarrow gathered pace. By the time the road levelled out in front of Eric's house, Mick's shoulder sockets were ready to pop. Attracted by the squeaking wheels, Eric looked up from his newspaper and his mouth fell open. His chair clattered against the wall as he jumped to his feet.

"G'day, mate," Mick called with a sheepish grin.

Eric's hand lifted instinctively in greeting. "Well I'll be jiggered." He whipped the front door open and yelled down the hall, "Lil, you've gotta see this."

Aunt Maggie sagged further into the wheelbarrow, arms loose over the sides, head lolling back. She'd make them pay.

The sight brought a shriek of laughter from Lillian. She shoved her hand over her mouth not wanting to offend Mick. "Poor Mick, ask him in for a cup of tea," she said, and headed for her comb and lipstick.

Embarrassed by Lillian's laugh, Mick decided not to call in and tell her that Aunt Maggie had said the house next door to her might become vacant and if so she'd need someone to look after her. It could wait until Lillian came to the shop next. After unloading Aunt Maggie, Mick turned the barrow towards the street.

"Hey, Mick, come and have a cuppa, Lillian's just made a cake." Eric held the gate open, his Colgate-white teeth flashing a huge grin.

Shit! You, blowhard tosser, Mick thought, pasting a smile on his face. It would look bad if he refused. Mick could never understand what Lillian saw in Eric, apart from his likeness to Clark Gable in *Gone with the Wind*.

"The old girl pulled one on you, did she?" Eric draped a solicitous arm across Mick's shoulders.

Mick stiffened. "I think the heat was a bit much for her."

"Pull the other one."

Mick's grip tightened on the handles. "She is an old lady, you know."

24

A Tussle

They entered the kitchen and Eric ushered Mick towards a chair. "Fill him up, Lil, he needs some strength to get back to his shop." In Eric's mind, Mick stole money off poor farmers, buying meat at rock bottom prices. He'd never had to scrabble for a quid. As far as Eric was concerned it served Mick bloody right getting conned by an old woman and he was going to rub it in.

"Nice day." Mick smiled at Lillian, his cheeks still pink from exertion, now turning a deeper shade.

"Lovely," Lillian said. She looked away, ashamed she had laughed at him. To compensate, Lillian had made the table look pleasing: set out her best cups, put cake forks on the bread and butter plates, dusted the teacake with sugar and cinnamon and put curls of butter in the Dalton china butter dish – the only remaining piece from the teaset her mother had given her as a wedding present.

While he waited for Lillian to sit down, Mick noticed the dark shadows under Lillian's eyes and the slump in her shoulders. He took in her firm round bottom and slender legs when she bent over the table to cut the cake. His glasses misted from the steam in the kitchen and he fumbled in his trouser pocket and pulled out a clean folded handkerchief and wiped them.

"Sit down, mate. Take a load off." Eric laughed.

"Yes, right." Mick could see he was going to be Eric's entertainment.

Lillian put a big slice of cake on a plate and placed it in front of Mick. Two pairs of brown eyes met and connected for one breath. Mick smiled into her eyes.

Suddenly Lillian became conscious of her faded housedress, bare legs and shabby shoes. Flustered, she picked up the teapot and poured Mick a cup of tea, spilling some in the saucer. "Oh, sorry, that was clumsy of me." She lifted the cup to empty the saucer.

Mick touched her hand. "Don't worry. It's just a drop. I do it all the time." She blushed and withdrew her hand.

Eric frowned at her clumsiness and turned to Mick. "Lillian and I were talking about how nice it was of you to bring the old girl home. You could have knocked me over with a feather when I saw her in the wheelbarrow. Is there a problem with the van? I could give you a hand fixing it." He grinned.

"No, it's on a delivery run. Lovely cake, Lillian," Mick said, refusing to be Eric's source of amusement.

"I'm sorry I didn't have time to ice it." She didn't look up from her plate. What an idiot she had been to avoid his shop in fear of all the gossip about Pixie and Eric. She wished she had an excuse to get out of the kitchen now though.

Not to be put off, Eric had another go at baiting Mick. "That was a sight for sore eyes. Gave Lillian and me a good laugh. Bet the old girl weighs as much as a bullock." Eric winked at Lillian.

184

Lillian gave Eric a reproving stare. Why was Eric being mean to Mick? "It was kind of Mick to put himself in that position. There are a lot who wouldn't."

Mick shifted in his chair. "Your aunt had one of her turns in my shop. She asked me to tell Lillian."

Eric threw his head back and chortled. "She gets a bee in her bonnet sometimes. Likes to make out she's hard done by and goes shopping to shame us. Wants a bit of sympathy so she finds a gullible audience and has a heart attack to get attention." The jibe rolled off Mick's back.

"She's certainly a determined old girl. Must be a bit of a trial, eh Lillian?" Mick's smile was sympathetic. Lillian couldn't help but notice his nice teeth: strong and even. She liked men with good teeth. He didn't smoke either. She'd never smoked and remembered how long it had taken her to get used to the smell of Eric's pipe. There were a lot of things she'd had to get used to, like cooking on a wood stove, washing by hand, wearing his sister's hand-me-downs, cupboards without doors and old settees with broken springs. She noticed the two men looking at her, waiting for her reply.

"Oh, she's not too bad really. Poor old duck, gets a bit frightened living on her own. She's scared of dying and no-one finding her."

"Nothing Lillian can't handle, though, eh Lil?" said Eric.

The compliment was lost on Lillian. She knew it was all blather for Mick's benefit. "I wish she'd get the electricity turned on," she said. "I worry Aunty's going to burn the house down one of these days. You should encourage her, Eric, instead of worrying about how much it will cost her." Put that in your pipe and smoke it, Lillian thought, knowing he wanted Aunt Maggie to spend as little as possible so there would be more inheritance.

"She's managed this long. A couple more years won't matter," Eric said, thinly.

"Actually, Eric, I just remembered that your aunt forgot to pay me for the mince. I didn't want to ask her while she was having an attack, so perhaps you wouldn't mind fixing me up. It cost one and six. I won't charge delivery."

Caught off guard, Eric gazed around the kitchen waiting for the money to materialise. He looked at Lillian. She shrugged and held out the palms of her hands. There was no way she was going to reveal the hard-won coins she'd filched from his pockets. Her stash had grown into fifteen pounds. It was in the post office with her ring money. She hadn't needed Eric's signature to open the account. She watched him make a show of patting his shirt pockets then his trouser pockets and looked away, embarrassed. "More cake, Mick?" she said, to distract Mick from Eric's ridiculous pantomime. Mick accepted the offered slice and devoured it in two bites, ignoring Eric.

The coins rolled as Eric slapped them on the table. Mick caught the coins and put them in his pocket, then withdrew a folded envelope, which he held out to Eric. "I may as well give you your account it will save me postage." Eric turned in his chair and reached into his bushman's jacket hanging on a nail on the door and grabbed his pipe ignoring the envelope.

The envelope grew large in Mick's hand. Embarrassed, he offered it to Lillian. "It's a bit overdue," he said apologetically. "Maybe you can drop by tomorrow and settle up?" As she reached for the envelope Mick pulled it back. They had a tug of war and Lillian giggled. She put the account next to the Bex on top of the fridge.

Eric watched the exchange with a sneer. Playing with women. A wonder he doesn't wear a frilly apron, the ponce. "Overdue? I'm surprised. Lil is usually on time with the bills." Eric pretended not to notice Lillian's frown. "Yes, must have been an oversight. Now don't forget, Lil. Put it where you can see it."

"I'm sorry, Mick." Why had she apologised? She didn't pay the bills. She was always saying sorry when it wasn't her fault, it sickened her. She glared at Eric.

"No problem, Lillian, I know you have a lot on your plate. I hear things in the shop." He gave Eric a knowing look and saw him shift in his seat. "Tell you what, I'm experimenting with a new sausage recipe. Spiced them up a bit. When you come tomorrow I'll give you a few to try." Mick winked at her.

Lillian bent down and poked at the fire, her neck and cheeks the colour of the embers. Mick had always teased her when she went into his shop but he'd never flirted with her, or had she read those little exchanges wrong? She needed another Bex.

Furious, Eric filled his pipe. What a bloody cheek. Mick cut up sheep's balls for a living. How dare he embarrass Eric in his own home, giving him a bill like that and telling him it was overdue while he accepted their hospitality. He clenched his pipe between his teeth and narrowed his eyes. "There're not many jobs around at the moment, Mick. Too many Italian immigrants. They'll do anything for money. I hear they sleep three families to one house in Melbourne. Everyone works shifts so the beds never get cold. When they go for a job interview they tell the boss they'll bring their brother along and he'll work for free. Unions can't do much about it. It's putting Aussies out of work. Not that I'd ever belong to a union, bloody communists. No offence, Mick, your Mum's Italian, isn't she?" He grinned over at Lillian. The kettle banged on the stove. Eric's eyes lost their crinkles at the corners.

"Spanish!" Mick shoved his chair back and stood up. The kitchen table rocked and the cups clattered. Bastard, he thought.

"There's a war on you know. The dagos from Ulladulla have fished out their grounds and come into Eden waters. One of our

187

fishermen shot their markers. Paddy was collecting guns for our blokes. I lent them my Grandfather's Purdy. Whose side will you be on?" The stove door clanged open and Lillian shoved a piece of wood in wishing it was Eric's head. How could he be so mean to Mick after he had brought Aunt Maggie home. What was wrong with the man? Mick stiffened, then smirked.

"The police are onto it. They confiscated the guns. That Purdy would have been worth a bit," he said with satisfaction. Eric paled. "Well the van should be back by now. I'd better get a move on. Thank you for the cake, Lillian. Delicious."

You're welcome, Mick. I'll see you tomorrow to pay the bill." Mick never hassled them to pay their bills; he had been very good to them.

Eric's lips stretched in a patronising smile as he stood up. "It was nice of you to bring Aunt Maggie home, Mick. Very gentlemanly." He opened the door and clapped Mick on the shoulder. "See you later, mate." He waited until Mick and the barrow had disappeared from view then shut the door and turned to Lillian. "Bloody rude, telling me my account's overdue while he's eating my cake. Who does he think he is? Bloody wog."

"His mother is Spanish," Lillian said, clearing the cups off the table. What was the difference between a dago, wog and a pom? Lillian wondered if her French father would have been a wog. She decided not to bring that up as Eric already had a low opinion of her mother.

Eric tried to remember which side the Spanish were on in the war. They're all the same anyway, he thought. It niggled him that Lillian seemed to be sticking up for Mick. He grabbed the account off the fridge and looked at it closely. It was those big roasts she cooked that cost so much. Half of it went to the dog. With a great flourish he produced his dog-eared chequebook and wrote a cheque in beautiful script. He admired his handwriting. It was even and had the correct amount of slope to the right to signify good character, according to his old school teacher, unlike Lillian's he thought. He put the cheque in the envelope with the bill and put it back on the fridge. "I'll be in the shed." He strode out of the kitchen.

It was a relief to see the back of both of them. They'd been sniffing and growling around each other like a couple of dogs and Lillian was exhausted from the strain of it. While Lillian washed the teacups her mind was on Eric's pettiness over the mince money. When they first met, Eric had reminded her of her father. In hindsight it was probably the sailor suit because her father had been a kind and generous man. The same couldn't be said about Eric. She'd have to think of a way to make it up to Mick.

25

The Horse and Cat

The sound of the dog chomping on a leg of lamb irritated Eric. He hurled the rasp he was sharpening the mower blades with against the wall above its head and noticed Bubs standing at the entrance of the shed with big solemn eyes.

"What's the matter, pet?"

"The pony I was saving up for has gone. Someone bought it." Her shoulders hunched and she started to cry.

"There'll be another one, pet. Don't cry." Eric ruffled her hair.

"I'll never save enough money."

Eric chucked her under the chin, wishing he could have afforded the pony. He'd always had a horse when he was a kid. He loved them. A thought struck him. He tilted Bubs's face. "Go and tell Mum I'll be gone for a while."

She dragged herself over to the kitchen. "Mum?" Lillian turned from the ocean view that massaged her senses and gazed at Bubs with dull Bex eyes. "Dad said to tell you he would be back later."

"Bully for him. Why the long face?"

"The pony's sold." Bubs's eyes wandered to the cake on the table. "Can I have a piece of cake, Mum?" Her voice echoed the loss of the pony. Lillian murmured in the affirmative and cut Bubs a large slice. "Will you play dominoes with me?"

"Sorry, love, I'm going to read in my room. Tell me when your father gets back. Have you any homework?"

"Just a composition."

"Good, write one about the pony. It will make you feel better."

The composition was nearly finished when Bubs heard her father honk the horn and whistle. She dropped her pencil and ran to see what he wanted.

The commotion outside woke Lillian. She sat up, blind in one eye, adjusted her glasses and swung her legs off the bed and headed for the kitchen to see what was going on. What in hell's name! A sad looking horse stood on the back of Eric's truck. Lillian pushed the window up.

"It's a horse, it's a horse!' Bubs yelled, jumping with excitement. Eric's smile was half a watermelon. The truck rocked.

Lillian's eyes crazed. Get a grip, she told herself, he's taking it to the farm. The old brown nag lifted his tail and crapped on the tray. Eric dropped the back of the truck, made a ramp with a couple of planks and led the horse off the truck. It ducked its head, sniffed the garden and curled its lips back for a nibble. "Hey," Lillian yelled, "mind my garden!" Eric tugged on the reins, but didn't look her way. A premonition of something ominous darkened inside Lillian. She watched him lift Bubs onto the ridge of bones already dipped from years of loads and saw Bubs lay her face along the horse's neck, arms hugging.

"Where did that come from?" Lillian shouted.

"He was impounded. Cost me a fiver." Eric stroked the horse.

"You'd better take good care of him, Bubs. He's an old fella." The beam on Bubs's face was Eric's reward; he loved his kids. If he ever won at the races he'd give them a farm each.

It would need a saddle and they weren't cheap. Lillian bit the inside of her cheek. A ridiculous thought struck her. She would ride the horse to Melbourne, take off in the night. Who would care? The only thing that Eric worried about was Aunt Maggie slinging him out of her will. Lillian's thought's stilled. What had Eric just said? He'd make a stall for the horse in the shed? Surely he wasn't planning to keep it here? He hadn't even asked her. Hadn't she enough to worry about? Had he forgotten she was dealing with an unwanted pregnancy? He was so thoughtless. Lillian could see the horse walking between the sheets on the clothesline, leaving its dirt and horsey smell on her clean washing. She imagined horse dung walked through the house via Eric's boots, as well as the plagues of blowflies. And what about her rose garden? Most of all why didn't he consider how it would affect her? It was all about making him look good. She yelled. "I hope that's going to the farm."

"It will keep the grass down," he shouted back, giving Bubs a reassuring pat.

The slam of the kitchen window sounded like an abattoir's stun gun. The look Eric had given her said killjoy. Lillian shoved some kindling into the stove's dying embers and watched the yellow curl ignite into an angry lick of flame. Tears of frustration streamed down her face. It was one bloody drama after another and she was losing her grip. She grabbed the box of Bex. Empty. Gone in two days. She needed to go to the doctor and get something stronger. A fly buzzed the kitchen. If she sent the horse away it would break Bubs's heart. But it couldn't stay, it wasn't fair on her. Nothing was bloody fair. Tied up in the shed, Jess barked in agreement.

On her way to the cliff, Lillian saw Aunt Maggie on her knees weeding the garden. They eyed each other as Lillian passed. It was obvious that she had heard the carry-on over the horse. She was probably expecting Lillian to rush over and cry on her shoulder. It was tempting, but there was still an outstanding apology and Lillian wouldn't renege on it for Johnny's sake. Also, after the umbrella incident, Aunt Maggie couldn't be trusted not to do something mad. No one in Eric's family ever apologised for anything. They all thought they were perfect. Lillian needed Aunt Maggie back in her corner and had to think of a solution.

While Lillian stood at the edge of the cliff watching the waves pound the rocks and picturing Eric beating his breast as he picked up her body, Aunt Maggie was trying to work out her own compromise. She had heard the exchange over the horse and felt Lillian's frustration. Aunt Maggie would hate it in her yard. One animal was enough, especially when it was sick and that horse didn't look too healthy. She went inside to check on Puss.

The cat lay on the chaise like a discarded muff. Aunt Maggie picked him up. The abscess had grown so big he couldn't open his eye. It wouldn't have gotten that big if Lillian had helped her lance it. She put the thought aside and rocked her old friend. He managed a small purr. If she could share something special with Johnny, he would know she was sorry and Lillian would be friends with her again. The cat's misery gave her the idea.

The next morning Aunt Maggie gathered the sick tabby in her arms and took him over to the shed where Johnny was repairing his billycart. Johnny cast a dubious eye towards her and hunched over the wheel of his billycart.

"I need you to do something for me."

"What's that, Aunt Maggie?" The pupils in his eyes shrank.

"Puss is sick. He has to be put out of his misery and I can't do it. I would if I had my gun." She looked around the shed accusingly and back at Johnny.

"You can use my slug gun, Aunt Maggie."

Aunt Maggie thought for a moment. If she used Johnny's gun he might have the cat on his conscience and she didn't want that. Besides, a slug gun wouldn't do the job. This was a humanitarian deed. It would also send Eric a message that she needed her gun back. "That's just a peashooter. I'm going to use the axe and I want you to hold him." When she smiled her glasses glinted in the sun.

A cold shiver went down Johnny's back. "What if you miss and hit me?" He touched the top of his head and felt the stubble.

"Don't be ridiculous."

"Why don't you ask Dad?" This could be the perfect murder.

"He's not talking to me, and your mother knows I can't manage on my own. We'll do it in my shed. I'll give you some money for a comic." Aunt Maggie smelt him teeter. "Come on, boy, I need your help. The girls are too squeamish."

Johnny swaggered to his feet. "I guess so." He picked up the axe and followed her to the coffin shed.

Half an hour later, Johnny was wishing a whale would swallow Aunt Maggie and she would die in its guts. He was dry retching as he ran across the yard to his mother.

The laundry was a steam bath. The big copper bowl brimming with boiling water and sheets sat like an inverted tit inside a chest-high iron drum. Under the drum a fire roared. Lillian wiped sweat from her brow and stabbed a sheet beneath the suds with her washing stick. The pregnancy was making her erratic. The soapsuds reminded her of sperm. Thoughts of Eric's infidelities plagued her. How many women had Eric shot his suds into? That waitress with the brown teeth; what had he seen in her, for God's sake? Her brain was an unused muscle but obviously her vagina wasn't. Lillian could still see those big udders brushing against Eric as she pretended to arrange his cutlery. She ground her teeth. One of these days she would snap his fork. There had been too many women. And that bloody horse had trampled her roses.

She scratched her hands and looked at the dermatitis from the new washing powder. Just keep it together, she told herself. Finish the washing and have a lie down. She hadn't been sleeping well since the shooting incident.

Lillian struggled with a double-bed sheet. Lifting it with her stick from the copper she dropped it into the first trough of rinse water and splashed Splinter who stood in the adjoining trough, stamping the soap out of another sheet.

"That'll do. Get out and I'll put it through the mangle." Lillian's words snapped. Splinter looked up, startled.

"Mum!" Johnny rushed into the washhouse white-faced and stood in front of her and gagged.

She looked up, mouth tight. "What now?" She slapped her wet hand on his forehead to check for a temperature.

"I k ... killed Puss."

"What!" Lillian pulled her hand back as though she'd been scalded.

"You killed Puss?" screamed Splinter.

"Aunt, Aunt Maggie tried herself, but I thought she wanted to kill me so I let Puss go and she missed his head, but she hurt him. He ran around the shed so I had to finish him off." Johnny wiped his nose on his sleeve.

"Dear God! She must be stark, raving mad." Lillian patted Johnny on the back. "What a dreadful thing to make you do."

"Sh ... she would have shot him if she'd had her gun."

Lillian went pale. "How was he killed?"

"With the axe." Johnny's shoulders jerked with sobs.

"Jesus!" The breath went out of Lillian's body. "What on earth has got into her?" She looked at Johnny's anguished face and pulled his skinny frame into her. "The demented old bugger."

Splinter sat on the side of the trough, knuckles white and gripping. "Puss was my friend," she wailed.

"Shut that noise up, Splinter." Lillian's eyes darkened. "Go and make yourself a Milo, Johnny. We'll sort this out when your father gets home." Lillian had to think, she didn't want to give Eric an excuse to have Aunt Maggie put away, she needed Aunt Maggie.

"Poor Puss, I'll have to help Aunty have a funeral for him," Splinter sobbed.

"You'll do nothing of the sort. Now get down from there and dry yourself. I need a hand hanging the sheets."

Sniffing back tears, Splinter jumped onto the concrete floor. "Ow!" She grabbed her foot.

"Bloody hell! What now?"

"Something burnt me."

Lillian looked at the red blister forming on Splinter's foot and saw the water leaking through a small hole in the copper. It settled into a puddle of steam on the cement floor. She gazed around the hut that stole her Mondays: thought of the roses she had nurtured; cuttings she'd stolen from wealthy gardens at night armed with Aunt Maggie's secateurs, the shooting and something broke inside her. Grabbing the wash pole, she charged the clothesline. "Ah!" Pinioned forms swung and jerked beneath her blows. Sheets wrestled the pole as she belted the blazes out of them. Her eyes were popping mad.

Splinter dragged the wash basket after her mother. "Mum, I'm sorry."

The backyard filled with barking and shrieking and Lillian unleashed her demons. The truck pulled up in the driveway. Eric jumped out and ran towards her. Lillian swung the pole back for the last mighty whack and collected him in the gut, knocking him off his feet. He lay on the ground winded, his eyes as big as the teacups she read.

"I want a bloody washing machine. I'm not washing another bloody thing 'til I get one. You hear me? Nothing! You spend our money on bloody horses that couldn't win a race out of a knackery. Bring home a nag that stomps my roses. You get days off when there's no machinery to mend and go to the Fishermen's Club but I don't get time off. I have to slave over washing and ironing. The poorest family in this town has a washing machine but you're just like your paltry, archaic family: too bloody miserly and self-centred to consider anyone. When I came to this country I knew life would be different but I didn't expect a life of drudgery, looking after your fossilised family. They're heartless and grasping and you're not much better. And your bloody Aunt made Johnny kill her cat. I've had it with the lot of you." The pole dropped from Lillian's hand and she shuddered with sobs.

Watching from the kitchen window, Johnny wondered if killing Puss had caused his mother to go off her head, and decided to make himself scarce.

Winded and red in the face, Eric clambered to his feet. He felt like a loser. All the stories he'd told her about what life would be like in Australia, he had believed. It wasn't his fault. Had the neighbours heard Lillian ranting? He craned his head to see if the good-looking headmaster's wife over the back fence was in her yard. She wasn't. Eric retreated to the kitchen.

Splinter wrapped her arms around her mother's shaking body. "You can have my savings towards a washing machine, Mum. I've got nine pounds from my babysitting jobs." Splinter led her mother into the kitchen. "I'll make you a cuppa, Mum." She busied around the kitchen, throwing dark looks at her father and crowding past him.

Eric packed his pipe and kept Lillian in his peripheral vision as he gazed across at Aunt Maggie's window, his face drawn and thoughtful. Was it true everyone in town had a washing machine? If Lillian didn't read all those damn books, she could wash twice a week and there wouldn't be so much in one go. Aunt Maggie didn't change her clothes often, or her sheets. He squirmed as he caught Splinter's accusing eye. It made him feel like a no-hoper. He sucked on his unlit pipe.

"Go outside, Splinter, I want to talk to your mother." Splinter looked from one to the other and Lillian nodded at her. She put a cup of tea in front of her mother, gave her father a furious look and left the kitchen. The cup of tea trembled to Lillian's mouth. All thoughts of Puss had gone.

Eric squeezed Lillian's shoulder. "Look, Lil, I'd buy you a washing machine if I could afford one. But where's the money going to come from?"

"You said Dingo Riley paid you well for fixing his trucks." She shrugged his hand off her shoulder.

Eric brushed his fingers through his hair and chewed the stem of his pipe. Why had he told her that? He walked to the fridge and switched the wireless on.

The room tightened around Lillian. She kept her back to Eric. "What happened to Dingo's money, then?" she said quietly.

A furtive look crossed Eric's face. Lillian never confronted him over money matters. He fished his brain for a way out and then spied the envelope with the butcher's account. He grabbed the account and waved it in the air. "It goes on bloody bills, that's where. Look at the size of this butcher's bill and you didn't pay it like I told you to."

Air hissed through Lillian's teeth. "I did, but you put the wrong date on the cheque. It bounced. It arrived back today." Her voice climbed an octave. "And I know you did it on purpose. Mick's been so good to us. I don't know how you could be so petty."

Eric winced and shifted his feet; he'd forgotten he'd put the wrong date on the cheque. He did it to spite Mick for being an arsehole over his account. He clucked his tongue and took the cheque out of the envelope, staring at it as though he'd discovered one of Aunt Maggie's worm-eaten ten-pound notes.

"What? No, I didn't. The bank must have made a mistake," he peered at the cheque. "Well I'll be! How could I have done that?" He took out his fountain pen. "What's the date today?" He knew what day it was.

Lillian snorted, "It's on your newspaper."

Eric picked up the paper and squinted at the date. Then changed the cheque with a flourish, and initialled the change. He flapped it in the air to dry the ink and dropped it on the table in front of her. "Take it up today."

"What about the washing machine?" There was a quiet determination to her voice.

"Yeah, Dad!" said Splinter, coming into the kitchen to see if her mother was alright and to get a Band-Aid for her burn. "Look, I got burnt by the water." She lifted her foot up for her father to see. "The copper's leaking water all over the washhouse floor."

"By jingo, I'd better put the fire out. If the copper empties it'll get red hot and could set fire to the laundry."

The laundry could burn down for all Lillian cared. The whole bloody house could go. Most of the things she'd owned and cared about had burned with their farm, including her feelings for Eric. His disregard of her. She knew he had played on her jealousy and used the waitress as a ploy to get her to go back to his mother's. She wasn't the gullible fool she used to be. And how could she ever forget him insinuating that she was a mental case. Who was sane in his family? One day the worm will turn, she thought and I'll get out from under. The bottle of cascara on top of the fridge caught her eye; she'd bought it when Bubs was constipated. Tonight she'd make a cottage pie and crush a cascara in Eric's portion.

Those harsh years had taught Lillian to squash her feelings but lately this was proving difficult. Maybe it was the pregnancy. A slow blowie looking for a place to drop its load received the brunt of her frustration from the end of a wet tea towel. In an effort to shake off her melancholy, Lillian fetched a *Women's Weekly* from under Splinter's mattress. Let him see it, she didn't care. The picture of a smiling woman sipping a martini by a swimming pool did nothing to help her mood. She flicked to the crossword. The words came easily, she filled it in, entered a competition then closed the magazine. She needed to get out of the house. In the bedroom Lillian changed into the dress she'd just finished making, applied some lipstick and powder, checked her image in the dressing-table mirror and picked up her handbag with Mick's cheque.

26

Delivery Run

The shop was empty when Lillian entered. Mick sharpened a knife and sliced six sausages off the string he'd just made and held them up to her. "Like to try a new sausage?" His eyes lit up. "Pretty dress."

Lillian blushed. "I've come to fix up the account." Her hand was shaking when she withdrew the envelope. What was wrong with her?

He noticed the shadows under her eyes. "How are things?

Lillian answered with a tremulous smile and nod of her head, not trusting her voice. She watched Mick pat the sausages into place and fold the butcher's paper around them. He had nice hands, long slender fingers. Nicer hands than Eric: his were stubby and his fingernails were lined with grease. To distract herself she lowered her eyes to the pendulum swing of the steel hanging from his belt. It bumped against the knives. She looked up to see him staring at her and felt her cheeks burn.

"Is Mrs Stewart still having heart attacks?" He grinned.

"No, but she just made Johnny kill her cat with an axe."

"Good Lord!"

"Eric took her gun after she shot at Johnny." Seeing the incredulous look on Mick's face, Lillian tried to cover up what she'd said. "She was shooting at a rat when Johnny got in the way." She hated telling lies.

"Good Lord." Mick couldn't think of anything else to say.

"I'm at my wits end to know how to deal with her." To Lillian's horror she began to cry. "I'm so sorry." She fished for her handkerchief.

"Here, take mine, it's clean." Mick pressed his handkerchief into her hand.

Lillian mopped her eyes. "It's not just Johnny or the cat, it's the copper and Eric didn't even ask me about the horse." She covered her face with her hands and sobbed. Why had she come here? The pregnancy had her emotions all over the place.

Mick lifted the counter. "Come inside and sit for a moment. I'll pour us a cup of tea." He filled two mugs from a thermos.

The hot brew was calming. Lillian put her mug down. "I didn't mean to burden you. I actually came to pay your bill. I'm really sorry it's taken so long." She wiped her nose on his hankie, avoiding his eyes. "Eric got the month wrong."

"Happens all the time. Don't worry about it. I knew you were good for it." Eric is a cunning shit. "Are you going somewhere? You look so pretty."

Lillian jerked to her feet. God, what was she doing? He was looking at her all soppy. "Ingrid Kasbauer isn't well. I … I thought I'd pop in." She prayed Ingrid hadn't been up the street today.

"Tell you what, I've got some deliveries to do and I'll be passing Ingrid's place. It's too hot to walk up that hill. I could give you a lift?" He wiped his hands on his apron.

Trapped in her lie, Lillian scrambled for excuses. "I don't know. What will people think?" Like any small town, Eden was starved for stories and there were plenty of willing tongues eager for some scandal. Eric had created his fair share but Lillian had never been on the radar.

"There's nothing wrong with accepting a lift on a hot day." Mick encouraged.

Her lips tightened. No one ever considered her. Since the shooting incident, a simmer of memories of all the awful things Eric's family had done to her kept popping to the surface. Lillian's saucepan was becoming too full to keep the lid on. Bugger the gossip and Eric. She'd feign a sore ankle when she got home. "Why not," she said, tossing her hair.

"Atta girl." Mick grinned. He turned the sign on the door to CLOSED FOR LUNCH, hung up his tool belt and wheeled the deliveries to the van. Lillian followed him.

The van was new and it gained a lot of attention. It was the first vehicle in town to bear an advertisement. The design was Mick's creation and he'd had it professionally painted in Sydney. He savoured the advertisement, MICK'S MEAT – THE HOUSEWIVES' CHOICE. A picture of a big pink sausage radiated beneath the words – it filled him with pride. He looked at Lillian to see how impressed she was, but Lillian was too preoccupied with looking around to see if anyone was watching her. Mick loaded the box and opened the passenger door. "I have one stop on the way."

The van pulled up outside the Eden Fishermen's Club and Mick jumped out. "Won't be long," he said, cheery voiced and grabbing a carton of meat from the back.

Lillian's gut flopped; she hadn't thought to ask Mick where he'd be making his deliveries. Now she was sitting in the main street outside the most popular venue in town. She put her hand to her face and shrunk in the seat and stayed that way until the van passed the Whale Museum and followed a line of ti-trees down the wharf hill.

"A penny for your thoughts?" Mick said.

The sea sparkled and a necklace of rocks gleamed in its sapphire setting. "I was wondering why some days the sea looks so beautiful and inviting and on other days, so cold and lonely."

"It depends on the company you are with." He gave her a wink.

Lillian picked at the raw skin around her nails. Mick was a sympathetic ear, someone to lift the valve on her pressure cooker. She would have to be careful. Their relationship mustn't get out of hand. "My father was French, you know. He drowned when his ship was hit by a mine, in World War One."

Mick wished he hadn't winked. He reached over and gave her hand a squeeze.

"I still dream about it sometimes." The sea lost its sparkle. She hadn't meant to tell him about her father's death; just that they both had foreign parents in common, that their relationship was a bonding of friends and nothing more.

He caught her sadness. "Half French? Hey, now I know where those lovely dark eyes are from."

Water slapped the barnacled pylons of the wharf and Lillian squirmed. She gazed up the wharf at a couple of fishermen mending nets. They looked up, too far away to identify her. She felt brave, they were nosey parkers. To hell with them. She sighed and watched Mick's hand whip through the gears, readying for the steep climb up the lookout hill.

"I've got a trip to Melbourne coming up, if you fancy another visit to your mother. You can ride shotgun with me."

"Melbourne!" Lillian nearly flew off her seat. "Really, Mick?" It would be perfect timing and all Eric would have to pay for was the abortion.

"Offer's open. I go to the Melbourne market four times a year."

Lillian considered it for a moment and then felt her enthusiasm wane. "Wouldn't the town love that. The Pommy upstart running off with the butcher."

"Is that a possibility?" He laughed.

"Of course not," she said, flustered. "I just mean that the CWA women want me to fall on my face. They think because I have an accent I'm stuck up." She gazed out of the window. "It's strange really, Australians ape the English, raising their pinkies and singing *God Save the King* with hands on their hearts when the flag is raised, yet they can't stand us."

"Oh, I wouldn't say that. It's just a chip on the shoulder from the stigma of being a penal colony. My mother had a rough time of it as an immigrant. Kids used to hold their noses when they saw her." Lillian tilted her head to one side and stared at him. "It was because Aussies don't eat garlic," he said. He noticed how tightly her hands gripped together in her lap. "My mother played guitar and danced to castanets in the kitchen when she wasn't throwing saucepans at my father and didn't give a hoot what people thought."

"I would have to ask Eric if he minded me driving to Melbourne with you. And Aunt Maggie of course." She didn't want Mick to know she was going to have an abortion. She thought for a moment. "You know, there's always someone you have to ask for permission to do things. It would be nice just to be able to please yourself."

"I please myself," Mick said. He looked across the bay and pointed to Boydtown and the imposing Seahorse Inn that nestled between a hug of hills and a long strip of sand. "Ben Boyd built that in the middle of nowhere. He pleased himself."

"It didn't work out for him, though, did it? He thought Eden would rival Sydney."

"He still did it, Lillian." Mick had no idea how difficult it was for women to follow their dreams.

There was a light in Lillian's eyes. "I'll give it a try and ask Eric if he would mind." He'd probably jump at the chance of a free trip that didn't mean a night on the road in a log truck. Her insides warmed. "You're a good man. You give the town drunk free steaks and donate meat to the fire brigade fundraiser. You're always helping someone out." It's a pity Eric isn't more like you, she thought.

Mick shifted in his seat and coughed. "I'll be leaving in two weeks so have a think about it. Eric gets a break every weekend at the farm. That's a lot of holidays. You've only been to Melbourne once in how many years? This is a free trip. Let him take care of the family. I'll take you out to dinner and a show if you come with me?"

"No! I mean, I'm sorry, Mick but I wouldn't do that." Mick's face fell. Lillian felt bad, but it was important Mick should know she wasn't the type to have an affair. Her life was complicated enough. If she and Eric should ever part ways Lillian doubted she'd want to fall in the arms of another man straight away. She'd like to be on her own with the kids, not have to answer to someone else. No one to quiz her on how much money she spent on food. She'd have her own money for the first time in her life. Would she be able to manage her own money? Why was she thinking about that? She wasn't divorced, not even close, and if she were, Eric wouldn't give her a penny. She shook her head to clear her mind. The events of the day were making her confused.

"Here we are." Mick said, pulling up in front of Ingrid Kasbauer's house. He leant across Lillian to open the door for her and his arm brushed her breasts. Lillian shrank back, not wanting him to touch her, scared that she had given him the wrong idea. She looked left and right, checking the street. It was as dead as the cemetery. No one had seen them. Lillian climbed out of the van.

"Thanks, Mick." Her smile met two pink spots on her cheeks. "You're a good friend." She emphasised friend.

"My pleasure, sweet lady." His foot pawed the accelerator and the van snorted away from the curb.

Lillian watched until MICK'S MEAT – THE HOUSEWIVES' CHOICE and the big pink sausage disappeared down the road.

27

Plonko and a Sing-along

On her return from Ingrid's, Lillian found a note from Aunt Maggie in her letterbox. It was an invitation to her birthday sing-along. Lillian smiled. It wasn't Aunt Maggie's birthday. It was an excuse to get them over there: a warm-up to her apology, no doubt. Lillian hadn't consoled Aunt Maggie over the loss of Puss, instead she'd written a letter saying how traumatised Johnny was over killing the cat and how she couldn't understand why Aunt Maggie had made him do such a thing. In reply, Aunt Maggie had said she'd wanted to erase any hard feelings that existed between her and Johnny and asking his special help was tantamount to letting bygones be bygones. Lillian hadn't responded. She put Aunt Maggie's invitation in her pocket. She must be getting desperate, Lillian thought. Lillian was still cleaning and washing and sending meals over, just not having afternoon cups of tea and feeding her the town gossip. If she was going to Melbourne with

Mick in two weeks she had to smooth things out so Eric would take care of her.

Feeling guilty about her ride with Mick, Lillian decided to make Eric a cup of tea and take it over to the shed. She'd tell him about Mick's offer, say he was making a delivery to Ingrid's and gave her a lift back to town. She carried the tea across to the shed, passing a clump of irises drowning in horse manure and put the cup on the bench next to Eric. "What are you doing?" she said, feigning interest.

The gun went still in his hands and he looked at the cup of tea with surprise. "Thanks for the cuppa." It was obvious she'd gotten over her grump. He wondered if she was after something and went back to the business of the gun. "Aunt Maggie wants her gun back. Read this. I found it tied to the motor I'm working on." He pulled the note from his pocket.

RETURN MY GUN. TOURISTS ARE THROWING BOTTLES .IN MY GARDEN AND COMING ONTO MY VERANDAH AT NIGHT. NEVER KNOW WHAT THEY'LL DO NEXT.

"All the tourists in town are making her nervous. I wouldn't mind shooting a few," he said, aiming the gun at the door and pretending to shoot. "They drive like maniacs, especially the ones from Melbourne. I'm doctoring the gun so she can't kill anyone." He checked to make sure he had left enough room for a cartridge then rammed another strip of his old shirt up the barrel and jabbed it a few times with a copper rod until it felt solid. He repeated the process until the barrel was packed tight.

Lillian took a note from her pocket. "Here, she left me one too. We're invited to a birthday sing-along this afternoon. It's not her birthday. I think she's trying to clear the air."

"I will give her the gun back when we go over. It can be her birthday present." Eric's eyes swept over Lillian; she looked

209

different, younger. Pretty. She was wearing lipstick and a nice dress.

"New dress?"

"I made it." She looked away.

"Very nice." His approval insinuated sex. Tonight, he might have a bath and give her a bit of the old one-two. He wiped the barrel of the gun and looked across at Johnny busy attaching a steering rope to the front of his billycart. Eric watched him with pride and felt glad he hadn't left Johnny with his sister, Mavis. He'd make a man of him. Not like that sissy school in Sydney Mavis had put Johnny in. Boys' schools create poofters. "Come on, Johnny, clean up, we're going to a sing-along at Aunt Maggie's. It's her birthday." He winked at Lillian. "We'll meet you over there, Lil. I'll bring the gun."

"Better shoot old Bully Beef first, Dad, he's eating Mum's garden." Johnny turned a cherub face to his mother and pointed at the horse, waiting for her screech. To his disappointment, she shrugged.

"Leave it. I'm going to have a lie down. I'm not feeling the best." There was a burning sensation in her solar plexus. She had noticed it happening after taking a Bex, which was what she had done before making her way over to the shed. It was to keep her calm so she wouldn't blush when she told Eric about Mick's offer. And now was the time. Lillian made to walk off and then turned. "Oh, I nearly forgot to tell you. I ran into Mick the butcher when he was dropping off a delivery to Ingrid. Apparently he's going to Melbourne in two weeks." She signalled Eric with her eyes that Johnny was listening. "He's picking up some specialty meats from the market. Going down in one day. He said he usually has four days in Melbourne. I mentioned Mum wasn't well and I was thinking of visiting her. He offered me a lift. Of course I said no, that you would insist I go by bus." Lillian watched Eric's face as he digested what she'd said. He frowned, stared into the distance and then shook his head at her stupidity.

"Why did you tell him I'd say no? All the money we spend in that butcher shop. The bastard owes us something. Tell him I insist he takes you. It will work with the other won't it?"

Lillian kept the smile off her face and looked at her feet. "I'm sorry, I just didn't think, and yes, the timing is right." Johnny grimaced. He didn't want his mother to go away, his father had given him a lot of jobs to do last time. He'd had to sweep Aunt Maggie's kitchen and change the flypapers.

"I'll see you over at Aunt Maggie's when Johnny and I've finished up. I'll bring the gun," Eric said.

"Pick those feet up, soldier, left right, left right," Eric chanted, marching with Aunt Maggie's gun over his shoulder on the way to the sing-along. Johnny lifted his feet high and marched behind with a piece of wood he'd shaped into a gun. As they approached the gate in the fence, Eric heard someone singing their way up the road. "About turn," he yelled, curious to see whom it was. They did a right turn, marched to the front of the house and peered down the street.

"Click goes the shears, boys, click, click, click ..." Plonko Bill warbled as he wove up the street. He drew level with Aunt Maggie's gate and put his hand up to open it.

"Why are you visiting my aunt, Plonko?" The drunk turned and saluted Eric.

"It's me barracks, sir."

Eric clicked his heels and saluted back. Johnny copied him Plonko swayed holding his salute.

"At ease, soldier." Eric's tone was clipped. They eyed each other. "It's not your barracks, soldier." A carload of louts came down the road and blasted their horn. Plonko threw himself on the ground, covering his head. The louts hung out the window and banged the side of the car, whistling and yelling. Plonko's body shook like the motor in Eric's shed. The car disappeared and Eric bent over Plonko. "It's okay, sport, all clear." He helped the drunk to his feet.

"That was a close one, mate." Plonko stumbled to get his balance. "See ya later, then."

"Sure, Plonko."

They watched him stagger up the road.

"Why did Plonko Bill lie on the ground and cover his head, Dad?"

"It was the war, buddy. He still thinks the Jerries are after him. He was a hero, you know."

"What did he do?"

"Dragged two wounded mates to safety while under German fire. After he got them to safety, he discovered he'd been shot three times."

"Cor!"

Plonko made his home in the boathouse on the beach, next to the cemetery. It was the beach where years earlier a killer whale, trapped in shallow waters, had been murdered by a vagrant. Plonko often heard the orca's spirit calling his pod. It was a sad and mournful sound that filled him with emptiness. On those nights even the flagon of wine he drank couldn't quiet its wounded cries. Nor did it dull the memory of the wounded soldiers who had called to him for help. On those occasions he would find a verandah to rest his head. Somewhere away from the beach. Usually Aunt Maggie's.

When they arrived for the sing-along Aunt Maggie was at the piano, hammering out *I'm looking over a four-leaf clover*. She had told Lillian the piano was to be hers when she died.

"Happy birthday, Aunt Maggie." Eric propped the gun next to the piano.

Aunt Maggie pushed the piano stool back. Her eyes dropped

to the gun and narrowed. Why had Eric kept it so long? He had no right to take it. If he thought she was going to grovel with gratitude, he had another thought coming. "I'm going to fetch the tea; we'll have it in here. Eric, get a chair from the other room."

"I think you should put the gun away first, Aunt Maggie." Lillian spoke with authority. Aunt Maggie swept up the gun and trotted off to the bedroom. A surge of pleasure filled Lillian. There wouldn't be any opposition to her going to Melbourne.

They sat around the piano drinking tea while Aunt Maggie cut the plum pudding. She handed Johnny a big slice and watched him over the top of her glasses. Johnny went still. His eyes darted from the pudding to Aunt Maggie and then to his mother. Lillian smiled at him, she knew what he was thinking. Poor kid. He was convinced Aunt Maggie wanted to kill him. Lillian helped herself to a slice and bit into it to reassure Johnny it wasn't poisoned. Aunt Maggie really had to apologise to Johnny to set his mind at ease. The sing-along wasn't going to be enough. The more she skirted around apologising to Johnny the more determined Lillian became. It was a battle Lillian had to win to gain more control over her own life. Aunt Maggie had to succumb and until then the children's visits would be restricted.

Still not convinced that his piece of pudding wasn't poisoned, Johnny held his cake out to Splinter. "Swap you. I'm not hungry."

Splinter changed plates and bit into Johnny's pudding. Her teeth hit something hard. She sucked the mixture off the shilling and held it up to Johnny, her face shining. "Look what I've got."

"That should be mine." He tried to snatch the coin but Splinter closed it in her fist.

Aunt Maggie's face fell; it had been her 'sorry money'. She must have given him the wrong slice.

Johnny leant towards Splinter with a glint in his eyes. "That's last year's pud and they aren't currants." He pretended to wave a fly away and drew his top lip back from pudding-pasted teeth.

Splinter gagged and spat her cake on the plate. "Mum!" She wailed, pointing at Johnny.

"Oh God!" Lillian didn't need this now. She grabbed Johnny by the ear and marched him into the kitchen. "I'm sick of you causing trouble. You're back on Aunt Maggie's dinner run, starting tonight, and for the whole of this week."

"What did I do?"

"You know very well what you did."

"That shilling was meant for me. I swapped puddings with Splinter."

"Why did you do that?"

"I thought it might be poisoned."

"Well it serves you right for trying to kill your sister."

The piano keys sank beneath the weight of Aunt Maggie's fingers. Her foot beat a rhythm on the pedal. Eric placed his hand over his heart and gave *Danny Boy* his best. At the end of the song Lillian stood up. "It's time for me to go and start dinner. Thank you, Aunt Maggie, it's been lovely." Her tone was formal. She turned to the children. "Help your aunt clear up before you leave."

"I've got some things to do, so I'd better make tracks as well," Eric said, annoyed Lillian had got her excuse in first.

When everyone had left, Aunt Maggie felt pleased. She'd enjoyed the afternoon. It was a pity Johnny missed out on his shilling but otherwise everything had gone well, with the children, anyway. Lillian had been courteous but hadn't offered to help which indicated she was still annoyed. It left Aunt Maggie feeling unsure. She'd never been in this position with Lillian before. In her mind, she'd apologised to Johnny, but she wasn't going to say sorry to Lillian. Give it time and she will come running, and no doubt Eric would need to borrow some money. Aunt Maggie picked up the gun, pulled back the hammer, aimed down the hall and squeezed the trigger. The hammer fell with a thud. Satisfied, she went to her bedroom, opened a small drawer in her dressing table and removed one cartridge. She cracked the gun barrel and dropped it in. Grim-faced, she snapped the barrel shut and slid the gun under her bed. A few nights ago she'd heard someone on her verandah. The prowler was back. It couldn't have been the family this time: she'd already eaten her dinner and gone to bed when she had heard his footsteps.

In the kitchen next door, Lillian berated Johnny for his bad behaviour. "I don't want to have to apologise to Aunt Maggie for you. Do you understand?" She shook her finger in his face. "She's not trying to kill you, but she does have to say sorry and that won't happen if you make trouble. Now, take her food over and don't touch it or I will kill you." Johnny glowered as he took the tray. He was more concerned about being at the end of Aunt Maggie's gun.

Johnny banged on the door and yelled, "Aunt Maggie, I have your dinner." He considered leaving the tray on the step and then he heard a noise coming from her dunny. The coast was clear. He raced into the kitchen and put the tray on the table, neck prickling. The cover slid off the rice pudding. Why did his mother always give her the biggest serve? He edged the table drawer open and withdrew a spoon. He cast a furtive look over his shoulder and dipped the spoon into the pudding. It was delicious. Using the bottom of his shirt, he wiped the spoon and placed it back in the drawer. He jiggled it shut and something fluttered to the floor. Five quid! He couldn't believe his luck. He pocketed the note and slunk off. Aunt Maggie owed him a lot more than a slice of pudding.

28

Red Satin

The sing-along olive branch needed a reciprocal gesture to get things back on an even keel before Lillian went away. Lillian knew Aunt Maggie was sorry because today she had actually thanked her for cleaning the house and given her a *Women's Weekly*. It had been hard not to give Aunt Maggie a squeeze and stay for a brandy, but she hadn't because an apology from Aunt Maggie was important to Johnny. Lillian couldn't have him going through life thinking his aunt tried to kill him. She took the cake she'd baked from the oven and put it on a cooling rack.

"Splinter, go and tell Aunt Maggie I won't be doing the washing because the copper hasn't been fixed yet." Eric wasn't getting any clean clothes until he fixed it. Ingrid had offered the use of her washing machine and Lillian was going to take the rest of the washing up to Ingrid's in a wheelbarrow just to shame him. "You're not to stay long. I'm coming over later to have a few quiet words with Aunty." It was time to tell Aunt Maggie she would be away for a few days.

Splinter found Aunt Maggie in the shed undoing the string on a brown paper parcel. "Mum said to tell you she's not doing any washing because the copper isn't fixed," Splinter said.

Aunt Maggie shrugged and tore the parcel open. Red satin glowed like a ripe tomato. She gathered it up and motioned Splinter over. "I want you to hold one end of the material for me."

They stood each end of the coffin holding the satin, then let it go. It sighed into the coffin and slipped over the thin horsehair mattress. Aunt Maggie took a packet of safety pins from her pocket, and pinned the fabric to the mattress. Then she covered in the sides, working her way around the rim of the coffin with a hammer and shoe tacks. When she had finished, she sat back and glowed in its reflection. Splinter clapped her hands and Aunt Maggie beamed.

"Take your shoes off and get in girl. I want to see what it looks like." Splinter climbed in and laid down with her arms crossed and eyes closed.

Aunt Maggie radiated. She would love to share this with Lillian.

Sick of waiting for Splinter, Lillian picked up the cake and followed the sound of voices coming from Aunt Maggie's shed. She stood in the doorway and smiled. "I thought you and I could have a talk over some afternoon tea, Aunt Maggie." Lillian's eyes dropped to the coffin and opened in horror. Suddenly she was back in the orphanage, standing in a line of children, waiting to kiss the face of a dead nun. She felt as though she was caught in a rip and trying to swim for the shore. "What on earth do you think you're doing? Get out of there, Splinter!" Splinter jerked to a sitting position, and climbed out. Lillian turned on Aunt Maggie. "How could you, Aunty? That's so morbid. She's just a child."

The sudden change in Lillian increased Aunt Maggie's heart rate. Her hand flew to her chest and she staggered backwards.

Lillian's eyes sparked. "Cut that out! I've changed my mind there won't be any afternoon tea until you apologise." Lillian was convinced that now Aunt Maggie knew about Eric's infidelities, she thought she could get away with anything. Well, she had to learn otherwise. Lillian stalked off with the cake leaving Aunt Maggie wandering around the shed with a face like a sorry dog.

Bad memories crowded in on Lillian. The orphanage and the war. She needed to get out of the house, clear her mind. She didn't have the energy to walk to Ingrid's and it was too late to fossick for glass on the beach. She'd visit Mick and buy some meat. And tell him she'd go to Melbourne with him.

Mick was putting the 'Back in half an hour' sign in the window when Lillian stormed in. "What's up?" He said, noticing her agitated state.

"All I wanted was an apology for the shooting. But I go over there with a cake and she's got my daughter in a coffin. Sorry, isn't in the Australian vocabulary. No one has ever said sorry to me. Giving up my home to come to this country where everyone looks at me with suspicion, being a nurse maid to Eric's bloody family." She shut her mouth at Mick's look of surprise and felt her face go red.

He took her hand and held it between both of his. "Come to Melbourne with me. If you have a break you'll cope better."

"I will come with you. Eric said it was kind of you to offer," Lillian said. Mick looked jubilant.

"Good on you." His grin faded. There's something I forgot to tell you the day I took your Aunt home. She told me she was going to look for another tenant because her family didn't care about her. It was probably said because she was in a stink, but better you know."

Lillian withdrew her hand. "She can get another tenant for

all I care." But the news shocked her out of her self-pity. Over the years Lillian had taken Aunt Maggie's dependency on her for granted, but since the shooting Aunt Maggie had grown more erratic. Lillian would have to watch her step. There was also another problem brewing – Mick was getting too familiar. She didn't want any problems on the trip. Rather than give him the impression she'd dropped by for a chat Lillian bought a leg of lamb to add to the one she'd bought two days earlier. "Sorry about the outburst, Mick. I'll need to know when you plan to leave and the departure time as I'll have to let my mother know." She sounded efficient. The bell on the door tinkled as another customer came in. "Well, I'd better get back and sort some things out." Lillian grabbed her parcel and left the shop in a dither.

When she arrived home Splinter was waiting for her with big sorry eyes. Lillian felt bad. She had overreacted with Aunt Maggie. "It's not your fault, love; it will all work out. We'll give Aunt Maggie time to think about things. She's the one who has to make amends." For tea, Lillian would make one of Aunt Maggie's favourites, lamb stew with dumplings, followed by a peach cobbler. If there was one thing that would make Aunt Maggie think twice about evicting them, it was her love of Lillian's cooking. Before Lillian moved in, Aunt Maggie had existed on watery mince and boiled potatoes.

"No visiting without my permission." Lillian lifted the tea towel off the cake she'd brought back from Aunt Maggie's. "You can have a piece of cake." She cut her a big slice then went into the garden to talk to her plants. Splinter followed.

Finding herself on her own with the cake still sitting on the table, Bubs cut two slices, eating one and taking the other into her bedroom. The newspaper and bottle money wasn't growing her savings fast enough and now Puss was dead she wasn't being paid to catch fish anymore. Her horse needed a blanket. Bubs sat on the bed and went through her financial possibilities. The stolen slice of cake lay untouched beside her. Could she sell the slice of cake to one of her friends for play lunch? But what if they all wanted it? She didn't want to lose any friends. She could have a tea party at Aunt Maggie's house and sell it to her? No, she'd think the cake was free and probably have a heart attack if she was asked to pay. Bubs giggled. Her friends were always asking about Aunt Maggie's heart attacks. An idea flashed. Maybe they would pay to see one? Maybe, Aunt Maggie would let Bubs have a tea party at her house and have a heart attack. Best of all, if Bubs gave her a tea party, maybe she'd say sorry to her mother. A shiver of excitement filled Bubs. She would write Aunt Maggie a letter, as she wasn't allowed to visit.

Rummaging through the big drawer at the bottom of the wardrobe, Bubs found her teaset still in its box. The cups weren't much smaller than her mother's best ones but the bread and butter plate was too small for the slice of cake. Taking nibbles around the edge of the cake, Bubs fixed the problem. She wrapped the cake in a hankie and slipped it into the dressing-table drawer. She took out the special forget-me-not stationery Splinter had given her for her birthday and wrote Aunt Maggie a note. Then she lay on her bed and wondered how many she should invite to the heart attack.

Still licking her wounds, Aunt Maggie picked the tea tray up off the step and slammed the door behind her. She had been waiting behind the door ready to give Lillian a piece of her mind if her food was late. She'd had enough of Lillian's ill treatment. A note skittled under the door and landed by her foot. Aunt Maggie picked it up and fetched her reading glasses off the sideboard.

Dear Aunt Maggie,
    I wood like to invit you to my tea party. Mum says you are incapisated so I will bring my tea party to you. Jimmy, Hazel and

220

Helen are coming to. Plese leave a note on the door saying COME
IN. Its after school toomorow. I have cake for you.
Love Bubs xxxx

Aunt Maggie considered the note as she placed the tray on
the kitchen table. Bubs was up to something. That was certain.
The mouth-watering aroma of lamb stew stole her thoughts.
She lifted the saucepan lid and viewed a gastronomic delight.
The saucer slid off the top of the peach cobbler. It was so
tempting Aunt Maggie wondered if she should start on that first.
Lillian was a wonderful cook – she really wanted to restore their
friendship. Perhaps Lillian had her monthlies and that's why she
caused a fuss over Splinter? Everything would have been alright
if Johnny hadn't missed out on his pudding shilling. The tea party
might be a good way to bury the hatchet, she thought. After
her meal Aunt Maggie wrote, COME IN and as an afterthought,
added, LEARN YOUR SPELLING, on the back of Bubs's note.
She made a hole in the paper and threaded it with string then
went outside and tied it to her door handle.

The birds had only just gotten up when Bubs checked Aunt
Maggie's door for her reply. She took the note down and skipped
home to get dressed for school, the story she'd tell her mother
already on her fibbing lips.

Beaming with excitement, Bubs burst through the kitchen
door. "Mum, you'll never guess what?"

"What?" It was an automatic response. Lillian was preoccupied
with thoughts of Mick the butcher while she stirred the porridge.
How could she dampen his ardour without losing his friendship?
They would be spending many hours on the road together.

"Aunt Maggie asked me to afternoon tea and she said I could
bring some school friends."

The wooden spoon went still. Lillian scrutinised Bubs. "When
did she ask you?" The children were only doing the dinner run,

221

not social visits and last night Lillian did the delivery to ensure Aunt Maggie's favourite meal wasn't sabotaged before it landed on her doorstep.

"Just now, when I went to put some flowers on Puss's grave." The fib would be taken care of when Bubs said her prayers before bed. She noticed her mother's lips seam. Maybe mentioning Puss hadn't been a good move. "Please, Mum. Aunt Maggie looked really sad."

"You don't say?" The wiles of her, manipulating the kids. On the other hand, if Aunt Maggie was looking for a new tenant Lillian had better keep the door open. Taking care of Aunt Maggie with all the tension between them was difficult. A ridge formed on the inside of Lillian's cheek as she chewed over the decision. "Oh, alright, I suppose it won't hurt. When is it?"

Bubs clapped her hands. "This arvo, after school."

29

The Tea Party

They huddled together outside their classroom and Jimmy held out his sixpence. "If she doesn't, I want my money back."

"She will."

"I haven't got sixpence but you can have my phantom comic." Helen reached into her schoolbag and took out a comic. Bubs checked to see if she'd read it. "It's a new one and you can use it for swaps or sell it." Helen's freckles were pink with excitement.

"Righto."

Helen's twin sister, Hazel, gripped the sixpence in her palm. "Howd'ya know she'll do it?" The sixpence was her milkshake money earned from selling newspapers.

"Cos she shot someone, but I can't tell about it," Bubs whispered. Hazel put her sixpence in her pocket, brown eyes wide. "It's okay. She won't shoot you. Dad fixed her gun."

After school they lined up at Aunt Maggie's back door. Bubs knocked and opened it just wide enough to get her head and the basket through. "It's me, Aunt Maggie, I've got the tea party." She held up the wicker basket she was carrying and entered. Jimmy, Helen and Hazel crowded in behind her.

Aunt Maggie was lying on the chaise longue. She lowered the newspaper she was reading and peered over the top of her half glasses. Bubs put the picnic basket on the floor, careful not to tip it. She cleared the books off the kitchen chair that served as Aunt Maggie's table next to the chaise longue and covered it with a white doily. She unpacked her teaset and arranged it on the doily then took the cork out of a medicine bottle she'd filled with milk and poured the contents into her teaset jug. A smile spread the cracks in Aunt Maggie's lips as she watched Bubs remove the teapot from a jumper she'd used as a tea cosy and pour tea into the cups. How sweet, she thought. Bubs passed her a cup. Aunt Maggie took it with her pinkie poised and waited for Bubs to serve her friends then sipped along with the children. When everyone finished their tea, Bubs brought out the plate of cake and gave it to Aunt Maggie who had a quick look to make sure it was cake and gave it a poke to see if it was fresh. The children watched and licked their lips as she popped it into her mouth. Her tongue flicked across her lips to clear the crumbs. Aunt Maggie noticed she was the only one with a piece of cake and her eyes moistened. How thoughtful of Bubs to include her in their game. She took off her glasses and dabbed her eyes on her sleeve.

"When's she gunna do it?" hissed Jimmy. Tea parties weren't his thing.

"Shhh," Bubs hissed back, giving Aunt Maggie a quick look.

The old lady's head tilted back. She lowered her eyelids and peered through slits. The four children lined up in front of her, watching, waiting for something.

"Are you feeling alright? Do you want some brandy, Aunt Maggie?"

Normally the question would trigger Aunt Maggie's reserve tanks of self-pity and start her heart flutters, but she was still smarting from the cold shoulder treatment she'd been getting from the family and was on the lookout for any slight. Ah! Aunt Maggie knew what her game was. The little minx. Well, she was going to be disappointed. She bet Eric had set Bubs up to it. He wanted everyone to think she was an alcoholic so he could have her put away. Aunt Maggie swung her feet off the chaise longue and stood up. "Get going you lot." The suddenness of the move made her dizzy. She tottered and put her hand out to steady herself.

Bubs jumped up and took her aunt's arm, relieved that everything was going to plan. "Hold onto me, Aunty."

"Is she doin' it? Is she havin' a heart attack?" Jimmy moved closer.

Aunt Maggie shook her off. "I'm alright, child." The impertinence of Bubs trying to make a spectacle of a sick old lady. She would give them a taste of her umbrella. Her mouth clamped and her hand reached for the umbrella stand.

Bubs glared at Jimmy; he was ruining everything. She needed to come up with something to trigger a heart attack or the kids would want their money back. Worse, she'd feel the sting of that umbrella around her legs. "Dad had maggots on his lamb dinner."

"What! What are you talking about? Maggots? When?" Aunt Maggie swallowed rapidly. Bubs watched her closely.

"When we had roast lamb just before Mum went to Melbourne, a fly had blown the meat. Did you find any maggots, Aunt Maggie?"

Aunt Maggie gave an involuntary shudder and gagged. Her hand went to her throat. The thought of flies breeding inside her was sickening. She didn't want them inside her even when she was dead. Every month she went through her instructions with Lillian to make sure her mouth would be closed after she died. She clutched her stomach. Her face contorted. "Pour me some brandy. Quickly!" Maybe she could drown the maggots before they became flies. She leant against the sideboard and released a series of belches.

The teacup Bubs handed her was full to the brim. Used to Bubs's small portions Aunt Maggie swallowed it in one gulp. The large shot caught her by surprise. She coughed and it came up the back of her nasal passage. She sneezed and a rubber band of snot swung from her nose. She tried to catch her breath, choked and thumped her chest. She let go of the sideboard, lost her balance and made a grab for Jimmy. He stepped out of her way and her arm landed on the chair, tipping the teaset onto the floor. The children gasped and drew back. Aunt Maggie managed to flip herself sidewards and landed on the chaise longue. A considerable amount of air expelled from her posterior.

Jimmy's face lit up. "She farted!"

Helen's eyes were as big as cups. "Is she having a heart attack?"

"Is she dying?" Hazel's voice was hushed awe.

"Are you alright, Aunty?" Bubs needed a bit more heart attack evidence. Aunt Maggie's face was purple and her nostrils flared like an angry bull. She tried to speak. Spit bubbles formed in the corners of her mouth and she gasped some incoherent words.

Jimmy leant forward. "She's saying somethin'. What's she saying?"

Aunt Maggie motioned Bubs towards her. Bubs held her breath and put her ear near Aunt Maggie's mouth.

The angry roar quivered Bubs's eardrum. "Make me a proper cup of tea and tell those little devils to clear off or I'll give them a whipping. And tell your mother I want to see her." Aunt Maggie cocked her hand and fired at Bubs. The friends disappeared with a "See ya later," shouted from the gate.

"Yes, Aunt Maggie. I'm sorry, Aunt Maggie." Bubs went into the kitchen and made Aunt Maggie a cup of tea. Then carried it back to the sunroom. "Do you want some brandy in your tea, Aunt Maggie?" It was something Aunt Maggie had never thought of. It sounded interesting.

"I'll give it a try but don't put any milk in it." Bubs tipped two spoonfuls of brandy in the tea and handed it to Aunt Maggie. Aunt Maggie sipped, her eyebrows went up. She had another mouthful. Bubs spirits lifted. "You can go, now but don't forget to tell your mother I want to see her."

"Yes, Aunt Maggie." Bubs ran home. She would give her mother a neck massage and forget to pass on Aunt Maggie's message.

The next day, suspicious that Bubs hadn't told her mother, Aunt Maggie wrote a letter summonsing Lillian to a meeting and put it in her letterbox. Lillian received it with a cry of triumph, stuffed the letter in her apron pocket and ran over to Aunt Maggie with a heart full of forgiveness.

By the time Aunt Maggie's prim lips had finished telling Lillian about the tea party, Bubs was in for it. "I don't know what got into her, Aunt Maggie, I'm sorry." The apology was hooked out of Lillian's throat. When she managed to look in Aunt Maggie's eyes, she knew she had lost her battle. Just wait until she got her bloody hands on Bubs. She knew it was the old biddy's obsession with death that romanced the minds of her children. They were hardly to blame but she was in such a temper, she had to vent her anger somewhere and Bubs was going to get it. Lillian left Aunt Maggie lying on the chaise longue like an overstuffed orca.

On window watch, Bubs saw her mother leave Aunt Maggie's and storm across the yard. She knew she was done for. Bubs tore past Splinter into the sitting room and crawled on her belly under the settee. Splinter followed her. "Please don't tell mum where I am, Splinter."

"What did you do?"

"Nothing, just don't tell."

"I won't." Splinter picked up her comic and plonked into a lounge chair.

Hornet angry, Lillian flew into the sitting room, head swivelling from left to right.

"She's under there." Splinter pointed to the three-inch gap beneath the settee.

"Get out here, Bubs." Lillian tapped her foot.

"You said you wouldn't tell, you promised," Bubs wailed.

"Out here, now!" Lillian got on all fours and eyeballed Bubs who lay as flat as a strip of liquorice. "Get me the broom, Splinter. I'll get the little rat." Splinter ran to do her bidding.

There wasn't enough space under the settee for Bubs to make a fast escape. She watched her mother's feet pace back and forth. "I'm sorry, Mum."

"You'll be sorrier when I get hold of you."

"Here you are, Mum." Splinter handed the broom over like a birthday present. Bubs hadn't been sent to live with Nanna.

The broom jammed into Bubs and she wriggled to the far corner where the broom had less impact. She trembled with fear; her mother had never been this angry with her before. She hadn't attacked Johnny when Aunt Maggie told her he had eaten her dessert or thrown crackers down her chimney. Maybe she had a migraine. "Get Mum a Bex, Splinter."

"What!" The broom froze. Lillian sucked air between her teeth.

Bubs took the pause as a sign her mother hadn't realised she needed medication and that it was safe to come out. She slithered from under the settee. It was a mistake.

Lillian hauled her up by the arm. "Get me a Bex? I'll give you a Bex." Lillian slapped Bubs's bare legs until her hand stung and Bubs's screams became hiccups. "Now, get in your room and don't come out until I tell you." Lillian pushed Bubs into her room and slammed the door. She leant against the door, shaking with anger. A wave of remorse tumbled over Lillian as she listened to Bubs sobbing. She wanted to go in and comfort her, say she was sorry, but she remembered her mother telling her, "never apologise to your children and never let them think you're in the wrong. Children don't forgive". Those words had been true for Lillian; her mother had apologised to her for putting her in the orphanage and although Lillian had said she forgave her mother, deep in her heart she hadn't.

"Here, Mum." Splinter handed Lillian a glass of clouded water. She took it and swallowed, a reflex action. The sharp taste cleared her head. She looked at her daughter and the Bex dregs in the bottom of the glass. Good God, her children had become her nurses. She would have to get a hold on herself.

Calmer when Eric came home, Lillian told him what Bubs had done. He fell into the fridge laughing. He thought it was childish of Lillian to keep the argument going. He didn't care about Aunt Maggie's apology as long as he could scrounge the occasional fiver.

Nettled, Lillian rounded on him. "It wasn't funny. I had to say I was sorry to the old girl and she lay on her couch so smug. She's the one who should be apologising to us for what she did to Johnny. It's alright for you; you don't have to wait on her hand and foot." She felt guilty for smacking Bubs. The tea party had been the straw that broke the camel's back plus the realisation that her children knew she couldn't get through a problem without taking Bex. She untied her apron. "I'm going out. You can get the kids to clean up."

Not even the beautiful warm evening and the smell of her rose garden placated Lillian as she left the house. Everything was getting her down. It was hard to believe that two months ago she had been in Melbourne relaxed and happy. She felt like she was heading for a breakdown. It must be the pregnancy, she thought. She pushed the abortion to the back of her mind. Right now, she would visit the draper's wife and read her tea leaves in exchange for a tarot reading. The day after tomorrow she would be going to Melbourne with Mick and she couldn't wait. As she closed her front door a cowbell clanged. Lillian looked across at Aunt Maggie's kitchen window. The blind was up and Aunt Maggie stood at the window waving the bell. What now? Lillian walked over to the gate in the fence. It stuck when she tried to open it. She gave it a kick and it sagged open. One of the hinges was broken. It was from the kids kicking it when they were carrying Aunt Maggie's dinner tray over. Lillian would have to get Eric to fix it. Aunt Maggie was waiting by the door when Lillian arrived. She thrust an envelope in Lillian's hand and stood back while Lillian read it.

> DEAR LILLIAN, IT WAS NOT MY INTENTION TO SHOOT JOHNNY. PLEASE GIVE HIM THE TWO SHILLINGS IN THE ENVELOPE AND TELL HIM I AM SORRY AND I DIDN'T MEAN TO HURT HIM. THANK HIM FOR HELPING ME WITH PUSS. YOURS SINCERELY, A.M.

Something tugged at Lillian's throat, she swallowed. "Thank you, Aunt Maggie. She stepped forward and gave Aunt Maggie a hug. "I must admit I haven't been myself lately. Can you spare a minute?"

"You're pregnant?" Aunt Maggie sipped her brandy, brow furrowed.

"I have to have an abortion because the doctor said it would endanger my life to have another child. I'm having it done in Melbourne. I'll be leaving in two days." Aunt Maggie got up from the chaise and trotted into the kitchen and came back with a packet of Epsom salts. She handed the packet to Lillian.

"Douche with this after the abortion, it will clean you out." Lillian smiled all the way to her tarot reading.

30

The Abortion

The butcher's van arrived and tooted. Lillian hugged her children and pecked Eric on the cheek.

"Make sure he pays for your lunch," Eric said, grinning. It served the wog right for embarrassing him over the meat account. The eighty pounds Eric had given Lillian for the abortion was safely in her handbag, she hadn't told Eric that Ingrid's doctor friend was only going to charge her fifty pounds.

"Take good care of Aunt Maggie and I'll see you all in four days." Lillian looked across at Aunt Maggie's kitchen window and waved. Aunt Maggie's hand lifted. Poor old duck, Lillian thought. She had promised to bring Aunt Maggie a bottle of good brandy, something she couldn't get in Eden.

The trip to Melbourne was easier than Lillian expected. Mick made her laugh with stories about his customers. Lillian talked about losing her father, life in the orphanage and the abuse she had suffered. And the ache of homesickness after immigrating to Australia. Mick listened in respectful silence.

"You must have had your confidence beaten out of you," was all he said, shaking his head. When they stopped for lunch, Mick got up to pay for their sandwiches and tea. Remembering Eric's mean comment about making Mick pay, Lillian put out a restraining hand.

"I'm having a free trip, Mick so you must let me pay." Mick shook his head and reached for his wallet. "Eric said I had to," Lillian insisted. Mick grinned and sat down.

"I can't fight Eric," he said.

It was nine o'clock at night when they arrived at Lillian's mother's place. They had left at six in the morning, it had been a long day. Lillian knocked on the door. Her mother opened it and Lillian grabbed her in a hug. They cried and laughed, then Lillian turned to Mick. "This is my mother, Louise McCrae. Mum this is Mick, the butcher."

Mick laughed. "Just Mick will do." Lillian blushed.

"You must come in for a cup of tea Mick, it's the least I can offer you," Louise said, holding out her hand. Mick shook Louise's hand. "Pleased to meet you Mrs McCrae. The cup of tea will be most welcome, thank you." He carried Lillian's suitcase inside.

"I've made a bed up on the couch for you, Mick," Louise said. "It's too late to find your hotel in the city at night." Mick opened his mouth to protest and Lillian's mother put up her hand. "I'm not listening to any protests. You are free to leave at whatever time you need to in the morning. The doctor is coming to see Lillian in the afternoon so there's no need to rush."

"Mum! Lillian said, sharply.

"Doctor? Lillian, you didn't say you were sick?"

"It's nothing," Lillian said, thinning her lips at her mother.

"Women's problems," Louise said quickly.

Mick nodded. "Then I'm happy to accept your hospitality for a night and I'll leave early in the morning for the Victoria Market."

After finishing their cups of tea, Mick turned to Lillian, "Are you free to catch up for a meal before we go back to Eden?" Lillian looked at her mother and blushed.

Her mother's eyebrows went up. She was quick on the uptake. "Leave me the name of your hotel so Lillian can get a message to you. It will depend on what the doctor says," she explained.

Mick looked at Lillian with concern. "Of course. I'll leave my particulars on the table before I go." He stretched. "If you ladies don't mind I think I'll hit the sack."

Alone in their room, Lillian whispered to her mother. "You shouldn't have mentioned the doctor. He thinks I came to see you. I don't want the whole town knowing my business."

"He likes you, Lillian. He seems a nice chap."

"I'm married, Mum." When Lillian had written to her mother about Eric's philandering, she had urged Lillian to leave him. Louise McCray had had three husbands. The war had robbed her of the first two and the last one she had divorced. At the time, it had scandalised her family and friends. A divorcee was a loose woman. Let them live my life, she would say if they turned their noses up at her. Lillian knew if she divorced Eric and settled for Mick her mother would applaud her. It wouldn't happen though.

"I've made a hair appointment for you in the morning. A nice new style will give you a lift. And in the afternoon the doctor is coming. I thought it best to get it over and done with so we can have time to ourselves without something hanging over our heads. When you're back on your feet we'll go shopping," Louise said. Lillian undressed, hopped into her mother's double bed and lay beside her listening to the trams rumble past, too happy to consider what would happen tomorrow.

The doctor had white hair and gentle blue eyes. Lillian sat hunched in front of him. She wished she could share her humiliation with Eric. Her fear. Her guilt. Her pain.

"This is not something I do regularly. It is only because Ingrid made a special request," the doctor said. "Now we must do business. "I vill need water to be boiled, and towels."

"There's towels on the bed and I have water boiling," Lillian's mother said. She knew the ropes.

"Then, Lillian, you will go and make ready for me while I vash my hands."

Although it was a cold day, Lillian lay on the bed covered in perspiration. She heard the chink of instruments as the doctor moved to the foot of her bed. A wave of nausea flooded her. She jerked to a sitting position, grabbed the bowl on the bedside table and vomited. Her mother handed her a warm face washer. Lillian wiped her face and looked at her mother, eyes large and dark. "Aunty Flo died from an abortion."

Louise patted Lillian's hand. "That was a few years ago and it wasn't a doctor that attended her. It will be alright, just try and relax." White-faced, Lillian lay back on her pillow and fixed her eyes on the ceiling and tried to still the trembling in her body.

"It will be over quickly," the doctor soothed. "Hold this to your nose and breathe deeply. Lillian held the ether-soaked wad of cotton wool to her nose and took a deep breath. The room swirled around her. Then something stabbed inside her and she descended into blackness.

When Lillian woke up the doctor had left and her mother was sitting beside her. A smell of ether lingered in the room. She dry retched, her body jerking. Cramps worse than her monthlies coursed through her torn uterus. She pulled her legs up and rocked, moaning in pain. Louise handed her the laudanum.

"I can't drink anything. It will just make me vomit more," Lillian said, pushing it away.

"Eat a piece of dry bread first and it won't upset your stomach so much." Louise handed Lillian a slice of dry bread that she had brought in with the laudanum. It had worked for her. Lillian took a small bite. "Let me check how much blood you're losing." Louise pulled aside a pad of gauze from between Lillian's legs. "It's normal. I'll fetch a hot water bottle. It will help with the cramps."

The next morning when the painkillers wore off Lillian felt an emptiness inside her. She sighed around the house in her mother's dressing gown, gloom and remorse clinging to her. What sort of a mother was she? She had just killed her child, used it as an excuse to visit her mother. Was it a girl or a boy? There was only one day left before she was due to return to Eden but she didn't feel like doing anything. The phone rang. Lillian's mother answered. She nodded into the phone, then looked across at Lillian, shapeless on the couch.

"Yes Mick, Lillian's in the bath at the moment, but I am sure she would be delighted to have dinner with you tomorrow night. Leave me your number and I'll get her to phone you back."

"No!" Lillian mouthed, shaking her head. Louise turned her back. "Yes we'll be in touch, thank you." She replaced the phone.

"I don't want to go anywhere. How could you?"

"You need to get out and enjoy yourself. And I hardly ever get to see you either. We only have tomorrow and then you're off back to Eden." She frowned, "You know I'll never be welcome up there. I want us to have a happy day together. Now, get dressed, we're going to Georges in Collins Street. You can wear my new hat and coat."

A spark of interest rose in Lillian. Georges was famous. The wealthy shopped there. It was like Harrods in London. Lillian's anger subsided – she didn't want to disappoint her mother and who knew how long it would be before they saw each other again.

It was an effort to get ready but Lillian did her best to brighten up for her mother's sake. She put on lipstick and her mother's new hat and coat and twirled in front of the mirror. She looked nice and her new haircut made her look younger. Her spirits perked up. They were soon in the city, jostling amongst the crowds and gawping at the latest fashions in the shop windows. Georges was dazzling, full of men in pin-striped suits and women dressed in silk, wearing diamond necklaces. Lillian bought a piece of lace to edge a handkerchief as a memento. They finished their afternoon with tea and scones at Myer.

The next day they went to the Botanical Gardens. That night Lillian went to dinner with Mick. He left the van at her mother's place and they took a tram into the city. Mick chose an Italian restaurant in Lygon Street. The best restaurants in Melbourne were in Lygon Street, he said. He'd been in the army and was stationed in Rome at the end of the war. He greeted the waiter in Italian, pronounced the dishes with a perfect accent. The food was delicious. Lillian loved the garlic and the herbs and wondered if she could get Eric to eat pasta. He'd probably order steak and chips, she thought. They drank red wine serenaded by a violinist and two singing waiters. Mick raised his glass to Lillian, she blushed and clinked glasses with him. He seemed so at home in the candlelight and music. Lillian hadn't had such a romantic night since she'd left England. In fact, since her wedding day when Eric had treated her and her family to cream tea at the Savoy. They'd had a pianist that day.

Their evening came to an end and Mick helped Lillian into the coat she had borrowed from her mother. She was sorry to leave. It had been a perfect night. She thought how silly she'd been for not wanting to have dinner with Mick. He'd been a complete gentleman. When they arrived back at her mother's the couch was made up for Mick.

"I thought since you had to leave so early in the morning you may as well stay here," Louise said. Lillian bit her lip. It wouldn't be good if Eric found out she'd been out to dinner and Mick had stayed over.

"That's very kind of you," Mick said. As if reading Lillian's mind, he added, "it might be a good idea if we keep this to ourselves, though. As harmless as it is, there are those who would love to make a fuss."

"Blimey." Lillian said smacking her head. "I forgot to get Aunt Maggie's brandy. Nothing will be open tomorrow, it's Sunday."

"There's another bottle in the cupboard she can have. I don't drink the stuff." Louise fetched the bottle. "It was a gift for some dressmaking I did." Lillian opened her suitcase and put the bottle inside.

"Thanks for everything Mum. I'm sorry I've been such a wet blanket. You'll have to come and visit me and stay for a few weeks. The children haven't seen you in ages."

"If we both save our pennies who knows? Maybe I can get a ride with Mick when he's next in Melbourne." Louise smiled at Mick.

"Anytime," he said, sincerely.

The next morning Louise handed Lillian a brown paper bag. "Some egg sandwiches for the road." Lillian took the sandwiches, and started to cry. Louise wiped her own eyes. They hugged and kissed and then Lillian got in the van. Mick put his head out of the window.

"Thanks for your hospitality, Mrs McCrae." He put the van in gear and they drove off.

Lillian was going over all that had happened the past four days, when Mick leant over and gave her hand a squeeze. "We should do this again some day," he said. Lillian snatched her hand away. What was Mick thinking? They could never do this again. It wasn't a holiday spree or a romantic interlude. She shouldn't have enjoyed her trip, that wasn't what it had been about. She had aborted her baby. Swamped with guilt Lillian, frowned at Mick.

His smile turned into a look of concern. "Oh! That was stupid of me. I know you came because you had a medical complaint. What I mean is, it's not a crime to have enjoyed a night out and each other's company in a city where no one knows us. I had such a good time, I guess I got a bit carried away. Alright?"

"It's fine, Mick." Lillian leaned back and closed her eyes, pretending sleep to avoid any further conversation about their good time. It made her feel guilty. She had ended a life. She shouldn't have been out enjoying herself. She wouldn't have gone if her mother hadn't encouraged her. If she'd had the baby would Eric have cared if she had died giving birth? What would happen to Johnny, Splinter and Bubs if she died? No doubt Mavis would take Johnny to Sydney to live with her. She'd like that, Lillian thought. She couldn't see Mavis spilling too many tears over her. She probably wouldn't take the girls, though. They would stay with Eric and wait on Aunt Maggie so he could safeguard his inheritance. "Oh, Good Lord!" Lillian shot up in her seat. She had never had a choice –her children's happiness would have been at stake.

"What?" Mick said, startled.

Lillian squared her shoulders and turned to Mick with a determined smile, "Sorry Mick I haven't been my usual self the last few days. It would be lovely to stop for a cup of tea at Lakes Entrance. Shall we do that?"

31

Breaking the Peace

The night in Lygon Street with Mick seemed a long way off as Lillian sat and listened to Aunt Maggie's complaints. "The prowler is back," she said, "While you were away, I heard him on my verandah three nights in a row. It gave me a heart turn." Aunt Maggie put on a sorry face and rubbed her chest.

"Did you tell Eric?" Lillian said. She knew it was nonsense, Aunt Maggie was only trying to make her feel guilty for being away. Well, she didn't feel at all guilty. She thought she would have, but she had looked Eric in the eye and said it had taken her the whole time to recover from the abortion. And that the doctor had told her she couldn't have sex for six weeks. She said she hadn't seen Mick from the time he had dropped her off to when he picked her up.

Aunt Maggie sniffed. "Eric didn't come near me, he only sent the children over. I kept an eye on him, mind you. He was busy in the shed most of the time." She gave Lillian a knowing look. "A couple of times he talked to the headmaster's wife over the back fence."

Lillian would have to keep her eye on the headmaster's wife, think of a way to warn Eric off without causing an issue. She smiled her appreciation and wondered what Aunt Maggie would say if she knew she'd had dinner with the butcher. "I brought you a present from my mother," Lillian said, reaching into the mop bucket she'd carried it over in. Aunt Maggie sat forward and beamed. Lillian handed her the bottle of brandy. Aunt Maggie smacked her lips. Lillian smiled. "There's something else in here too." Lillian pulled a roll of wet newspaper out of the bucket. "I also sneaked some rose cuttings for you from the Botanical Gardens." Lillian tore the wet newspaper off the cuttings. Aunt Maggie took them from her and inspected them, eyes gleaming. "We'll plant them tomorrow," Lillian said. Aunt Maggie patted Lillian's arm. "I'll see you tomorrow, then." Lillian picked up the bucket and left.

The wet cloth steamed as Lillian pressed the crease down the front of Johnny's shorts. Tomorrow she would buy another lottery ticket. The weight of the iron was making her wrist ache. She put it back on the stove to re-heat. It was two months since her tarot reading and she was still waiting for the money the draper's wife said she would win. Moths made a bull's eye out of the light bulb above the chessboard Bubs and Eric were hunched over. Only one more move and Bubs would have him and he'd have to pay her threepence. Lillian caught her eye and gave her a wink. Bubs ducked her head into her shoulders and grinned. *Volare* played on the wireless, Lillian hummed, it was one of the songs she had been serenaded with in the restaurant. Her thoughts blew apart with the gun blast and scream. It was a déjà vu moment. The hair stood up on Lillian's neck and she did an automatic headcount, holding her breath. "That sounded like a …"

"Bloody gun!" Eric shot to his feet.

"It came from Aunt Maggie's." Lillian's voice hushed. "I think I heard someone scream." She looked towards the open window. The kitchen filled with Jess's barking.

"What in the blazes has she done now? Where's the torch?" Eric pulled a drawer open, felt around and slammed it shut. "Get the bloody torch, Lil." Lillian scrabbled on top of the fridge and handed Eric the torch. He turned it on and ran out of the kitchen. Lillian rushed after him, the children in her wake.

"Quiet, Jess." Eric swept the torch along the fence and marooned a figure scrambling for his life. Eric held the torch on the intruder who seemed to be having difficulty getting to his feet.

The intruder lifted up his hands and held them next to hair that looked like it had been excavated by a bandicoot. "Get them search lights off me."

"Plonko! What are you doing you silly old coot?"

"I was takin' a bloody piss and a sniper nearly got me. Saw a flash of fire, and boom!"

"Why were you pissing in Aunt Maggie's, for Christ's sake?"

"It's me barracks. I was on manoeuvres."

"Christ almighty!"

"You can say that again."

Fear gripped Lillian. "Go and see if Aunt Maggie's alright. She's probably terrified."

They all followed Eric to the back door. Johnny kept at a safe distance so he wouldn't be the first in Aunt Maggie's sights.

"You there, Aunty?" Eric tried the handle. "It's locked."

"What about the kitchen window?" Lillian said, clutching Johnny.

In the torchlight the window was cracked just enough at the

bottom for Eric to get his fingers under. "Here, hold the torch, Lil." He passed her the torch and pushed the window up then stuck his head through. "Shine it around the kitchen." Lillian flashed light around the room. "It doesn't look like she's in here but I can't be sure. I'll have to go in. Keep the light inside so I can see where I'm going."

Plonko craned his neck around Eric. "I'll go in, fella. No need for you to get shot."

"Bugger off, Plonko. You've done enough bloody damage." Eric shouldered him out of the way and threw his leg over the sill. "I'm coming in, Aunty." His body clogged the window and illuminated in the torchlight. "Don't shine the bloody thing on me, Lil, she could be hiding somewhere with a knife. The old bugger might've gone off her rocker."

Eric dropped through the window onto the floor. "Hand me the torch. I can't see a damn thing." He swung the light around the room. "Seems clear."

"Let me in the back door and I'll check the bedroom, she won't be scared of me," Lillian said. "You kids wait outside while Dad and I have a look." Eric opened the back door and handed Lillian the torch. She pushed past him.

"Take it easy," Eric said. He pulled a box of matches from his pocket. "I'll light the lamp in the kitchen."

The torch shook in Lillian's hand as she made her way down the hall. "Are you there, Aunty?" The torch dimmed and died. "Blast! Bring the lamp up here, the torch has died." Eric held the lamp up and Lillian made her way into Aunt Maggie's bedroom. "Put the lamp on the washbasin and tell Johnny to run home and get the two spare batteries off the top of the fridge." She glanced around Aunt Maggie's bedroom. The bed was still made. A pair of satin gloves, draped over the bed end, made giant hands on the wall. "Eric, she's not in bed," Lillian yelled down the hall. Eric hurried back. "Maybe she's hiding in the cupboard scared out of her wits," Lillian said. The wick did a fire dance. Lillian felt a breeze. "Her window must be open, the wick's moving. Eric, take a look on the verandah, she might have panicked and climbed out of the window. I'll check the wardrobe." Lillian opened the wardrobe door and felt inside.

Eric crossed the room to check the window. His foot bumped something solid. He looked down. Christ almighty!"

"What?" Lillian's heart jumped in her throat.

"Bring the light over here."

Heart pounding, Lillian went around the bed and held the lamp up. Aunt Maggie lay on the floor, her burial bonnet tangled around her neck. Her eyes were closed and her tongue protruded from her mouth. The shotgun was clasped in her arms. The burial dress lay crumpled at her feet. "Holy Jesus!" The lamp shook in Lillian's hand. Eric dropped to his knees and lifted Aunt Maggie's arm. It was loose and floppy. He eased the gun out and laid it beside her.

Lillian sat on the floor and cradled Aunt Maggie's head in her lap. Johnny, Splinter and Bubs crept over. Johnny clutched the torch batteries, open mouthed.

"Is she dead, Mum?" Splinter cried.

"You shouldn't be in here," Lillian said. "But since you are, go and get the candles out of Aunty's kitchen cupboard, light them and stick them on saucers." Lillian stroked Aunt Maggie's face, it felt like crumpled linen under her hand. "Don't worry, darling, I'm here." There was a tremble in her voice.

"Give me the batteries, son," Eric said, taking them out of Johnny's hands. Eric fumbled with the torch. "Shit, it's bloody hard without electricity, old miser. She should've put it on years ago."

"Well, you didn't encourage her. And don't call her names." Lillian looked at the old face in her lap. "Don't take her, God," she prayed.

The beam from Eric's torch made a cameo of Aunt Maggie's face. Tiny pustules of moisture popped through the pores of her skin. "Can you hear me, Aunty?"

"Of course she can't hear you! She's unconscious!" Lillian snapped.

"What's that smell?" Eric sniffed the air. "Something's on fire." He shone the torch on the floor next to Aunt Maggie. A thin trail of smoke floated upward in the beam. It was coming from the gun. "Shit! The shotguns on fire." He grabbed the jug off the washstand and poured water down the barrel. Then broke the gun open and removed the smouldering cartridge. It burnt his fingers. He cursed and dropped it on the floor.

"Eric, leave the bloody gun and help me move Aunt Maggie onto the bed. Johnny, hold the torch up."

Johnny raised the torch and gasped. Aunt Maggie looked old, rumpled and fragile. Johnny's lip trembled. He kept the beam steady while his parents tried to lift her onto the bed.

After two attempts, Lillian eased Aunt Maggie's feet back to the floor. "I can't lift her; she's a dead weight."

"I'll have to get Plonko to give me a hand." Eric straightened up slowly, rubbing his lower back. A few falls off a horse and a tree he'd felled the wrong way had left their legacy.

"Plonko can hardly hold himself up, let alone lift Aunty. Leave her with me and go and ring the doctor and the ambulance."

"Righto, yes." He stood up and stared at Lillian. There was something else he had to do but he couldn't think what it was.

"Get a move on, man."

"Yeah, right." He hurried from the room.

"I've got the candles, Mum," Splinter said. Bubs and Splinter held a candle in a saucer in each hand. "Where do you want me to put them, Mum?"

"Spread them down the hall, we'll need to light the hall for the doctor and stretcher."

245

Splinter stared down at Aunt Maggie, cradled in her mother's lap. "Is it a real heart attack?" Her voice was just above a whisper.

"Looks like it, pet. Hurry with the candles. Johnny, fetch a glass of water and a spoon." She might have to spoon the water in Aunt Maggie's mouth. Lillian took stock of the room, noticing Plonko hovering in the doorway. "Plonko, why don't you wait in the back room so you can let Doc Smith in when he comes?"

Plonko shuffled into the sunroom. The decanter caught the candlelight and sparkled like the crown jewels. Plonko had a closer look. "Now, aren't you a beauty." He picked up the decanter, removed the stopper, sniffed and salivated. He poured a shot into the glass next to it, raised the glass to his lips and lifted his pinkie. "Don't mind if I do, Colonel," he giggled. It was a long time since he'd tasted brandy; cheap plonk was his poison.

Aunt Maggie's breaths came in long shudders. Johnny returned with the water.

"Thank you, pet." Lillian spooned some water between Aunt Maggie's lips. It slopped from her mouth, unable to pass her swollen tongue. Her eyes remained shut. They had been rehearsing Aunt Maggie's death for so long and now the possibility was here, Lillian was afraid.

A trail of cars pulled in behind the ambulance as it came to a halt in Aunt Maggie's driveway. The driver, and Sluggo, the local policeman – who had been playing cards with the driver at the time the call had come through – jumped out. Doc Smith arrived with his bag. Constable Sluggo thumped the windows of the cars that had followed the ambulance. "Get the hell out of here you pack of galahs," he shouted. "We need to get the ambulance out." A line of cars reversed and jockeyed for position in the street.

Doc Smith pushed passed Plonko in the doorway and raced down the hall. He squatted next to Aunt Maggie and felt for a pulse in her neck while she lay in Lillian's lap. He tried to see in her eyes but the candlelight reflected in her pupils and gave him a false reading. "I need a torch." Lillian handed him the torch. He snatched it from her. It was hard to understand how Lillian could allow the old lady to live without electricity. He lifted Aunt Maggie's eyelids and flashed the torch across her eyes. "How long has she been like this?" His voice was sharp.

"We phoned you straight away. Let's see, maybe half an hour." Lillian removed her glasses and wiped her eyes on her sleeve. "She's going to be alright, isn't she?"

Doc Smith heard her concern. He knew Lillian had been good to Eric's Aunt, cared for her for years and he felt bad that he'd been so short. His tone softened. "I'm not sure. She may have had a heart attack or a stroke. I need to get her to hospital."

Constable Sluggo picked up the gun that lay next to Aunt Maggie. It felt warm. He frowned, cracked the gun and felt for the cartridge. There wasn't one. He sniffed the barrel and it smelt of gunpowder and burnt cloth. The pungent odour made him cough. He went over to the window to check for a bullet hole. Nothing. He looked around the room, now crowded with people, their faces ghoulish in the strange light. They were from the cars that had followed the ambulance and had sneaked in unnoticed during the chaos. Constable Sluggo's eyes became gun barrels beneath the slab of his forehead. It was time to take charge. This was not an ordinary accident. "Bugger off outta here, you goggle-eyed dingo bastards." He waved the shotgun at the crowd. The constable was a bullish man: jutting jaw, flattened nose and a scar that cut through one eyebrow. In his youth he'd toured the territory with a boxing troupe. The constable was a man to be obeyed. The crowd left. Decanter in hand, Plonko followed and sat on the back step.

Eric danced on one foot, then the other, watching Constable Sluggo and waiting to be asked about the gun. It came after the room had cleared.

"Can I've a word, Eric? Maybe in private where there's some light?"

Eric led Constable Sluggo into Aunt Maggie's sunroom where a runway of candles lined the floor. The chaise lounge sunk beneath Eric's weight, dropping him below the constable's eye level, forcing him to look up. Constable Sluggo leant forward on the straight-backed chair.

"Any idea what Mrs Stewart was shooting at?" He tapped the ends of his fingers together.

"She thought Plonko was a prowler." Eric crossed his legs and quickly uncrossed them. He didn't want to look like a poof.

"Right. Know where Plonko's got to?"

"Outside, I think."

Constable Sluggo went to the back door and shouted into the darkness, "You there, Plonko?"

"Shh … shh … sure am, Mister Copper," came the slurred voice from the bottom step.

A sigh escaped Sluggo, he'd had many run-ins with the drunk and he knew he was harmless. He usually bought him a packet of fish and chips before he put him in the clink for the night. "I want you in here, mate."

"At your shervice, sir." Plonko staggered into the sunroom with the now empty decanter and attempted several times to place it on the sideboard. Constable Sluggo relieved him of the decanter and had a sniff to see what Plonko was drinking. "Stealing is an offence, Plonko." He put the decanter on the sideboard.

"I only borrowed it, sir."

"Why were you prowling around Mrs Stewart's?"

"I was jush takin' a piss."

"Where, exactly?"

"By the barracks window."

"Plonko. The war's ended, mate."

"Not on your bloody life, a sniper took a shot at me!" He

straightened up. The moment was sobering. He'd seen the gun flash and thought there may have been a couple of them waiting for him. When he'd taken a look, he hadn't been spying. He was just interested in why there were still lights on in the barracks during a blackout. An image popped in his brain. He had seen someone inspecting some money. "I think I surprised a forger."

A siren went off in Eric's head. He didn't want anyone to know about Aunt Maggie hiding her money. If it got out half the town would turn up with spades. "Yeah, right, Plonko." Eric gave Constable Sluggo a knowing wink.

"Don't go anywhere, Plonko. I'm going to have to take you in until you sober up." Constable Sluggo turned to Eric. "We'll need a lift to the police station; I came here with the ambulance. Can you?" He raised his scarred eyebrow.

"No need to ask. I'll give you a lift, Sluggo."

Sluggo cleared his throat and looked gruff. "The name's Cliff, Eric. I'm on duty." He didn't like Eric; he was sure he had stolen McKenna's cattle.

"Oh, sorry, Cliff."

"Constable Cliff."

There was something in the policeman's gaze that unnerved Eric.

"I'll take the gun with me, if you don't mind." It wasn't a question.

"Not at all, help yourself, Constable." He could feel a trickle of sweat run down his back.

"I'd like to go now."

"Yes of course." Pushy bastard, Eric thought, clenching his teeth.

The roar of the truck made it impossible to talk. Eric pulled into the police station and Constable Sluggo got out and dragged Plonko after him. A pungent smell of piss filled the truck's cabin.

Eric noticed a puddle where Plonko had sat and cursed him under his breath.

Constable Sluggo tipped his cap. "Thanks for the lift and come by the station tomorrow so we can have a chat."

"Done." Eric waved and sped off, his mind busy with the gun.

Lillian rubbed the pins and needles in her leg from sitting on the floor next to Aunt Maggie and watched as the ambulance driver, Doc Smith and two onlookers lifted Aunt Maggie onto the stretcher. "Are you going with her?" the ambulance driver asked Lillian.

"Of course," Lillian said without hesitation. She knew Aunt Maggie would be frightened waking up in hospital.

"You can sit in the front of the ambulance, Lillian." Doc Smith patted her hand. "I'll ride in the back with Mrs Stewart."

Unaware of Eric's difficulty, Lillian's mind was on Aunt Maggie as the ambulance siren wailed. She remembered all the fake heart turns and the times when she had wished Aunt Maggie's heart attacks had been real and felt guilty. What was going to happen if Aunt Maggie died? It was inevitable of course, she was old, but Lillian depended on her, had tried hard to keep her in the best of health, at least until the kids were old enough to make Eric think twice about what he did. She realised how unlikely that was, he'd never considered anyone but himself and Lillian had no more independence than she'd ever had. Apart from a roof over her head nothing much had changed. Eric was going to inherit money if Aunt Maggie died, but that meant he'd buy the farm and Lillian would have to move to the farm. It was the last thing she wanted. Eric's womanising had stopped, thanks to Aunt Maggie and her umbrella. He would get up to it again, Lillian had no doubt. And Lillian still wouldn't have any money to leave him and take the kids to Melbourne. All Lillian could do was pray her protector wouldn't die.

32

The Interview

The next day at the police station, Eric sat in front of Constable Sluggo, hands clenched between his knees and a pool of sweat in his bum crack. He looked around the room, eyes settling on Plonko who watched him from the lock-up, sober. If it hadn't been for pissing Plonko, he wouldn't be in this fix and Lillian too preoccupied with Aunt Maggie to be concerned. Eric crossed his ankles, pasted an inane smile on his face and looked across the desk of neatly stacked files, into the Constable's penetrating gaze.

Constable Sluggo cleared his throat. "It looks like the barrel was packed with cloth to stop the shot or blow up the gun. The kick from the gun would knock a man over, not to mention the fright Mrs Stewart would've gotten when it caught fire, enough to give the old lady a heart attack. I know you poured water down the barrel to put the fire out. What I want to know is who tampered with the weapon in the first place, and why?" Constable Sluggo was enjoying the fear in Eric's eyes.

"No idea. I found it smouldering so threw some water down the barrel in case it set something on fire, but that was all, Constable Cliff." Eric chewed his words like a piece of gristle. Did this plod think he was Dick Tracy? "I mean, it's as old as the hills. I think it belonged to her father. Fought in the Boer war, he did. Maybe the Boers did it."

"Bloody foreigners!" Constable Sluggo blinked like a machine gun. His wife had run off with an Italian.

"That's it, then?" Eric said.

"If she dies there will be an inquest, of course."

"That's normal," Eric said.

Seeing the relief on Eric's face, Constable Sluggo added, "Don't leave town."

"Now look here, Sluggo …"

Constable Sluggo's eyes narrowed. "You'll inherit from your aunt won't you?" He'd make the bloody cattle thief sweat. And Lillian must have known what was going on, the stuck-up Pom, always keeping to herself. He'd take her down a peg as well. It might be worthwhile chatting to young Johnny, but he would need to get him without the parents. It was illegal to interview kids. It wouldn't be an interview though. Constable Sluggo stroked his chin. Then he nodded Eric towards the door.

Tired after spending the night at the hospital with Aunt Maggie, Lillian had come home for a change of clothes and to get the children off to school and found Eric in a panic. The floorboards squeaked under his pacing. "Why didn't you tell the truth to start with? They all know Aunt Maggie is eccentric."

"It's all right for you. If she dies I'm the one who could be charged with attempted murder. And where would that leave you?"

The worry lines on Eric's forehead aroused Lillian's sympathy.

"Well, she's still alive so maybe you're worrying about nothing," Lillian said. She looked at the clock. Mick was doing a delivery to Pambula and said he'd give her a lift to the hospital after lunch. She needed to put her head down for a couple of hours. "You'll have to see to the kids after lunch because I'm going back to the hospital."

It was just after lunch and Lillian and Mick were alone in the shop. Mick drained the last of his thermos into her cup. "How is Mrs Stewart?"

"They're keeping her sedated." She wouldn't mention Eric's problems with the gun. Lillian finished her tea and looked at the clock. "It's time to go."

The trip to Pambula took half an hour. Most of it Lillian spent in silence planning Aunt Maggie's future living arrangements. She wouldn't be able to live on her own. Splinter would have to move in with Bubs and she and Eric take Splinter's room. Then Aunt Maggie would have a fireplace and enough room for an armchair. If she dies, Mavis will be down like a shot. Before Lillian had moved next door to Aunt Maggie, Mavis had been content to send Christmas cards. She had visited every year since, scared that Eric might benefit more than her in Aunt Maggie's will.

"It's funny how death brings out the graspers in families," Lillian said, thinking aloud.

"We all have them," Mick said.

"Eric's family are a weird lot. Mind you, they had a hard time growing up with that mother of theirs. She was a cow to me." Lillian packed her mother-in-law away. One shouldn't think ill of the dead. "His sisters call me 'The Pom' behind my back."

"My mother was called a Dago," Mick said. They sat in silence. "What will happen with your house if she dies?"

Lillian's brow furrowed. "I don't know. I just hope Eric doesn't buy the farm. I don't want to move out of town. It's too isolated." How would she manage Eric without Aunt Maggie? It was too disturbing to think about.

Mick patted her hand. "Let's not jump the gun, life is unpredictable, one door closes another one opens. How are the kids taking it?"

"They're at school. You know kids, it's all a bit of an adventure for them." Lillian was tempted to tell Mick about their predicament with the gun. She wondered what Eric was telling the police. They'd probably interview her. She wouldn't be able to lie. What a fiasco. Why the dickens had they hidden Aunt Maggie taking a pot shot at Johnny? It would have explained the gun. The police enquiries were just routine. There was nothing to worry about, Lillian told herself. She was glad the children hadn't been too affected. Kids were resilient. They couldn't wait to get to school to tell their friends about Aunt Maggie. It was the first time Lillian hadn't had to nag Johnny to hurry up.

Johnny stood outside the school gate surrounded by a group of boys. Constable Sluggo was parked near the gate watching them. He got out of the police car and walked over to the group. "What have you got there, son?" Constable Sluggo leant over Johnny's shoulder. The group of boys surrounding Johnny moved away. "Mind if I take a look?" He took the bullet out of Johnny's hand and turned it around. "Where did you find this?" It was illegal to interview a child without a parent present, so Constable Sluggo wanted to sound friendly.

Johnny squirmed. He'd found the cartridge on the floor in Aunt Maggie's bedroom and put it in his pocket to show his mates. Was he going to go to gaol for doing that? He hung his head and looked at his boots. "I don't know," he mumbled. Constable Sluggo frowned.

"You know what I reckon? I reckon you found it in your Aunty's bedroom. How's that for a guess?" He grinned at Johnny.

"Can't remember, sir." Johnny quaked. Constable Sluggo patted him on the shoulder.

"No need to be nervous, son. We're just having a friendly conversation. Hey, aren't you the lad who dropped the double bunger down the RSL chimney?" Johnny went pale. The constable laughed. "Frightened the daylights out of the boys, you did. They reported you to me and I told them to forget about it, that I admired your spunk." Johnny's shoulders went back. He grinned up at Constable Sluggo.

"Gosh, if they had caught you they would have put you in a reform school. Too fast for them, you were. I bet you played a prank on your aunt and stuffed the gun barrels with cotton wool, too. You little rascal." Constable Sluggo grinned.

"No, I didn't. Dad did that," Johnny blurted. His eyes widened when he realised what he'd said. He had sworn an oath to his father that he wouldn't tell anyone. It was the mention of the reform school that had made him nervous. He'd heard tales about reform schools.

"Is that right?" Constable Sluggo gave a tight smile. "You won't mind if I keep this then. It might be important evidence. You should consider becoming a detective when you grow up." He patted Johnny's shoulder and looked towards the school gate where Johnny's friends were waiting. "I'd better not keep you. I have to get back to work, can't stand here chatting all day."

Red-faced from being driven through town in the police car with the siren on, Eric was as angry as a trapped snake. He leant across Constable Sluggo's desk, knuckles pressed into the wooden surface. "You can't question my kid. It isn't legal."

"I didn't, just happened on him showing his mates a cartridge and I asked him where he found it. It was just a friendly chat. Doubt you could prove otherwise." The constable removed his cap and threw it over his shoulder, without taking his eyes off Eric. It landed on the hat stand behind him. "Stuffing a gun barrel with the intent to kill someone isn't legal either." He held up a fragment of scorched cloth. "And don't tell me it was the Boers who did it. They didn't have Pelaco labels in those days."

Eric's shoulders sagged. "Look, Sluggo, I only did it to protect my kids."

"Sit down. I need a statement." He put a piece of paper in his Burroughs typewriter and hit the keys.

33

Following Instructions

It seemed strange laying out Aunt Maggie's burial clothes. The satin smoothed under Lillian's hand. All those weeks of worrying over living arrangements and Eric's culpability if Aunt Maggie died and Aunt Maggie had had a second heart attack, taking them all by surprise. It was fortunate, really, because it wasn't attributed to the shotgun, so Eric was let off the hook.

The old lady had been an enormous presence in Lillian's life and she was going to miss her. Under Aunt Maggie's protection Lillian had felt safe, she'd even stood up to Eric. Now that she was gone Lillian made a vow that she wouldn't revert to allowing Eric to browbeat her and fill her with guilt. The sun beamed through the window throwing light on the cream satin dress. The image filled Lillian with peace, driving away her anxieties. She sensed an inner strength; a knowledge that if Eric fell into his old womanising ways, she would be able to deal with him without Aunt Maggie's protection. Thank you Aunt Maggie, she said under her breath.

Lillian picked up the bonnet and smiled. "This will hold her chin up and keep her mouth shut. Poor old thing had such a phobia about flies." Eric didn't answer. He was too busy tapping at the walls and listening. He felt under the wash table. Lifted the mattress and checked to see if it had been mended anywhere. He examined the back of the flower lithograph on the wall while Lillian folded the dress and bonnet, placing them in a brown leather suitcase. The rest of Aunt Maggie's clothes she put in a tea chest for the rubbish tip.

"Only ten quid in a shoe. There has to be more somewhere," said Eric.

"I'm going to empty the food cupboard and clean the kitchen." Lillian left Eric to his money hunt. Aunt Maggie had only died a couple of hours ago and he'd begun searching as soon as they got back from the hospital. It sickened her.

He followed her into the kitchen. "I'll give you a hand."

Every packet and tin Lillian put on the kitchen table, Eric searched. There was nothing. He looked up the chimney and felt inside. A rain of charcoal dusted his boots. "Don't make a mess, Eric. I haven't got time to clean." Lillian frowned at his footprints.

He wiped his black hand down the side of his trousers, and looked around the kitchen. Then bent and opened the oven door of the stove. A handful of notes lay in the oven and his spirits lifted. "Look at this. Aunt Maggie must have missed some." He put the notes on the table, held each one up to the light and examined both sides. A few had lace holes where the numbers had been. He threw those in front of Lillian and pocketed the rest. "What a waste," he whimpered, booting the oven door shut. Lillian gritted her teeth and didn't look at him. "You'd think she'd have left a letter or a map to show me where she's hidden her money." Flummoxed, he stared at the floor. "Mavis arrives tomorrow and I know she'll have a good look around. I'll spew if she finds something. She's never done a damn thing for the old girl." He wasn't looking forward to his sister's visit.

"That's it, then. The kitchen cupboard is empty." Lillian put the last packet of weevil-infested porridge in a box ready to be dumped over the cliff into the sea. She looked around the sunroom. There was nothing she felt like taking: maybe the sideboard and the painting, and Aunt Maggie's chaise longue, but the rest of it was heavy old stuff that required a lot of dusting. Lillian had grown up in England surrounded by antiques and ancient buildings. She liked modern things but Eric had never bought a stick of furniture. Everything they had was second-hand and full of woodworm. Stuff Eric's family hadn't wanted. Aunt Maggie's house would get sold and the money split between Eric and his six siblings. The only thing that worried Lillian was what would happen to the house they were living in. The reading of the will was tomorrow. She turned towards Eric who stood like a stunned mullet, wondering where Aunt Maggie's money was. "Can you get rid of this box? I'm going to cut some roses for Mavis's room. She'll be here in a couple of hours."

Eric picked up the box and put it in the wheelbarrow. He was thinking he'd tackle the shed next, though apart from the coffin there wasn't much in there. His mind was going over all the places he hadn't searched, while he wheeled the barrow of rubbish towards the cliff.

Lillian cut a few roses for Mavis's room then she dug at an obstinate weed next to the bush's roots. Ching! Her trowel hit something hard. She scraped the earth away and uncovered a brick. It had emerged like an omen and for a moment she felt sick, remembering the smell of brick dust as she lay under her bombed home. She cursed the brick, snug in the earth. She dug it from the ground, tossing it as far away from the roses as she could. She turned back to the cavity in the soil. Snow-capped

259

mountains and a gorgeous blue lake fringed in fir trees peeped up at her. It was an unusual place for a tin of Arnott's biscuits. Easing the earth from around the tin Lillian lifted it from the soil. The lid was rusted. Using the point of the trowel, she managed to prise the lid off. Inside, tied with string, in neat bundles, were notes of different denominations. Lillian's mouth dropped open. There must be a few hundred pounds, she thought. Her hands trembled with excitement as she put the tin in the bucket next to the cut roses. Moving further along the garden bed, Lillian attacked a few more weeds, digging deep between the bushes. The trowel struck another hard surface. Fever gripped her. She dug faster, reaching another brick. She pulled it free and hurled it aside. The large tin of chocolates, resplendent with painted red roses, beamed up at her. She prised the lid off. Tightly rolled bundles of notes packed its interior. It was a dream. The trowel picked up pace, racing along the rest of the rose bed until it unearthed a third brick weighing down the lid of a Bushells tea tin. Her heart was racing as she put the tin in the bucket with the others to be examined later. She placed the cut roses on top of the tins to conceal them.

The squeak of the approaching wheelbarrow added to the tingle in Lillian's nerve ends. Her gut lurched. Panicked, she patted down the soil and sat back on her haunches, heart beating.

"What are you up to?" Eric said, as he drew level and rested the barrow.

Guilt flushed Lillian's cheeks. She quelled her nerves and looked him straight in the eye. "Tidying up the roses and getting some flowers for Mavis." She hadn't lied. Later she would show him the money, but for the moment she wanted to feel its power. It was the first time in her life she'd ever had money that was hers to do with as she liked.

"Don't make her too comfortable or she might want to stay longer," Eric said.

"I doubt that. She'll be glad to go home after she's helped me get the wake ready." Lillian couldn't have given a hoot about Mavis.

"I'm going to have a quick look in the shed. How about making a cuppa? I've been up since sparrow fart." He picked up the barrow and headed for the shed.

She'd make tea and bake scones. Give Mavis a rousing welcome. Try not to arouse suspicions. In a state of ecstasy, Lillian collected the trowel and bucket and floated across the yard. The day was bright with colour. What would she do with the money? Tell Eric? Not yet. She had better find a good hiding place while she thought about what to do. She couldn't believe her luck. But what if Aunt Maggie had said where the money was hidden in her will? Eric was sure to rush home and dig it up before Lillian could put it back. Perhaps she should tell him now? An inner voice urged her not to. How would she explain a new washing machine away? Think, woman, think!

The kitchen smelt of baked scones. "Now, you kids mind your manners. Aunty Mavis will be here soon." Lillian was finding it hard to act normal, as though the greatest gift hadn't just fallen in her lap.

"Where's she sleeping, Mum?"

"Aunt Maggie's."

"What if Aunt Maggie's ghost is there?"

"Don't be silly, Splinter, she died in hospital."

"I don't want Aunty Mavis to kiss me. She nibbles like a goldfish." Bubs made fish lips in the air.

"That's enough. Now go and clean yourselves up."

"Do you think she'll bring me a present?" Johnny's eyes shone.

"Don't you dare ask her, Johnny. Do you hear me?"

Johnny nodded. He couldn't wait for Aunty Mavis to arrive. After his mother and father, she was his favourite person. He

261

went to his room and got out the stamp album she had given him and took it to the kitchen.

"What if she finds something?" Eric put two sugars in his cup of tea and stirred it absently.

"What could she find? You've already been through the place."

"I'll have to get a spade into the garden."

"Maybe she burnt it all." Lillian said. It was too late to admit the truth now, he would think she'd tried to keep the money for herself.

"I'm thinking of giving Mavis the worm eaten money I found in the stove. I'll tell her Aunt Maggie burnt the rest and that might stop her looking." Eric said.

"How much of it was any good?" Lillian asked.

"None of your business," Eric growled. He had to take his disappointment out on someone.

"What are you going to do with your money, then?" Lillian leant against the wall with her arms folded. She knew it wouldn't include her and the kids.

"I'm thinking about it."

Good. She would think about her buried treasure.

Eric glanced at his watch, the figures hardly discernable under the scratched glass. "I'd better get going, the bus is in." Eric looked at his watch with its peeling leather strap. "What did you do with Aunt Maggie's jewel box?"

"It's on my dressing table. Mavis said Aunt Maggie had told her she was going to leave it to her."

"Don't give it to her before the will reading and check if my father's fob watch is in there. I could use it."

"She'll know if it goes missing."

"A watch isn't jewellery. What would she do with a man's watch?"

"Even so, it's not right to take it."

"Don't tell me what I can and can't do with what's rightfully mine."

"If you find the money, you won't need her old watch. You can buy a new one. A gold one."

"I guess you're right." He looked at his wrist and imagined a gold watch.

Johnny looked up from his stamps. "Dad, can I come with you to fetch Aunty Mavis?" Lillian felt a pang of jealousy at Johnny's fervour. She set the table up for afternoon tea.

"Something smells wonderful," tweeted Mavis as she fluttered through the door. She gave Lillian a hug and peck on the cheek. Lots of squeals and arms reached for her and she disappeared into the clump of children like a little sparrow.

"Let Aunty Mavis sit down and have a cup of tea and I'll give you all some scones and jam." They rushed to their chairs and grabbed a scone from the silver platter that Mavis instantly recognised as Aunt Maggie's. Her bird-like eyes quizzed the kitchen, not missing a thing. She pushed away her irritation and dropped into a chair.

"Lordy me, you lot have grown." The scone had golden warmth: it was light and buttery soft and the homemade jam from the farm blackberries glistened on the top. Mavis took a bite. "Have you chosen a coffin yet? Not too expensive, I hope."

"She made her own," Eric said.

Mavis put the scone down and stared at Eric, a piece of blackberry jam stuck to the corner of her lip.

"You can't possibly bury her in that thing."

Scenes from coffin practices and funeral clothes flicked behind Lillian's eyes and Aunt Maggie's instructions echoed in her ears. "We are going to bury Aunt Maggie the way she wanted, Mavis, in her coffin."

Mavis looked from Lillian to Eric, open mouthed. "Don't be ridiculous. What will people think?"

"Eric agrees with me, don't you, Eric?" Although she sounded convinced, Eric hardly ever backed her up where his family were concerned.

Eric frowned. "It is what Aunt Maggie wanted." He resented Mavis putting in her two shillings worth, interfering in everyone's business. The family know-it-all. Eric hoped she wouldn't find out about the police enquiry he'd been put through. Aunt Maggie's death was a sensation in town. "Everyone knows she built her own coffin; they'll want to see it. I'm not going to do the old girl out of her moment of glory. Are you going to pay for a new one?" He added.

"It can come out of the estate like all her funeral costs." Mavis knew the ins and outs of deceased estates. She had inherited twice already. Her tongue flicked out and licked the piece of blackberry jam off her lip. It was ridiculous. What were they thinking, burying her in that thing? Eric and Mavis had never agreed on anything and she wasn't going to give in on this. She knew Eric was selfish with his money and it was evident in the clothes Lillian wore: usually cast-offs her mother sent her or frocks she'd made herself. Mavis wondered if Lillian still had the silk blouse she had given her. Mavis had cut the pearl buttons off the blouse and pocketed them before handing it to Lillian. She told Lillian they would be wasted on her, living in the country. The pretty dress Lillian was wearing caught her eye. Either her sewing had improved or she had wheedled the money out of Aunt Maggie.

"I'm not sitting in church next to a piece of homemade junk that a pauper wouldn't be put in," she retorted. "If you can't get another coffin at short notice, find a carpenter to cover that monstrosity and make it look presentable or you'll be the laughing stock of the town."

"It's not our choice, Mavis, Aunt Maggie was very specific about what she wanted," Lillian said, sticking to her guns.

264

"It was the wish of a senile old woman and anyone carrying out such a wish must be off with the pixies. Anyway, this is a family matter, between Eric and me."

Lillian went red. "She put me in charge of the funeral, you know."

"Good Lord!" Mavis put her hand to her mouth and covered a titter. It was impossible to think Lillian could be in charge of anything. Look at how she left Bubs in bed with a broken leg for a week. Poor Eric, he'd had a lot to put up with.

"It's not a joke, Mavis, ask Eric." Lillian looked at Eric and felt her heart squeeze. He was grinning at her.

"I don't think she meant it," he said. Lillian wanted to cry. Mavis had won.

"Are you getting all the jewellery, Aunty Mavis?" Johnny beamed.

The tea took a wrong turn in Eric's throat and was violently rejected down his shirt front. He went into a spasm of coughing and Lillian leant forward and gave his back a hard whack. He pulled away and glared at her then waved his arm towards the children. "You kids nick off," he coughed, eyes leaking.

Mavis looked at Johnny shrewdly. "I'll come and see your stamp album later, pet.

Lillian squashed her anger and switched the conversation to safer ground. "Are you sure you'll be okay staying at Aunt Maggie's? It's so dark over there."

"I've stayed there before. All I need is a torch and some candles."

Good bloody riddance, Lillian thought. "Johnny can light the kerosene lamp for you and Eric will take your bags over." She looked across at Eric who coughed an exit, grateful for the excuse. "I'll get the chip heater going if you'd like a bath, Mavis?" Lillian offered.

"No thank you, I'll just take a pot of hot water over and have

265

a wash." Mavis had experienced the chip heater before. It was a kerosene drum rigged to the main water tank by a connecting copper pipe. Another pipe went from the drum through the timber wall and into a tap that stuck out a foot above the bathtub. A fire under the drum heated the water. When the water boiled, the drum vibrated against the side of the house like a washing machine off balance. It made the tap shudder and splutter rusty water full of mosquito wrigglers into the bath. It terrified Mavis. She thought the bathroom would blow up. Baths were a once-a-week occasion. She'd have one when she returned home to the luxury of her own bathroom and gas hot water.

34

Outside Aunt Maggie's Bedroom

Eric was light on his feet. He crept onto Aunt Maggie's verandah and crouched beneath the window peeking under the half-mast blind. The kerosene lamp on a chair next to the bed lit up the room. A pile of clothes on hangers lay on the floor in front of the wardrobe. Mavis's backside and stocking feet were framed in the door of the wardrobe. She was on her knees inside, examining its walls. Eric smirked. There was nothing in there. He'd done a thorough job.

She backed out of the cupboard, dusted her knees and made her way to the bed. She picked her handbag up from the bed and rummaged through it, withdrawing a small packet. Eric squinted to see what she was holding but the light was too dim. Why in God's name hadn't he encouraged the old girl to put the electricity on? His breath ghosted the window. He covered his hand with his shirtsleeve and wiped it clear. A board creaked under his feet and Mavis looked up. Eric ducked below the sill and held his breath. A high sea pounded the shore.

He heard Mavis walk to the window and pull the blind down. It rolled back up with a loud thwack! He heard Mavis curse. She pulled the blind down again. This time it held, leaving a slit of light near Eric's feet. On his knees there was just enough gap left under the blind for Eric to see Mavis open a pocketknife. What's the sly cow going to do with that? He didn't have to wait long to find out.

The blade thrust into the side of the mattress and slit the seam, opening it up like a skinned sheep. Eric's jaw unhinged. Mavis inserted one arm up to its pit and moved along the mattress, feeling as she went.

Caesar's bloody ghost! He hadn't gone that far. Nerves gave him the sudden urge to wee. He shifted his weight, but the sentinel board creaked another warning. Bugger! If she put her head out the window he would make a run for it. Hopefully, she wouldn't recognise him in the dark. He saw her stare at the window, head cocked to one side and brushing coils of horsehair off her sleeve. Eric drew to the side, flattening against the wall and listened. Body poised. After counting to seven he peeked under the blind again. In the flickering light he saw her take a long darning needle and a reel of cotton from a packet. She threaded it and began to sew up the slit in the mattress. He eased himself away from the window and tiptoed off the verandah.

The bedside lamp was on and Agatha Christie was winding up her plot. Lillian had her money on the waitress, though everything pointed to the butler. She didn't look up when Eric entered.

"We've got to do something." He combed his fingers through his hair. "Mavis is pulling Aunt Maggie's place apart. What if she finds something?"

Lillian coughed back a laugh. Perhaps she should put him

out of his misery and tell him what she'd found. She packed the thought away. "You gave the place a thorough going over and you didn't find anything."

"I didn't slice the bloody mattress open."

"Dear God!" But why was she surprised? Lillian stared at the worry grooves between Eric's eyebrows – the need for reassurance in his eyes – and wondered if he would have done the same. She came to the conclusion that he probably would have if he'd thought of it. "Well she'd better put everything back together. I'm not doing it. I hope no one saw you peeping through her window; it might take some explaining." Lillian giggled and went back to her book.

It puzzled Eric. How she could make a joke of it. "I'll buy you a washing machine if I find the money."

"I'll hold you to that." Her eyes slid back to the book, more from guilt than the need to find out who the murderer was. She tried to bend the creased corner out of the page.

He undressed, folded his clothes on a chair and got into bed. He squeezed her breast.

"That hurts." She pushed his hand away. "I have my monthlies." She didn't look up from the page.

The bed bounced when he flipped onto his side and reached to turn the light off. The movement made her feel nauseous. "Not yet; I've only got a couple of pages to go."

He jumped out of bed and grabbed his dressing gown. "You're bloody frigid!" The bedroom door slammed behind him. Lillian marked the page and put her book on the floor. She slipped her hand under the mattress and pulled out a half-eaten bar of chocolate, broke off two bits and tucked it back, then switched off the light. Lying in the dark, sucking on the chocolate, she thought about their sexual encounters. He was a thoughtless lover, taking what he wanted and never bothering if she was satisfied. His idea of a wife's role was servant to a man and sex was to be available whenever he wanted it and that was twice a day, every day, regardless of whether they fought or not. The only thing that held him off was her period or if he had another woman. And there had been plenty of them until Aunt Maggie had clumped him with her umbrella. Lillian fell asleep thinking about Aunt Maggie.

She woke in the morning with Eric banging around the room in a foul temper. It was to be expected, he hadn't had sex. She ignored him, her mind on the funeral preparations. Dawn lifted its skirts and showed a slash of orange, the colour of Aunt Maggie's knickers. Lillian watched it bloom into a new day without Aunt Maggie. She gazed at the sea and it was as flat as she felt. The Cadbury Roses tin sat on the kitchen table, empty. It was going to store a cake for the wake. Its earlier contents were tucked under Lillian's mattress, next to the bar of chocolate. If only Eric knew what he had been sleeping on. She gave a wry smile and her mind went to planning the day. The wake and the funeral would be perfect, just like Aunt Maggie wanted it. She had put her faith in Lillian, the only one in Eric's family ever to do so, and Lillian had something to prove.

She went into the kitchen and lit the fire in the stove and put the kettle on. Plans for the wake bubbled along with the tea water while she made porridge for the kids. Eric didn't speak to her. He didn't wait for the porridge. He took the cold leg of lamb from the fridge, inspected it with care and gnawed in silence. When he'd finished he wiped his hands on a tea towel and opened the kitchen door. Flies buzzed in.

"Will you be back before lunch?" Lillian asked, waving a tea towel at the intruders. Eric nodded and grumped out of the kitchen. Good riddance, Lillian thought. It wasn't her fault she had her period or that Mavis was as sneaky as him.

"Mum, can we go swimming?" Johnny sat down at the breakfast table dressed in his swimsuit with a towel draped around his neck. Splinter and Bubs joined him also in swimsuits with towels in hand.

"We want to go swimming at the wharf. All the kids from school will be there. We're going to have races. Can we?" Splinter pleaded. Lillian could do with Splinter's help. She eyed them thoughtfully. With the tension in the house it would be better to get them out of the way. One never knew what they might come out with in front of Mavis. It was going to be a hot day. The kitchen was already a buzz of flies. Lillian decided she would make some pancakes for lunch to put Eric in a better mood. His silences worked on her nerves. Tiptoeing around him when she had so much to think about would bring on a migraine. Lillian wondered how much he was going to bet this weekend. He'd probably try and talk Bookie Jim into taking the worm-eaten fivers he'd found in the oven. She hoped he'd have a win and not be surly towards Mavis and that Mavis wouldn't be too tired to help with the baking for the wake. The children fidgeted, waiting for her answer.

"You can go for a swim after you see if Aunty Mavis wants some breakfast."

"Thanks, Mum," they chorused. They gulped their breakfast and jammed through the door, elbows extended.

Puffy eyed, Mavis stood in Aunt Maggie's doorway looking at the three cheerful faces before her. She was exhausted; the night's search had revealed nothing and it had taken ages covering up her tracks. The last thing she wanted was to be surrounded by children, as much as she loved them.

"Do you want to come swimming with us, Aunty Mavis?" Johnny wanted to show her how well he could dive.

"No, pet, I'd like a nice quiet day."

"Mum said she'd make you brekkie if you want."

"Tell her I'll be over shortly."

"We're going to swim at the wharf if you want to come later." Johnny's eyes shone with hope.

"That's lovely, dear, but your mother might need some help. I'll see you when you get back." Mavis stifled a yawn, closed the door and wondered how she was going to get through the day. She had better do a final check to make sure everything was in order. She didn't want Eric accusing her of snooping, though she suspected he'd already been through everything. The silver scone platter was an indicator. Aunt Maggie had told her on her last visit that Lillian was getting the furniture but the silver and crystal couldn't be called furniture. Mavis made a note to discuss that at the will reading. She straightened the Dante Gabriel Rossetti print. It was nice and she liked the frame but she didn't have any wall space in her house. She'd checked the back to see if anyone had pulled it apart and resealed it but the dust and webs behind the picture proved it hadn't been moved in years. She hoped no one would notice it had been disturbed. If they did, she'd just say she banged into it in the dark. She gave her hair a comb and went to breakfast.

"Sleep well, Mavis?" Lillian lifted the kettle off the stove and poured boiling water into the teapot, noting the dark circles under Mavis's eyes. Serves her right for creeping around all night, Lillian thought.

"Not really. I couldn't stop thinking about dear old Aunt Maggie." She touched her nose with a lace handkerchief. It was the one Lillian had given Aunt Maggie. She had edged it with the lace she had bought in Georges.

I bet you couldn't, Lillian thought. She gave Mavis's hand a pat, jammed a thick slice of bread on the toasting fork and shoved it in front of the embers.

"Haven't you got a toaster?"

"Eric thinks they spoil the taste of the bread." The heat of

272

the fire added to Lillian's flush of annoyance. She would love a toaster.

Mavis tutted. Eric's meanness came from their father. She was happy she'd missed the trait. "Too paltry to buy one, you mean."

That was the pot calling the kettle black. Lillian swivelled, nailed Mavis with a look and then turned back to the fire.

Mavis gave a self-conscious cough. "So, how's the silver and china going to be divided?"

There had been no enquiries from Mavis as to how easy or difficult Aunt Maggie's passing had been, no show of sympathy. Aunt Maggie had been a trial but she'd also been Lillian's friend. "That, you'll have to ask Eric. Aunt Maggie left us the furnishings but I only want the sideboard and the chaise longue, and maybe the picture in the sunroom. I'd rather talk about it after the funeral." Tendrils of smoke rose from the bread. "Damn." Lillian pulled the toast away from the coals, scraped the charred area, turned it around and put it back in front of the embers.

"Don't worry, I like dark toast," Mavis twittered. A heavy silence settled in the room. Mavis pleated the edge of the tablecloth with her fingers. It was her duty to find out what was what and she wasn't going to be put off by Lillian. "I didn't see Aunt Maggie's jewellery box in her room." Mavis noticed Lillian frown. "Not that I was looking," she said hastily. "It was just that I needed somewhere to hang my dress and I know she kept it in the cupboard. The last time I visited she showed it to me and said she wanted me to have it. The jewellery of course, not just the box," Mavis allowed a break in her voice. "The dear old soul." When she dabbed her eyes the light caught her diamond rings and flared a rainbow.

Nothing caught the light on Lillian's work-worn hands. The thin gold ring of servitude looked bare as she took Mavis's toast off the fork. "The jewellery box is on my dressing table. I moved it in case someone broke into Aunt Maggie's house. Everyone in town knows the place is empty." And that was the first thing Eric had grabbed. They were as bad as each other, Lillian thought, giving a tight smile. The only piece of jewellery Lillian had ever valued was her own engagement ring. She hoped it would bring the butcher's apprentice more luck than it had her.

35

Tea Leaves and Coffins

The jewellery box sat open on the kitchen table and Mavis
sorted through the contents. "I'm not an admirer of her taste
in jewels but it's nice to have a keepsake. It will make me feel
she's near me." The diamond-bright fingers pulled Aunt Maggie's
handkerchief from her sleeve and dabbed her eyes.

Would it just. Lillian slapped a lump of butter on the toast
and clattered a plate in front of Mavis.

The smoky toast oozed butter and Mavis crunched into
it. "Mmm, Eric's right, it does taste nicer than in a toaster.
I wouldn't mind another piece."

Lillian wanted to tell Mavis to make her own toast, instead
she jammed a slice of bread on the fork and squatted in front of
the fire. A wicked urge nudged her. "Aunt Maggie was probably
near you last night," she said. A glow of satisfaction filled Lillian
when Mavis's head jerked up, toast halfway to her mouth.

"What do you mean she was near me?"

"Pardon? Oh, I sensed Aunt Maggie when I was cleaning her room. It unnerved me at first. I felt like her shadow had crept over me. I went really cold and then I had a lovely warm sensation of being hugged." Lillian checked the toast and pulled it off the fork. "I think Aunt Maggie came back to thank me for looking after her for so long. I wouldn't be a bit surprised if her spirit stays around for a while."

Mavis's eyes shot around the kitchen. "Where?"

Lillian tilted her head and looked reassuringly at Mavis. "Not here. I meant in her house, until after she's buried. I didn't say anything last night because I didn't want to frighten you. I'm glad she wasn't angry with me. Angry spirits attach themselves to people, you know." Lillian sucked her cheeks in to stop herself smiling at the startled look on Mavis's face. She put the toast on a plate, poured two cups of tea and pushed one towards Mavis. A spider knitted its web along the wall.

A tingle ran up Mavis's spine as she stared into her sister-in-law's dark eyes. Eric had told her Lillian went to tarot readings and read tea leaves for her German friend. He said Lillian had dreams that she claimed came true. Some of the dreams Lillian had written in depth to Mavis. Of course Mavis had never encouraged her and didn't refer to the dreams when she wrote back. That sort of mumbo jumbo attracted the devil. Mavis shivered and tried to ignore the prongs of curiosity that pricked her. But she couldn't help herself.

"Strange, I did have a sensation that someone was watching me last night. I even heard the verandah creak." A tremulous giggle escaped Mavis. She waved her hand as though dismissing the sheer ridiculousness of such a notion. If she'd been a Catholic, she would have crossed herself. It was Lillian's fault. God would understand and the devil had many disguises. The teacup shook in Mavis's hand. She sipped her tea, noticed Lillian's eyes on her cup and gripped it tighter. One time Lillian had read Mavis's tea leaves, an indulgence Mavis regretted, and saw a gravestone in her cup. Two days later Mavis's friend died.

When Lillian finished drinking her tea, she swirled the dregs around in the bottom of the cup and turned it upside down on her saucer. She righted the cup and peered into it. A smile of tea leaves greeted her. "That's a good omen." Lillian put the cup down.

Mavis rolled her eyes and drained her own cup, taking care to sieve the liquid through her lips so the tea leaves would stay behind.

Lillian held out her hand. "Let me have a look."

"Oh, really." Mavis tucked her chin in and crimped her lip, but handed her cup over anyway. Tea leaf reading was against the Jehovah's witness religion and she always made a point of telling Lillian before she offered up her cup. Today she forgot to mention it.

The full treatment was coming Mavis's way. Lillian placed her palm over the top of the cup, left it there for two minutes then rotated the cup three times to disperse the leaves in the bottom. The cup was then turned upside down with the handle pointing towards Mavis. Mavis hunched forward, hands clenched in her lap. Lillian strung Mavis out a few heartbeats longer and peered into the cup.

"Oh, dear!" She frowned, rotated the cup and viewed it from another angle.

Mavis's hands went clammy. "What?" She gave a derisive laugh and shifted in her seat. Lillian looked solemn.

"What?" Mavis tried to see over the rim.

"It's ... you've ... oh, nothing." Lillian pushed the cup away and gave a shudder.

What had Lillian seen? Was Aunt Maggie watching her? Should she ask? No, it was sinful!

The opposing forces wrestled on Mavis's face while Lillian struggled with the urge to laugh. She collected their cups and made for the washing-up bowl. Standing at the window, Lillian gazed out at the stretch of blue and stationary fishing boats. "Tch!" She scratched at the window. "Damn flies, they leave their dirt everywhere." She picked up a tea towel and rubbed the window, clamping Mavis in her peripheral vision.

Head bowed, Mavis tapped her heart and her lips moved in silent prayer. *Thou knowest this to be the work of the devil, oh Lord. Free us from our sins.*

Got her. Lillian's scheme was bearing fruit. She picked up Mavis's cup again, felt her tense, pressed back a smile and stared into the cup. She turned to Mavis and gave her a penetrating look, opening her mouth to say something. Mavis stiffened and Lillian held her gaze and then closed her mouth with a worried frown. The look on Mavis's face, as she was about to receive her fate, nearly undid Lillian. She turned away and wiped the door of the refrigerator. Now that the fish was on the hook she was going to land it. Mavis had earned this and it would work to Eric's advantage even though he hadn't supported her over Aunt Maggie's coffin.

Loyalty was something Eric was missing when it came to Lillian. He discussed her with his siblings and it galled her. He never took her side and made them think she was a crackpot because of her interest in religions. Mavis couldn't talk; a Jehovah's Witness had converted her on her doorstep. If she spilt salt she threw it over her left shoulder and she cried if she broke a mirror, so who was the crackpot? It was payback time and Lillian was enjoying watching Mavis squirm. She put the cup in the washing-up bowl and looked across at Aunt Maggie's kitchen window. She craned forward and frowned. "Did you lock up when you left?"

"Yes, I think so." The hair frosted on the back of Mavis's neck. "Why?"

Lillian shook her head and laughed. "My eyes must be playing tricks on me. I thought I saw someone at Aunt Maggie's window." There was a muffled squeal from Mavis. Lillian felt a rush of satisfaction and continued to stare at Aunt Maggie's.

"Would you mind if I moved over here for the next few days?" It was the second time Mavis had said it. She scraped her chair on the floor to get Lillian's attention.

Lillian turned, eyes soft with sympathy. "Did you say something? Sorry, I was somewhere else."

Mavis drew a deep breath. "I'd like to stay here if you don't mind. Not that sleeping at Aunt Maggie's bothers me although it is more convenient having electricity." She fiddled with the rings on her finger.

"Of course I don't mind. You can have Johnny's room. He can sleep on the settee." Lillian put her arm around Mavis and gave her a squeeze.

They look pretty cosy, Eric thought, as he entered the kitchen. He wondered what they'd been talking about while he had been out coffin hunting. You couldn't trust women. He'd had a good morning, won twenty quid and found a coffin. Two wins in one day, not bad. And there was more to come when the will was read. But it didn't alter how pissed off he still was with Mavis.

"Morning, Mavis. Sleep well?" His tone was sarcastic and his eyes icy. She looked pretty ragged. Eric smirked. He'd got out of bed a few times and saw a candle moving from room to room behind Aunt Maggie's blinds. The good thing was Mavis didn't look chirpy. He knew her well enough to know she couldn't disguise the thrill of finding some money, however tired she was. But it didn't make up for having spent half the morning trying to sort out the coffin problem. If it had been up to him,

Aunt Maggie would have got her wish. Waste of bloody money burying good wood.

"Mavis is going to sleep here tonight," Lillian said casually. She added some more hot water to the teapot and poured a cup for Eric.

"Really?" Eric's eyes narrowed. He was about to reply, when he saw Lillian raise an eyebrow with an imperceptible nod. What was going on? He wasn't very good at the subtleties of body language. He took out his pipe and gave it a suck to clear the stem and buy some time.

"What for?"

"She thinks Aunty Maggie was watching her last night." Lillian winked as she handed him a cup of tea. Eric examined his pipe.

"That has nothing to do with it. I'm scared of falling asleep and not blowing the candle out." Mavis sat straight-backed, hands clasped in her lap.

"Well I'll be blowed. Why do you think Aunt Maggie was watching you?"

Mavis squirmed, remembering how she and Eric had made fun of Lillian behind her back. Were they doing it to her? "It's nothing, just a feeling I had. I'm probably thinking about Aunty too much." She took refuge in her handkerchief and blew her nose.

Eric grimaced and stirred a second spoonful of sugar in his cup. He knew his sister was trying to work out how she could get her greedy hands on Aunt Maggie's money. It was good she was moving in with them. He'd be able to check Aunt Maggie's ceiling undisturbed. Eric realised Lillian was behind Mavis's decision. She was pretty astute sometimes; he'd give her that. "I wouldn't put anything past Aunt Maggie. She certainly didn't like visitors. Tried to kill Plonko Bill, didn't she?" He grinned inwardly and watched his sister over the rim of his cup.

A shiver went through Mavis. It was hard not to believe in

ghosts in this town of her childhood holidays; where sightings of the murdered orca that plagued Plonko's inebriated nights, were said to bring disaster. She had dreamt about the creature last night and wondered if a dream counted as a sighting. A cold sweat made her blue and white striped dress stick to her back. *Dear Lord, free me from superstition. Cleanse me of my sins.* The sooner she was out of Aunt Maggie's house, the better.

"Perhaps you'll help me bring my stuff over today, Eric?"

"Glad to, Mavis. By the way, I've just found a coffin that could solve our problems. Remember old Tiny Rob, Lil? His family had a special coffin made because he was so big and then he came out of his coma?" Lillian gave a curt nod. "Well I did a bit of negotiating and the undertaker said we could have it at a good price."

How dare he! Lillian seethed. "You're burying Aunt Maggie in a second hand coffin. Is that any better than burying her in her own?"

"It's being delivered here this arvo."

"Here?" Mavis and Lillian said in unison.

"Yep. It's big enough to fit Aunt Maggie's coffin inside and that way she will be buried in her own coffin, and look respectable." His head wobbled with genius. Lillian turned her back on Eric and felt on top of the fridge for the Bex. "I'll have to put them together here and then take the coffin to the undertakers where they will load Aunt Maggie's body."

It wasn't long after lunch when the horn blared, announcing the arrival of the coffin. Lillian watched Eric guide the truck down Aunt Maggie's drive from the kitchen window and wished it was Eric being buried.

The truck jerked to a stop. The cabin door swung open and Cocksie's small frame followed his oversized boots onto the ground. "I'll need a hand unloadin' this, mate. It's a real blighter."

The top plate of his false teeth dropped onto his lower lip, pushed out and sucked back to emphasise the difficulty.

The huge mahogany coffin had ornate gold handles. Aunt Maggie would have hated that, Lillian thought. She opened the kitchen window to eavesdrop.

"She's a beauty," Eric said proudly. "My aunt would have been happy with this." He was going to kill two birds with one stone. His shoulders squared.

"Must have cost you a packet, mate. Pretty generous." Cocksie's teeth moved as he spoke.

"The least I can do for her, sport. I've looked after her for years." Eric shone with goodness.

Lillian wished she could kick him square up the arse. She saw Johnny and Splinter walk around the truck and was about to call them in when she thought better of it. Rather not let Eric know she could hear them.

Johnny eyed the handles. "Are they real gold?"

"Aunt Maggie won't be too fat for that," Splinter said.

"We'll need a ramp to slide him off," Cocksie said.

"Come on, let's see what they're doing," Mavis said, pulling Lillian away from the window. Reluctantly Lillian left her post.

As they approached, Eric swept his arm towards the coffin and made a mock bow. "Ladies, behold the royal box." A multitude of expressions collided on the faces of the two women.

"She won't like you using that," Lillian snapped, pointing at the Persian carpet they intended to slide the coffin on. If only Eric had backed her up instead of giving in to Mavis. The coward.

Mavis walked around the truck. "Heavens, it's enormous."

Eric checked his fingernails. "Aunt Maggie's coffin will fit inside it."

Lillian wasn't placated. She gazed at the spectacle. "That'll never fit in the hearse."

Eric's grin disappeared. It hadn't occurred to him that the

hearse could be a problem. Trust Lillian to put a dampener on it. She was right, though. They would never get it in the back of a hearse. He tugged his ear.

"We could decorate the truck like they do on Anzac Day for all the wounded soldiers and carry it on that," Splinter said.

There's a possibility, bright little girl. "I was just thinking the same thing, Splinter." Eric turned to Cocksie. "You up for the truck then?" Cocksie's truck didn't rattle and smoke like Eric's.

"You can't be serious." Lillian glared at Splinter.

Cocksie hitched his testicles. An unfortunate habit he had when women were present and he never knew what to do with his hands. "Sure, mate. Cost ya, though."

"Where will you get enough flowers to cover the back?" Mavis sneered. It was ridiculous and she was glad she lived in Sydney.

The muscle in Eric's jaw twitched. "We could get some wattle from the bush. It's only to cover the truck. There'll be wreaths inside the church." He watched lines compress on his sister's forehead and saw the slight shrug of annoyance she always gave when she didn't have a comeback. He grinned into the stem of his pipe.

"Wattle?" Lillian spat. "Aunt Maggie was allergic to wattle."

Eric's eyes narrowed, "Well she isn't now," he snapped. Mavis grabbed Lillian's arm and nodded towards the house. She knew her brother's temper. And Aunt Maggie's ghost wasn't going to blame her for this charade.

36

Coffin Fit

The lip around the inside of Tiny's coffin was a problem. So was the lid that didn't go back far enough to allow Aunt Maggie's coffin to go inside. And Lillian enjoyed every truck-thumping, tyre-kicking curse that came out of Eric, as he battled to fit the coffins together. She heard Eric apologise for banging the truck's roof with his fist, and watched Cocksie check it for a dent. Hiring Cocksie's truck had irked Eric. He'd always referred to Cocksie as having a window missing from his top storey, yet Cocksie wasn't the one with the dilapidated heap parked on the road. If Mavis hadn't been busy going through Aunt Maggie's crystal, she might have questioned Lillian's sanity had she seen her giggling at the window. "It serves him right, Aunt Maggie," Lillian said under her breath. She really should get on with making cakes for the wake and was about to close the window when Eric yelled.

"Another two quid! That's robbery it's not even dented."
He aimed a boot at the coffin. "Bugger you, Mavis!" Had Eric
looked towards the kitchen window, Lillian's smile would have
sliced him in half, but his attention suddenly diverted towards
the back fence. He raised his arm and jumped off the truck and
disappeared from Lillian's view.

Antenna up, Lillian hurried outside on the pretext of picking
flowers to see what was going on. The wife of the headmaster
was at the fence passing on her condolences to Eric. Lillian knew
she should go over and join them, make small talk to let Eric
know she was onto them, but she didn't have the courage, scared
he would say something to demean her, like blaming her for the
coffin debacle. She filled the watering can and observed without
being noticed. Their heads were close as they chatted. Embers
fanned in Lillian's heart. A leopard doesn't change its spots, she
thought, and now Aunt Maggie's no longer a deterrent, this was
how it was going to be again. The headmaster's wife disappeared
and Eric went back to his coffin problem. Lillian walked over to
the truck.

"How's it going," she said.

"I'm going to take the base out of Tiny's coffin and fit it over
Aunt Maggie's, then put the base back," Eric said.

"Why don't you just give up and do what Aunt Maggie wants
and blow what Mavis thinks."

"I've paid good money for Tiny. I've got it sorted." Eric
inclined his head towards the house. "Haven't you enough to do
in the kitchen?"

"It won't work. I've got a feeling." Lillian wasn't going to be
dismissed.

"What would you know," he said with a pained look.

"You'll see," she said with a lift of her chin. She didn't know
what he'd see, but he'd see something. She went back to her
garden and pulled at a few weeds, still within hearing range.

Eric shook his head at Cocksie. "Women! Bloody interfere in everything. Especially Poms," he said loudly. He picked up the hammer and banged into the base. One of the boards split. "Shit!" Lillian had jinxed him.

Cocksie shifted his teeth. "You can't use that plank again, mate."

Furious, Eric stamped the base out, cracking another board. "Let's just fit the blighter over."

The veins bulged on Eric's forehead. They couldn't lift Tiny higher than Cocksie's knees. "Shit a brick! You'll have to put the mongrel down, it's too bloody heavy." Eric stood back and observed the coffin in silence. Lillian tossed a few weeds in the air.

"We could take it down the wharf and get one of the tuna boats to winch 'er over," Cocksie said.

Eric thumped his forehead with the palm of his hand. "I've got a block and tackle in the shed."

When the truck reversed into Eric's shed Lillian stood at the entrance with her arms folded.

The gleaming mahogany box dropped over Aunt Maggie's old bedstead like they'd been made for each other. Eric turned towards Lillian. "See," he gloated.

Her shoulders sagged. Why couldn't it have worked out in her favour just once? They turned the coffin on its side and Eric nailed two palings lengthwise along the bottom. No one would see the underneath if it was carried by the handles. Eric patted the coffin, pleased with himself.

Lillian tilted her head to the side, thoughtful. "What are you going to do with it tonight? The undertaker's closed." When you die I'm going to give you a Viking funeral. All I'll need is a boat, she thought.

The muscle in Eric's jaw went to work. He didn't miss the edge of triumph in her voice. When Mavis goes, he was going to let Lillian know who was boss. She didn't have Aunt Maggie to hide behind now. He looked across at Cocksie. "We could swap trucks. It's just one night?"

Cocksie eyed Eric's wreck and chewed his falsies. "O'right, but it'll cost ya."

"Give me a minute and I'll get your dough." He turned to Lillian. "Is Mavis in the kitchen?

Lillian nodded. Her day had improved. She hummed as she followed Eric.

Reluctantly, Mavis pulled the purse from her bag. "This wouldn't have happened in Sydney." She held the note tight so Eric had to snatch it from her hand.

"Ingrate," he said. He read Lillian's smirk as agreement and crumpled the ten-pound note in his fist. He wrote a note to the undertaker and strode outside. Cocksie left with the tenner and the letter to the undertaker. Eric felt proud, he'd managed everything perfectly, Lillian couldn't complain now. But something was already on the boil in Lillian's pot.

That night, to ensure Eric slept well, Lillian crushed three sleeping pills in his rice pudding and to make sure, stunned him with a rollicking session of sex that Eric took as recognition of his superior problem solving abilities. Then armed with a torch and a leg of lamb, Lillian made for the shed. Jess wagged her tail and went to work on the lamb while Lillian surveyed the coffin. It taunted her from the back of the truck – for two pins she'd pick up that crowbar and smash it to pieces.

37

A Weighty Problem

The dining room table looked a treat. Aunt Maggie's best china gleamed in the centre of the white linen cloth. Iced cakes sat on silver cake stands good enough for royalty. Egg and parsley sandwiches, cucumber and vegemite, cheese and tomato, corned beef and pickle, filled Aunt Maggie's Victorian silver platters. Crystal glasses surrounded the sparkling decanter, full to its brim with brandy. Aunt Maggie would be so proud, Lillian thought, looking across at the chaise longue Eric had carried over. He'd wanted to dump it but Lillian wanted to remember Aunt Maggie and it looked nice in the sitting room. She could see her lying there, nodding with approval. It was going to be the best funeral ever. Just like Aunt Maggie wanted. Except for the coffin. Lillian's plan hadn't worked and she regretted the sex.

"Johnny, Splinter, Bubs, come in here and let me have a look at you." They jostled through the door, pressed seams, starched organdie and mirror shoes. Lillian licked her fingers and patted Johnny's hair. He pulled away and tugged at the crotch of his shorts, he was fourteen, too old for short pants. Lillian smacked his hand. "Don't do that."

"They're tight."

"You can put up with it for a couple of hours. Loosen your braces and pull your shorts down a bit."

"How do I look, Mum?"

"Lovely, Splinter. Doesn't she, Mavis?"

"Very nice indeed." Mavis put her hand up to her neck and touched Aunt Maggie's locket. The gold bangles on her wrist clinked.

Lillian's eyes narrowed. She could have waited. "Where's Eric?"

"Trimming the wattle for the truck which should be back from the undertaker's any minute." Mavis couldn't wait for the day to be over.

"Right." Lillian would make herself scarce. The thought of the truck being decorated in their yard while Aunt Maggie lay in the coffin on the back, wasn't something she wanted anything to do with. Her nerves were already on edge. She eyed her children. "Now, make sure you behave yourselves. No running around outside the church and definitely no giggling. Just remember, everyone will be looking at us today." The realisation filled her with apprehension. Better take a Bex to get through the funeral. Lillian mixed the powder in a cup and brought it to her lips. She knew she shouldn't take it. That she needed to be present for the funeral, not off with the fairies. Aunt Maggie always said she was a daydreamer and didn't like it. She tipped the Bex out. Today she was going to be aware of everything. Lillian took a compact out of her handbag and dabbed her nose. "I suppose it's time to go, then."

Vases of roses, hand-picked and arranged by Lillian, lined the altar, their perfume an offering to God. Tears filled Lillian's eyes, as she looked around the church pews, solid with townsfolk. There wasn't much entertainment in the town and a good funeral was always welcome. It gave the women an opportunity to show off their best dresses and the single men could check out bride prospects.

A horn signalled the arrival of the coffin. The organist pulled out the stoppers and pushed her feet into the bellows. It reminded Splinter of Puss kneading his paws in Aunt Maggie's lap.

The truck was done up like a float in a whale festival. The coffin, taking up most of the truck's tray, sat in a bed of golden wattle. Ten men lined up to unload it. Plonko, dressed in an army uniform and a chest full of medals, swung both the church doors open. Today, he would stay sober. He felt a bit responsible, even though the old girl had been the victim of friendly fire.

At the sound of the door opening Lillian turned and looked outside. A crush of disappointment filled her at the sight of the coffin. "Sorry, Aunty," she said under her breath. A handkerchief fluttered at the corner of her eye. She looked at the waver. The headmaster's wife gave her a sympathetic smile. Lillian forced her lips up in acknowledgement. Hypocrite. She turned her attention to the truck outside. Eric stood on the back, instructing the men, full of importance. He looked handsome in his new suit, the heir of a rich old lady. Lillian screwed her handkerchief in her lap and watched.

"Right, let's get this mule moving." Eric commanded.

There were eight men hauling on the rope while Eric and Cocksie struggled amongst the wattle, nearly horizontal as they pushed with their shoulders, grunting like constipated bulls.

When the coffin was off the truck, five pallbearers lined up either side and grabbed the gold rails, hands red from rope burns.

"Ready, on the count of three." Jaws clenched, biceps taut,

they lifted the coffin free of the ground, took a breath and marched towards the church steps.

Constable Sluggo turned to Eric. "It won't clear the steps. Better to get it up on our shoulders. We can carry more weight that way."

Eric glowered. Sluggo could go and root himself. The price of the rustled calf and heifer was coming out of his inheritance. It had been the only way Eric had got Sluggo to close his investigation of the gun and keep his mouth shut. There was no way he was taking orders from Sluggo. "A couple of us can get underneath and lift it clear of the steps with our backs."

Sluggo looked pained. "Only a bloody drongo would do that." The pallbearers all nodded in agreement. Eric's neck reddened.

Cocksie munched on his teeth. "Ya know, mate, no one will see the shitty underneath if we all keep together. Our heads will be in the way."

Seething inwardly, Eric agreed. "Alright, but keep close, boys. We had an accident and I had to do a quick repair." As they heaved the coffin onto their shoulders, Fraser Bigall, the local carpenter, snuck a look at the base. The mesh and planks of wood reminded him of his chicken run.

"Onward Christian soldiers, marching as to war," the congregation sang. They watched the ten sweating pallbearers weave down the aisle.

Lillian bowed her head. She had failed Aunt Maggie. She wiped her tears. The pallbearers reached the front of the church and stood to attention, knees trembling, coffin biting into their shoulder pads and waited for the hymn to finish. At the last 'Amen', a sound, like nails being pulled by a claw hammer, squealed above the hushed bowed heads. One end of Eric's planks pulled free of its nails and clattered to the floor. A gash of bed mesh squeezed through the gap like the guts of a slaughtered cow. Suppliant heads shot upright and swivelled towards the coffin. A congregation of gaping mouths depleted the oxygen with uniform gasps. Lillian's eyes widened in horror.

A loud crack filled the church and Eric's other support gave up under the strain. They dangled under Tiny's coffin like two broken legs. Aunt Maggie's red satin mattress on its wire-mesh base sagged through the bottom and rested Aunt Maggie's buttocks on the floor.

"Look, it's Aunty." Bubs yelled, standing up on her seat.

Lillian grasped the back of her seat and rose halfway to her feet. "My Lord!"

Kids clambered up on their seats to have a look. Heads ducked and wove behind large hats to get a better view. Sybil Tomkins' eyes rolled back in her head and she collapsed onto the floor. Her husband pushed her under the pew to avoid being trodden on and climbed on the seat next to his son.

A high-pitched wail escaped Mavis. This was the worst experience of her life.

Lillian observed the congregation as though she was watching a stage performance. Aunt Maggie was getting a standing ovation. Everyone was standing on the seats. She watched the pallbearers stagger around trying to gain control of the coffin. Lillian covered a hysterical giggle with her handkerchief.

"Put the bloody thing down," Eric hissed, his muscles screaming under the weight.

Cocksie's bandy legs became the mouth of a cave. "I can't. Me fuckin' coat's caught on the handle." The congregation gasped.

"Bluey, put your end down."

"If I do, that loose paling might spear someone's feet, mate."

Eric's face was puce. "I don't give a fucking dingo's arse. I can't hold it up any more," he shouted. Some parents covered their children's ears, but Eric was beyond caring. "Jim, you and the boys lower it your side." Eric tottered sidewards and the nine pallbearers stumbled after him.

Dumbfounded mourners squashed to the end of their pews to avoid being slammed by the coffin. It was a battering ram gone wild. Cocksie tugged at his coat and the coffin smashed against his shoulder, sprawling him to the floor. The pallbearers lost their balance and let the coffin go. It hit the floor with a thunderclap, landing on its side. Aunt Maggie bulged through the bottom like a popped boil and the congregation screamed. Splinter buried her face in Lillian and Johnny led a rush towards the coffin to get a better look. Constable Sluggo took off his jacket and covered Aunt Maggie. The organist struck up *Swing Low Sweet Chariot* in an effort to calm the people.

Cocksie rolled in the aisle nursing his arm. "Me bloody arm's broke."

The minister closed his gaping mouth, put his bible down and stepped forward. "Now boys, mind the language, you're in the house of God."

"I don't give a fuck 'oose 'ouse I'm in, you fuckin' shit chimney, me bloody arm's broke."

Eric, close to vomiting with embarrassment, jumped on a pew and waved at the crowd. "Everyone out. Only men who can help, stay." He looked across at Mavis, whose hailstone tears were soaking Lillian's shoulder, and harpooned her with his eyes. It's all her bloody fault.

Lillian knew that accusatory look. It was usually directed at her. If only he knew what she had done. She hadn't meant to sabotage the funeral and turn it into a farce. In fact, when she'd loosened Eric's planks with the crowbar, she thought it would come apart at the funeral parlour and force Eric to bury Aunt Maggie in her own coffin.

"Come on, kids," Lillian said, pushing them ahead of her while she led sobbing Mavis outside with the rest of the mourners. The crowd increased while they waited for the funeral to continue. Inside, the church echoed with banging.

Hearing the laughter and noticing the growing crowd, Lillian remembered her words to Aunt Maggie: "I want the children to respect death, not make fun of it."

Mavis clutched Lillian and sobbed into her handkerchief. "I'll never show my face in this town again," she moaned.

"Shut up, Mavis!" Lillian shrugged her off and reached into the store of promises she had made an anxious old lady. "You kids stay here with Aunty Mavis while I go inside and see what they're doing in there."

Lillian marched up to the closed church doors. Plonko swung them open and bowed her through. The two coffins were separated and Fraser Bigall was inspecting the bottom of Tiny's coffin to see how he could mend it. Lillian walked over to Eric. "What's going on?"

"We're going to bury Aunt Maggie in Tiny's coffin."

"You'll do no such thing." She elbowed her way into the centre of the men grouped around the coffin. Incredulous, Eric stared after her. "Aunt Maggie will be buried in her own coffin as she wished. Fix the base on her coffin." The men all looked at Eric for direction. "Don't look at him, Aunt Maggie legally appointed me to carry out her last wishes. This has happened because no one listened to me."

"You'll be breaking the law if it's been stipulated in a legal document, Eric," Constable Sluggo said, enjoying the moment.

Eric gave Lillian a withering look. "If you think you can do better, go ahead."

The red satin lining caught Lillian's eye. "Constable Sluggo, if we could borrow the flag from the police station we could drape it over the coffin."

"Splendid idea." Sluggo ran to do her bidding. The Pom had brains.

Twenty minutes later the minister appeared on the church steps and addressed the crowd. "Thank you for your patience.

Please make your way to the cemetery. We are reconvening at the gravesite."

Aunt Maggie in her homemade coffin, carried on the shoulders of six men, came out of the church draped in an Australian flag. She was loaded onto Cocksie's truck and driven by Eric through the town to the cemetery with Cocksie nursing his shoulder at his side. Lillian rode in the front of the police car. Mavis sat in the back squashed between the children. People with cars followed, stopping to pick up interested townsfolk on the way. Others saluted the flag as it passed. It was the biggest funeral in Eden.

At the wake, one of the CWA women asked Lillian if she'd go on their planning committee.

38

The Will

The solicitor, Peter Turnstile, a tall thin man in his fifties, had the look of a mortician, as he stood by the door in his black suit. He shook Mavis's hand and showed her to one of the three seats in front of his over-large desk. "My condolences at the loss of your aunt, she was an interesting woman." An image of Aunt Maggie taking a wad of worm eaten ten-pound notes from a biscuit tin and paying his account floated before him.

"Thank you, Mr Turnstile, she meant a lot to me." Mavis dabbed a dry eye with one of Aunt Maggie's lace handkerchiefs.

When Eric and Lillian had taken their seats next to Mavis, Peter Turnstile flashed a gold-toothed smile beneath a thin moustache and settled down for another boring day. "Let us proceed." He opened the file in front of him and withdrew a document then peered at the three faces before him over the top of horn-rimmed spectacles. "This is the Last Will and

Testament of Margaret Elizabeth Stewart. I appoint as my executor my solicitor Peter Turnstile to carry out my wishes as follows in regards to my assets, including my two properties at Number 6 and Number 8 Sea View Street. It is my wish that my house, Number 8 Sea View Street, is to be divided between my nephews and nieces … "

Mavis stopped dabbing her nose with her handkerchief and leant forward. The solicitor must have missed a line, she thought. "Excuse me, what about the other three houses she owns in Sea View Street?" she asked.

The expression on Peter Turnstile's face was long suffering; there was one at every will reading. He tapped his fingers on the desk. "Mrs Stewart sold the other properties over a period of years prior to her death. She's been living off the proceeds. Now, if you don't mind, I'll continue."

Mavis whirled on Eric. "Why didn't you say something? Why didn't you tell me? You could have declared her incompetent!"

Eric's mouth hung open; he'd been as surprised as Mavis. All he could do was shake his head.

"May I proceed, madam?" Peter Turnstile frowned at Mavis and returned to the will. "The abode at Number 6 Sea View Street, currently occupied by my nephew, Eric and his family …" Eric squared his shoulders and smiled. "… I leave to his wife, Lillian, in its entirety."

Eric shot to his feet. "What! Lillian? How? That's not legal she's my wife. Aunt Maggie's made a mistake."

Peter Turnstile pursed his lips. "These are the wishes of the deceased. Now, if you will kindly sit down and allow me to proceed."

A ship pulled into the harbour of Lillian's mind, waiting for her to get on board. Had she heard right? The storm in Eric's eyes told her it was true. She actually owned her own home. Apprehension filled Lillian. There would be a row over this later, for sure. She would have to keep her wits about her. No more Bex, she vowed. She sat back stunned.

"To my great-niece, Louise, alias Splinter, I leave my red bloomers and lace shawl for future ballets. I also leave her my gold locket …"

"No!" Mavis clutched the locket around her throat. It was the most valuable piece in Aunt Maggie's jewel box.

The solicitor's head snapped up. "Enough! Any more interruptions and you'll have to make another appointment and pay for it." He glared at Mavis. Her head shook with indignation. "To my great-nephew, Johnny, I leave the Persian carpet he wiped his feet on, my gun and tools. To my great-niece, Maureen, alias Bubs, I leave my eggshell tea set, tapestry cushion with the camel on it and five pounds to buy a fishing rod."

"Ridiculous, you can tell the woman was incompetent. I'm going to contest the will." Mavis gave the still gaping Eric a look that could gut a whale.

"And …" Peter Turnstile said loudly, "my two final requests are that I shall be buried in the coffin I built and that Lillian will transplant the roses by my back door into her rose garden."

Lillian's eyes opened wide as Aunt Maggie's bequest dawned on her. The roses by the back door were where she had found the money. Aunt Maggie had left Lillian her money in secret. Lillian had been left the bulk of Aunt Maggie's estate. She valued me. She cared. Lillian pulled a handkerchief out of her sleeve and mopped her eyes. Peter Turnstile nodded approvingly at her.

"Tch!" Mavis crossed her ankles and jiggled her foot. Lillian hadn't reacted to the house news, so why all this emotion over roses? She never did have her feet on the ground. Fancy snivelling over roses.

Lillian and Aunt Maggie had forged their relationship over their rose gardens. Lillian had dug while Aunt Maggie knelt beside her on a sugar bag, pulling weeds from the garden bed.

"That's enough for today. I think we've earned a cuppa." Lillian always noticed when Aunt Maggie was getting tired. They'd pack up the gardening and go inside. Lillian would make tea, while Aunt Maggie settled herself on the chaise longue. They would have their cuppa and chat.

"Did you buy the latest Yates catalogue, Aunt Maggie?"

"I did and we'll keep it here. I don't want Eric throwing it away. I also bought you a *Women's Weekly*."

"You're a brick, Aunt Maggie. I'll hide that at home. There's a good competition in it this week."

Lillian and Aunt Maggie poured over the Yates catalogue and sipped their tea. "That's the same rose as the one Mum had in her garden in England."

"Write the catalogue number down."

"Thank you, Aunt Maggie, what are you choosing?"

"I want a red rose like the one on the Cadbury's tin."

Lillian turned the page and pointed. "They look the same, what do you think?"

"Put me down for two bushes."

The order was filled out and tallied up. "That comes to three pounds ten." Lillian said.

"I'll give you the money for a postal note tomorrow and you can send it off."

They would grin at each other like a couple of naughty kids. Then Aunt Maggie would want her reward. She'd lean back with her hands folded in her lap, eyes sparkling, and say: "Now, tell me about that floozy waitress again or Cora." She loved Lillian's stories about Eric's infidelities and Lillian enjoyed having a sympathetic ear. Aunt Maggie was the only one she'd told her secrets to and likewise Aunt Maggie had shared some of her own.

The reading of the will had stopped while Lillian's tears flowed. Tears of gratitude, relief and loss.

Mavis gave Lillian's shoulder a sharp poke. "This is ridiculous. Pull yourself together." Jealousy was eating Mavis.

The sting in Mavis's voice cut into Lillian's memories. She turned red swollen eyes on Mavis. Pinch-lipped disapproval smacked back at her. Embers of injustice from years of ridicule by Eric's family fanned into a fire. Lillian leapt to her feet and stood over Mavis. "How dare you sit in judgment of me, you shallow avaricious cow. What do you know about my feelings or the relationship I had with Aunt Maggie? Don't think for a minute she didn't know you were only nice to her because you wanted her money. Despite what you think, she was a clever old woman. If she left Splinter the locket it was because Aunt Maggie loved her. Splinter visited her every day, not once a year. She did her shopping, danced and read for her. All my children have done more for her than you ever have."

Mavis looked like she'd put her finger in a light socket. Her mouth dropped open with shock. Outrage reddened her face. "They were well paid, no doubt." Her voice dripped with sarcasm.

Lillian's eyes bored into Mavis. "Trust you to think that. Not everyone's the same as you. I know Aunt Maggie paid your bus fare when you came to visit. My children acted out of kindness. The gifts she left my children and me are gifts of appreciation. Aunt Maggie was my friend: a much better friend than you ever were. Don't think I don't know how you laughed behind my back to your sisters. Eric told me you think I dabble with the devil."

Mavis's eyes tightened the perfectly ironed collar around Eric's neck. Red-faced, he looked across at the solicitor, eyes pleading for a call to order. But Peter Turnstile was noticing the claret lights in Lillian's hair and the majestic height of her chin.

Eric put his hand on Lillian's arm in a feeble attempt to calm her. "I know Aunt Maggie's death has been hard on you, Lil. On all of us." As soon as he said 'us' he regretted it.

"Hard on you two! Don't make me laugh. The pair of you ransacked her house before she went in the ground. Mavis even slit the mattress open and sewed it up again. You told me you saw her through the window."

Mavis spun on Eric. "You sneak!"

"Don't call me a sneak. You took all Mother's jewellery. You knew Howard sold the farm. He paid you to look after Mother. Did he tell you what they did to Father?" The colour drained from Mavis's face.

Lillian put her hand on Eric's arm. "That's not the issue here. You can sort that out between yourselves later." Lillian wasn't going to get side-tracked by Eric's father's death.

"The issue here is that you two don't think I deserve to inherit anything and yet I was the one who took care of Aunt Maggie. She was my friend." How much of a friend Lillian hadn't realised. "The only friend you didn't try and mount," she said, turning hot eyes on Eric.

Eric put a finger inside his collar and stretched his neck. There was something in Lillian's eyes he hadn't seen before. It made him nervous. He dug at a mark on the carpet with the toe of his black polished shoe. Mavis grabbed her handbag and rummaged through it like a mad woman then withdrew a handkerchief and blew her nose. Silence filled the room.

Peter Turnstile emerged from the furniture and shuffled the papers on his desk. "I believe that's the end of the reading." It was all he could think to say. Lillian was quite a woman.

With a toss of her head, Mavis got up and strode towards the door.

"Just a minute, Mavis." Lillian's voice lassoed her exit. "I think you have something that belongs to Splinter." Mavis went rigid. Without turning, her hands rose to her neck and unclasped the locket. She held it out to Lillian. "Thank you, Mavis." Lillian took the locket.

The following day Mavis departed. There was no wave of her hand as the bus pulled away. She sat in her seat, tight lipped, clutching her bag and looking straight ahead. In her mind she saw Lillian and Aunt Maggie cosy together. How could she not have seen it before? To think that Aunt Maggie had never claimed a pension or had a bank account and Eric had never done anything about it. All those years Mavis had visited the ungrateful old witch. Even if Aunt Maggie had paid her fare, it was a long tiring trip from Sydney to Eden. She bet those two connivers wheedled all the money out of Aunt Maggie. Mavis fished in her handbag for heartburn lozenges.

There hadn't been many words exchanged between Eric and Lillian since the reading of the will. A sick hollow feeling lived in Eric's chest. He'd gone over the previous day in his mind so many times and still had trouble believing it. A brown scum had formed on top of his cup of tea and he chewed the stem of his unlit pipe. What could he do? He carried his cup of tea into the lounge room where Lillian was polishing Aunt Maggie's sideboard.

It had him jiggered that his own aunt would leave this house to his wife. It was demeaning. He'd have to win Lillian around. His share from Aunt Maggie's house wouldn't be much after it had been divided between him and his six siblings. The realisation that he might not have enough to buy the farm was like a kick in the guts. If he could get Lillian to sell the house, she'd have to put the money in his bank account. She didn't have one of her own. He quelled his panic and told himself to take it easy. Use the old charm. He'd still get what was rightfully his. He wasn't going to miss out, again.

39

Who Cared?

The news blared on the wireless – Princess Elizabeth was going to be crowned in Westminster Abbey in June. It would be exciting to be in England now, Lillian thought. She twiddled the knob and found some music. The muscle in Eric's jaw tightened. He liked to listen to the news during meal times. It covered up the sound of the children chewing. It was his wireless and Lillian had moved it into the sitting room. He quelled his annoyance and nuzzled around the subject he wanted to raise and decided on a direct approach.

"I can't understand why Aunt Maggie didn't just leave the house to me. What was the point of giving it to you? You can sign it over to me; I'll speak to the lawyer next week. I'm the breadwinner, damn it."

"What's the difference who owns it? We still live together. I've never owned anything of value. Not a washing machine, not a bed, a sideboard, a chair." She paused and shook her head. "Not even a bloody chamber pot. Everything we've got has been leftovers from your family and most of it, worm-eaten." She put a doily under the decanter.

His jaw set. "I want to buy the farm, so we'll have to sell or mortgage the house." Lillian turned a stone face towards Eric and he changed tactics, looking contrite and lowering his head. "I know it hasn't been easy for you, Lil, and I'm sorry, but we could make a go of the farm." As he took her hand he felt like Jess begging for a bone. "You did a great job at the funeral by the way, saved the day. All the fellows said I was a lucky bloke to have you."

Lillian took a deep breath and gave Eric a steady look. "I'll have to think about it." She didn't want him to confuse her.

He nodded. The old charm never failed.

Two envelopes arrived for Lillian the following week. The official one, she put in her handbag and another in her own handwriting, she tore open. Her eyes scanned the typewritten page a second time. She let out a yell and ran across the yard waving the letter. Jess barked and jumped about on her chain.

"What the blazes is going on?" Eric leant the spade against Aunt Maggie's shed. Her backyard looked like a plague of bandicoots had been through it. He approached Lillian. "Are you alright?"

"I won, I won, go and bite your bum." She sang at the top of her voice and waved the letter under his nose.

He took the letter. "Well I'll be..."

"I entered the *Women's Weekly* competition. I won a washing machine."

"So you've been wasting money on those rubbish magazines." He felt bilious. He wanted to cry. It was all so bloody unfair.

Lillian gazed at him and drew a deep breath. He was being petty. It was the disappointment over the house, she knew that, but he'd controlled her for too long. "Come and have a cup of tea. I have something I want to discuss." After Eric was settled in his armchair with a cup of tea, Lillian told him what she'd found.

"In the rose garden?" He shook his head, voice quiet, too flummoxed to realise she'd watched him dig up Aunt Maggie's yard for days.

"Yes, she meant me to have it." She saw his face close over and her insides roiled at what she was about to do. "You know, if I give you the money, you should be able to buy the farm once you get your share from the sale of Aunt Maggie's house." She watched him absorb what she'd said, saw his lips lift in a small triumphant smile and allowed him the moment before she drew her bow. "But I'll only give you the money if you agree to a divorce on the grounds of your adultery." Her arrow skewed Eric to his chair. He stared at her, slack mouthed in disbelief. When his eyes turned colourless, her chest tightened and the room grew smaller. Lillian watched him measure and weigh her words, calculating his reply and saw he was unsure of her. It was a good sign.

"Yeah? And how do you intend to manage with the children? Sell jam?"

His nasty response was expected. Lillian's chin went up. She swung her foot. The post office bonds she had found in the Bushells tea tin were now safely deposited in her new post office account and it hadn't required his permission. She leaned against the cushions, draped her arm along the back of the chaise longue and swirled the ice cube in the small glass of brandy she held. "I'm thinking of taking in a boarder. The girls can move into our room. I'll take Splinter's room and rent out Bubs. It's the closest to the bathroom. I've already been approached by the new hairdresser in town." She took a sip of brandy and felt Aunt Maggie's nod of approval. Lillian watched Eric's mouth open and shut, and warmed to her task. You can drop your washing off. I'll have a machine." The room suspended oxygen.

"Like hell!" Eric's fist came down on the arm of his chair and he jumped to his feet. "This is my house, you are my wife and you'll do as I say. You are not going to cheat me out of what is rightfully mine. If you had tried harder with my mother in the first place, we'd be sitting pretty by now."

Lillian's heart skipped a beat but she didn't flinch; Aunt Maggie had left her protection. Her eyes narrowed. "Aren't you forgetting we left because of your paedophile brother?" She saw his jaw clench. "You've always blamed me for the loss of your family farm. Thought I should have tried harder with your mother, but it was already left to Howard. If you had let me in on your father's death I might have understood more." Eric's eyes widened. He opened his mouth to speak and Lillian put her hand up; Eric was going to hear it all. "I know about your father."

His face registered shock. "Who …"

"Aunt Maggie told me. She trusted me, more than you ever did." Eric paced the room. "What your father did all those years ago changed all your lives. It wasn't me. The only thing wrong with me was I was gullible: a refugee, homesick and worried about my family being blown apart in England. And you didn't help me with any of that. We made a go of the farm together. We were happy until you slept with Cora. Then there was the waitress when I had just lost my home."

Ashes piled around Eric's feet. "The waitress was only …"

Lillian flicked his excuse away. "I don't care anymore. Nothing was ever right about me. You criticised me for reading, for having religious interests and yet it was the only consolation I had, isolated on a farm without friends. I was dying of loneliness, Eric. You always put your family and your own needs before mine. They didn't think I was good enough for you, for them, but I was. It wasn't me who created scandals wherever we went. I hardly stuck my head outside the door, I felt so humiliated. And on top of all that I still had to deal with being called, 'The Pom'. Did you ever think of how I felt?"

Eric looked across at Aunt Maggie's sideboard where his trophies sat, dull next to the crystal decanter. They hadn't been polished in a long time. He fished around for something to say in his defence but nothing came to mind.

"Aunt Maggie was the only one who appreciated me. I deserve what she's done for me and I'm not going to let her down." Lillian saw the clench of his fist. She was nearly at the finish line. Only one more hurdle to go. Her voice was quiet. Steady. "And don't even think of raising your hand to me or I'll sell the house and move to Melbourne." She might anyway.

Eric blanched. He looked at Lillian draped on the chaise longue and realised Aunt Maggie had always been in Lillian's corner. He remembered the clout on the head with the umbrella and the fiver she had given him to move Bubs's horse to the farm. He sagged in the chair. "If that's what you want," he said. He gazed across at Lillian, her new hairstyle suited her, her dark eyes held a challenge, she still had her English complexion. The new dress she was wearing showed off her good figure. Everything tumbled inside Eric.

"First I'm going to visit Mum for a couple of weeks. Mick has offered me a lift." There wasn't going to be anything in it for Mick yet, maybe never. She needed to organise her life without complications.

She stood up, walked over to the sideboard and picked up the box of Bex. Lillian handed the box to Eric. "Here, you might need these." She wouldn't need them anymore.

Acknowledgements

I started writing this book a long time ago in the wonderful Holmesglen TAFE creative writing course in Melbourne where I had exceptional teachers and great classmates. Sadly the course was closed down due to lack of funding, but even after the closure, my teachers, Kristin Henry, Gary Smith and Teresa Cannon continued to support me when I asked for their advice. I hold them in a grateful heart.

The book had long bouts of inactivity after the course ended and I filed it away to concentrate on my art career. Then my husband died after a long illness and I opened the book up again. I struggled with it for a few years and then Teresa Cannon introduced me to author Jennifer Dabbs. It was Jennifer who got me on track. Thank you, Jennifer.

To my friends and family, who read my drafts and gave their valued opinion. Annette Sonego the first reader of the first of my ten (maybe more) drafts. Diane Kilderry who helped with the full stops and commas and never stopped prodding me. The avid reader Joyce Spiller, with her keen eye and aversion to the overwritten. The positive assessment of Hilary Dobson. My five children, with a special emphasis on Penny and Jean-Paul who I trapped in the toilet or shower so they would be forced to listen to the latest page I had written – eventually they moved out of home. Christine Walker who did the tedious line check for my submission draft, a submission that found a home in the caring hands of Susan Hawthorne and Renate Klein. Both of these women support women writers and are editors of Spinifex Press. Also special thanks to Pauline Hopkins from Spinifex Press who edited my novel. My gratitude to Spinifex Press is boundless. Thank you for taking a chance on me. This is my first novel and I am seventy-three. Never give up on a dream.

Other books available from Spinifex Press

Locust Girl, a Lovesong
Merlinda Bobis

Winner, Christina Stead Award, NSW Premier's Literary Awards

Most everything has dried up: water, the womb, even the love among lovers. Hunger is rife, except across the border. One night, a village is bombed after its men attempt to cross the border. Nine-year-old Amadea is buried underground and sleeps to survive. Ten years later, she wakes with a locust embedded in her brow.

This political fable is a girl's magical journey through the border. The border has cut the human heart. Can she repair it with the story of a small life? This is the Locust Girl's dream, her lovesong.

ISBN 9781742199627

The Happiness Glass
Carol Lefevre

The literary longings of a studious girl born into a working class family, hot afternoons in a dust-plain Wilcannia schoolhouse; the temptation to stay, and the perils of breaking free—*The Happiness Glass* reflects complex griefs in the life of Lily Brennan.

Lily's story allows the author to navigate some of the difficulties of memoir, and out of its bittersweet blend of real, remembered, and imagined life, the portrait of a writer gradually emerges.

In fiction that forms around a core of memory, life writing that acknowledges the elusiveness of truth, Carol Lefevre has written a remarkable, risk-taking book that explores questions of homesickness, infertility, adoption, and family estrangement, in Lily Brennan's life, and in her own.

ISBN 9781925581638

The Floating Garden
Emma Ashmere

Sydney, 1926, and the residents of the tight-knit Milsons Point community face imminent homelessness: the construction of the harbour bridge spells the demolition of their homes. Ellis Gilbey, landlady by day, gardening writer by night, is set to lose everything. Only her belief in the book she is writing, and the hopes of a garden of her own, allow her to fend off despair. This beautiful debut novel evokes the hardships and the glories of the 1920s and tells the little-known story of those who faced upheaval because of the famous bridge.

ISBN 9781742199368

Dark Matters: A novel
Susan Hawthorne

When Desi inherits her aunt Kate's house she begins to read the contents of the boxes in the back room. Among the papers are records of arrest, imprisonment and torture at the hands of an unknown group who persecute her for her sexuality and activism. Scraps of memoir, family history and poems complete this fragmented story as Desi uncovers Kate's hidden life. Can Desi find Kate's lover, Mercedes, who had escaped from Pinochet's Chile? Where is she and can she help unravel Kate's story?

ISBN 9781925581089

*If you would like to know more about
Spinifex Press, write to us for a free catalogue, visit our
website or email us for further information
on how to subscribe to our monthly newsletter.*

Spinifex Press
PO Box 105
Mission Beach QLD 4852
Australia

www.spinifexpress.com.au
women@spinifexpress.com.au